THE KISSING FENCE

CAITLIN PRESS INC.
8100 Alderwood Road,
Halfmoon Bay, BC VON 1Y1
www.caitlin-press.com

Text design by Shed Simas / Onça Design
Cover design by Vici Johnstone
Cover image C-01724 from the Koozma J. Tarasoff Collection,
courtesy of the Royal BC Museum and Archives
Edited by Meg Yamamoto
Printed in Canada

Caitlin Press Inc. acknowledges financial support
from the Government of Canada and the Canada
Council for the Arts, and the Province of British
Columbia through the British Columbia Arts Council
and the Book Publisher's Tax Credit.

 Canada Council Conseil des Arts
for the Arts du Canada BRITISH COLUMBIA
ARTS COUNCIL Funded by the
Government
of Canada

LIBRARY AND ARCHIVES CANADA CATALOGUING IN PUBLICATION
The kissing fence / B.A. Thomas-Peter.
Thomas-Peter, Brian, author.
Canadiana 20190172665 | ISBN 9781773860237 (softcover)
LCC PS8639.H605 K57 2020 | DDC C813/.6—dc23

the
KISSING
FENCE

by B.A. THOMAS-PETER

CAITLIN PRESS

This novel is dedicated to the Doukhobor people of Canada. The stories I have drawn on—while changing identities and creating drama and fictitious characters for literary purposes—are largely true. Some are drawn from first-hand accounts spoken directly to me by those who experienced them. I am grateful to both the orthodox Doukhobors and those from the Sons of Freedom for their generosity, for inviting me into their homes, and trusting me with their stories. The contemporary storyline is entirely fiction.

Thanks also to my wife, Kate, who helped in the field research, and for reading the first draft. Others were also generous with their time and support. I hope they know of my appreciation.

1

West Vancouver, November 17, 2017

HER SHOULDERS FELL AT THE SIGHT OF WILLIAM IN THE RIDICULOUS shoes and clinging clothes of the cyclist. His genitals protruded in three conspicuous lumps. "Are you going out again?"

"I won't be long," he said to his wife. "I had to drive to work today, so I need the exercise."

It was an easy tale, not quite a lie and not something he wished to explain. He should be hungry and tired from a long day at the business, and pleased to relax at home with the family. Instead he was setting off into a damp evening with more relish than could be justified, except with what was nearly a lie.

"Where are you going?" Julie asked. "There's ice on the roads."

"I'm not going far, just along Marine Drive."

"Please wear your helmet," she said, as he pulled on his merino wool hat and stretched the band of a headlight over it. "Will you be back to see Kelly into bed?"

"I should be," he said. "Just an hour or so." She turned away from him, his padded bottom reminding her of a filled diaper, and he clip-clopped into the garage.

The bicycles, cleaned and ready, waited patiently. He touched the sensor to open the garage door and lifted the bike he loved the most from the rack. It rose without effort and the wheel turned at a touch. There was something magical in the featherweight carbon frame and titanium engineering designed to such dedicated purpose. Dust on his daughter's bike rankled, and he pursed his lips. *I'll get rid of it. She'll never use it.* Kelly's sight was failing. There was nothing to be done about it and within years, months, perhaps weeks, she would see nothing but diffuse light. It was a blessing, he thought, that she was a cheerful girl.

William checked chain and derailleur, stepped over the machine, clipping his shoe into the pedal, and pushed out along the drive and down the hill toward Lions Gate Bridge. The bicycle ticked and hummed under him. The rain fell gently through the mist, but it did not matter that it was cold and damp. He gripped the handlebars, his quads took up the strain and he was on his way. The sense of freedom came with the spit of rain and wind on his face. He could go anywhere he wanted, but now there was only one place he needed to be.

In three minutes he arrived at Lions Gate Bridge and began powering up the ramp, gathering speed as the bridge swooped down into the park. At the first opportunity he turned right to join Stanley Park Drive. It was a long road on which travellers moved only counter-clockwise around the park. Everyone in the flow of traffic could be seen. He slowed, allowing cars to pass, and considered if he had seen any of the cars or occupants before. The caution seemed excessive but he had agreed to it, and in some way it excited him.

At the southerly entrance to Stanley Park, before the apartment blocks began, he turned into Park Lane, timing his turn to maintain the steady rhythm, crossing the stream of cars, their lights catching him briefly. His attention lingered behind, anticipating the lights of a car following him. There were none, but even so there was always reason to be cautious. He turned right onto the cycle path and headed toward the city lights, stopping after twenty metres where the footpath intersected another at the beginning of Comox Street. Switching off the light strapped to his head, William watched. He was alone with the darkness under the late autumn skeleton of an old magnolia tree. The rushing noise of a few cars travelling on moist streets could be heard. Breath plumed in front of him. A hundred metres away a man shuffled along, pushing a shopping cart. William watched the little wheels tremble across the street. Large bags of clanking bottles and cans jostled for position to remain on the cart. He thought of all the man's possessions being pushed along in the rain.

Pathetic, he thought. *A life wasted.* A car passed along Park Lane and he looked carefully. It was nothing. The tall buildings at the edge of the park were settling down for the night. There was no danger he could see.

With headlight on, ears tucked under his hat and a shoe clipped into a pedal, he pushed off again along the footpath, past the No Cycling sign, and headed north toward Coal Harbour. It was quick and effortless in the cold air and empty streets of the late evening. At the end of the underpass of Lions Gate Bridge Road two raccoons scrambled out of his way and into the darkness. They watched warily as he flew by. He turned left onto the unused road and powered up the hill toward the outdoor theatre. At the next junction he turned right toward Brockton Oval, crossing the road leading up to the aquarium, and started the short climb to the crest of Brockton Oval Trail. Already the park had enveloped him in deep quiet. Just the crunching of stones under his wheels could be heard as he pushed on, unsettling patches of mist drifting in and out of his path.

The mist thickened. Branches snagged him and he moved to the left. Again a thorny branch caught him, digging into his scalp, and he moved to the right. Once over the summit, he accelerated. His hat and headlight suddenly lifted from his head. The beam of light careered in all directions. He grasped for it, catching the branch as it snatched his headgear away, pulling his arm straight. He twisted to look up. The thrashing light caught images of a great feathered crucifix looming over him, brilliant white against the black sky. In another sweep of the light an owl stared down at him.

He bundled the hat, light and leg of the beast in his fist as the bicycle trundled downhill. The owl lifted and pulled him forward into the blackness. He felt the control of his fate slipping from him. Only the owl's strength kept him upright. The talons tried to pull away and he shifted his grip as the bike wobbled. He tried pulling himself upright and wondered, momentarily, how this would end. The front wheel veered and buckled suddenly, launching him through the air into the darkness. In his head he shouted, *I can't be late*, and realized he still had the hat. Noise of bushes being disturbed all around him began, scratching and whipping at clothes and face. Then everything stopped.

WILLIAM DANGLED BELOW THE OWL AND LOOKED DOWN AT STANLEY Park, nearly black below him. Silver-grey mist lay in the crevasses and on the water all around. To the right, Vancouver sparkled like a party dress. To the west, the black jagged ripple of Vancouver Island stood on the horizon. Ochre and blue painted the sky, and lights from the North Shore were approaching.

"Where are you taking me?" he asked the owl. Its wings washed cold air over his face. "I don't want to go."

The owl gawked at William. He had a choice to go with the owl or let go of the hat. The hat was worth nothing, but still he did not want to give it up and neither did he want to fall.

William said, "I can't be late for the meeting. I'm never late." There was no reply.

Lit pillars of Lions Gate Bridge poked through the mist. Heavy wings of the owl pulled on the hat, lifting and lowering William, causing him to swing in the cold air. There was so much he did not want: to leave, to give up the hat, to be late for the meeting and to fall from the sky. They all seemed so important.

VOICES OF MEN SURROUNDED HIM IN THE DARKNESS. TWIGS BROKE AND rough hands brushed leaves from his face, forcing his eyes to squeeze tight and then open. Flashlights backlit a scrum of steaming ogre-like figures smelling of earth and sweat.

A light blinded him suddenly and an ogre spoke. "Don't move. You fell off your bike and we don't know what you've done to yourself."

William grimaced with the pain in his head and stiff discomfort. Strong hands of the ogre pressed on his chest. "Stay still till the ambulance comes, and let them deal with you."

"I have to get up." More hands pressed him down. He struggled against them. The pain rose again, this time in his shoulder. He searched for his left arm and tried to move it, but it was lost to his senses. Only pain registered.

"Just stay still now," said the ogre. "You've done something to your shoulder and banged your head. Just stay still and you'll be okay." Someone laid a coat over him. "What's your name?"

"William." The pain was clearing his head. "My name is William. Who are these people?"

"Rugby players. It's training night. We train over there." He gestured with his head to a field somewhere down the path. "Someone saw the bike, then we found you."

William groaned. "How long have I been here? What time is it?"

"I think it's about seven thirty."

He closed his eyes and recalled the plan should something like this happen. He had never thought it was to be used to make up for a failing of his. He hated the idiots who found reasons not to deliver what they said they would, and who tolerated disappointing others.

Pain arrived in another wave, and he began anticipating what would happen now that the meeting had passed. A small group of steaming ogres would stay and be kindly in the cold evening until the ambulance arrived. He dreaded being manhandled into the ambulance and having to go to the hospital, waiting for his turn to be prodded and X-rayed. His schedule would be lost. It was not what he had planned.

High above him it seemed as though a star moved one direction and then another. Again it moved, this time in an arc.

"Where's my headlight?"

"Didn't see a light," said the ogre. "We'll find it when the ambulance guys move you."

They would not find it, thought William. He could see it in the sky: a small sparkling dot circling above.

Something buzzed underneath him and a cowbell repeated. His iPhone vibrated in the small storage pocket at the back of his cycling jacket.

"Would you get my phone please? It's my wife."

November 20, 2017

IT WAS THE SUDDEN, UNEXPECTED JOSTLE AS HE LOWERED HIMSELF INTO Julie's car that sent his mind elsewhere with pain. Sleep had been impossible. Now, even with the sling to inhibit movement, there had been several knocks of the elbow causing him to suppress a yelp. Julie noticed this occasion and shook her head in disapproval.

"Why can't you do what everyone else would do and just stay home, at least until you can drive?" She continued to ease William downward into the seat.

The ache radiated from his shoulder in all directions. "You know I can't leave the office." William wondered if her irritation was about having to drive him to work. Two days had passed since the fall, and she had reached the end of sympathy with him. The passenger-side door closed.

"I don't see why not," said Julie as she stepped into the driver's seat. "You've had a concussion. It'll be a few weeks before you're ready to do anything."

She was right, he thought. Of course, he should have a few days off. "It's just a bad time to leave it. Something always goes wrong when I'm not there."

"They can manage without you for a week."

"No, they can't." For the first time William noticed a high-pitched hissing in his ears and pulled at the lobes with his good hand. "I can't risk an order being messed up, or someone being careless and giving our secrets away."

"What secrets does the company have? You import bicycles and sports gear. How secret can a bicycle get?"

The mocking tone enraged him. It was never good to talk about the business with Julie. It must have been the pain in his head that disoriented him. Her contempt for what he did was normally the end of talking, but today was different. He exhaled slowly to give himself time to respond in a way that did not bring another question.

"You're not a business person, Julie. You don't understand what the competition is like. The competition would love to know about our contracts and how we manage the business. They all want to know how we do it. If they did know, we'd be in serious difficulty and suddenly it would be gone." Not yet at work but he felt exhausted.

"Sometimes, I think it would be good if it was 'gone.'"

Nothing of his efforts, he thought, was what she wanted. "You can't mean that."

"I do mean it! It would be better if it all went up in flames."

"That's hard to believe." Anger caused his head to pound. "No second car or personal trainer, living in the valley next to a mall, Kelly in public school and waiting for the sales to buy your shoes. I can't see it working out … can we talk about this later? I'm really not up to it today."

Julie ignored him. "You're married to the business and your bicycles. It's all you think about. Sometimes I think I'm just something on the side, cooking dinner, looking after Kelly and keeping the bed warm." She paused.

"Not very warm," he said. He had strayed onto unforgiving ground and waited for the retort. Then it came.

"It needs a spark to start a fire."

It was true, uncomfortably true, that he had not been interested. He had never understood how his voracious appetite for women had melted in the years since Kelly was in kindergarten. It was easy to believe that Julie's ambivalence had switched him off, or that he had been busy developing the business, but no other woman had generated interest of any kind in that time. It was not what his youth would have predicted.

"I should have told you that we have a special order coming in this week. High-spec bikes with tight distribution arrangements. I can't leave it to anyone else." He thought the concession might be enough to divert her.

"You mean you won't leave it to anyone else."

It was time to say nothing more. William watched the passing of cars and shops. There were glimpses of Burrard Inlet toward Stanley Park as they drove along Marine Drive. The traffic thickened as they passed the main road feeding the bridge. He speculated where the owl had dropped his headlight.

Julie turned south off Marine Drive into the industrial district, east of the bridge. After a few blocks she turned left and pulled up outside the office.

William recognized a car across the road. A man sat motionless within it. "Thanks for the ride," he said, and opened the passenger door with his good arm.

"Let me help you out," she said, opening the driver's door.

"No, I'll be fine."

She turned toward him. "Don't spend all day at work."

He could hear the frustration in her voice. "Okay. Just a few hours and I'll get a taxi home." Carefully he swung his legs into the street and lifted himself out, resisting the temptation to check the car across the road. "Thanks," he said, before walking toward reception.

Through the glass doors Dennis, the warehouseman, came scampering down the stairs from the office. William thought it a little odd that Dennis was upstairs when all his work was in the warehouse. "Morning, Dennis," said William as he came through the doors. "I'm just coming in to see you."

"Morning, Boss." The warehouseman spotted the sling. "What happened to your arm?"

"Nothing serious, just a fall from the bike. Has the delivery arrived this morning?"

"Not yet. It's too early. Not sure when it's coming."

"Find out and let me know."

"They said it would be today but didn't give a time."

"Get them on the phone and tell them if they want the next shipment contract, they better give us a time, and it better be this morning."

"Yes, Boss."

William turned to go out the door, thinking how good it was to employ someone with an army background. They were not always bright, but they did what they were told without complications. He made his way up the stairs to his office. Each tread assaulted him with a jostle. Cathy, his admin assistant, should be in by now and would have dealt with the mail and, with any luck, made the coffee.

"My goodness!" Cathy said, standing. "What happened?"

"I'm fine. I just fell off my bike. Any messages?" Cathy's face was red and blotched, and he thought it was better not to ask.

"I'm not often in before you, so I knew there was something."

"What's in the post?"

"I'm just going through it now," said Cathy. Her voice changed and she looked down. "Sorry, I haven't been in long myself."

William heard something, an invitation to inquire or perhaps an excuse to be offered, but let it go. At forty-two years old, Cathy was not very different from him in age but had never started life. If it wasn't a problem with the loser she had married, it was her children demanding everything of her. There was always a sorrowful tale in the family: an injustice of some kind, an unwanted pregnancy, a debt owed, medical investigations needed. It was terribly complicated in her world, but William thought it was simple to understand. Cathy was not up to life as an adult and preferred to create the intensity of a television soap opera rather than accept responsibility for her own life. Her neediness and availability had not always disgusted him, but it did now.

Cathy said, "I've just been talking with Dennis. There's been a message from SynchronoX, asking if their shipment has been received. I said it hasn't come."

He could see now what the puffy red face was all about; Dennis was snuffling at the trough. He knew it would only cause drama and suck energy out of the firm. *She may have to go*, he thought, but right now he had to deal with the man in the car.

"All right. There's not much for me to do until you've gone through the mail. I'll get some coffee. Try to be done with it before I get back. I have my iPhone with me if you need to call." William moved to the stairs. "The accountant is coming at eleven today. We need to be ready to screw Canada Revenue." William smiled as if it were a joke. "He'll want to see the books too, so I want to go over the last three months before he arrives. So, deal with the mail and filing, then get the books out."

Leaving the office, he looked up and down the street, avoiding eye contact with the man in the car, and began walking slowly to Tim Hortons just a few blocks away. His head and shoulder pounded with each step. Behind him a car door opened and closed.

The morning coffee queue in the Tim Hortons was five people long. The small athletic man who had followed stood behind him. William turned his body and spoke quietly, seeing Uri for the first time.

"What are you doing here? It's not what we agreed."

"You didn't come to the meeting, William. We cycled the route three times trying to find you. We were worried about you. What happened to your arm?" There was no hiding the Russian in his voice.

"We have a protocol for that and I was going to use it." William drew breath. "I was five minutes away from the meeting when I fell off my bike. I'm fine. It will be a couple of weeks before I can meet in the usual way."

Uri nodded. "Sorry to hear it. I'm glad all is well with you."

"Uri, your delivery hasn't arrived yet. I'll let you know when it has."

"William, why are you upset with me? I just want to make sure you are well."

"You know I am well, Uri. You were outside my house when I got back from the hospital. You watched my wife help me out of the car. If I hadn't recognized you, we would have called the police." The two men shuffled up in the queue. "That would have drawn attention to all of us."

Uri said, "We were worried about you. Nothing wrong with that."

"We have an arrangement. Everyone does well out of it, but you have to keep to the protocol. We don't have an arrangement if you don't keep to what we agree."

"You're right, William. It is good that you want us to take care of each other."

"I have to be able to trust you. It's always about trust in business, and being reliable." William knew it was useless trying for the moral high ground with someone like Uri.

"William, it is not me you talk to if you want to pull out of a deal. You understand." His apologetic tone did not alter.

"We have an arrangement, but you must not come to my work again, and never to my house. Can we agree to that?" They shuffled forward.

"Yes, we can agree, William." He shrugged. "But there are others."

"Tell them, Uri. Never to my house."

"I will speak with them for you. These people, William, they understand. People always have limits, but they understand."

"Next, please." A smiling young woman in a brown uniform and netted hair spoke to him from the counter.

"A double-double, please." William handed change to the woman and walked to the end of the counter to pick up his coffee. With his one good arm he dropped the cup into a cardboard sleeve and covered it with a plastic lid. When he turned, Uri was gone.

William thought he had already done too much. His head felt bulging, the light of the day was incandescent, and the thought of drinking his coffee was nauseating. He sat in a corner away from the window, allowed a wall to take his weight and closed his eyes. The grey light penetrated, saturating his view. An ocean wind whistled in his ears. He squeezed his eyes shut and shielded them with his good hand. Gradually, as he remained still, the pain and intense light ebbed away, leaving a grey mist. Something small, in the soft grey distance, between eyes and lids, moved.

"You okay?" A gentle hand touched William awake. "Everything all right?"

"Yeah. It's just a headache." William saw with disgust the dishevelled young man inspecting him. It was the second time in two days he had been roused by a young and filthy man smelling of earth. He stood up to leave.

"Your coffee!"

"Keep it," said William. "Looks like you need it."

November 21, 2017

WILLIAM LISTENED TO KELLY ASKING HER MOTHER, "HOW'S DAD?"

"Don't worry, he's fine. Nothing broken."

She would never be a high flyer, he thought. She would soon lose the power of focus and nothing would be clear. If she were really bright or gifted in some way, it might be different. She was a nice girl, for whom private schooling was a waste, but she was happy, it was what her mother wanted, and there were opportunities for her to try things out and build her confidence.

Kelly said, "Tell me about the owl."

"An owl tried to steal his hat and knocked him off his bike," Julie said.

"Do they do that?"

William entered the room. "It was a surprise to me. I thought I was getting caught in the bushes as I cycled along, but there was an owl pulling my hat off." Kelly gasped and giggled at her father. "Then I was flying through the air."

"Like the owl! What kind was it?"

"I don't know."

"Did it fly away with your hat?"

"No, I held on. It got my headlight though."

Kelly asked, "Why, Dad?" She looked toward him with unsteady eyes. "Why did you hang on to it?"

"I don't know. Maybe I thought ..." He hesitated. "I don't know. I just did, without thinking." There was a moment of awkwardness. "Your mother tells me you're playing soccer."

"Yes, and we have to go," said Julie. "I'll get my coat. Do you have your soccer kit?"

"Yes, it's here."

William said, "I haven't seen you play. How do you know where the ball is?"

"There's a bell in the ball and we hear where it is. I see a little but mostly I hear it. I don't need to see it."

"Hmm. I wouldn't have thought that was possible. I couldn't kick a ball that I could only hear."

"Yes, you could. You can tell where it is. It just needs practice."

Julie's voice came from the hall. "Come on, Kelly."

"Why were you in the park? Mum said that you were just going along Marine Drive."

"Well, I just got into a rhythm, you know. It felt good so I went over the bridge." It was a necessary lie, but only a little one. "Your mum is waiting. You better go to practice. Play well."

"Bye, Dad."

The door to the garage opened. A car started and moved off and the door closed. Mother and daughter were gone. He had not spoken so many words to his daughter in weeks, or was it months? The household was unfamiliar even when they were there. The routine was not his and, sitting in the living room, he had a sense of being superfluous to it all. Kelly was changing, becoming a teenager. She had never questioned him about something he had done. More challenges would follow. Soon there would be boys at the door and the task of protecting her would take a new turn.

In the quiet of his house he lifted his noise-cancelling headphones and placed them on his head. The outside world disappeared as he switched them on. He had not realized how much noise there was to cancel in the quietness of his house. For the first time William heard, with perfect clarity, the rushing noise that had bothered him since the fall. There was nothing to interfere with it. He listened and concentrated to hear every strand and whisper. Would it go away, he thought, or would he struggle against it always?

His iPhone buzzed. The number was unknown. There was a message waiting. He pushed his headphones aside and lifted the phone to his ear.

"Hello? … Yes, it is." He listened to the hospital receptionist. "I understand if the doctor thinks it's necessary … how quickly can we do it? … I think that will be fine but I will have to check my diary … would you send me an appointment? … Thank you. Goodbye."

More tests meant less time at work. He checked the message that waited for him. It was an emoji, the absurdly innocent signal from Uri. He knew what it meant.

The ringing in his ears would not stop.

November 22, 2017

THE YOUNG MEN FINISHED UNLOADING. DENNIS SUPERVISED THEM AND kept a running total in his head as they worked. Now he returned from outside the delivery bay, having squashed the end of his cigarette into the concrete with his boot. Stacks of boxes in the delivery bay towered over him, each one marked with the garish yellow and black logo of SynchronoX. He began counting again, in earnest. At the bottom of each stack he used his pencil to softly write the accumulated total to keep track of the inventory and check the numbers against the order. Satisfied that the total was correct, he returned to the beginning and began checking the white sticky label on the side of each box to compare each serial number with that provided by the manufacturer, just as he had been instructed to do. The delivery man waited patiently for the signature he needed to move on. It was never quick enough for him, but for Dennis, it was a process of ritual importance to get right. He was, after all, the person responsible for deliveries and dispatches, and should there be an error, it could be only his. Now especially, with the boss off work for a few days, he had to ensure everything was done as it should be done.

Dennis inspected and checked each box, confirming the serial number against the delivery note in his hand. The sequence of serial numbers suddenly discontinued and started with a second series. He double-checked against his record and, having satisfied himself that all was well, continued on.

He walked through the delivery bay to the truck's cab. "Okay," he said to the driver. "Thanks for waiting." He reached to sign for the delivery. "Sorry to hold you up."

The driver said, "I guess if I had just spent a couple hundred grand on a pile of bikes, I would want the numbers to add up." The two men smiled. "See ya next time."

Dennis reached in his pocket, retrieved his phone and called the boss.

WILLIAM WAS STILL HOLDING HIS IPHONE, CHECKING HIS CALENDAR AND entering the hospital appointment, when it rang.

"Hello," said William. "They all arrived as we ordered? ... Good ... oh, you did ... no, don't do anything more tonight ... we're a little late with the order, not your fault, so one of the retailers is coming in over the weekend and arranging their own transport ... no, no, nothing needs to be done. I'll come in and open up ... that's kind of you but you don't have to come in ... I'll be all right. You have a good weekend ... oh yes, I should be in on Monday. It's feeling better already ... bye, Dennis. Thanks."

November 25, 2017

WILLIAM WAITED IN THE KITCHEN FOR THE TAXI. JULIE STOMPED AND clattered as she cleared breakfast away.

"Why are you going into work on a Saturday when you still can't drive, or even cycle? You lasted one hour—one hour!—just a few days ago. You've done nothing but sit in that chair and sleep since then."

"It's the special delivery. It arrived yesterday and has to get out today. There is transport coming for it this morning. I have to go." There was no defence, especially today.

Julie announced, "I'm taking Kelly to soccer. She said you wanted to see her play. Will you get to the game?"

"I'll try," said William.

Kelly arrived in the kitchen. "Are you coming to watch me?"

"I'll try, Kelly. I have to go into work first." He turned away from her disappointment.

"Get your soccer kit together, Kelly," said Julie. "We have to go soon."

"My taxi's here," said William. "I better go. Might see you later."

It was a relief to be out of the house and on the way to work. His shoulder had settled a little but his head still throbbed with every movement. A North Shore soaker hammered the roof of the taxi, masking the hissing wind in his ears, and his mind wandered. The rain and endless rhythm of the wiper blades reminded him of the trips into the valley to see his father in Riverview Hospital, the large mental asylum far enough from the city to be neglected. It had been a relief when he had left his father and driven away, as it had been when his father had passed. Was it odd, William thought, to feel relief driving away from those who should be dear to him? It had always been so, but William knew there was something wrong in feeling relief.

Perhaps, he reasoned, it was inevitable that distance from family would grow if he wanted to be successful and secure their future. It was what men had to do if they were to prevent being stripped naked and buried by those that ran the province to suit themselves. His father being sent to Riverview was what happened to men not able stand up to those with enduring power and authority to do as they liked. William resolved never to allow it to happen to him.

The taxi stopped outside the reception of his warehouse and office. The driver watched William in silence, waiting for payment. William paid with cash and stepped into the street, putting his face to the sky. The cold rain soaked his hair and face in a second, distracting him from the throbbing. He thought of Kelly at her soccer match. How would she hear the soccer ball in all this rain? It might be indoors, but he did not know.

A large white panel van, parked down the street from the warehouse, watched him enter the building. William opened the door with his key and walked into the hallway, stopping briefly to turn off the alarm. He took the stairs cautiously to the first landing and kept a steady rhythm on the second flight to the first floor. The pain could be managed if he moved carefully. In the large outer office he went first to Cathy's desk. It always annoyed him that the keys to the steel security cabinet enclosing the CCTV recordings could never be found when he wanted them. Cathy would put them in the drawer, in a pot on her desk or among the pencils. Finally he located the keys and knelt at the cabinet, opened the door and switched the security cameras off.

Downstairs in the warehouse, he pressed the release of the overhead roller door. The white van moved to the warehouse door. Three men emerged onto the street and ducked under and into the warehouse as the door rose. They headed for the boxes.

"Wait," said William. "Not all of these are going. I'll tell you which ones."

The men stood while William found the manifest hanging on the wall, removed a document from his pocket and began comparing the one in his hand with the one on the wall. The two documents were identical in every way except the manifest on the wall had nearly double the number of serial numbers. He inspected both documents and, having counted twice, turned to the waiting boxes. William saw quickly that they had not been stacked in order of serial number. He would have to find each one.

"You're expecting twenty-five units, correct?"

A man nodded in agreement and signalled to his companions to start loading.

"Wait," said William. "You'll take the ones I give you. It's going to be complicated. All the boxes look the same, but they're not the same. They've been mixed up. I'll point out the ones on your order." By the time they finished, it would be as if the twenty-five bicycles being carried off in the van never existed.

William speculated that they would not be finished in time for him to get to the soccer game. It was unlikely. He would have to wait to see the shipment out of the warehouse, shred the manifest listing the extra units, turn on the security cameras and lock up before getting a taxi to the school. The game, inside or out, would be all over by then.

December 8, 2017

WILLIAM SWITCHED OFF THE TESLA AS THE GARAGE DOOR CLOSED BEHIND him. He should have taken Julie to the appointment with the doctor. She would complain again, but this time with good reason. It would be a weightier complaint than he had anticipated, since he had not told her of the neurological investigations that had been hastily arranged, or even that there was something to investigate. Julie would be angry with him for keeping it quiet. That would be the focus. Not the concern for his health, the operation that he needed, only that he did not include her from the beginning. She would be right to be cross, but it rankled that he would have to explain himself before the tumour in his head was acknowledged at all.

William tried to let the thought go and got out of the car. He took a moment to appreciate the orderly place he had created for his cycling gear and the neatly stowed household clutter, and then winced as he closed the car door. Kelly's dusty bike reminded him of a challenging conversation he would need to have with her. How was he to tell Kelly of the tumour? Maybe Julie could help him. She was always able to speak to their daughter in a way he had not found.

He dispensed with his coat and made his way to the kitchen. Dinner was over. He walked into the living room. Julie sat in front of the television with a glass of wine in hand.

"Dinner's in the oven," she said without turning from the TV. "I didn't know you'd be late."

"I should have told you." William found the wine, poured himself a glass and trailed into the sitting room.

Julie glanced at him briefly. "Not hungry?"

"Not really." William sat in his usual spot. The television noise filled the space. Already he was impatient for the right moment. "How was your day?" It was the familiar and safe inquiry.

"Just the usual," said Julie. "Nothing to report."

"Where's Kelly?"

"She's upstairs with some homework. She wants to go out later, so she's getting it done early."

"Where is she going?"

"I've already said she can go." Julie's expectation of his objection arrived suddenly for both of them. She hesitated. "She's going to a party, at Michael's house."

"Do you know who's going to be there?"

Julie turned on him. "Of course I do. It's Friday night and she's going with her thirteen-year-old friends to a party. I'll be driving a few of them." The air was suddenly hot. She sipped wine to cool it.

"Maybe I should drive her," he said.

Julie stood and marched into the kitchen. William stared at the television without watching, wondering what had happened. He listened to his dinner being pulled from the oven and shovelled into the recycling bin, and then he followed her into the kitchen, perched on the bar stool, leaned on the granite countertop and waited.

Julie stopped banging around the kitchen. "I'm just tired of being questioned, like I've done something wrong, when you come home from work. I've been here all day and I'm not one of your employees."

William stayed quiet. There was nothing he could say that would not inflame Julie further, but there were still things he needed to tell her.

He allowed a little time to pass and then said, "I do have something important to tell you." Julie continued to work in the kitchen. "It really is important."

She stopped. "What's important to you that you want to tell me?"

William ignored the scratch in her question. Her eyes looked tired. He could see she did not want to hear him. There was no point in trying to be sensitive. "I have a brain tumour. A small one, but it has to come out." There was a question on her face that could not find words. "After I fell off my bike I had some tests."

"I know," she said, "but they didn't say anything about having more tests then."

"When I went back a few days later for a follow-up, I was referred to a neurologist and arranged to have the tests done. I got the results today." Julie's brow furrowed.

"Is it cancer?"

"They're not sure but think it's unlikely. Apparently the tumour is underneath my brain, not actually in the brain. Anyway, I need an operation to have it out." He waited for her to catch up. "Apparently it's on my pituitary gland."

"What does that mean?" Julie asked. "Will you be all right?"

William tried not to think of what she might mean, but it came too easily to cast off. What was she really concerned about? She had long ago lost interest in him. "Apparently it's a common operation, and they seem very confident they can do something for me."

"There haven't been symptoms, have there? I haven't noticed anything."

He thought, *What would you have noticed, unless the money ran out?* but managed not to say it. "The neurologist said that I've probably had it for years. It may have affected me. He won't know until he does some tests on it. I wouldn't have noticed anyway. It happens gradually. The effects are hard to spot."

"What sort of effects?"

"I'm not sure. My hormones have been messed up in some way. The problem is that it'll get bigger, and I may get worse if I don't have something done about it."

Julie sighed. "Why didn't you tell me?"

"It wouldn't have changed anything. I didn't want to worry you, or Kelly."

"For God's sake, William. You don't decide what we can know or not know. You don't decide." She sighed again. "Sorry, I don't mean to be angry. This is about you getting well, but I don't like … waiting to be included."

William watched Julie's exasperation play out. She was right. He was not good at sharing feelings, kept things to himself, but mostly he neither liked nor trusted her sympathy. It was more than he could tolerate. Julie would never understand how pointless her concern now seemed, when he had to dislocate a shoulder or have a tumour in his head before she showed any sign of being interested in him.

Julie asked, "What will we say to Kelly?"

"I don't know."

"You need to talk with your daughter about this. I can mop up during the day, but it really has to come from you."

William felt helpless. "I'm not sure how to tell her." It wasn't just the helplessness of not knowing what to say to Kelly; it was having to ask for guidance. Having to ask would confirm his absenteeism and line him up for another judgment, now or later. The wind whistled in his ears and he pulled at them.

"Well," Julie began. "She knows you've been injured. Perhaps you could tell her what a lucky thing it was to have happened."

"Lucky?"

"Yes."

"You mean, lucky because they found something serious."

"Yes. I think if you tell her how lucky you have been that they found something when it was small and they can operate, she might be happy about it. Not so worried."

It was simple and obvious. He had not thought of it. "That sounds good. I'll try that."

Julie came to him and put her arms around his waist. He stiffened. It was unfamiliar. William remembered that she could embrace with her whole body. He had managed to hold all of that at bay, but she was too quick, and in any case perhaps he should allow it. He put his arms on her shoulders and patted her.

"I'm all right," he said.

"I expect you will have that written on your tombstone." For a moment it was like they had been before Kelly arrived.

"I better go speak to Kelly."

He tried to pull away but she clung to him. "Tell her after the party. Maybe tomorrow. I haven't finished yet. You may not know you need a hug right now, but you do. So do I."

December 11, 2017

JUST A FEW KILOMETRES FROM THE ROAD HE TRAVELLED, SKIERS PLAYED on Cypress and Grouse Mountains, under floodlights. In North Vancouver, the temperature remained above freezing and for a few hours the rain had given way to dampness. William felt the weakness in his legs as he tried to power over the bridge into Stanley Park. Just a few weeks of being idle and muscles were no longer what they were. Even so, it was good to be on his bicycle again. He got into cruising mode as he slipped off the bridge into the park. It would be a difficult meeting, but there were a few minutes' cycling time around the edge of the park to work out how to play it. By Second Beach he pulled off the road onto the cycle path and rolled along the side of the empty playground. He moved slowly along, as was the arrangement, waiting to be joined.

The whirring sound of another bike lifting moisture from the path could be heard approaching from behind. The new rider settled in for-mation beside William as they swooped through the underpass on the way to the lake. Two more riders held position ten metres back.

"It's good to see you, William," said Uri. "How are you?"

"I'm all right. And you?" asked William.

"Very good. And your shoulder?"

"I'm not ready for mountain biking yet, but if I keep to smooth pavement, I'm okay."

"That's good, William."

"How was the shipment last month? Was it all that you wanted?"

"Everything was good. William, thank you for arranging it. We know that you were not well. It was appreciated."

William said, "There is a problem this month." Uri was quiet. "I need an operation."

"What kind of operation is this, William?"

"I've had some tests, and I have a small tumour in my head. Nothing to worry about, but I have to have the operation before Christmas, on the twenty-first."

"But William, the shipment is coming. The shipment doesn't turn around. What will you do?"

The pace and urgency picked up alongside the rhododendrons.

"What do you suggest?"

"It is for you, William. This is your part of the business. We can do nothing until it gets to you."

William tried to concentrate through the discomfort of his shoulder being jarred by every little bump on the path. He had cycled too far. "There is no good time to have an operation like this, but if I have it before Christmas, I'll be pretty well recovered by the new year and be able to manage the January shipment."

"So soon?" Uri asked. "William, this is brain surgery. Will it not take a long time?"

"Apparently not. They won't have to cut into the brain, just near the brain. If I wait until January to have it, I might not be ready for the shipment, and we will be in the same situation. I should just get it over with as soon as possible."

Uri was quiet for a hundred metres. "So, someone you trust will take delivery at the warehouse?"

"Yes. I've got a good man in the warehouse. Ex-military. Reliable. Does what he's told. He was there to receive the last SynchronoX delivery."

"But he doesn't know to give our part of the shipment the following day," said Uri.

"That's true, but if I have the manifest before I go into hospital, I can instruct him on separating your consignment from the rest. To get it out the next day, I'll have to give everyone the day off, leave the security cameras off and give you keys for the front door and alarm. The alarm needs a key and a code. The warehouse door can be opened from the inside."

"William, you won't mind me being at your work?"

"This is different. I don't want the consignment in the warehouse for more than a day. You will be there for only half an hour if we arrange it well. The consignment will be stacked and ready for you. You just have to load and lock up."

Up ahead the Stanley Park Causeway underpass approached. Uri was thinking in silence.

"Okay," he said. "We will do as you plan. Have you keys?"

William sat upright on his bicycle and pulled a length of ribbon from his jacket pocket and passed it to Uri. "The alarm code is on the ribbon."

"This must work, William. Dennis must make it work for you."

"He will."

"I'm sure it will go well." Uri grinned. "With the operation and the delivery."

Three cyclists moved to the right of the path as it ran under the causeway. William watched them turn toward the city before he turned west along the seawall. He allowed himself to slow and stop. His shoulder ached and his ears rang. He got a last glimpse of three riders moving silently away from him along the path into Coal Harbour. William had more than one thought about the plan working. Not everything was within his control and he would be in no position to respond to anything that went wrong. It would rely on Dennis doing exactly as he was told.

A current went through him. He searched his memory for any recollection of having mentioned Dennis by name when speaking to Uri. There was nothing he could recall. Maybe he had mentioned it. The doubt bothered him as much as not knowing what else Uri might know.

2

Perry Siding, BC, September 9, 1953

GERRY FLANAGAN LOOKED OVER THE WOODEN BRIDGE INTO THE CRYSTAL cold water of the Slocan River. It reminded him of his time in Ireland as a boy. Thirty pairs of police-issue boots rattled over the bridge but the sound of water over stones could still be heard. Ahead, on the west side of the bridge, more men waited. A group of them turned to watch their fellow RCMP officers arriving. Just three years had passed since the provincial police in BC had been disbanded, and many officers from the old guard neither understood nor accepted the takeover by the RCMP. Their resentment lingered. They huddled together, inspecting the arrival of the outsiders. As the groups joined, the trundle of boots on boards gave way to the mournful sound of singing from the next field, south of the road.

"You failed the first test. Late and missed the briefing," Sergeant Benson, a small and wiry man something over fifty, said in greeting.

"Sorry, Sarge. Bus was late."

Benson reached into a crate. "It doesn't matter. Here," he said, offering Flanagan a brown bottle of beer.

"No thanks, Sarge. I don't drink." Flanagan saw bottles in the hands of his colleagues and wondered what was going on. None of the men made eye contact and a few muttered quietly like embarrassed schoolboys.

"You'll need it, son," said the sergeant, holding out the bottle. His thick Borders accent made it sound like an order. The tilt of his head suggested any man who would not drink with him could not be trusted.

"Not for me, thank you," said Flanagan. He knew it was a mistake not to take it. He had failed the first test, and the second.

"Suit yourself." The sergeant tossed his empty into the field and took a long swig from the fresh bottle.

"What's the plan, Sergeant?" Flanagan asked.

The sergeant eyed him. "We're going into that field," he said, pointing with the nose of the bottle toward the singing, "and we're going to arrest every one of these Russian protesters, because they think the laws in Canada don't apply to them." The sergeant stared into Flanagan's eyes. "That's the plan, son." He paused to lift the bottle to his lips and continued to watch Flanagan.

Both men could hear the singing and each knew what the other was thinking. Flanagan asked, "What resistance are we expecting?"

"Whatever they offer, we'll deal with."

"What are we arresting them for, Sarge?"

"The protesters are naked. That's the complaint."

From across the field Flanagan could see nothing. "Someone complained?" he asked.

The sergeant studied him again. "You're the new boy from Ontario, aren't you?"

"Yes, sir. I've been here a week."

"Irish?"

"I am, Sergeant."

"Republican or Loyalist?"

"Irish, Sarge."

The sergeant's question said everything of the past that Flanagan's family had tried to escape. His family had left Ireland for Canada because of turmoil, but history would always follow them. He had not been alive when his father was interred by the Black and Tans, who marauded unchecked through the streets of his homeland, searching, beating and arresting anyone who looked part of the Republican Army, and every Catholic did. It had embittered his nation, his community and his family. The question also told of the sergeant's past. A soldier, certainly, but his connection to Ireland was less certain. Maybe he had felt the spitting contempt from one side or the other, or seen too much of the war.

The sergeant eyed him with more suspicion. "Well, 'Irish,' either way you won't know much about what's been happening here, will you? In this province, nudity is a serious crime. Punished by three years in prison."

It was too late for Flanagan to prevent his eyebrows lifting in surprise. The sergeant approached to within a few inches of his face. "Is that a problem for you, son?"

"It seems a long time, sir. That's all."

"That's not our concern, is it?"

"No, sir."

"Your job, if you expect to get to the end of your second week, is to follow the orders I give you."

"Yes, Sarge."

The sergeant tossed the second bottle after the first and caught the attention of the officer behind Flanagan. "You stay with our Irish colleague with the fine sensibilities, and make sure he does his part."

"Yes, Sergeant," came the reply, as the sergeant walked off.

Flanagan looked over the hedge toward the white tents in the next field. The prayer songs drifted toward him on smoke from their fires. The images were too far away to see what was going on. There was movement. Children played, and he could see a few larger pink figures.

The voice from behind said, "You'll see plenty in a few minutes, and you'll not want to remember any of it. None of us will."

Flanagan acknowledged the man standing behind him. "I don't see any protesting." There was no response. "What are we waiting for?"

"Transport's coming to take them away. Adults head to the railway line on the trucks; children without parents and mothers with babies go north to New Denver on the buses."

"What do you mean? Are we arresting the children?" asked Flanagan.

"Just the adults. The children won't have anyone to look after them, so we pick them up."

"Christ!"

"Anyway, it's not our responsibility. We've had orders from Victoria just to round 'em up and get them on the transport."

There was more Flanagan wanted to know but the group began stirring. Officers muttered about the buses arriving. Bottles flew over the hedge and men began arranging their gear.

"Form up! Form up!" shouted the sergeant, and men arranged themselves in rows. When they were roughly settled, he said, "You'll cross into the top field at the first gate. Move right along the hedge and stay in two ranks."

The troop moved sluggishly.

"Move yourself!" the sergeant shouted, and they stepped up. "I expect everyone to do their part," he said, fixing on Flanagan. "No exceptions. There'll be no shirkers here today. You'll do what you're fucking told."

Flanagan moved off with the others. The momentum had started and whatever was going to happen could not now be stopped.

Two lines of officers arranged themselves loosely inside the hedgerow, across the grassy field from the tent village. Behind them a smaller number were armed with rifles. The phalanx of black uniforms started walking toward the tent village, where people scurried back and forth, alarmed at the advance. The Russian harmony got louder as they approached. Large, naked, pendulous women and tall, thin, naked men began watching them.

Flanagan felt a push in the back. "Your baton, get it out. Get it out!"

"We don't need batons—they're naked for Christ's sake."

The officer behind jabbed Flanagan hard in the shoulder with his stick. "We're all in this. All of us," he said.

Flanagan scrambled for his baton and saw the others gripping theirs. He looked again at the naked people in front of him. They were helpless and unarmed. Then he scanned the taut faces down his rank. Faces of men steeling themselves, as one sporting team would brace against the impact of another. Why, he wondered, *are they angry with these people? It's madness. They must all know this is madness.*

A lean naked man, bearded and fierce, stood his ground and the lines of police hesitated. "What do you want?" he said. An officer stepped forward and struck him on the side of the head. His scalp opened as he fell. A woman ran screaming toward him but fell from a blow to the back of her head. Shrill screams of terror emerged from the children who ran for cover into the tents. A few men emerged and were knocked to the ground, some broken, others unconscious within moments. The right flank of RCMP advanced into the prayer tent and the left rushed into the others. Batons swung, thudding on flesh and bone, bringing terror to adults and children.

Inside the prayer tent Flanagan saw children huddled as far from the entrance as they could be. Mothers stood defending them with pleas of mercy, but the advance of his colleagues continued. Parents fell, twisting to escape the blows, freezing the children. The black threshing line came ever closer until the children understood only the danger they were in, scampered under the skirt of the tent and ran for their lives toward the tree line.

Flanagan followed under the skirt and shouted after the children. "Stop! Stop! I won't hurt you," he said, and then understood running added to their fear. In any case, he remembered, they did not speak English and would not understand his reassurance.

Thirty feet away a little one tripped on the path as Flanagan pulled himself out of the tent. She was five or six years old, and the older girl helping her could only have been nine or ten. She looked back at him as the little one scrambled to her feet. He flapped his hands after them and they disappeared into the forest.

Another policeman came round the tent and gave chase.

"Don't bother," shouted Flanagan, but his colleague continued into the woods. "You'll never find them."

"Orders," said the colleague. "We have to round 'em up."

NINA PULLED AT THE HANDS OF HER YOUNG COUSIN ARINA AND HER friend, one on either side of her, dragging them along as fast as they could go. Over her shoulder a uniformed man squeezed himself under the skirt of the prayer tent, just as the children had done, and was getting to his feet. The policeman was shouting to stop, and something else about not hurting them. Her mother's lessons had taught her to understand English, and her father's lessons had taught her to distrust all the English had to say. She would keep running. Her lungs burst with new effort. Arina stumbled, but Nina did not let them stop. She pulled the child up with all her might until her bare feet made contact with the ground. Another glance back and Nina thought she had misunderstood what was going on. The policeman had stopped. Their eyes met. He pushed his hands forward, as if shooing her away, until another officer appeared at a gallop. Gathering the children in each hand, she pulled them into the forest.

They would be caught. Surely they would be caught, thought Nina. Without explanation she scrambled the two little ones into the thicker undergrowth and followed them in. The children had played in these woods. It was their one advantage. The den was just tall enough for her to lie flat on the ground, while the younger ones sat cross-legged.

Touching her mouth, she whispered, "Be very quiet, just like mice." The boots and legs of police officers were on the path and near them. They watched through the sticks and stems and from under the leaves of their den. The men were panting and pushed into the undergrowth, first one side of the path and then the other. Now they stood quietly, waiting for the sound of frightened children.

Nina felt her foot being nudged and froze. Then again she felt it and peered down the length of her body toward the path. The dark leg of a policeman could be seen. The boot swivelled on its heel and tapped her bare foot sticking out of her hiding den at the edge of the path. Quietly she drew her leg up.

A voice said in English, "We're wasting our time out here. Let's get back. There's more to do in the camp."

IT HAD NOT TAKEN LONG. THE MORNING WAS NOT YET OVER. THERE WERE still children on the run but most had been gathered, as had the adults. Children were bundled onto buses. The parents moaned and nursed themselves carefully up wobbling boards onto the open trucks. Flanagan held the hand of a shaken woman balancing up the plank. She was twisting to see a child getting on a bus.

"Pavel!" she shouted, followed by something in Russian. It must have been final guidance or reassurance, or whatever message a mother would give to a child at the moment of separation. Perhaps, Flanagan thought, it was a simple statement of love. He imagined saying something to his children about taking care of themselves and also that he would find them. Whatever she said, he knew it would not be enough.

He felt the heat of his tunic and wanted to fall into the Slocan River to cool and soothe himself. As he reached for the next person in line, his attention was grabbed by a bus leaving for New Denver. All the children and some of the mothers with young ones were heading there. Flanagan caught sight of a particular boy on the New Denver bus whose nose was pressed to the window. He traced his stare to the woman he had helped onto the flatbed a minute before. The boy must have been the Pavel she had shouted for. With all of these parents looking at all of these children, each connection was unmistakable.

When Flanagan was a child, his mother would say to her children that they should not worry because the sun would shine and the sky would be blue in the morning. Whatever troubled him no longer mattered when it was said. For these children, Flanagan thought, the sun would shine, the sky would be blue and even the Slocan River would ripple over rocks, but nothing would ever be the same. It would always matter.

A rough grab lifted his sleeve and turned his hand.

"There!" said the sergeant, twisting Flanagan's arm to inspect the outside of the palm. Both saw the dried stain of blood smeared from his cuff along his finger. "There's no one to look down on now, son. Is there?" The sergeant glared in triumph before returning Flanagan's hand to him with a shove.

Flanagan wiped the stain on his trousers but it would not budge. In desperation he licked his fingers and rubbed furiously at the stain. Without thinking he again put his fingers to his mouth and tasted the Doukhobor blood on his hands. It was enough to make his gut convulse, and in a moment he was helpless, leaning against the truck, heaving his bitter breakfast onto the grass.

It's true, thought Flanagan. He was part of this, just as every British hand that had confounded the politics of home was responsible for all that had happened to his father and his people. There would be consequences for this too. When he came to account he could only say he had caused no injury and, adding to the inventory, he had prevented three children from being taken. It was lame and quickly he knew it would not be enough to balance these books. Flanagan wished the children he had left in the forest would be well and find their way to safety. It would be his fault if they did not.

The truck he leaned on came to life, noise drowning out the crying of men and women. Diesel fumes added to his nausea. The buses with children began pulling away from Perry Siding. Children and parents would travel up and down the Slocan Valley, in opposite directions.

If the trauma of their history were not already carved on the hearts of these people, the injustice of this day would stay with them always. It would torment those needing sleep, stand between people at every conversation, erode lives and spew anger into the air at all things easily misunderstood. He had seen his parents embittered, families broken and the weave of his community decay until anger was all that remained. The children would grow troubled and misshapen, just as they had in Ireland. The distrust and hate for RCMP and government officials of all kinds would remain tightly gripped among them like a treasured stone until someone could relieve them of the burden. In a few years the identity of all of them would be shaped around that stone. The injustice would be deified. It would offer purpose in every day, kudos from friends in taking the weight of it and martyrdom when it crushed them.

He hoped an anguished hope that someone would do something.

NINA GESTURED TO THE GIRLS TO STAY QUIET FOR A WHILE LONGER UNTIL the sound of police moving off faded to nothing.

The immediate danger had gone. The sound of shouting, mothers wailing and children crying had ended. In the distance diesel engines of long buses had roared into life and moved off with nearly everyone they knew. Now, with just the sounds of birds, whispering trees and the ripple of water, it was strange to be alone in the forest. Nina shuffled out of the den and brought the little ones with her. Some of the tents were still up and they walked carefully toward them.

"Don't worry," she said. "We'll have to do some walking to find our parents." It was untrue, but it was all she could think of to say. The closest place she knew of was Krestova, if only she could remember how to get there.

The prayer tent was standing but leaned awkwardly. Under the canvas, the late summer sun brought the temperature up. Nina and the two little ones kicked through the debris of clothes and shoes on the ground. They were clothed well enough for a summer day, but they searched for something to wear when the sun fell. On the little table that had stood between women and girls on one side and men and boys on the other as they sang, the symbols of faith remained undisturbed: a small round loaf of bread, a jug of water and a small cup of salt. It was all that had not been unsettled and all that Nina would need to keep their spirits up on the way to Krestova. She bundled the bread into the tablecloth and gave the children a drink of the fresh water before setting off.

"We better get started," she said, offering her hand to Arina. "Don't worry. We'll be all right."

Krestova, BC, January 18, 1955

AUNTIE'S HOUSE AND WHAT REMAINED OF KRESTOVA COSSETED NINA LIKE the blanket she pulled over her shoulders against the morning chill. There was a familiarity to everything in this communal house. It was identical to hers in all but detail. Just the push and shove between characters was new. Two brick houses in mirror image stood forty feet apart. Behind them a row of buildings, bathhouse, barns, workshops, spanned the width of both houses and the gap between them, creating a courtyard and a sense of function and purpose. There was nothing here without function. Outside of the courtyard, orchards and fields for planting had been established. Everything, bricks and bread, had been created by the endless toil of the Doukhobor people.

Through the back door of either house were two rooms. On one side was a dining room with a long wooden table and benches, enough to seat twenty people. On the other side was a kitchen dominated by a bread oven standing five feet high, creating a platform between it and the ceiling, where the old and very young sometimes kept warm at night in deep winter. Past the dining room was a larger parlour that opened into the hallway, where stairs led to a wide corridor with bedrooms on either side. Everything was here for a peaceful life. "Toil and a peaceful life" was the mantra of all of these Doukhobor communities.

Already, before the light of day, the house was alive and the smell of bread from the kitchen brought memories of Nina's home. The clatter of wooden spoons on the large dining table, clanking of steel pans and endless chatter invited her to get out of bed and go downstairs. It reminded her too of her parents, still in prison. She had come to know it was not good to lie in bed thinking of them. In any case, breakfast waited, and then morning jobs were to be done before lessons. She swung out of her bed, reached across the room and jabbed Arina awake through her blankets.

After breakfast there were chickens to feed and eggs to gather for Auntie. Nina and Arina headed for the barn. The morning light was just arriving as they picked their way across compacted snow in the courtyard. At the edges of paths snow piled in shovelled lumps, but against the buildings wedges of snow drifted five feet against windward walls.

The children entered the barn and collected feed for the chickens while Arina stumbled in the darkness. The sound of people running between the outer buildings toward the communal houses caught their attention. From deep in the barn they watched silent men in black uniforms rush toward the kitchen doors. Some had rifles; others held truncheons at the ready. Nina pulled Arina to the hay piled on the floor of the barn and gathered it around them. There was banging on doors and shouting from inside the house. Women shouted and children screamed. The volume of indignation excited the dogs to bark and the hens to cluck and flap.

From the kitchen door two officers emerged holding a boy wrapped in a blanket. Auntie's father, an elder of the house, wearing only underwear, followed, shouting and grappling to get hands on the boy. An officer turned and wrestled him away, and both fell into the deeper snow against the house. The boy escaped and set off running in his pyjamas and bare feet. One officer chased while the other struggled to get away from the clutches of the elder. A fierce elbow connected with the cheek of the elder, whose body melted before limbs stiffened in spasm. Arina jumped to go to her grandfather but was held by Nina. The officer rose and joined the chase for pyjama boy, leaving the elder to quiver in the snow. Auntie's cries for her father filled the courtyard and others came, soothing, lifting the old man.

One by one children were taken from the houses, some crying, others reassuring their parents to subdue their fear. Nina remembered the turmoil and shouting of Perry Siding and knew parts of what had happened before she was born. Three hundred fifty Doukhobor children had been taken just like this. The children were sent away; some died, while others were never heard of again. They had been taken and lost. Now it was happening again.

Every Doukhobor adult and child lived with knowing English Canadians were capable of this. It was part of the folklore of betrayal, the narrative of English-Canadian entitlement. The recollection was fearful enough, but to see and hear the cries of this new generation of children bundled into cars found instant location in the Doukhobor memory, confirming what was already believed, swelling emotion beyond simple terror.

Nearly an hour had passed. The commotion had ended. Nina and Arina shuffled in the cold, peeking out to see if it was over just as Auntie came to the kitchen door and shouted, "Arina! Nina!" Both children ran into the hugs and warmth of the communal house. Inside, women tended to the elder, now sitting up with blankets draped over him. Others sat inconsolable at the dining table where arms held them tight. Some prayed quietly.

"Where's Peter?" asked Nina, thinking of pyjama boy.

His mother lifted her head from her hands. "They have him. He's taken."

Nina said, "No, he's not. We saw him get away and run. He had pyjama bottoms on." The room looked at her. "Nothing else."

Uncle stepped toward the door. "Which way did he go?"

"I don't know. We just saw him get away." Everyone in the room except the elder and the most desolate flooded out the kitchen door and spread out toward the outbuildings, gripped in the new panic of finding the lost boy. A few rounded the corner of the houses and headed uphill toward the forest, everyone shouting for Peter.

A child's noise surfaced through the shouting. The community was in silence, listening carefully for the quiet sound of one precious boy in danger they might save. From the snowy wedge that had drifted against a wall of the house, sounds of struggling could be heard. Several of the men ran toward it and began digging with their hands. In seconds, Peter was pulled from the snow. His skin was blue. The tip of his nose was white with the first signs of frostbite. Everyone knew what had happened. Escaping from the police, he had managed to be out of sight long enough to jump into the snowdrift and be gone. It was an act of desperation that might have killed him, but the risk saved him from a fate thought worse than that. The men hurried him into the house.

March 14, 1955

NINA NOTED THE HELPLESSNESS IN AUNTIE'S EYES. SHE ROLLED UP THE brown paper bag holding their lunch, handed it to Nina and asked, "Will you have enough food?"

"You always give us plenty."

"You'll be safe in the forest today, won't you?" said Auntie. There would be nothing she could do once Nina and Arina stepped out the door and trudged through the snow up the gentle slope to the wooded hills behind the house.

"I know the woods," said Nina.

"Will you be all right, you two?"

"We'll be all right."

Auntie grasped the edges of Arina's coat, pulling them together, inspecting, before squeezing love into her with the strength of a bear. "Stay with Nina. Don't be going off on your own." Then she turned to Nina.

"Stay in the woods till the police have gone."

"We will."

"And don't go too far."

"I won't, Auntie. Don't worry." Suddenly Nina's face was grasped and her cheek squashed with thick Russian lips. "Thank you, Auntie."

Auntie grabbed the cuff of Nina's coat and rubbed it between her fingers. "Your coat needs mending."

"It will be fine for today."

"I'll make you a new one. Off you go now. God protect you."

The door opened. Hand in hand the two girls left the house. Arina waved wildly at Auntie; Nina walked without looking back. The sky was blue and the sun, shining from the southeast, warmed her through the layers. She loved being free and outside, but the early excitement of days in the forest had faded. The elements never bothered her but the prospect of being in the woods for the day caring for Arina caused her feet to drag in the snow. She wanted to know what her friends were doing and even if they were friends still, after all this time. Who had they become in New Denver? And did they ever think of her? The big sky felt empty and the massed conifers were overwhelming. It would be difficult being in the forest today.

Arina said, "You're lucky. My mother's going to make you a new coat."

Nina perked up remembering her auntie's promise. The new coat would be made for her. It would be warm and last forever.

October 10, 1955

THE RHYTHM OF THE HOUSE WAS COMFORTING, HER PLACE AT THE TABLE assured, but something about this morning dulled her enthusiasm. Nina sat at the edge of her bed but could not fully wake. She had not seen her friends in over a year and she missed them, sometimes more than she missed her parents. There were a few other children but those from her communal house were gone. She had no desire to wake up and think of them all together in New Denver without her. Neither did she wish to pad through the house, past the bustle of activity downstairs, just to pee. By lifting her feet from the cold wood floor and toppling over, she could put off the day a little longer. Her head landed on the pillow moments before sleep found her.

From outside the house the noise of someone shouting reached her and was gone. Another noise, but now from inside the house. Chairs moved across floors, doors rattled and banged shut, voices lifted. Nina did not want to allow it in. There were feet on the stairs, running. Now on the landing they came tapping toward her room. The door flung wide, but still Nina would not allow it through her haze.

"Nina! Nina, wake up!" Auntie's voice pressed into her sleep. Her blankets pulled away and she coiled against the fresh cool of morning. "Nina! You must hide! The police are coming to take you. You must hide." Inside her sleep, it did not seem so bad to be taken, to be with her friends again. Strong arms heaved her curled body to a sitting position. "Help me, Nina, please!" They were shaking her now and more voices were in the room.

Uncle's voice came. "Open the cabinet and take the door."

His huge carpenter's hands gathered her off the bed, shifting her easily into his arms, and for a moment she was warm against his body and clung to him. In his arms she flew, knowing she would land in the special hiding place through the large cupboard in her bedroom. The wall at the back had been removed and the space behind it would fit one child. It was a space with spiders and only darkness, but it was safe from English-Canadian police.

"Nina, listen to me," Uncle said. She squinted at him knowing the drill they had done so often, but never at this time of the morning. "Shuffle back and take the handles."

Her job was to grip the handles on the inside and pull the wall panel into place, bracing herself with her feet against the frame. The cupboard doors would be closed, but even when opened, the look and feel of the wall would not give her away. "Quickly now. Stay until we come for you. You understand?" She nodded.

Robust knocking on the kitchen door vibrated the house. Voices shouted in English to be let in. Outside, between the houses, children and women began screaming. Uncle's eyes showed his alarm. She pulled the panel toward her, submerging herself in darkness. It was cold, and she wished she had gone out to pee before all of this.

GERRY FLANAGAN WAS THE LAST OF THREE UNIFORMED MEN POUNDING in sturdy boots up the stairs to the bedrooms. He stood at the top of the stairs with his flashlight. The uniformed men split up and searched quickly in all of the rooms. A man and a woman stood on the landing in their underwear, holding candles, and watched them barge into each room, flashlights glaring, beaming under the beds and behind the doors. The three officers emerged onto the landing. Without discussion two of them entered the first room and began a more thorough search, yanking blankets and mattresses off beds, emptying drawers, disturbing everything. Flanagan stayed outside, watching for movement and listening for noises that would give the children away.

"You have no right to come into our house," said the man in his underwear. "You have no right."

"We can do what we like." Sergeant Benson's voice came from the stairs and surprised everyone. "You don't have to be here. If you don't obey the laws of the land, then go back."

The man said, "I've been here fifty years—longer than you!"

"We obey Jesus Christ," said the woman next to him. "No worldly laws are above his."

"That may be, but he is not here to tell us. Is he?" said the sergeant.

"He's in every man," the man said. "Maybe not you."

The sergeant turned on him. "I have the law with me. I am the law. Just stand there and let my men do their work. You have nothing to worry about if God's with you."

The two police officers emerged from the first bedroom. Without breaking stride they entered the room across the landing and began again. Flanagan noticed the man and woman shuffle and exchange a glance, before a squeal emerged from the room.

"Arina!" the woman shouted, and pushed forward. Flanagan wrapped his arms around her.

Her husband pulled at her to free her from Flanagan's grip.

"Take your hands off my wife. You have no right."

The three shuffled back and forth on the landing in a drunken dance until the slapping sound of a riding crop lashing the man's face caused him to let go and stumble backwards. It was an animal cry of pain and outrage that emerged from him, drawing his wife to his aid. The girl, Arina, emerged crying and frightened from her bedroom, held by a policeman with a broad smile on his face.

The policeman said, "She was in the mattress, buttoned up the side."

"Take her to the cars," said the sergeant. "Keep searching."

The woman hustled forward, barging the officer aside. Mother and daughter clamped arms around each other and began crying, sobbing. Officers grabbed them and tried forcing them apart.

"Wait, wait, stop!" said Flanagan, pushing the officers away.

"What's this, Irish?" asked the sergeant. "Have you forgotten what side you're on again?"

"Just wait," he said, shaking the sergeant's grip from his tunic. "Let me talk to them." Without waiting for a reply Flanagan bent down on one knee, his head level with theirs. His hands rested on the shoulders of the mother and daughter. "We have seven men in this house. Some have batons, some have rifles and we all have orders. School-aged children are being taken to New Denver, today, right now. If you struggle to stop us, people will be hurt, your daughter will be upset and she'll go to New Denver in these clothes and without anything to eat. If you get some clothes on her and give her something to eat for the journey, at least she will be warm and not hungry. Then you can go to New Denver and see her." Arina continued crying, but her mother listened to Flanagan's soft, reasoned tones. She looked toward her husband, who was still holding the side of his face. He nodded and the woman turned to Flanagan.

She asked, "Have you children?"

"Two daughters," he replied.

"So, you understand the feelings?"

"I do," said Flanagan.

"If you understand, and still do this," she said, pausing, "how will you be forgiven? God will not forgive you."

There was no escaping the horror and sadness in her eyes. Her horror was not for herself, her daughter or even her being taken. It was knowing Flanagan was outside of forgiveness. Flanagan felt the words breach the moral cloak of a uniformed defender of the law, finding him unprotected, naked to a simple truth.

"I know," he said, "but there is no choice for either of us."

She lifted Arina, as if protecting her from a terrible darkness in the room, and carried her into the bedroom.

"Stay with her," the sergeant shouted at an officer. "Now, finish the search." Looking at the girl's father, he said, "You, come downstairs with me."

The turmoil in Flanagan's head calmed enough for him to think about the task. He gestured to his colleague to follow him into the next room. Quickly they opened everything, felt the mattresses and checked again under the beds. Nothing. The next bedroom was a family room with a large double bed, a single and a baby's cot suspended from the ceiling. The bed was cold, but they tossed it anyway. They shone their flashlights into the corners and under the beds and rummaged in the hanging cot before hurrying to the next room. Flanagan opened the door. Two single beds and a cupboard.

IT WAS COLD HIDING IN THE WALL BEHIND THE CUPBOARD. NINA'S LEGS trembled with the chill and the strain of bracing the door shut. She had heard the muffled sounds, each arriving with more alarm than the one before. Every sense strained for more information. There were banging footsteps, shouting on the landing, her uncle had wailed with pain, Auntie and Arina were crying. Now there was quiet, save for the sound of police searching room to room.

The door of her room opened abruptly and she held her breath, listening to each noise, calculating how many there were and what they were doing. One leg began trembling beyond her control. She so wanted to pee, and the cold and strain of holding the door had made this worse. As her fear rose, she ached to let it go.

A voice in the room said in English, "The bed's warm. There's clothing for a child."

It was too much to hold on to, and out it came. The relief caused her to exhale and the trembling leg eased, but the sound of pee draining from her caught her attention—so much, and it kept coming, soaking her clothes, adding shame to her fear. The cupboard door opening startled her. She imagined a policeman in the cupboard moving clothes, searching. At the bottom of the panel she held shut was a gap large enough to see a strip of light from the room—enough for her to see her legs still pressed on the frame, and a growing puddle running from her hiding place, between her feet, under the door and into the cupboard, where the policeman searched. A new flashlight beam reflected off the puddle into her eyes.

WHILE HIS PARTNER LIFTED THE MATTRESSES, FLANAGAN PULLED AT THE clothing in the cupboard and tried not to think about the little girl being dressed in the bedroom across the landing. He worked his way from the top shelf down, moving quickly to be done with this business. Finally he pointed his light to the bottom corners of the cupboard. A puddle spread from the wall toward him. Flanagan put his hand on the panel and tried to shift it, but it would not move. He shone his light, trying to make sense of why water was running out of the cupboard, and then put his head closer. The smell was all he needed.

"Anything?" asked the sergeant entering the room.

"Nothing, Sarge." Flanagan stood and closed the door of the cupboard. "Two more bedrooms to do."

"Well, hurry up and get on with it."

"Yes, Sarge."

September 3, 1956

NINA KNELT AND ADMIRED HER CONSTRUCTION OF BROKEN STICKS AND spruce boughs. It had taken most of the day but had kept her occupied. She imagined her friends coming to play and how excited they would be to find a secret den in the woods. By now, she thought, Arina had become part of the secret world of New Denver, and may have carried the memory of her to her friends.

Shadows had begun reaching into the valley from the crest of the hill behind Auntie's house. The attraction of building a den had passed and it was time to go home. There was always tomorrow to refine her forest hideaway.

Nina crawled out through the small opening into the late afternoon light and admired her work. Until the fir needles turned brown you could walk by it without ever seeing it. Inside, it was large enough for three or four children to play in secret.

The den moved and creaked, as if at any moment it would collapse under its own weight. Branches rustled behind it. The head of a bear emerged above the den with a guttural snort. Nina turned and ran. In two steps her heart pounded and her chest heaved, her attention narrowed to the single task of getting away. The forest thrashed at her face and arms, snagging her clothes and holding her back.

Distance from the bear became enough to think of where she was going. Through the rasp of her own breath she listened for noises of the bear following her. Sounds everywhere were unfamiliar. The bear was quick enough to be behind or in front of her. Branches fell and birds startled into the sky; everything was a sign of danger. Staying in the woods as darkness arrived was not a choice to be made. The only option was getting back to Auntie's house, and to do that she would have to go past her den and the bear or take a long route around and risk not getting home before the cold and dark overtook her. It had to be the long route.

An hour had passed. Nina had given a wide berth to her den, moving as quietly as she could, listening carefully to every sound of the forest. Long shadows reached into the valley from the west, but lights from Auntie's house could be seen through the brush, just down the hill. The crackling sound of treading on forest mulch held her still. She listened for another sound and suppressed the urge to run wildly toward the light. Another noise from a different direction could be something, or nothing. She waited for more, but nothing convinced her it was safe to go or to stay. It was time to break cover and run for the house.

In the open, past the tree line, Nina was sure she would make it. There were no sounds of grunting breath or snarling anger chasing her. With every stride she felt more confident in seeing Auntie again. The house was clearly in view and she angled her run to take her to the kitchen door on the other side. Her body relaxed and suddenly she could acknowledge the stinging scratches on hands and face from running through the bush. Thirst clawed her throat and her legs ached, but it was over now. She was home.

As she passed the outside corner of the house on the perimeter of the group of buildings, a black car came into view between the outbuildings. It took her three long strides to come to a halt. The police were there. Nina flattened herself against the wall of the house, knowing they had come for her.

She edged along the wall to see into the yard. Across the courtyard, through an open door of the barn, lit up like a nativity scene, a police officer was shifting hay with a pitchfork. Nina watched carefully. He was not shifting but stabbing the hay, stepping along and stabbing again, in search of children, looking for her. Auntie and Uncle would be inside worrying, hoping she would not come home just now or be hiding in that hay. Up the hill toward the forest it was now foreboding black under deep azure sky. Other officers began walking across the yard to the outbuildings. In seconds she would come into view. It would be easy to stay still and be taken. Being endlessly watchful, hiding, days spent alone in the forest could all be over if she waited a few seconds longer. The idea came with relief, and the prospect of joining lost friends brought a sudden sense that all of this would finish. Nina still watched the nativity scene.

The officer thrust the pitchfork into the hay, walked two steps and thrust again. Nina wondered if he would really do that if he thought she was hiding there, and then the realization came to her. He did think she might be hiding in the hay. There was no other reason to search for her there.

When the RCMP officers walked past the edge of the house and flashed their beams, there was no one to be seen. Nina was well into the darkness, heading for the tree line, taking her chances with the bear, believing Auntie's assurance that God would protect her in the forest. It seemed inevitable that she would be taken, but not this day, not squealing in terror at the point of a pitchfork.

3

Vancouver, December 21, 2017

IT WAS COOL IN THE ROOM WHERE HE WAS BEING MADE READY. PATIENTS waited, hidden and helpless. William hated the garb everyone was forced to wear in hospital. It was convenient only for those who wanted to get at you.

The surgeon arrived, brushing aside the curtain that surrounded the bed. Dressed in clogs and green pyjamas, he began speaking through a mask over which his nose protruded.

"Remember me?" he said cheerfully. "I'm Dr. Franklin. How are you feeling?"

"Fine, thank you."

"We'll be ready to take you into the operating room in a few minutes. I thought I would come by and answer any last-minute questions you might have." His eyes smiled. William did not answer. "Let me just refresh your memory of what we are doing and what to expect. Today we are going to make a fairly small incision under your eyebrow," said the surgeon, drawing an arc with his finger, "and remove that tumour we found on the pituitary gland. This method is called transsphenoidal because we are going through the sinus behind the nose. What it means is that we don't have to open the skull, and we don't have to navigate through brain tissue, and there will be almost no scar. Of course there are always risks with any operation, but we've done this operation many times and it's very successful. You'll have to take it easy for a couple of days, but you shouldn't feel too uncomfortable. Do you have any questions for me?"

"How long will it be before I start noticing differences? I don't really know what to expect afterwards."

The surgeon rocked his head back and forth. "It's difficult to be sure about that. You've had the condition for ten years or so. We don't know what you would be like had you not had it. You also have your routines and habits, like we all do. Don't expect these to change overnight. There are lots of men with the symptoms you describe without your condition, so I don't think there will be dramatic change."

"I didn't even know they were symptoms." William shrugged.

"Things happen slowly, so you wouldn't notice changes. Remember, you are a busy man with responsibilities and lots of stress. Why would you notice?"

"Put like that, it hardly seems worth doing something about it."

The surgeon's eyes smiled again. "Well, it all depends on what type we are dealing with. We're more concerned about preventing something worse happening. It's only little, as adenomas are, but too big to be in your head. Eventually it could affect your sight and other things. And it has probably been upsetting your system for a long time. It's worth it. Believe me."

"Thanks." William grimaced politely.

"No need for that," said the surgeon. "It's all part of the service." His eyes smiled again over the mask as he moved toward the opening at the end of the bed. "The anaesthetist will be along shortly, and I'll see you again in theatre. Rest now."

William waited in the cubical. Through the gap in the curtains at the end of his bed he could see people enter and exit his field of vision in not much more than a blink. Soft voices drifted to him from all directions. Trolleys moved. He shifted his head back and forth to widen the angle of view. Two nurses stood in their hospital fatigues behind a counter, huddled over a clipboard. He thought there was something holy in all of this cleanliness, reverence and quiet murmurings like the voices of churchgoers. He hated the helplessness of waiting for others to act.

The small gap in the curtains opened suddenly and the anaesthetist swept in with a nurse.

"Hello," she said cheerfully. "All ready?"

William nodded. "Yes, I think so."

"Good. We can give you something to relax you before we take you into theatre," she said, turning his arm over and exposing the back of his hand.

She held his forearm and rubbed his hand. Her touch was unfamiliar and discomforting but he allowed it. He was always wary of being touched and it was made worse now that he was helpless. She produced a syringe and secured the cannula with tape to his hand. "You'll feel a little warm and pleasant when this takes effect."

He watched her attach a syringe and inject something into him, bracing himself for the intrusion. The warmth came and he struggled quietly against it.

The nurse said, "We'll be taking you to theatre now." Someone kicked at the legs of his bed and suddenly it was moving. The anaesthetist walked beside him along the corridor. Lights above him passed quickly. Looking up he could no longer make out her features against the light. A wide door opened into another room. There was bustle and conversation. It did not seem to matter what was being said.

The anaesthetist's voice retrieved him from the warm comfort that was embracing him. She held his arm again, did something with the cannula on the back of his hand and said, "Count backwards from a hundred for me."

"One hundred, ninety-nine, ninety-eight, ninety-seven, ninety-six ..."

He was being shaken gently and spoken to in a soft voice, interrupting the warmth. The voice was concerned but not urgent. Inside, William tried not to listen.

"William. William. Wake up. You're in the recovery room; everything went well." The shaking continued; it did not feel to be his body rocking. Inside, it was still. The cocoon of anaesthesia allowed him to hear but not care about the note of urgency now creeping into the voice asking his body to wake. It was too soon to emerge. Something else had to be dealt with before he came back to the world. *What was it?*

TREETOPS FLASHED BY. THE OWL'S FLIGHT LEVELLED AND THE GROUND appeared through the trees just below them. William searched for a place where he might land if he were to let go, but each time he saw a chance, it rushed beneath him and was gone.

William said, "You're going too fast. I can't let go, and I can't be late."

"And you don't want to let go of your hat," said the owl.

"I have a meeting to go to."

"This meeting," said the owl. "It doesn't happen before you arrive?"

"No, it won't."

"It cannot happen until you arrive?"

"Of course not!" said William.

"Then how can you be late?"

"Because I'm supposed to be there at a certain time."

"Is that a rule?" asked the owl.

"I suppose it is."

"Whose rule is it?"

"Well, mine, I guess."

"Then," said the owl, "make a new rule, so it does not matter."

"What's the point of a rule if you just make up another rule when it suits you?"

"What's the point of a rule if another one suits you better?"

"That's madness," said William.

"Perhaps," said the owl. "What does it matter if it's the first or second rule you make? It's what you choose."

"It isn't what I do."

"WILLIAM, OPEN YOUR EYES FOR ME. WAKE UP." THE INSISTENCE STOPPED and the voice moved away from him. "No," said the voice, "he isn't coming round. Perhaps you should get the anaesthetist." Footsteps left them. He could be alone for a time.

His head was being moved, light forced in his eyes. The anaesthetist was talking. "I don't think there's anything to worry about. He just seems to be taking his time. William. Try and open your eyes." Her hands stroked his shoulder.

From inside the cocoon, William appealed, *Not yet. Please don't wake me yet.* What was it that could not be grasped?

"Try!" His voice breached the surface.

"Oh," said the anaesthetist, "you're back with us. We thought you might sleep till tomorrow. You're in the recovery room. Everything went as we wanted. The nurse will be along to see you and then we can get a drink for you. I'll check on you later."

Footsteps left and others approached, two people walking with quick steps. He had not remembered what he wanted to deal with. Maybe, he thought as his eyes opened, it was nothing, but he was not content. William closed his eyes and tried to find the thought that evaded him.

"Don't go back to sleep on me, William." The nurse's hand came to his face and rubbed him gently, smudging out the last chance of recovering it. He was awake now. It was gone.

DENNIS CLOSED THE WAREHOUSE DOOR AND TURNED TO THE STACK OF yellow and black SynchronoX boxes. Cathy was upstairs in the office, but she would have to wait until he had sorted the boxes as the boss had instructed.

He lifted the manifest from the wall and began inspecting the box ends. The first he found within seconds. It was high in the pile and it slipped out with a tug. Dennis carried it near the warehouse roller door and began a new stack. The second took another minute to find and was lower. At least ten bicycles lay on it, and it needed coaxing out. He pulled at one corner, pushed at another and steadied the swaying boxes on top of it. Again he pulled, pushed and steadied until the target box balanced those above it on an edge. Upstairs a Christmas treat was waiting, and he cursed himself for cutting corners. He began easing it out an inch or two at a time. It was the only choice.

Gradually the box moved out and the stack leaned gently back and forth several times, until three boxes slid off the top and split open on the concrete floor. The clattering sound of boxes opening and titanium parts spilling out was unmistakable. Dennis knew the damage without seeing it.

He could hear Cathy coming down the stairs. Quickly he pulled the target box out of the stack; from the doorway all would seem normal.

"Are you all right?" Cathy asked as she came through the door.

"Yes. Why?"

"I heard a noise."

"So did I," said Dennis. "It must have been someone next door or in the alley."

Cathy hesitated. "Do you need help?"

"No, thanks. I'm doing fine with this." He smiled at her. "I might need some help a little later."

"I can only stay till twelve. Don't be too long." The door closed as she left.

Dennis walked around to the back of the stack. Two boxes had split open and one was compressed at the corner. He started gathering the parts. It was not as bad as he had thought. The carefully engineered pieces had been in form-fitting polystyrene and in individual plastic bags. He just had to gather up the parts and push them into their rightful place and claim the shipping company had done the damage to the boxes. There was no one to say otherwise. The army had taught him not to confess to anything unless he had to, and he would not change the habit on this occasion. He would, if he had to, apologize for signing off on the delivery without inspecting each unit, but if there was no damage to the contents, there should be no problem.

Dennis crouched on his haunches and picked up two sprockets with the same part number stuck to the two plastic bags containing them. He looked for anything to match each with the right box, but there was nothing. There was something unusual in their weight. He inspected them. They were marked the same, but one sprocket was heavy and the other light. It might be, he thought, that they were from the same box. He laid both boxes side by side and opened them both. The preformed polystyrene packaging had space for only one large sprocket in each box. Each part had a number, and one of each number was associated with each box, but the parts were different. The bikes were labelled the same on the packaging but were not the same in the box. *Jesus!* he thought. It was time to close up the packages and get on with the separation as the boss had asked him to do.

As the cardboard lid came down on the last box, he checked the number against the manifest. It was one of those he was to separate out. Then he saw it, written in pencil, on the bottom corner at the end of the box: the number fourteen, in his handwriting. *For fuck's sake! What is going on here?*

The separation was complete and the new stack of twenty bicycles sat by the roller door of the warehouse. The separation had not taken very long, but it had offered enough time to think through the implication of what he had stumbled on. It was an opportunity if he could avoid blowing the chance.

The camera in the corner of the warehouse, at the junction of wall and ceiling, watched. It would have caught everything. No problem. He would delete the tape and say nothing. *No one checks it anyway.* A random period deleted this close to Christmas would go unnoticed, and in any case, the video recorder would start its cycle again and no one would suspect anything. He would go upstairs and see that Cathy was content, as if nothing were unusual. She was not expected to be at work anyway, which meant she would say nothing about the noise of crashing boxes. It was a plan likely to work, especially with the boss in hospital.

He washed his hands, pulled off his overalls and walked up the stairs.

"Hi," he said to Cathy. "Sorry it took so long."

"I'm still here."

SHE SMILED NERVOUSLY AT HIM, SMOOTHING OUT THE RIPPLES OF HER skirt along her thighs.

"That was nice," said Dennis. "Can you show me where the security tapes are?"

"You'll get me in trouble. Why do you want the security tapes?"

"Well, you came into the warehouse this morning, and in reception." He could see it made no sense to her. "Are you supposed to be in today? Because there's a record of you and me being in the building at the same time, when you are not supposed to be here at all. Someone might think that you're here because you're being very naughty. Could that be true?" He walked toward her with a sway of someone who knows what will happen next.

She lifted a key ring from a pot on her desk and selected a key for him. "Just there," she said, nodding toward a steel cupboard low to the floor.

"I'll wipe the tapes when you go. I can lock up." He kissed her. She was soft and warm. "Merry Christmas," he said. "I think you better go before we get started again."

"Then I better go now." She lifted her coat from a chair by the door and left him in the office.

He turned to the camera recorders as she left the building. There was a rack of three recorders in the cupboard. It took a minute to work out that it was a series of VHS recorders, each with two tape decks, each recording two cameras—an antiquated system, but effective. The recorders were labelled with the camera they tracked. *That's peculiar,* he thought. They were all turned off. *Why would they be switched off over Christmas?* Cathy might be in trouble for forgetting to turn them on. He pressed the power and the record buttons. The lights came to life and the machines began humming.

One last job to do. He pulled the manifest from his pocket and went to the photocopier.

December 22, 2017

IT WAS QUIET, DARK AND TOO EARLY FOR MORNING TRAFFIC. THIRTY metres from the reception area, Uri watched the van arrive at the delivery door. He moved quickly from his car to the doorway and put his key in the lock. The door opened; he moved to the alarm panel, inserted the key, punched in the code and waited for the panel lights to turn green. Inside, the layout was just as William had described, and in a moment he was in the warehouse with the lights on.

Uri took stock of his surroundings. Two stacks of SynchronoX boxes, one large and one small, waited. He opened the delivery doors, and men emerged from the van and began loading the smaller stack.

They were done quickly. Uri closed the delivery doors as the van departed, and recalled the remainder of the plan. His job was to set the alarms and lock up. William would be back before Christmas to start the security tape recording. He scanned the office and decided there was nothing else to be done. Quickly he set the alarm and closed the front door behind him.

"HOW ARE YOU FEELING?" ASKED JULIE. SHE SAT NEXT TO THE BED.

His forehead throbbed front and back, and his ears rang constantly. He reached for the apple juice remaining on his lunch tray and sipped tiny amounts through a plastic straw. His throat was raw and the taste of blood was constant. William peered through swollen eyes and a dressing taped under his nose, and spoke carefully.

"Better than I thought I would."

"You look like you've gone ten rounds with a boxer."

"I feel like I have." William allowed his head to fall back against the pillow and then lifted it quickly to prevent a new slug of blood sliding into his throat.

"That's honest," Julie said, and then hesitated. "I am pleased it's Christmas. The office is closed. All the deliveries made. You can be off for a week or so ... and let yourself recover."

William heard the emphasis in her words. She continued, "When you're home and feeling a little better, I want to spend some time talking."

"Do we have something we need to talk about?" It did not come out as he expected.

"We haven't spoken in years. Yes, we have some things to talk about. Now, you're not in a state to argue. You can't even ignore me and cycle off. Anyway, I have to get back for Kelly. She really wants to see you. I'll let her know how you look, so it doesn't come as a shock. She might be able to see the colour. Maybe you could phone her and tell her you're okay, and I'll bring her tomorrow when we pick you up." She stood and began putting on her coat.

They did not seem to be the whining or complaining words he normally heard. "When?" He asked.

"After lunch. They've said about two o'clock. I can come and get you, providing you're okay."

"No, when did you get unhappy?"

Julie let her coat hang on her arms and shrugged. "Oh, I don't know. When the business really took off; four years ago when your dad died; ten years ago when you"—her voice broke suddenly—"lost interest. It's hard to say when the change happened. When did you?"

William shook his head. It was a perplexing question. He had never thought of being happy or unhappy. In any case, he could not find words to reply.

"Well, I better get going." She pulled her coat over her shoulders. "Kelly will be wondering where I am." Julie stopped at the door and turned to him. "See you tomorrow."

William smiled as best he could through the gauze. It was not intolerance or contempt in her voice or in how she looked at him from the foot of the bed. Was it sadness or pity? How could it be that she had become sad, with all that he had provided and after all his effort?

Lying helplessly in a hospital bed, he imagined his father watching as he left one of the terrible Riverview Hospital visits. Was there sadness or pity on his face as he left his father's room? Did his father see it or know of his anger and disappointment? A twitch of anguish cracked a crust of scab at the tip of his nose and brought moisture to his eyes. The thought of adding a burden to his father's torment discomforted him. He closed his eyes and turned his face away to escape the thought. A clot of blood slipped into his mouth. William reached for the polystyrene cup and allowed the slug to drip from his lips. There was something about being alone and helpless that kept drawing his mind to his father.

Suddenly a gush of liquid filled his mouth. He spit into the cup. It was clear, and it was something he knew to be watching for. William reached for the nurse alarm and in a few seconds he arrived.

"Look," he said, lifting the cup toward the nurse.

The nurse looked into the cup and then at William. "How are you feeling right now?"

"I have a bad headache."

"Where's the headache?"

"Forehead ... and the back's throbbing." He reached behind his head and rubbed his neck.

The nurse asked, "Are you stiff?"

"Yes."

"Okay, I'm sure everything is fine, but let me get the surgeon to see you."

William said, "Can you just pass me my phone? I have to let my daughter know I'm okay."

"WILLIAM. WILLIAM. WAKE UP PLEASE." THE NURSE WAS GENTLE AND insistent.

Inside, William struggled for words, and a grunting noise emerged.

"There you are. Good. How are you feeling?" William groaned and blinked. "Can you hear me?" He nodded. The nurse's hand lay on his shoulder and she tilted her head to look directly into his face before speaking again. "You had the little repair we talked about and we borrowed some fat from your tummy to make a plug, so you've had a stitch there. It can come out in a few days. The operation went well." She smiled. "We're going to keep an eye on you for a few days, but we might get you home before Christmas."

Christmas, thought William. *There's something I'm supposed to do before Christmas.* It was something to do with visiting.

WILLIAM'S HEAD THROBBED, HIS EYES BARELY OPEN, AND HIS BLOODY ears hissed as if cruising in a jet. The pieces of the plan with Uri began assembling through random thoughts. By now the special dispatch of bicycles would be over. Dennis would have done his work too. William just had to get to the office and turn the security cameras on. Why was it important to turn the cameras on? What part of the plan was it? It came to him: without CCTV he was not insured. Christmas was a dangerous time to go without insurance. The thieving bastards from the valley came into town to have their way when everyone was celebrating. He would not get into work now until Boxing Day or maybe the twenty-seventh. His mind stumbled forward and a fix came to him.

Cathy—he could text her and ask her to drop in to the office. She could do it.

Christmas Eve 2017

CATHY WANDERED, KILLING TIME, IN THE STORES, WEIGHED DOWN AND hot with people picking at all they encountered. She thought it was crazy to shop on the day before Christmas but it was a welcome distraction. The text from the boss had given her reason to spend the day away from Christmas in her apartment. Finally, her meandering put her at the corner of the street where the office waited for her and she turned, walking quickly to complete the chore. A man watched her from a car parked across the street and twenty metres past the entrance. He tapped his phone and put it to his ear.

Cathy opened the front door and went to the alarm panel. It was already switched off. Odd, she thought, and cursed Dennis, who had promised to turn it on before leaving after their last encounter. There was sudden anticipation of Dennis being there. Maybe William had asked him to come to work and he would be waiting. She picked her feet up on the stairs and burst into the office.

One man sat at her desk; another knelt at the cabinet holding the CCTV equipment. Neither took an interest in her arrival. The door to William's office was open and a small man with dark hair walked out.

"You are Cathy?" he said, smiling. "We have not met." She was unable to speak and stared at him. "Don't be alarmed. We are friends of William. It will be okay."

Speech returned to her. "Who are you? What are you doing here?"

"Please," said the little man, "sit down. You may help us before we go. It won't take long." He took her arm and led her to the office chair. The large man moved off to accommodate her.

She sat, trembling, waiting. The man at the recording cabinet was pushing all of the security tapes into a bag.

"Why are you here today?" asked the little man.

"William asked me to come and switch on the security tapes."

"How is William? I am concerned that he gets well. Have you spoken to him?"

"No. He sent me a text yesterday asking me to come and switch the tapes on."

"May I see it?" Uri waited for Cathy to search her bag and hand him her phone. He read the text and handed the phone to the large silent man now perched on the end of the desk. "Thank you, Cathy. It is just as you say. Why would he ask you to do this?"

"I don't know. Perhaps he forgot to turn them on. He has a lot on his mind right now."

"What do you mean? Has he too much stress? It is never good for business."

"Well," began Cathy, "he's been in hospital for some surgery, but there has been a complication and he needed a second operation quite quickly. He hasn't come out yet. I really don't know how he is." Fear washed over her and tears were not far away.

"Oh, I am sorry to hear that. I expect you are fond of him. These things are upsetting. You mustn't worry." He laid a gentle hand on her forearm and smiled. She watched him, appealing in hope through red eyes that it would be all right, that she would be fine.

"Cathy, tell me, when did you last come to work?"

"About three days ago."

"Was that the twenty-first?"

"Yes, I think so. I'm not sure."

"But was the office not closed on that day? Why were you in?"

"I sometimes come in when I'm asked to if there's a big order or something important going on, like today. William asked me if I would."

"It is important that you tell me, Cathy. Who asked you to come to work three days ago?"

She hesitated, flustered and reddening. The name jumped from her. "Dennis." Cathy doubted she had done the right thing in saying his name.

"Ah, Dennis. The warehouseman, yes?"

"Yes. Please don't tell William." Her eyes appealed to him. It was what she always did. "I'll lose my job. Please don't tell him. Please."

Uri spoke to the room. "Dennis is special to you. I understand this. It happens."

"He's married," she said, as if a further confession would convince him she was being co-operative and oblige the little man in a confidence between them.

"So are you, Cathy." He fixed her wedding ring in his gaze and smiled. "So are you."

It was hopeless. Cathy was naked before them. Nothing that happened now was in her control. The little man knew things about her, could take away her job and her lover. What pleasure would she have in her life without—her thoughts faltered—something for her?

"Don't worry, Cathy. This can be between us." He smiled again. Her loyalty grew with the hope he offered. "We can help each other. A partnership. You must tell me things, and William will not know. Your family will not know. Dennis will be our secret."

Cathy nodded, grateful. The relief spread over her like cool air from a window.

"You must say it, Cathy. Do you understand?"

"Yes," she said. "I understand."

"Good. But Cathy …" Uri leaned over her shoulder and put his face close to hers. His breath smelled of something, vegetables. "Everything about our partnership is secret. Like it did not exist. Do you agree with this?"

"Yes." She nodded again.

"You must answer the phone when I call you, and do just what I ask you to do. Do you understand, Cathy?"

"Yes, I do."

"This is good, Cathy." Uri stood behind her and rested his hand on her shoulder. "Thank you. If your phone rings and you don't know who is calling, it could be me, and you must answer it. Okay?"

She nodded.

"Good." He patted her shoulder gently. "We are in partnership now. So," he continued, "what's my name?"

She craned her neck to see him and tried to think of a name. "I don't know your name."

Uri's hand slipped from her shoulder and gripped her right breast, bundling and twisting clothes and flesh together as if turning a door handle. The pain lifted her upright in the chair and against him, still standing behind her.

"Cathy, you have not understood our partnership. How can you know the name of someone who does not exist?" He smiled. "Let's try again. How many men are in the room?"

"Well," Cathy started, the pain rising in her, "three."

"You have forgotten our partnership, Cathy." The smile had gone. "Less than a minute, and the partnership is gone. What am I to think?" He squeezed harder, until she threw her head back and yelped, before releasing some pressure. "Now, Cathy, another time. How many men are in the room?"

Through layers of pain and confusion her voice emerged in a low growl. "No one. There's no one in the room."

"Good, Cathy." He allowed the breast to unwind but held his grip tight. "That's what is true, because I want it to be true. You understand?" She nodded. "Now, what do I want to be true when I ask, 'What do I look like?' What will you say, Cathy?"

Cathy tried to gather herself and concentrate, knowing what would happen should she get it wrong. "I haven't seen you." He squeezed. Her voice became louder. "You were never here." The twist began and she was lifted from the desk. Her voice rose in crescendo. "No one was here." The pain left her and her voice returned to near normal. "I was here. Only me."

"Very good, Cathy. I think we do have a partnership. Thank you." He released the breast and pulled away from the desk. "I'm sorry about this," he said, gesturing at her breast now held tight by her hand. "So hard to be sure if we understand each other without it." He smiled again. "Would you like one of the men, who were never here, to bring you some video tapes to put in your machine?"

Cathy nursed her breast in her hands and watched him take her phone from the quiet man and place it on the desk in front of her. She had begun to understand how far down the rabbit hole she had fallen. All she could do to keep some control of it, and keep away from these men, she must do.

"No. I can do that."

"Okay. I will leave it to you. Will you remember to switch the machines on after we are gone, before you leave?"

"Yes."

"Good. I am glad I can rely on you." The three men moved toward the door, before the little man stopped. "One more thing, Cathy. The machines were on when we came today. Why would William ask you to turn them on if they were already on?"

"It must have been Dennis," said Cathy. "Last time we were here, he said he would wipe the tapes so no one would know we were both here. He would have started them again."

"Thank you." He smiled again. "Merry Christmas, Cathy."

She listened to them walk down the stairs and out onto the street, before moving. The pain in her breast had not fully ebbed away. She understood the brutish calculation of men and knew this pain was there to ensure she understood there was nothing arbitrary about the little man's intent. She was supposed to feel the visceral terror of help-lessness. There would be no mercy with him. She could not rely on a change of heart or his better nature. Neither could she open her legs for him. Men like that only wanted what they wanted. She drew a long breath. *Somewhere,* she thought, *someone will be cooking that fucking little man Christmas dinner. I hope he chokes. I hope they all choke.*

4

New Denver, February 10, 1957

WHITE CLOUDS DRAGGED ACROSS THE MOUNTAINS ON THE FAR SIDE OF the lake, leaving snow on high ground. Silver frost tipped the trees to water's edge. It was winter in New Denver and no mistake. Pavel and Paul stood together, watching from inside the chain-link fence, the wire thickened by frost. They waited in silence for the arrival. The two boys had always been tight friends. They could have been brothers had they not shared the same Russian name. One chose to remain Pavel, and the other had the English version, Paul, ensuring their separate identities were never lost or confused.

This visiting day felt awkward, as both knew it would end differently. Neither had the words to speak of it. There was joy for Paul having reached the age of sixteen, and no longer obliged to remain at New Denver Dormitory, and sadness for Pavel at his friend's departure.

"I bet you can't wait for lunch today," said Pavel. "Your mama will make you something special."

"I'm gonna eat so much, I'll need new pants!" They laughed like boys. Paul continued, "It won't be long before you're out too."

"A year and some," said Pavel.

Younger children huddled for warmth in dormitory doorways, waiting for the arrival.

"Are they coming?" asked a boy of six years, shouting from the dormitory step.

"They'll be here soon," said Pavel, loud enough to encourage the little ones.

Cold wind carried the sound of singing and the children rustled. They came off the step, bundled in coats, scarves and hats, to join the line of children at the fence, like soldiers at the firing line. The singing was louder and some of the children pushed forward.

"I have to get my stuff," said Paul.

"You better go," said Pavel, as Paul turned away toward his dorm room.

Pavel shouted after him, "Eat some for me, will ya!"

"I'll eat for all of you!"

"You'll get fat."

"I will." Laughter stretched out between them, and he was gone.

Pavel reached for the shoulders of two little ones, gently pulling them back. "Careful, you boys. Don't put your face on the fence." They stared at him without understanding. He knelt and removed a glove. "I'll show you what will happen." Pavel brought his hand to his face, licked a finger and touched the bare metal wire. The children watched his finger stick, frozen to the fence. Pavel pretended to pull and yank until the children laughed. "Look!" he said, showing the back of his hand with four fingers extended and the index finger bent at the knuckle and hidden. The children were transfixed and horrified at the missing digit, and then searched the fence to see if it was still hanging. "Here it is. I found it." Everyone laughed. "You don't want your lips or tongue to stay on the fence, so be careful. Look!"

The children looked up to see the pink faces and sturdy frames of their parents walking toward them, men on one side and women on the other. The sound of their singing was upon them and brought familiar warmth and comfort of home, but they could not wait for the singing to end. Older children standing in their usual spot waved at parents and parents waved back, while newcomers frantically searched to find their own at the fence. One of the small boys stood motionless. Pavel knelt to him. The boy was crying.

"Don't worry. Your mother is coming." It did not help. "What are you crying about? Your mother doesn't want to see her boy crying."

"How will she kiss me?" His cheeks were already wet and frost gathered on each eyelash. "I don't want my lips to hang on the fence."

Pavel regretted his warning to the children and his mind raced to soothe the boy before his mother found him at the fence. "You can do it like this," he said, bringing the tips of his thumbs together and touching forefingers to make a diamond. He placed the flat of his hands against the fence, covering a single diamond shape of the chain link, and put his lips into the shape. "You see?" he said, turning to the boy. "It's a kissing fence. You just have to have your hands together like this." The boy stopped crying and Pavel gently wiped the tiny icicles from his face as best he could.

A young matron swooped in from behind them. "What's the matter?" she asked, as if the cause of a child crying on visiting day could be a surprise.

Pavel said, "He can't find his mother. It's his first visit."

"Oh dear," she said. "Shall I help you find her?" The young matron put her arm around the child and held him close. "She'll be here somewhere. Let's try this way first." Standing up, she grasped the boy's hand, smiled at Pavel and began walking along the fenceline.

Pavel expected the boy's mother and father would come and pass food for him over the fence, dropping it to one of the taller children or RCMP officers overseeing the meeting of innocents. The smell and taste would comfort the boy for a few hours after his parents had gone. Pavel knew well how this would go and reminded himself to find the boy when his mother had gone.

He began walking the line to find his father at the usual place. Some of the parents draped blankets over the fence to provide shelter for the children. A police officer tucked the corners of a blanket into the chain link around two young girls so they could shelter from the cold wind while facing their parents through the fence. It was another small act of kindness, and Pavel hoped that none of the children were fooled. The parents would not be. At least it allowed them to speak their own language. Russian words overheard by matrons could mean punishment on a bad day, and yet some of the parents and children, especially the newer ones, spoke nothing else. Huddled under the blanket, they could whisper without fear.

Pavel scanned up and down the fence. He turned at the bottom of the line and walked back toward the other end. On the top step of the dormitory Matron MacDonald stood, glasses like butterfly wings, hair set, certain in manner. She scanned the scene like a border guard. Pavel watched her without looking, as did all the children who knew the danger. Some of the matrons and teachers with smiling faces seemed to enjoy the children, but they were not all smiling.

"Pavel Korenov! Pavel!" The shout came from beyond the fence. His father's closest friend waved and walked quickly toward him. "It's good to see you, Pavel. How are you?"

"I'm well, thank you. Is Father with you?"

"Your father can't come today, but I have something for you. I have some pastry for you." From under his coat he conjured two slender packages wrapped in thin cotton tied at each end with string, and began clearing the frost from the fence. "The women made them small to get through the fence. Better than throwing it over and the pastry breaking."

The enthusiasm and grin were intended to distract, but neither was convincing. He began feeding the floppy sausage shape through the diamond openings. Pavel pulled gently, glumly, on the other side.

"Thank you," said Pavel, trying to smile. "It's kind of you, and there's enough to share." The community had not forgotten him, even when his father was not there to remind them. He knew there was something to be grateful for, but he could not grasp it. "What has happened to my father?" He asked. "I am old enough to be told."

There was quiet between them as the man looked intently at Pavel, measuring the new heft in the boy. "It is right. You are old enough to know things. You're a man now. It happens quickly these days."

"Is he safe?"

"Yes, he's safe, but he was taken. They came for him, and many others." It had been expected. The community had hidden him until so many were taken that there were too few to conjure a plan to hide him. As with the children, it became a matter of attrition until the RCMP found him and took him away to prison.

"Do you know where he's been taken?"

"No. Not yet."

"What about Mother? Any news?"

"There's no word on any of them. Your mother and sister are with many of our people. They have God in their hearts and remain true." The two nodded at each other, understanding the importance of holding true to faith. The work of passing the second package through the fence continued.

"There are more children here this time," said his father's friend, scanning up and down the fence. "How many are there?"

"It's hard to say. A few come every week; others leave when they get outside school age."

The older man said, "Our leader, Sorokin, has said our path back to Russia will be through the prisons of Canada. Be strong. Think of this place as part of that path. And look after each other, Pavel. Keep safe. We will come when we can. I must find my children."

"Thank you," said Pavel, turning and walking away. He had no understanding of Russia or desire to go there, except the language was familiar and the stories enchanting. The idea of returning there was bewildering. He was just a boy and knew nothing but British Columbia, his love of home and hatred of this place. Sorokin was just the name of a man who lived thousands of miles away, of whom people talked as if he was their leader and for whom money was collected. His parents always gave what they could.

Within a few strides he realized there would be no more family visiting him at the fence, and steeled himself to show nothing of it. He began walking toward the dormitory, thinking of his father in custody somewhere. Only his faith would sustain him now. He had to be in this place, do what was needed to avoid trouble, but reject all their

teachings to stay true. All their history of kings and queens, great bat-
tles, colonial dominance and industrialization was not his history, not
the Doukhobor way. He would keep the true way safe inside him, ready
for when he emerged from this.

PAVEL FELT THE GAZE OF MATRON MACDONALD AS HE APPROACHED THE
dormitory. Large, white and starched, she stood on the veranda looking down on everyone. There was something indomitable about her,
and now, at the top step, bundled in a large coat, her size and authority
seemed titanic. He forced himself not to look up to her as he reached
the bottom step. She would never get that from him.

"Your father not come today?" she asked.

At the top step, where he nearly matched her height, he turned to
her. "He sent a message and some food to share."

"Maybe he's off burning someone's house down. I expect he's on
the run like the rest of them." Matron's contemptuous eyes wandered
to the fence and back again before falling on the cotton-wrapped rolls
of pastry.

"Pastry from home," said Pavel, anticipating her demand for an
explanation or inspection, anything to display her dominance of him.
He clenched his gut to control his nerves. "I'll open them later with the
others who didn't get visits." Pavel felt the ripple of anger in Matron
at his defiance.

"You know that food not eaten during visiting has to go to the
kitchen. We can't have rats in the dorms again."

If the pastry went to the kitchen it would not be seen again by
him or any of the children. Just as the factories, houses and flour mills
his people had built were taken by the English Canadians, so it was
that whatever the Doukhobor children had could be taken. The children would watch the matrons consume it without shame. She could
remove the pastry this minute and consume it in front of everyone.
Seizing his pastry would go unchallenged, and protest from him or
other children would bring only the strap. She had all the authority

there was to have, but in this moment, over these pastries, Pavel and Matron were connected in a tug-of-war.

He said, "They'll be gone before lunch."

It did not matter how small it was; he felt it was in his grasp to choose the outcome, if only he could hold his nerve and his temper long enough.

"Be sure they are." Matron MacDonald turned away disdainfully as if she had never been interested.

Pavel entered the dormitory, undid his boots and left them behind. It was nearly as cold as outside, but at least it was quiet. Two long rows of beds, each with allotted space and bedside locker, stretched the length of the room like berths in a harbour waiting for ships to return. He slipped down the central passage on shining linoleum to his berth and put the precious pastry on his locker. An hour would pass before the children returned. There was time to be alone without the clatter and chatter and questions for which he offered comforting answers to little ones, without really knowing the answers they wanted.

His little defiance had soothed the turmoil of learning of his father's capture and Paul's leaving, but had not cleared the contempt of Matron's remarks. He allowed himself to fall back on his bed, close his eyes and remember his family. His mother's face was getting more difficult to recall, and he tried to imagine it. His mother had told him to remember only the smiles, the warmth of family, playing in the fields and lessons from their worship. He was not to spend time worrying about them or to dwell on where he was, because he carried God with him always. From outside there was just a murmuring of seventy children and a hundred or more parents and relatives speaking at the fence. The snow dampened sounds of laughing and crying from the yard.

"Hello," a soft voice said in Russian.

Pavel sat up quickly. "Who are you?"

A girl about his age stood several beds away, layered in clothing. He could see a long, white, thick cotton dress, a plaid shirt and a grey sweater. She had wrapped a blanket over her shoulders and had pulled her head scarf from her hair and held it around her neck like a tether.

Even from that distance her blue eyes startled him. She smiled, offering a hint of how he imagined her running in the fields on a sunny day, short blond hair tossed with every stride. The image passed.

"I'm Nina! Don't you recognize me?"

"I've never seen you with short hair," said Pavel. "It's nice to see you. Haven't seen you since … I was taken. When did you get here?"

"Today. Matron cut my hair as soon as I arrived." Nina pushed at her hair. "It made me cry."

"Don't be crying here. It's fine," said Pavel. "Never show weakness to them. Have you been given a number and a bed?"

"Yes. I'm Girl Ninety-Five," said Nina, waiting for his number to be volunteered.

"I'm Boy Twelve."

"You were taken at Perry Siding?" Nina asked. Pavel nodded. "That will be more than three years," she said in surprise. "It's a long time." Nina approached his space.

He nodded again. "It will be four years in September. How did you escape the police for so long?"

"I hid in the woods, mostly, and my uncle made a hiding place inside. Even if they came in the night I didn't have to run and hide. I was hidden in less than a minute."

"How did they find you?"

"I was outside close to the house, too close. My uncle saw them and shouted, 'Politziya! Politziya!' They heard him shouting and lots of them came for me. He meant to warn us, but it just told them where we were." She smiled again. "He was so upset."

"They're devils."

"They are not all devils. A policeman found me before but pretended not to see me."

"So why did he take you this time, if he is not a devil?"

"He wasn't there. Lots of them came and saw me. They were all coming."

Pavel had heard too many stories of young children being pulled from their parents or dragged from under beds with too much relish to find goodness in any of the RCMP. "You'll learn they're all devils. They see what they want to see and do what they want to do. God doesn't guide them." Pavel realized that he was being unfair to Nina. It was too early to talk like this with the newcomer. "Sorry. My father couldn't visit me today. He was taken. Are you hungry?" He tried to pick up his enthusiasm and reached for the pastry. "I have pastry. Would you like some?"

Nina nodded and sat on the end of Pavel's bed as he undid one of the parcels. "I was watching you at the fence. Who was that little boy?"

"He just arrived last week, picked up the day after his birthday. It's his first visit from his parents."

"But why was he crying?"

"He wasn't sure how his family would kiss him without getting his lips stuck on the fence."

"What did you say to him?"

"I told him it was a 'kissing fence.'" The children smiled at each other. "I showed him how to hold his hands, like this." He put down the pastry, spread his hands wide and connected his two thumbs and then both forefingers to make the diamond shape. Nina copied him. He held his hands up, as if pressing them flat on the fence, and their palms touched. "Through there," he said, gesturing with a nod to the gap in their hands.

"That was nice of you. Have you become the father of the little ones?" She had allowed her hands to linger on his without intending to. Neither understood the current flowing between them.

"No, not their father," said Pavel, handing her a pastry. "Everyone needs comforting here. They like to see us laugh and play. They think if we play, we're not missing home. Sometimes they say, if we laugh or seem happy, we are better off here than at home. It lets them say our homes were not good, our families are criminals." His anger flashed. "But underneath, no one is happy here. I let them see nothing."

Nina stared at him. "Sorry," he said. "Please eat, or Matron will take it. Never give them what you don't have to give, and never give them everything."

"They take our food?" she asked.

"All the time. They eat it where we can watch them. So we know they can do anything they like. I shouldn't be talking like this. You've only just arrived. There's plenty of time to learn these things."

"I want to know," she said, breaking the pastry and putting it in her mouth. "The sooner I learn, the better."

It was Pavel's turn to look hard at Nina. She had just arrived after hiding from the police for three years, and now she sat at the end of his bed without a sign of fear or wretchedness, as every other child arriving at New Denver had shown. She was different. Not just the eyes and straw-coloured hair, but the bearing of her shoulders could be seen through the layers of cloth. The confidence of her gaze revealed something he had not seen in other children.

"Okay," said Pavel. "The first thing to know is that Russian is not allowed here. You'll be strapped at school or punished in the dormitory if they hear you. But, there is no rule about singing. So we sing messages to each other."

"It sounds like fun," said Nina.

"Be careful with it. You have to look like you're really singing—a hymn or something." Nina soaked in his words. "The other thing is you can say anything in English to Matron or teachers, but it doesn't mean a thing. Talk about their history and their lessons, agree with them, let them speak badly about our people, it doesn't matter."

Nina was concentrating with an intensity that made him self-conscious. She asked, "Why doesn't it matter when they say bad things about us?"

Pavel could see the confusion on her face. "When we speak in Russian, it's different. We never lie when we speak Russian."

"So, when you speak English to me, it means nothing?"

"Sometimes, when we say something in English, it is a way of saying the opposite. English people hear the English words and think we're behaving well, becoming 'good Canadians,' but what we hear or say in English isn't important. It doesn't change us. We can share stories of home with the young ones, but only in Russian, because this is true speaking. When you speak English it isn't true speaking. It doesn't matter what you say in English, except sometimes when it means the opposite in Russian."

"How will I know when it means the opposite?"

"You'll know."

The door of the dormitory opened and Matron said loudly, "Nina! You mustn't be in the boys' dormitory." The winter cold from the open door touched everything.

Both children stood behind the bed as Matron approached.

"I'm sorry. I didn't know," Nina said in English.

"Well, you do now. But you," said Matron, glaring at Pavel, "you know perfectly well."

"Nina was here when I came in. I was just giving her some pastry before she left."

"Make it quick, and get back to your dorm, Nina."

Pavel gathered up a few more pieces of pastry in both hands and dumped them into Nina's. Crumbs fell between them and they began giggling at the clumsy transfer under the scowl of Matron.

"Hurry now. Don't make a mess."

Pavel turned to Matron MacDonald. "She'll just be a second." The nervous giggling continued. "And she won't come in here again. Promise." He turned to Nina, his hands still securing the crumbling pastry in hers. "You won't, will you? You won't come back and see me in here again, will you?"

It was as clear an instruction as there ever was. Her blue eyes sparkled with understanding.

"Never again. I promise."

February 15, 1957

IT WAS INEVITABLE, THOUGHT CONSTABLE FLANAGAN, THAT HIS SERgeant would have his revenge, shunting him away from real police work to manage a desk or, as chance had it, escorting Doukhobor children to school in New Denver. The irony of the posting was not lost on either of them. Nor was the impact on Flanagan's career misunderstood. His new responsibility of taking charge of this detail was the kiss of death. His card had been marked. He was finished.

New Denver was tucked in a valley on the east side of Slocan Lake. The southern part of the town was laid in a grid. Four avenues divided the space between Galena Avenue in the south and Third Avenue in the north near the river that divided the town. Running north-south, four streets completed the grid, between Union Street on the east and Josephine Street on the west. Farther west, a long open field sloped gently down to Slocan Lake. In the north, over the Union Street bridge, the grid continued as if uninterrupted. The school was in the north, on Seventh Avenue.

Twice each day Flanagan walked with the children from their fenced enclosure south of Galena Avenue, at the southern edge of New Denver, across the Union Street bridge to the school on Seventh Avenue in the north. At lunch and at the end of the school day he would walk them back. The children hardly needed escorting, let alone by an armed policeman. There was no risk of them running off into the hills or forest, where winter would freeze them solid and summer would starve them. New Denver was too far from anywhere for the children to walk out on the unmade roads running only north and south.

As they tramped home from school in the last light of a winter's day, across squeaking packed snow, the children were in a shouting mood. Flanagan walked behind an excited group of children. Each was bundled in winter gear, the young being walked along by brothers and sisters. Older boys clustered together, as did the girls. Endless taunts, snowballs and jibes flew between them. Flanagan's task was to herd the children over the Union Street bridge. From there, all were hungry enough to head for the dormitory, eventually.

As they crossed into the south side of the town, a few children slipped off Union Street toward the lake. Flanagan turned away to avoid seeing them go. He had a rough idea to which house they were heading, between Josephine and Kildare Streets on Third Avenue, but not what they were up to. It did not matter, he thought. They were just kids.

"WHERE ARE WE GOING?" ASKED NINA.

"You'll see," said Pavel.

Pavel's friend Marko chimed in. "We're going to the Green Witch's house."

"The Green Witch?" asked Nina.

"It's not like it sounds." Pavel smiled at Nina, who did not yet know this particular secret.

The children often went to where the Green Witch lived. She was a grey, stooped lady always seen in a green sweater. The long-serving children called her the Green Witch to frighten the newcomers and put them off the treats she could offer. It also allowed them to keep secret the Green Witch's dry cellar, where boxes of candy and Russian food were stored in neat rows, each labelled with the initials of a child. It was their secret stash from home, kept safe from the matrons by the foreboding image and rumours of the Green Witch.

Nina, Pavel and Marko arrived at the Green Witch's door and knocked.

"Thanks for coming with me," said Marko. "I'm always scared about coming here. She scares me."

"She's not that frightening." Pavel's eyes searched the street behind them. Not all the children in New Denver could be trusted. The small, like Marko, and the young were easy targets.

The door opened. A woman, short, stooped and rounded, stood silhouetted by the light of the room. Grey hair escaped from the bundle tied at her back. Pavel envied the simple comforts he could see. A fire, cloth-covered furniture, a cushion and a few pictures reminded him of home. A dull light came on over the door. She wore multiple layers topped by the green sweater that gave her her name.

The woman said, "Go ahead. You know where to go. Don't touch anyone else's box, now, will you?" The Green Witch turned to Nina. "You're new."

"I'm Nina."

"Good for you. I hope you're not here long enough to go mean."

Nina said, "I won't be mean. I'm not mean."

The Green Witch glared at Nina. "Remember you said that, young lady. You remember it. Let me know if you want a box." She turned and closed the door.

Pavel said to Marko, "We'll wait here. Don't be long." He peered again into the darkness. Figures moved in the street and it was only a matter of time before others came.

Nina felt the tension and began searching the darkness without knowing what she was searching for.

Pavel tried to explain to Nina what was happening. "She lets us keep boxes of things, so they don't get stolen by the matrons. Some of the children keep food here to stop them taking it."

In her own gruff way the Green Witch loved the Doukhobor children as she had loved the Japanese children interned at New Denver two decades before. They all needed comforting, and the Green Witch defied all their captors in providing a little of what the children needed.

"Don't you want to get to your box?" Nina asked.

"Don't have one." Pavel put his head into the cellar. "Marko! Hurry up," he whispered hoarsely.

"What are you doing with the girls, Pavel?" The unwelcome voice of a boy called Sam came from behind Pavel and Nina, and they turned to face him and three others. "Have you stopped being one of the boys? You've never been one of the gang, have you?"

"Not your gang, no."

Sam had arrived in New Denver in 1955 in the first days of the raid on Krestova, or Operation Snatch, as it became known. Angry and frightened, he quickly learned how to use his size to survive. He and his group of friends developed their own idea of sharing among the children. It amounted to taking what they wanted. Everyone was terrorized by the tax he demanded on everything the children had. Now Sam and a group of boys stood between the house and the dormitory, while Marko rummaged in the cellar for his food.

"Who's this?" asked Sam, gawking at Nina.

Pavel said, "She's new. I'm showing her around." He felt sudden anger for explaining himself to Sam.

"It's Nina, right?" Sam said. Nina nodded. "The girls say your English is so good, you must be a spy. Is that true?"

"No, it is not! Who says that?"

Marko emerged from the cellar. "I've got chocolate!" he said, holding a thick bar in his hand. He stopped when he saw Sam and the three other boys.

Sam stepped forward. "I hope you have some for me."

"It's Marko's stuff," said Pavel, bracing himself to fight the larger boy.

"It's okay," said Marko. "I'll give some to anyone who asks." Marko broke a piece from the bar and offered it to Sam, who took another step forward, reached past the offering and snatched the remaining bar from Marko's hand.

"Give it back!" shouted Pavel, now in the fight, gripping the hand with the stolen chocolate. Sam's three friends shouted and cheered the larger boy, who pulled, yanked and pushed Pavel into the snow. Sam and friends stood over Pavel, giggling and sneering at the ease with which Sam shook Pavel off. Pavel began to stand but a push stopped him. Again he tried and a push tumbled him down.

The door of the house opened suddenly and the Green Witch emerged with a wooden spoon raised in her hand. "Get away! I've told you before not to come here. I'll paddle your backside next time I see you."

Sam and his friends were already backpedalling as the door opened and began running toward the dormitory as she approached.

The Green Witch returned the few steps to her door and asked Pavel, "Are you all right?"

"I'm fine. Thank you," he said, getting up and brushing the snow off.

"You?" she asked of Nina and Marko.

"Yes, thanks," said Marko, and Nina nodded.

"What did they get?"

Marko said, "Just a bar of chocolate. It's okay."

"Wait here," said the Green Witch.

The three waited outside the door like carol singers while the Green Witch went inside. When she returned, she said, "Be careful when you come here after dark. That mongrel and his pack of wolves are always about. Here, fresh today." She gave each a round biscuit and a yellow-toothed smile.

"Thanks," said Marko, grabbing the biscuit and recoiling from her. In surprise and horror, he began running.

Pavel took his, saying, "Thank you," before chasing after Marko.

"Nice to meet you," said Nina. "And thank you." She raced to catch the others.

None of them understood why they were running and stopped two blocks south at Galena Avenue.

Marko bit into his biscuit and said, "She still scares me. Nice cookie, though."

"It's not her you should be scared of. She saved us that time," said Pavel.

"She saved you!" said Marko. "I wasn't gonna fight Sam. He can have the damn chocolate."

Nina was surprised to hear Marko swear and said to Pavel, "You were very brave."

"Brave enough to get your teeth knocked out," said Marko. "I'd feel terrible if you got your teeth knocked out for a bar of my chocolate."

Marko was ungrateful but it was not that causing Pavel's sudden irritation. Once again he had chosen a hard path, putting himself in the way of harm for reasons that were obvious to him and yet unseen by others. *Why don't they see?* It was never "just" a bar of chocolate.

"It just made me so angry," said Pavel, "having to stand there while he took things from us. He might as well be one of them. We might as well burn all we have, if it's so easy to take things from us." The image of burning belongings was too close to the long history of their people to let pass. It surprised them and they fell into an awkward silence.

"Mind you," said Marko, grinning like an ape, "you did impress Nina!"

Pavel's hand reached out and snatched the toque from Marko's head as he ducked and bolted, still grinning.

From five yards away Pavel threw the toque back to Marko, who said, "Thanks for coming with me. I'm still hungry. I'm going in," and stuffed the last of the biscuit in his mouth. "See you inside."

Nina stopped with Pavel as Marko walked on. "Why don't you have a box in the cellar like the others?" she asked.

"We should be sharing things, not hoarding them for ourselves. It's just selfish." Pavel felt the discomfort of knowing that explanation would not do. "We just end up fighting if some have more than others. Like with Sam."

"Is that what the green woman meant when she told me to not be mean?"

"Maybe," said Pavel. "It's hard not to be selfish here. I guess that's where the meanness starts. They've turned us against each other." That explanation, he thought, was enough. He had been accused of being too high and mighty and wanted to avoid that with Nina.

He said, "You've survived your first school day. How was it?"

"Not too bad. Thanks for showing me around." Nina's voice faltered. "You don't think I'm a spy, do you?"

"No, I don't. Don't listen to anything Sam says. He's a bully. Only says things to look tough."

"You stood up to him."

"It was stupid."

"No, it wasn't. Brave, not stupid. Someone has to stand up. It's important. Not everyone can do it. Just try not to get your teeth knocked out." She smiled at him. Even though it was near dark, he could make out the colour of her sharp blue eyes. They saw more than his appearance. They saw through his frustration and anger to what was important. She was without challenge or criticism of him. There was nothing to defend against with her.

"See you tomorrow," he said as she turned away. Something changed in his breathing. The next breath filled his lungs with cold fresh air, and he let the weight of his shoulder and chest clear it all out. The tension of the day left with it.

CONSTABLE FLANAGAN ROUNDED THE FINAL BEND AT THE END OF UNION Street next to the dormitory. Nearly all the children were back. The others would be back soon enough. He could make out a group of four boys crossing Galena heading for their building. Ahead, a small security hut, usually occupied by Mr. Nori, the Japanese security guard, stood in isolation next to the eight-foot chain-link fence. He stood outside greeting each child with a wave or smile. Two children approached him with excitement. The prospect of cadging a nickel from him was on their faces. Mr. Nori looked around as if keeping care of a secret and pulled off a glove to find his pocket. The children waited.

"Shh! Mustn't say anything," Mr. Nori said with a stern face and then pressed a nickel into each of their palms. Flanagan turned away. Only Matron MacDonald would object to his charity.

It was easy to see why the children loved Mr. Nori. On weekends small groups of children would surround the hut, urging him to come out and simply be with them. Sometimes they were rewarded with the change from his pocket, before rushing to spend it at the candy store. He gave what he had and accepted each child without question.

February 22, 1957

"ARINA! WAIT FOR ME." NINA SAW HER COUSIN AHEAD NEAR THE BRIDGE on the way to school. She ran to catch up. "How are you? We haven't really spoken since I got here." Arina's eyes moved up and down the street, avoiding her. "What's the matter?" asked Nina.

"I can't talk with you," said Arina.

"Why not? We're family."

"Everyone says you're a spy."

"You know I'm not a spy." Nina emphasized the word to mock Arina with the absurdity of it. "We lived together and spent hours in the forest together. I looked after you. How can I be a spy?"

"Keep your voice down. We did live together, but I was caught and you weren't."

"So what?"

"So, why was I caught and you stayed free?"

"Arina! What have they been saying to you? I was in the wardrobe and you were in the mattress when the police came. It could have been you or me, or both of us." Arina was ten years old but had become older, more cynical than Nina could ever have imagined her becoming.

Nina continued, "I'm shocked at you. Who's been saying these things?"

"It's what everyone's saying."

"Well, it's not true. You know it's not true."

"What were you doing in Matron's office this morning? You were seen going in and talking a long time with her," said Arina.

Nina scrambled to connect the pieces. "She called for me after breakfast. Your mother and father brought my clothes. She told me they all had to be cleaned before they would give them to me, and some things I wasn't allowed. That's all."

"You won't see any of those again."

"What do you mean?" asked Nina.

"Tell your people not to send you anything like clothes or shoes. If it's good, they won't give it to you."

"They're not 'my people,' they're your mother and father! What would they think of you?"

Arina's eyes watered. It was enough, thought Nina, to jolt Arina out of the crazy notion a group of younger girls left alone had conjured.

"I'm sorry," said Arina. "They'll be mean to me if I go against them. I know you're not a spy, but you have to be careful. Don't talk to the matrons."

"It's a good tip, but what must I do to stop them from thinking I'm a spy?"

"I don't know. Don't give them anything to talk about."

Nina thought for a moment. "We better not talk again until it's safe. I hope it's not long. I've really missed you."

"I've missed you too."

The two girls risked walking near enough to each other to rub shoulders for a few steps. It connected them without giving too much away. They had reached the small white church and turned the corner of Union onto Seventh Avenue. Opposite the school a car stopped. A girl got out and began making her way into the school.

Nina asked, "Who's that?"

"She's one of the matrons' daughters. Why do you ask? Don't make friends with her, will you?"

"No, I won't make friends with her, but ..."

"But what?"

"She's wearing my jacket. The one your mother made for me."

"See what I mean?"

February 25, 1957

IT WAS NEARLY TIME FOR LIGHTS OUT. THE END-OF-DAY HUBBLE-BUBBLE of a dozen boys decompressing from school, clattering mealtimes and raucous playground noise rose up from the dormitory, drifted over the lake and was lost. There was nothing to contain it. No comforting advice for tomorrow's trials or making sense of a confusing day. All that happened, good and bad, had equal, unmodulated volume. Only the older children mitigated the blizzard of noise, helping the younger ones to find stability in routine and anticipate what was to happen next.

Years of residential schools for Indigenous children across the province had equipped New Denver with the skill of occupying the time of children in custody. There were chores, demands and expectations, allowing only the time before sleep for contemplation. For some there were too many idle moments, allowing heads to fill with lost family. For others it was a time to restore fading memories, of reclaiming what had been bullied out of consciousness with the fear of being strapped with the length of rubberized canvas hanging in every classroom, with national anthems, flags and someone else's history.

Pavel began walking between the beds, speaking quietly in Russian, encouraging the boys to get out of their winter clothes and into pyjamas before the night matron, Matron Cody, came to turn off the lights. It fell to Pavel to anticipate her displeasure and get the dorm moving toward bedtime.

In winter, it was an easy task to get everyone to bed. No one stayed out of bed very long. The boys would make ready their pyjamas, undress at the speed of light and pull them on before scrambling into bed. For the slow, it could mean a quicker hand whipping away a pyjama top, leaving the victim naked in the cold, chasing his thin cotton covering as delighted children hurled it from bed to bed. The slow would learn to be quick, and the game would remind children they were on their own.

Marko braved the cold and rushed barefoot to the toilet one last time. Yuri asked if his wash bag had been seen in the showers and everyone groaned. There was always something Yuri had lost. Others wriggled and rubbed their limbs between the sheets to brush away the chill. The volume began falling steadily before the night matron's arrival.

The door opened without a knock and in she came. Karen Cody smiled broadly at the doorway, made up and on the edge of middle age. No one was sure of her. She spoke nicely, smiled always but dished out too many punishments to be trusted. Often it was the whole dorm punished for the misdemeanours of one or two.

"Everyone ready for lights out," she said. "Where's that one?" She pointed to the empty bed just as the toilet flushed behind her and then Marko appeared. He tried to skip by Matron but she managed to swat the top of his head as he scampered toward his bed. "You know what time you have to be in bed!" The rustling stopped. All was quiet. "Remember, there's to be no talking. You all have school tomorrow and need your sleep. Don't keep each other up. Good night." The lights went off and she stepped out, closing the door behind her.

The children waited to hear her footsteps move from behind the door, but they did not. Pavel knew the night matron was outside listening for a reason to come back in. All the boys listened to her stealth, waiting for the creaking floor to give her away or the door to fly open and lights to be turned on. Finally she moved away and the whispering began.

After a whole day spent struggling in English, now the sound of their mother tongue floating from pillow to pillow consoled everyone. Pavel let the whispered Russian comfort him and thought of Nina. Nearly every minute not taken by something else was spent thinking of her and how he might arrange to see her: an accidental encounter, a game in the yard, a moment in class. Mostly, he was concerned with what she was thinking.

In the darkness, a boy's voice was heard. "Pavel, will you tell us more of the story?" he asked in Russian.

Pavel struggled to connect to the tale he had been telling by instalments. The stories of their past were known in part by the children, and Pavel would fill the gaps in his knowledge with made-up links in order to hang on to the fragments of their history. The stories they could not remember and the songs they could not sing eroded in memory.

"Not tonight. The guard's patrolling outside and Matron is keeping an eye on us. We better be quiet." He tried to return to Nina. Her face came to mind, her smile, the hair, those eyes. It made him long for morning and feel guilty about it. He should be worried about his father and be upset with no longer having him visit every two weeks, but now only Nina occupied him.

Another voice came. "Please. The one about the queen."

The stories Pavel told filled the evening space with something. Even if he was unsure of how true his stories were or if he was getting the story right, at least it was something of who their people were.

"Okay, just a few minutes." Some of the children, wrapped in blankets, padded softly to his bedside. They shuffled together on the next bed and settled like squirrels in a nest. Others curled in their beds and waited for the story to bring them sleep. Pavel calculated that Matron would be seeing others to bed for about thirty minutes. It should be safe. He brought to mind the story of Queen Lukeria and remembered the gestures his father would make to add to the drama. It was dim in the memory, but his friends would not know or care if what he said was true.

"A hundred years ago in the south of Russia," he began, "there was a girl born who became known as Queen Lukeria. As she got older, the people, our people, thought she was more than a normal person. They thought she had special gifts to make the crops grow and people contented. They believed this because everywhere she went there were beautiful flowers growing. Some said the flowers grew in her footsteps as she walked, and when she visited a village, the harvest gave more than the village could eat. People would come to her angry with their neighbour, upset with something or even crying without reason, and she would speak with them. Always, they would leave smiling. She could help people see God's work and what must be done to have a better life."

The moon bounced off the snow outside. Its light painted the dormitory and eager young faces blue grey. Marko asked, "Did she live in a palace?"

"Oh no," said Pavel, remembering a photo he had once seen. "She lived in a simple house: two storeys with a balcony all around the second floor."

"Why didn't she live in a palace?"

"Because it is not our way."

"I thought all queens lived in palaces."

"Many queens do, but Lukeria was not like them. She was only a queen because the people loved and looked up to her, not because she was born into a noble family with money."

"I'd live in a palace if I was a queen—or king."

A flurry of insults erupted. "Be quiet, stupid!" "Listen to the story." The bed jostled with nudges and pushing.

"It's my bed!" said Marko.

"Shh!" Pavel sighed. "We have to be quiet. Maybe we should sleep and have stories another night."

"No, no. Please," said a whispering voice. "Just a little more." The boys settled in the blue light, and Pavel struggled to conjure his enthusiasm again.

"Well, if you really want to know ..." He hesitated as his father would have done. "When people came to her village, it was not only flowers, fruit and wheat they saw, but every house was painted and cared for. The animals were fat. Every child had shoes and a shining face. They played in the fields, helped their mothers and came home to plates stacked high with food. Everyone had a place at a table, no one in Queen Lukeria's village was poor and they were all happy."

Pavel was at the end of his fragmented recollection and searched for inspiration in the quiet faces of his peers. Marko's pyjama top was opened from waist to chest, the buttons lost to tugging and roughhousing.

"Important people from villages all around would come and ask how it could be. Queen Lukeria would ask them, 'How many buttons have you on your shirt?' They would be surprised, and some would reply, 'What have my buttons to do with the hunger our villagers feel in their stomach?'" Pavel looked intently at those listening on the next bed, delaying his story until he worked out what to say. "Shall I tell you why the buttons are important?"

"Because they could eat the buttons!" said Marko.

There were jostles, and a chorus responded with "Idiot!" "Stupid!" and "Be quiet!"

"Shh!" Pavel put his finger to his mouth. "Shh." It was enough time for an idea to emerge. "Queen Lukeria would say, 'Do you have more buttons on your shirt than your neighbour?' But they could not answer. She would say, 'Is the cotton of your shirt thicker than your neighbour's?' Then, 'Is your house warmer? Is your barn bigger?' The important men from the villages would begin to understand and tears would run down their faces, but she did not stop. 'Are your animals fatter? Have you more seed for next year's planting?' Finally they would cry out and ask her to stop, not ask but beg her to ask no more."

"Why were they crying?"

"Because Queen Lukeria helped them to see they had lost the true way." There was confusion on their faces. "Our way is not to have more than another. If you have something, you must share it. You mustn't own more than others, and there's only one way to prevent this from happening, by owning nothing and sharing everything. This is the Doukhobor way. The true way."

"But," said another whisper, "Queen Lukeria's village was lucky because things grew wherever she walked. They had lots to give."

Pavel searched his memory for a reply his father might give. He was on his own. "That's not what the story tells us. They had much to give because they shared." It didn't make the sense he wanted but it was the best he could do.

"But—"

"The village got stronger because—"

At the crunch of snow and beam of light outside, everyone froze. It was the night guard patrolling. A small group of men in half-hearted uniforms took turns patrolling the outside of the buildings, as if there were a risk of one of the children making a break for home. Quietly the boys gathered their blankets around them and tiptoed across the freezing linoleum to their own beds. Pavel listened to the night patrol crunch off toward the next building.

Pavel signalled there would be no more story tonight with "*spokoynoi noch.*" Whispered "Have a peaceful night" returned to him from the beds.

Marko stared at him from the next bed and Pavel waited.

"I'd like to be a king or queen. A king, I guess. Kings live in palaces, don't they?"

"*Spokoynoi noch, Marko.*"

February 28, 1957

PAVEL HAD BEEN THINKING ALL DAY, WHENEVER THE IMAGE OF NINA escaped him, of the story he had promised to tell in the dormitory that night. They had asked for a new one and he had searched his memory of Father's tales not yet told to the boys with whom he shared the night. Now they waited for it to begin.

"Can you tell us another one about Queen Lukeria?" asked a boy, repeating the request of yesterday.

"Yep," said Pavel. The chatter stopped and the silence waited for him to begin. "This is the story of the Burning of Arms." It was a phrase often used, and Pavel hoped he had enough of the tale.

Marko chirped, "What's it about?" The children looked at him like the fool he could be and Pavel continued as if he had said nothing.

"Not very long ago, about the time our grandparents were born, there was a terrible war between Russia and a country called Turkey. They had been fighting for nearly as long as the oldest man alive. Our people were asked to fight in the army for Russia."

"Why were they fighting?"

"Over land," said Pavel. "It's always over land." It was a good enough answer for him to continue. "Anyway, the Doukhobors don't fight to defend one country against a different country just because a person says we should."

"Canadians fight," said a young voice.

"My teacher says we are Canadians and we should behave like all Canadians," said another. "She said there was no excuse not to."

"We came to Canada with permission to farm the land and not to fight or be like the English." Pavel felt his father's anger rise and fall within him.

"Let him finish the story."

"I wanna know why we don't fight and Canadians do."

Pavel felt the confusion of the unexpected. He had assembled the ideas he could remember about Queen Lukeria, but why it was that Doukhobors did not fight had not been part of it.

"Okay! Be quiet. Shh. I'll tell you why and then we can have the story.

"The church in Russia had mountains of gold. There were big palaces with treasure and gold and jewels. Churchmen wore beautiful clothes made of silk and the best wool. They wore tall hats with gold braid. But outside the churches, the people had no food. Children were always hungry."

"I'm always hungry," said Marko.

"Not like this." Pavel tried to keep the momentum. "Lukeria told our grandparents that God isn't in gold and fancy clothes. God should be inside people. We should keep God in our hearts and sing."

"What's that got to do with fighting?"

Pavel realized that he did not know where this was going. He was lost. The bridge between singing hearts, tall golden hats, Canadians fighting someone and Doukhobor grandfathers not fighting the Turks had been carried away, leaving just a vacant space in his mind.

A voice emerged from the darkness. "If God's inside you, you wouldn't be able to kill anyone. You'd have to be kind to them, wouldn't you?"

"Yes," said Pavel. "That's right. That's why Doukhobors don't fight and Canadians do."

"Don't Canadians have God inside them?"

"Not like our people do."

"Let him get on with the story!"

"The czar—"

"What's a czar?" asked a boy across the aisle in the darkness.

"He's like a king. The czar told Lukeria that if she stopped the Doukhobor men from being taken into the army, he would send his best solders, frightening men on horseback known as Cossacks"—Pavel lifted both arms to emphasize the size and waved an arm over his head as if swinging a sword—"to destroy her villages and take all their land. What do you think she should do?"

"Tell us," said a face washed in blue light.

"Queen Lukeria wanted to save her people and agreed to do what the czar asked. She told the Doukhobor men that they must join and be good soldiers for Russia."

"But they can't fight."

"Yes, but later, when the czar had gone, she told them to shoot their rifles over the heads of the Turkish soldiers so they wouldn't be hurt."

"Isn't that a lie?"

"Well, yes, I suppose so, but you can lie to people who don't have God inside them. That's okay."

"Is it? My papa said I must never lie."

"How do you know?" asked Marko.

"How do you know what?" replied Pavel.

"If God is inside someone. You could lie to the wrong person."

"Just be quiet. I haven't finished the story."

"Yeah, let him finish."

Pavel took a breath. "The Doukhobor soldiers couldn't pretend to be soldiers, so they decided to pile up their rifles and set fire to them. Then they threw in their Russian uniforms. The fires could be seen from one great ocean in the west to another in the east, and burned for two days and two nights." Pavel stopped, hoping no one would ask which oceans they were. Nor did he want to tell his friends what happened next.

"Go on. Then what happened?" asked Marko.

"Well," said Pavel, "when you see our houses burning and our people stripping off their clothes and throwing them in the fire, you will know why." He did not know how these dots connected, or if any of it was true, but was hoping the scraps of information he had strung together were not completely misleading.

"Why?"

"Because the soldiers had to stop being soldiers and find the true way by burning what they had, their guns and uniforms." It did not make complete sense to anyone, but it was getting late and Pavel was at an end with it.

Night Matron Cody came through the door. Fierce white electric light had the children squinting and covering their eyes. "You've had your warning. If you want someplace to talk and be up at night, I'll give you one. Up, everyone up! Into the shower, right now!" she said, clapping her hands. "If you need help, I'll help you or get the guards to do it." In a single movement she peeled the bedclothes from the nearest bed, exposing a squirming boy on a white sheet.

The boys slipped slowly from their beds to avoid the same fate and began making their way to the shower. It was a familiar routine.

Marko said, "I don't need a shower." The other boys smiled or giggled, shaking their heads at him. Matron, even in this mood, knew enough of Marko to ignore it.

"Keep your pyjamas on. You're not having a shower, Marko. You'll stand in the shower room until you can learn to be quiet at night. Come along," said Matron. "You can talk all you like when you get there. Not you, Pavel. You can stay on your bed. I need to talk to you."

Pavel stopped by his bed and exchanged glances with the others as they filed out. They all knew the routine and what was to happen, but Pavel had not been singled out before and did not like being separated from the others. They would wonder why he was not being punished with them. It was a division that would be hard to explain.

The shower room was large enough to have the children standing or sitting under the bright lights and showerheads. If the floor was wet, they would stand in bare feet and endure the cold of the tiles, huddling together to preserve what warmth they could generate. If the floor was dry, some of the boys would stand or sit on their pyjama tops in a tight group and hope the punishment for speaking Russian would not last until morning. It was enough to stop the numbing of toes for an hour or so.

Karen Cody followed the children toward the shower and switched the dormitory light off as she left. Pavel listened to her admonish them one last time, then a door closed and footsteps returned to the dormitory. He expected the lights to come on, but Matron crossed the floor of the dormitory in the half-light and sat beside him on the bed.

He asked, "Why can't I be with them?" He was unsure whether to be indignant or frightened.

"Because I wanted to talk with you privately."

"What about?"

"You're their leader, Pavel. They respect you. I can see that; so can you. You're responsible for keeping your friends up at night with stories. I've heard you whispering in Russian to them, night after night. You know it's not allowed, don't you? They need rest, and you tell them stories and keep them up. They're so tired they can't concentrate at school, and now you're responsible for them standing in the shower. They might be there all night, until they learn their lesson. Unless," she paused, "you can learn to be responsible for them."

"What do you mean?"

"You are a young man and they're still children. You could teach them to go to bed and get their sleep and how to behave, just like I could teach you things. I wouldn't have to punish them if I could rely on you." Pavel cocked his head as if to concentrate on a signal he was not quite hearing. Matron saw it and picked up the invitation.

"You're growing up. I've seen the changes happening in you."

There were no words to be found. He could not see what she meant or where this was heading.

She put her hand on his shoulder and said, "I've just seen you with your new friend and thought you must be feeling confused right now. And you might need someone to talk to about it."

"What new friend?"

She smiled. "I think you know. We've all seen you when Nina's around. You can't take your eyes off her. These are new feelings for a young man, exciting and confusing. It's best if someone talks with you about it and helps you through it."

"I want to be with the others. What has Nina got to do with them?"

"You don't have to be shy. That's what I wanted to talk with you about. These things are normal. As normal as the hair growing where it didn't before, or your voice breaking, getting lower, and you're stronger." She gripped his biceps with both hands and smiled at him. Pavel looked past her to the door leading to the showers. "Don't worry about your friends. They can come back to bed just as soon as we finish our talk."

"I should go to them."

"But you don't want them to stay in the cold, even with you. You're a brave young man, Pavel. I'm impressed. They don't have to be in the shower very much longer. Will you be able to teach them to behave?"

There was something in her voice urging him to comply, but he could not grasp it yet. He got enough to understand the danger of not going with her.

"Yes," he said.

"Good. Then they can come back soon. Providing you and I can have our talks from time to time, I'll leave you to keep your friends in order, tell them stories if you like. They won't need me to teach them lessons, because I'll rely on you. Is it a deal?"

Pavel was paralyzed with confusion and said nothing, knowing that the longer he was silent, the greater confidence Matron had in their agreement—if only he understood just what the agreement was.

Matron pushed him gently to lie down on his bed, and suddenly he knew. His friends would be standing in the cold shower room longer for every moment of his resistance, so he allowed himself to lie back on the pillow. With one hand she pulled at the string of his pyjamas, exposing him in the half-light. With the other, she brought his hand between her legs. It was strange she was not wearing stockings on such a cold night, but he now understood that she had come to do this. It had never been about speaking Russian or needing sleep. Of course, she had been thinking about how to do this, listening at the door, watching him, planning, and now the understanding crept over him like Matron's hands in the dark. He could keep his friends safe and know they would not suffer in the showers, take the strap on their hands or much worse, if he allowed this. A choice against his friends, his people, could not be made, and he tried to resign himself to her agreement. His father would say it was what the English did. It was how the English said one thing and meant another. They could be trusted to do only whatever they wanted.

So many thoughts and feelings began. He should not be doing this but could not stop Matron from touching him, nor could he prevent his body from reacting to the hand kneading between his legs. Every muscle in his body strained for and against it.

"No need to be nervous," she said. "No one will ever know about our talks and our arrangement. I'll never tell. And don't be embarrassed. It's normal. It's what every strong, young body does."

He struggled to push Nina from his thoughts. The prospect of her finding out what Matron was doing, what they were doing, was too much and he wrestled to distract himself. Outside there must be sounds of the night, which he strained to find. Pavel stared at the purple blue through the window and thought he heard, a long way off, an owl hooting. It was enough to hold onto and avoid giving Matron Cody everything. He would keep separate from this, what he was thinking and the sweetness of Nina. All of that would be kept for himself and other times, if he could keep it away right now and focus on that haunting noise. The buttons of his pyjama top were now undone, his skin blue in the moonlight. He was naked before her.

5

Vancouver, Christmas 2017

DIRTY SNOW EDGED THE ROAD AND THE QUIET STREETS WERE WET WITH melt. William sat in the passenger seat of the Tesla. "Thanks for coming to get me."

"Kelly will be glad to have you home on Christmas Day. She's been worried about you." William heard that Julie might not be, but tried to ignore it. "You had us all worried for a while."

"I didn't mean to."

Julie smiled. "I can be angry with you for lots of things, William, but having a brain tumour isn't one of them." The blood cracked at the end of his nose as they both smiled.

"How is she?" he asked.

"Kelly's fine. Happy with her new snowboard; can't wait to use it." William heard Julie hesitate. "If you're okay, I think she's going up the hill tomorrow."

"Are you taking her?"

"No. One of her friends will be. I might drive them to the mountain."

William's head felt thick. He imagined being blind on the mountain. "I haven't seen her on the mountain. How does it work?"

"Not that complicated really. She follows someone and listens. Sometimes there'll be someone trailing behind giving her directions. Her friends just kinda do it, without much instruction. On a wide piste, her peripheral vision is good enough to see light and dark."

"She must trust them."

"She couldn't do a lot of things if she didn't." There was gentle quiet between them. "We're so lucky that she has so many friends. They don't seem to notice she can't see very well." William struggled with the idea of good fortune but thought better of challenging Julie on Christmas Day. There was nothing good about being blind as a teenager. It was hard enough with all your faculties.

"It would be good if you spent some time with her while you're off."

"I wouldn't know what to do with her. Anyway, it sounds like she'll be too busy for me."

The quiet hardened.

"It's up to you. She'd love to spend time with you. Why don't you take her into work sometime?"

"Maybe." He thought it was a crazy idea. He did not want her to know the source of all their comforts.

The Tesla came to a stop in the garage and began dripping on the floor as the door closed behind them. It was good to see the bikes lined up in their rack. It reminded him that the bicycle delivery and dispatching should have happened by now at the warehouse. William hoped it had gone as planned. The implications of something going wrong could not linger in the mind. Kelly could never know about such things. It was another reason to keep her away from work.

William eased himself out of the car and followed Julie into the kitchen. The house was quiet. Christmas lights cheered the room. William could see through the living room into his study. The light was on and he followed it. Kelly sat cross-legged in his chair, noise-cancelling headphones on, head nodding to the time of the music on her phone.

William bent into the edge of her vision and spoke. "Hi." Kelly pulled off the headphones and reached to him. "Careful now. I'm still delicate."

"Merry Christmas, Dad." It was an awkward embrace, and unfamiliar. Headphones, iPhone and body angles conspired to prevent an intimate exchange.

"Merry Christmas." William could feel the urgency of her affection and it surprised him. "Don't be worried. I'm fine now. I just have to get rid of these panda eyes and I'll be back to normal."

"I thought you might not come home."

"I was always coming home." Bending over made his head pound and his legs unsteady. He tugged himself away from her and perched on the filing cabinet beside the desk. "I'm fine. Really."

"You just say that. That's what you said after falling off your bike, and the first operation. You always say you're fine." It was an echo of her mother.

"Sorry," William said. "I didn't want you to worry."

"I was worried, so it didn't work."

"Would it be better if I said I was having some brain surgery and there are risks?"

"It would be true."

"Sometimes, being 'true' isn't the only thing that's important."

Kelly pouted in mock defiance. "That's what people say when they don't want to be true."

William felt humbled at his daughter's clarity. A few months ago, he would have dismissed her words as naïveté, but they were familiar now and landed on him like a dead weight. "Maybe you're right. I wanted you not to worry. Sorry."

"Well, I want to worry. Just like you worried about your dad."

The reference to his father came unexpectedly. "How did you know I worried about my dad?"

"You took me once, when I was about seven, to that place. It was autumn."

"Riverview Hospital."

"It had big trees. You wanted me to see the colours. Maybe you thought I'd better see them while I could."

"I'm amazed you remember."

"You were so sad. You pretended you weren't, and I pretended to be happy, to cheer you up." She smiled.

"I didn't fool you," he said, perplexed at her understanding.

"No. It made me feel ... terrible, I guess. I never wanted to go again. Did it always make you sad to visit your dad?"

"Yes, it did." William pondered how much to say. "It was always sad. He was angry at everything. He just couldn't be happy."

"Why was he angry?"

"So many things." He paused, trying to shorten the story. "He and my mother were taken from their parents to live with other children. It was a bad place where they went, and lots of bad things happened there. He never really got over it."

"Why were they taken?"

William could see the momentum of her interest rising and needed to escape it. "I'm really tired. Would you mind if we talked about it later? I need to rest awhile."

"Oh, Dad! I never knew this stuff. I want you to tell me."

"Perhaps later. Now, let me sit down and you go help your mum."

She slipped off the chair, reached the door and stopped. "What was the name of the place they were taken?" she asked.

"It's called New Denver."

"I won't forget." Kelly transformed to cheeky girl in an instant. "You said we'll talk later." She was gone.

Like so many of his people, his father had been tormented by anger, betrayal and finally depression. William knew there would have been no forgiveness or consolation in his father's last thoughts. The Canadian government, the Province, the Mounties and finally the hospital had taken everything from his father, because he was not strong enough to see the writing on the wall. His stubborn allegiance to a way of life was a frailty. As a young man William had promised himself he would never succumb to it, but now there was room for conjecture about his father. *What would such a man think of what I have become?*

Boxing Day 2017

HE HAD SETTLED TO RESTING. SLEEPING WHEN NEEDED, FORAGING IN THE kitchen for leftovers, watching television. There was little point in trying to concentrate on work or finding something else to do. He could do nothing but be there, with them. It was easier than he had expected, and he was expected to do nothing. Kelly had not pressed him on the subject of his father, but it was coming, he knew. Any moment now, Julie and Kelly would come in the door with tales of adventure on the mountain. With luck Kelly had not broken her leg with the new snowboard.

The iPhone dinged with a message, an emoji, followed by an unknown telephone number. He knew who it was. William called the number and waited for the connection to be made.

"William, Merry Christmas. How are you?" Uri's voice was full of cheer.

"I'm recovering. Still feeling a little slow. I'm not sure how long we have to speak. How was the shipment?"

"There were problems, William. We need you to find out what happened." There was no alarm in his voice, but a tremor rippled through William.

"What happened?"

"Some of the boxes had been opened and pieces from one box had been changed for pieces from another. We have one important piece missing."

"How could that have happened? You watch it until it gets to me and I have it for less than a day." The implications were clear in his words.

Uri said, "You understand, William. It's important that you find out what happened and return the piece."

"What's the piece?"

"A large sprocket."

"Okay. I'll look for it." William hesitated. "Just to be sure, you're saying one of your boxes has an original sprocket, and one of the real boxes now must have the counterfeit sprocket."

"I think that's correct, but we should not talk of details on the phone," said Uri.

"I understand, but why is it so important?"

"William, you must find it and tell me why it was moved." William listened. "There are people who need to know. We need to know what dangers there are and what we must do. It will be a test for you."

"What do you mean, 'a test'?"

"Every relationship is tested. William, you know this. It is a test of our partnership. We need to know it is a good partnership, that we can rely on it."

"I understand." His head thumped with his heart. "I need a few days."

"Okay, William. A few days. In a few days I'll send you another number." The line went dead.

William deleted his call history, opened his messages and deleted the number he had called, doubting his caution would do any good if it came to it. There was menace in Uri's calm. William thought Uri was giving him directions not to be ignored. There was nothing else to do but find out what had happened.

He would have to go into the office, and his family would not like it. A plan came to mind. The ringing in his ears seemed prominent now. He had thought it had almost left him. Maybe it was always there, but he had not been listening to it.

December 27, 2017

"BUT YOU'VE ONLY BEEN HOME A FEW DAYS." JULIE APPEALED TO WILLIAM not to drive, but he could hear it was without conviction.

"I'll be fine. I feel much better."

"I know, but it's been just a week and you haven't driven at all."

The new number from Uri had not arrived, but he could no longer pretend that there was time to spare. It had been easy to ignore the trouble brewing.

"I'll drop Kelly off, get into the office for an hour or two and then come home. It'll be good to spend some time with Kelly."

Julie smiled at him and approached. "I like having you home. Kelly's liked it too. Let me see you." She inspected his face, outlining the bruising with her finger and touching his cheek. "You've gone from blue to yellow. I guess that's progress. Have you been getting any fluid in your mouth?"

"Nothing."

"You will drive carefully, won't you?"

There was, strangely, a pleasure in being treated like a schoolboy. He had always disliked relying on others, but now he felt the need for someone to take care of him, just for a few days.

"Will do. Promise." For a moment he thought she would kiss him, but it passed. "I better get going."

NO HEATING FOR A WEEK HAD TURNED THE RECEPTION HALLWAY TO A fridge and the warehouse to an icebox. William kept his coat on, inspecting the stacks of bicycles. The clipboard hanging on the wall gripped the manifest that Dennis had left. William released it and checked the consignment of SynchronoX bicycles. The count was right. Then he began looking at the serial numbers. Each one of the genuine bikes had a number listed on the manifest, as did the counterfeit bikes that had already gone, but these were in sequence. He matched the list with the boxes and all was well. The manifest could be destroyed, and the real one filed upstairs.

From the back of the stack he scanned up and down. At the top he could see two boxes with crumpled corners, and he shifted the rolling ladder into position to get them. William opened the first box where it was and picked out and inspected each part. They were matte black, perfectly engineered and light. They were genuine. He shifted the box to one side and turned to the second, and knew immediately that it had been opened. The matte patina of the large sprocket was grey rather than black, and the weight, four times that of titanium, gave it away. At least he had secured it and Uri would be reassured that it had been found. He might even return the real one, and the bicycle could become part of the consignment shipped across the continent.

William tried to piece together how a counterfeit part had found its way into an original box. The crumpled corners of the top boxes suggested an accident. Genuine and counterfeit boxes had fallen and spilled open, and in the process of returning parts to boxes, a mistake was made. It sounded simple enough and plausible, but he had to check the security tapes before connecting the dots finally. He slipped the sprocket into his pocket and descended the ladder.

Upstairs William went through the outer office to his. There was nothing on his desk. It was just as he had left it. The shredder was always ready, and the manifest was pulled through it quickly. He picked some paper from the scrap pile and fed the machine before opening the storage bin, mixing the shreds with his hands and lifting the tangled ball onto the desk. From his pocket he pulled a plastic bag and filled it with the shredded paper. It would find a home in one of the garbage cans or dumpsters on his way home and then on to landfill or incineration. The sprocket was then the only physical connection he would have to the counterfeit bikes. It too might be disposed of on the way home.

William could feel the fatigue setting in, but there were security tapes to deal with. He found the key from Cathy's desk and opened the doors of the cabinet. Every tape deck hummed and twinkled blue light. He stopped the warehouse and reception tapes and pressed rewind on both. The high-pitched whirring reminded him of the wind in his ears. They clicked to finish and he pressed play. Both tapes were started on December 24, just before 5:30 p.m.

On the reception tape Cathy could be seen entering the picture from the stairs, going to the security alarm and setting it, before walking out the door. Through the glass she could be seen locking the building. William wound the tape back to the shot that captured her face and paused it. She looked terrible. He increased the speed of the replay and raced through hours of video. There was no one else coming or going. There was no point going through the other tapes if no one had entered the building. William pressed rewind on all the tape decks and stood up, waiting to restart the recordings before he left. Just the effort of squatting and standing caused him to feel dizzy.

The lid of the photocopier was up. A green light blinked. There was nothing on the glass or in the trays. Normally, Cathy would turn off everything but the cameras before leaving, especially over a holiday, but why would she be using the photocopier when her errand was simply to turn on the security cameras and leave? There was something to figure out.

William struggled to recall how to interrogate the machine. It had come as a surprise when the copier salesman told him that most photocopiers had hard disks and stored data of the documents they reproduced. He had set it up to do just that, but had not used this feature before. He pressed Menu, then Options invited him to cycle through a series of choices: History, Servicing, Troubleshooting. He returned to History. The first choice was Pages, then Last 24 Hours, Last 7 Days, Last 30 Days, Select Time Period, Delete All. He selected the time period and fiddled with the arrow buttons until he had isolated December 24, then clicked OK. Nothing. He went back to Pages, selected Last 7 Days and clicked OK. One photocopy had been made in that time period. William scrolled back to History. The second choice was Documents. He clicked OK. A list of dates emerged and he scrolled to December 21 and clicked. One document was shown. OK. Two choices appeared: Print, Delete. He selected Print and pressed OK.

The photocopier spread light through the outer office, casting a shadow that ran the length of the room and back again. A crisp sheet of paper emerged and the machine went quiet.

William read from the sheet but could not fully comprehend it. Fear rose from his gut and pulsed in his chest. The manifest confused him. Original and counterfeit bicycles were listed, connecting him, the company, and the abyss. It was out, and no longer in his control.

The panic subsided enough for William to think. December 21 was the day Dennis was to have separated the consignment. William recalled walking into reception the morning after falling from his bike and seeing Dennis skip down the stairs, and then finding Cathy flushed in the office. Dennis knew his way around upstairs. It was also possible that Cathy had come in to see him. Either could have photocopied the manifest. William pulled out his phone.

"Hi, Cathy ... yes, I'm fine. Recovering well. Have you had a good Christmas? ... Good ... yes, I did too, thanks for asking. Sorry to bother you, but I need to ask you something ... no, no, the cameras are working fine. It has to do with something else. Do you remember when I asked Dennis to come in and do some work before Christmas to get a dispatch of some SynchronoX units ready? ... That's right, the twenty-first. Did you come in that day?" The noise from Cathy's end was unclear. It first sounded like a muffled whimper and then there was movement. She came back on the line. "What are you saying sorry for? ... Why are you crying? ... Cathy ... Cathy, stop for a second, just stop. Take a breath. Tell me about that day, what happened ... I'm not going to fire you ... tell me what happened." His head was pounding and he closed his eyes to concentrate. "You've been seeing Dennis ... I suspected it. I'm glad you told me ... no, I don't have to tell anyone else. When you came in that day, did you use the photocopier at all?" There was a pause. "Are you sure? ... Okay. What about Dennis? He left after you ... you can't really say if he did or not, but he could have ... thanks for speaking to me. Don't worry about the other thing. Enjoy the holiday. We'll talk again in the new year. Thanks ... okay. Bye."

He believed her. It left Dennis as the most likely explanation, but why would he photocopy the manifest? The adrenalin from the panic was wearing off and he could not trust himself to think. The call to Dennis would have to wait. He closed the photocopier, turned on the security cameras, picked up the bag of paper shreds and headed downstairs to lock up. The tin noise of a cowbell rattled from his iPhone.

"Hi ... I'm just on my way home now. No, I'm fine. Getting tired but I'm fine ... I'll be all right to drive ... yes, I'm sure ... milk? Just milk? ... 2 percent, organic ... okay, I won't be long ... bye."

Walking to the car took more effort than usual. William felt the fatigue in his back and hips causing him to walk like an old man. His nerves were jangled and he started at the noise of passing cars and sudden appearance of people walking past him. Inside the Tesla it was quiet, save the hissing in his ears. The drive to the supermarket and then home would be a challenge. He started the car and rolled into the street, trying to decide which supermarket to go to, and to remember where he had seen a dumpster.

Wet snow fell outside the Save-On-Foods on Marine Drive and caused him to hurry back to the Tesla. The four kilometres to his house in West Vancouver seemed a long way. He would have to conceal his current state from Julie when he arrived, but first he had to get rid of the evidence in his car and in his pocket. He felt exhausted, closed his eyes and let his head fall back against the headrest.

"WILL IT GET ME?" HE SAID TO OWL.

"What?"

"Will the fire get me?"

"It's coming," said Owl.

William and Owl looked behind. The forest glowed with red-yellow flame roaring and crackling through the valley as fast as they flew. Dark smoke billowed above them.

"Go faster!" said William.

"I'll go faster if you let go!" said Owl.

"I have to hang on, or the fire will get me."

"It might get us both if you don't let go."

It was true, thought William. It would be a kindness to the owl if he let go of the hat. "Why don't you let it go?" he asked Owl.

"The fire will take you."

"But you'll die if you don't let go of me."

"Maybe," said Owl. "It's a choice both of us make."

William could taste the smoke in the air and feel the heat chasing them.

THE KNOCK ON THE TESLA WINDOW BROUGHT WILLIAM TO ATTENTION. Outside, the snow had turned to rain and a man in uniform peered in. Drops of rain formed on his glasses and dripped from his nose.

"Sir! Can you open the window, please?"

William turned on the ignition and slid the window down. "What is it?"

"Sorry to disturb you, sir, but are you okay?"

"Yes. I'm fine. Why?"

"Someone reported you being unconscious in the car. We thought you might have been injured or sick."

"No, I'm fine. I've had some surgery"—William gestured to his face—"and felt a little tired, so I closed my eyes. That's all."

"That would explain the bruises." The man in uniform smiled. "You do look a little beaten up."

"Thanks!" The milk and the paper shreds were on the passenger seat. William was relieved to see it was a security guard, not a policeman.

"You okay to get home?"

"Yes, thanks. I'll be fine."

"Well, sorry to disturb you. Have a good day."

"Thanks for your concern." William waved him off and started the engine. He needed to get to that dumpster and be rid of the evidence before going home.

December 28, 2017

THERE HAD BEEN NO COMFORT IN BED. NEITHER BODY NOR MIND WOULD settle enough for proper sleep. William could not force himself to think each element through. The usual method of identifying the problem, what could be done and the implications of each option eluded him. Every path found a monster, too frightening to face in the night, and his thoughts bounced to something else. So it went on. By morning there was only hope that a conversation with Dennis would relieve the wildness in his head and thumping in his chest. William checked his watch. Dennis would be at work by now. So would Cathy. They would both be expecting a call. Maybe, William thought, it would be better to go in and have the conversation face to face.

WILLIAM SAID, "DENNIS, HOW WAS YOUR CHRISTMAS?"

"It was good. Very good, thanks. And happy new year to you." Dennis seemed cheerful. "Your operation went well? Just a little bruising left."

"Actually, they had two tries at getting it right, but I'm fine now. By the way, thanks for coming in and sorting the SynchronoX consignment before Christmas."

"I'm always glad of the work." Dennis was different. There was a swagger in his manner. The usual reference to him as "Boss" had been dropped in favour of something more familiar.

"Two things," said William. Dennis turned his head. "Did you have any problem separating the shipment?"

"Why do you ask?"

"Some of the boxes were damaged." William watched Dennis shrug. "The customer reported a piece missing. I thought maybe there was an accident and some pieces fell out."

"Oh," said Dennis.

"Can you help with that?"

"I don't think I can. Who is the customer?" His lip curled into a smile.

"Never mind about that." William forced himself to stay on top of this conversation. "Did you use the photocopier when you came in on the twenty-first?" It got his attention.

"What's the problem?"

"Someone may have, perhaps innocently, copied confidential documents. Perhaps they were thinking they were doing the right thing and didn't know how serious it was. It's the kind of thing that could lose someone their job. But, if it was innocent and we get the copy back, no harm done. It won't be a problem."

Dennis stared. "I don't think I need to worry about losing my job." William waited for him to explain himself. "You're up to something."

"What am I up to, Dennis?"

"Did you know that some of the SynchronoX bikes that came into the warehouse this month are in the same boxes that I counted last month? I guess they were the same bikes too."

"No, I didn't, but how would you know that?"

"I mark them when I'm counting, with pencil. The marks I made came back to the warehouse this month. How can that be? We sent those bikes all over Canada, but they arrived again the following month. Seemed odd to me."

William calmed himself. "What do you make of it?"

"They were all the boxes you wanted me to separate for a special dispatch. The same boxes that mysteriously left the warehouse without anyone in the building to open up. The same boxes going in and out every month tells me, well, something strange is going on."

"Something strange."

"Look, I don't need to know exactly. It doesn't matter to me if you are into fake bikes or something else. All I need to know is you'll be in shit if anyone finds out. Police, Revenue, I don't care."

William tried to ignore the pounding. "You would need proof of something."

"Yes, I would."

There it was. Dennis did not flinch and stood steady, confident. It was Dennis who had copied the manifest.

"What are you after?"

"I don't want anything to change. If it goes badly for you, I lose my job. Let's just say I'm pleased to be a valued employee. I think I'm due a pay raise, that's all. I don't want the boat to rock."

"So." William released a long breath and nodded. "You're still Dennis in the warehouse, and I'm still the boss?"

"Yes ... Boss."

"Okay, Dennis. That sounds fine. What about Cathy?"

"What about her?"

"It's not good for business."

Dennis shifted his weight from one foot to the other and adjusted his gaze enough to suggest he was at the edge of his confidence. "I didn't think I was treading on your toes."

"You're not. Just leave her alone, and let her down gently." William turned, full square to the younger man. "If this is going to work, I can't have you being disrespectful in public or in private, and I can't have you fucking my secretary. It shouldn't be too hard to understand." Dennis had not seen anger flash in his boss before and stepped back. "So, are we agreed on how this has to work?"

"All right. Agreed." Dennis was not happy with the idea but knew he was pushing his luck, or William was bluffing.

"Good. I had better go upstairs and catch up. Has the second batch of SynchronoX been dispatched yet?"

"No, Boss. It's to go this week."

"I've put one box aside. Seems to be missing a sprocket. We'll have to get a replacement."

William made his way upstairs, conscious that energy would fail him soon. Cathy was in and would be waiting nervously.

"Morning, Cathy."

She watched him carefully as he walked past her desk and into his office. "I am so sorry."

William stopped and interrupted. "Cathy, I don't want to hear any more about it. I'm only in for an hour and I've got too much to do. Just ... just ... get on with your work." He walked into his office and closed the door.

William took his coat off and tried to let the steam dissipate. He regretted saying to Cathy that he would not fire her, and wished he had smashed Dennis into the ground with a mallet. He hated personal lives being brought to work. *Of course life gets complicated,* he thought. *But why the fuck can't they just get on with their jobs!* He wasn't paying for their personal life. It happened all the time, especially among the younger employees, but Cathy should know better.

A buzz in his ears distracted him, and his fury fell away. Within a few breaths, William relented. He had been too quick with Cathy and began thinking about how to approach her. Without a plan he opened his door.

"Cathy, I didn't mean to be harsh with you."

She remained still. He was lost for something to say. Normally he would leave her to recover her composure and then he would behave as if nothing had happened. It was a tried and tested method of drawing a line between someone's emotions and the tasks he was paying them to do. He had always believed it helped them draw the same line and become more professional in their work, but now, without a reason, he stayed with her. Then, without thinking, he put his hand on her shoulder. The touch settled her.

"I'm just a little upset," she said. "Christmas is always a difficult time."

"It must be," he said without knowing. "I think I better go home." She acknowledged him with half a smile. "Will you manage without me?"

"Yes, we'll be fine," she said.

As William left the office a message arrived with a ding from his iPhone. It was the emoji and a code, "R4-2day." William recalled the time and location of the fourth cycle route arranged with Uri and the timing that went with it. Uri had chosen a gentle route in West Vancouver. He might be able to persuade Julie that he was up to riding a short, local route without raising suspicion. He deleted the message and speculated as to why Uri had not sent a number to call. There might be a reason he wanted a wheel-to-wheel meeting, and his heart thumped with the thought.

William had always seen the need for caution, but now he was becoming aware of the subtle strength of their arrangements. There was never a meeting place, a record of a meeting or preparations to meet. They had always been arranged by a simple sign and message from a throwaway phone, and even if a message was found on his phone he would have no problem denying knowledge of it, safe in the understanding that it would lead nowhere. The counterfeit bicycles were gone, the false manifests destroyed and the sprocket dispensed with. His tracks were covered. It was only the copy of the last manifest that exposed him. There was nothing else. There was just Dennis to keep sweet, and Uri.

WILLIAM APPROACHED THE NORTH END OF MCKECHNIE PARK HEADING west. They were to meet on a turning circle as the road ended. Uri would arrive from the west at about the same time from the unmade road separating the two parts of Mathers Avenue. There was no traffic and little sound; mist hung from the bushes. He was nervous. The arrangement between them had worked without problems for several years and suddenly there were interruptions, changes in plans, and now, a breach had occurred. The road abruptly opened into a turning circle. William stopped. There was nothing. It would not be long before the cold penetrated the technical layers of his clothing. William recalled the night he fell from his bicycle. A few stars found their way through the wisps of cloud in the early evening, but nothing moved.

"William." Uri's voice emerged from the track. "I'm glad you could come tonight." Two other bicycles pulled up behind him. Steam lifted from the three like smoke from an engine.

"You've had a workout."

"Yes," said Uri. "All this Christmas eating. We need to get rid of it, and keep warm. But you're cold. Let's get going."

William turned his bike around and they set off east along Mathers Avenue. He and Uri took the lead.

"William, how is your family?"

"Good, thank you. What about yours?"

Uri sighed. "I am not as lucky as you. No wife, no family. No complications." He smiled like a schoolboy. "It is easier for me this way."

William had never extracted information from the little man, but occasionally there was something curious in his conversation. What, he wondered, was easier for Uri without a family? The wheels turned on the damp streets.

"I have something to tell you. You won't like it," said William.

"I like it when you say what is going on. It's better when you tell me, so don't worry."

William began. "We have a problem with the warehouseman."

"Is that Dennis?"

"Yes. He's complicated our arrangement. When I asked him to deal with the last consignment, he did as I asked, but there was an accident. Some of the boxes were opened and he noticed something unusual."

"You have discovered why there were pieces changed?"

"He knows they are not the same. He's also been counting the boxes in and uses a pencil to mark the boxes as he counts. It seems you've been using the same boxes over and over again. He noticed the pencil marks."

Uri seemed unmoved. "So, Dennis thinks he has discovered something."

"He says he doesn't know what's going on, but he thought Canada Revenue or the police would be interested."

"He has threatened us?"

"I don't think he will be a problem. He just wants a promotion and to keep his job."

"And what do you want, William?"

"I think we should keep him sweet. Find some way to draw him in and give him good reason to be quiet."

"That would be clever. But William, it is never good to widen the circle of trust. Why should we do anything? He doesn't have the boxes now, or the bicycles. There's no evidence."

"That's the problem." William hesitated. "I think Dennis photo-copied the manifest after doing the job. He's got a copy of the false one. There is a copy of the real one on file in my office, and the manu-facturers will have a copy." They were silent as the four men passed Thompson, heading to Thirty-First Street.

"It is a problem, William. A big problem. What will you do?"

"Increase his salary. It's what he wants." It sounded lame as he said it.

"It's not a solution, William. The others will not be happy with this."

"What do you want?" asked William.

"The plan was yours. You must fix it. You must get the manifest and make sure it's the only copy. Then we decide what to do with Dennis."

"I'm not sure how I'm going to get it from him." They hovered at the top of the hill leading down Thirty-First Street. Uri lifted a foot off the pedal and stopped.

"William, please understand. You must do what must be done. Shall I ask my colleagues to help you?" He nodded toward the lean, quiet men who had stopped ten metres behind.

"No. Let me deal with it."

"Good, William. We have confidence in you." He smiled. "We are still partners and I will tell the others that there is a small problem, but everything will be taken care of. Now, give me the sprocket."

"Don't worry, I got rid of it," said William, adjusting his bike to set off.

Uri's hand reached William's arm. "William, I asked you to find the sprocket and return it to me. I must have it. You must get it back."

William felt the urgency in Uri's grip. "It's fake, useless, weighed four times a real one. What does it matter?"

"It's true. It weighs more than four times what a real sprocket weighs, but it matters." The smile had gone from Uri but making sense of what was being said was still difficult. "Let me help you understand. This piece has value to us."

"What is it?"

Uri had William fixed in eye contact and appeared to be calculating the implications of what he would say next. "Gold, William, ten ounces of gold. Each of our special bicycles has twenty ounces, in various parts, worth about four hundred thousand Canadian dollars, in each shipment. We use the special packaging and false bicycles many times because together, with the gold, they weigh exactly what originals weigh."

"I agreed to help you clean your money for a cut. Nothing was said about gold."

Uri shrugged. "What is gold, if it is not money? Surely you understood that we would not be taking such risks for a few thousand dollars. There are bills to pay. Did you not ask yourself why we're paying you so much each month?"

William could not respond. The full knowledge of what had been going on had evaded him and the implications could not be settled in his mind. He tried to calculate the amount of gold that may have trickled through his warehouse in three years. His ears buzzed with fear of the calculation but the amount was in the millions, tens of millions. It was enough to send him to prison forever and take everything from his family.

Uri allowed him time to absorb the magnitude of his involvement and recover. "You see why the sprocket has value, not just because of the gold, but because if it is found, it will be known how it moves."

"Yes. I see," said William.

"And the manifest? You understand why we must have it."

"Yes. Of course."

"Good, William. Thank you." Uri shuffled a little closer, steam rising from him like smoke from a demon. "You have taken a step today, closer to the centre of our circle of trust. Everything is more important now, there is more responsibility, and you must be more careful to do exactly what you agree to do. The stakes are higher for all of us." He offered his hand and smiled as if congratulating a graduate.

William shook the hand before Uri adjusted himself onto the bicycle seat.

"One week. We will meet in one week. Enjoy the new year, William." Without a sign between them, the three left William standing and slipped down the hill.

One week, he thought, was not very long. He watched the red lights of the trio sink into the darkness.

6

New Denver, April 13, 1957

NEW DENVER WAS NOT WHAT NINA HAD IMAGINED. SHE WAS STILL A SPY in the eyes of the girls and therefore alone on a Saturday morning, shunned by the others without redress. Only Pavel and some of the younger ones risked talking to her. There was much to contemplate in passing the time. Green shoots and early daffodils gave the impression of summer coming, but not yet. Snow still lingered on the slopes and chill could be felt as quickly in shade as the sun felt warm in the open. At night the temperature fell to near freezing.

From the lake a brisk spring wind whipped the BC flag. Nina watched it furl and unfurl. English school had instructed her on the meaning of it. The flag, she had learned, was a British ensign: a Union flag on a blue background with the provincial shield of arms in the middle. At the top of the shield was another Union flag with a golden crown in the centre. At the bottom of the shield the sun radiated, depicting the age-old maxim that the sun never sets on the British Empire. It revealed what had been said many times in her hearing: that British Columbia was for the British.

More disturbing to Nina were the words and symbols like *arms, shield, crown* and *empire*. They struck horror in the hearts of Doukhobors in a way that she had not understood until coming to New Denver. The ideas were simply incomprehensible. They were a perplexing, reviled anathema of everything her people stood for. It was the reason

Doukhobors turned away from the Orthodox Church in Russia, with its icons and grandeur, and from the czar's nationalist imperialism nearly two centuries before. Nina's spirit had been soaked in this history even before she was born.

Pavel had taught her to question what people said and trust the evidence of her own eyes about the world they now lived in. It was a history repeating. She could now understand why her parents could not tolerate sending their children to English school, refused military service, and declined to register anything with government authorities. Before, it was a childish acceptance of religious mantra, but now it was real and she was alive to it. She was fixed to the bedrock of her people's struggle. Even the language of her childhood teachings had new meaning. Governments, she now understood, served only worldly interests. They preferred the symbols and strength of their authority to all that was important to her people.

The cackle of the flag in the wind, mocking all but the British, became irritating. That flag and all it stood for was the cause of her people's hardship. It was the reason she was separated from her family, the cause of all the children being taken and of the divides among her people, and why she sat alone in a place where she had thought her friends would welcome her. It all started with the laughing flag they were told to cherish. Anger grew quickly and Nina searched for a target on which to vent the frustration foaming within, but she was alone, completely alone in the courtyard. Her disappointment spawned another thought.

A FEW CHILDREN SAW NINA WALK TO THE SHORELINE, GATHER SEVERAL medium-sized rocks in a large piece of blue cloth, push a simple rowboat into the water and begin rowing. No one knew her purpose.

Arina arrived as Nina's boat pulled out of reach. "Where are you going?" she asked. "It's too cold to swim."

Nina smiled, put a finger to her lips and lifted a corner of the flag into view. Arina's eyes bulged in alarm.

The dormitory buildings south of Galena Avenue sheltered the shoreline from the bitter wind from the north. For twenty-five yards into the lake there was calm on the water. Nina rowed close to the wind line, where the ripple began, and shipped the oars. Between her feet she pulled the corners of the flag together and settled the stones at the bottom before using the flag's lanyard to tie the corners together. The last thing she wanted was for the flag to be found floating at the surface, implicating her unexpected paddle. There would be terrible consequences, but the fear was lost in the strength she felt surging through her.

As Nina finished the knot, there was a moment of doubt. *What would my parents think of me?* She had always been a dutiful child, helping others, doing her chores without complaint. Her mother and Auntie had often told her that she was a good girl. Now she was a thief, a vandal, no longer the sweet child her Auntie smothered in kisses. The thought of leaving that behind mattered more than anything that might happen to her in the dormitory. She looked left and right along the shore. Pavel could not be seen. At least he would not be involved if it all went wrong. In any case, she thought, this must be done alone. Only Arina was watching.

She lifted the sack over the gunwale and let it go. It was gone in an instant. On the shore Arina's arms were held high in excitement. Nina stood in the rowboat, lifted an oar over her head and roared. Her defiance and exultation crossed the lake. She was thrilled with the sound of growing up and shouted again for good measure. Arina celebrated with her, the two howling at the top of their lungs.

Mr. Nori heard the shouting and arrived at the south side of the compound in time to see the boat ease across the wind line and wobble. Nina bent her knees to stop it, but too late. She was in.

Surprise came with shocking cold, and then the inability to breathe. Once back on the surface she could neither inhale nor exhale. Her chest seemed only to be squeezing the life from her. The fall had pushed the boat away toward the southern edge of the lake. Her shoes were dragging on her, and her clothes restricted the movement of her arms. She struggled to pull free of her jacket but managed only to trap her arms behind her. She kicked to stop from sliding under again but could not prevent it.

From under the surface Nina saw the light of the sky. She kicked with desperation and then, with great sadness, thought she would never see Pavel again.

NINA WOKE SUDDENLY. SHE WAS IN A BED IN THE SICK BAY: A FEW ROOMS smelling of disinfectant, with sagging mattresses and crisp white sheets. It was dark outside and quiet, save for the distant after-supper bustle in the dining room across the courtyard. An office light was on where the nurse normally sat, but Nina was alone. Recalling the shoreline, to where she had been dragged just hours before, caused her to shudder. It was bad enough to have nearly drowned, but to be rescued, and then vomiting out all that was inside her, in front of the children was nearly too much. But now she was hungry and climbed out of bed to find food. Mr. Nori, the Japanese guard, had laid her face down on the stony beach, leaned heavily and repeatedly on her back, and pushed the water from her lungs. Now her ribs ached with each movement. With a blanket over her shoulders Nina made her way to the dining room, hoping she was not too late, passing the flagpole on the way.

From outside the door, Nina saw a meeting in progress. Matron MacDonald, the principal and an RCMP officer stood with their backs to the door. The children sat at tables in front of them.

"Children," Matron MacDonald began loudly. She waited for the clamour to end. "Something very serious has happened today, so I have sent all the younger children to bed early to talk to you." A buzz began. They would be taking the boats away, or some suggested Nina might have gone to hospital, or she might have died. "Children!" The buzz stopped. "Today is Saturday and tomorrow, you all know, is visiting day. But I have decided to cancel all visits because of what has happened." Another swell of noise began and stopped as Matron MacDonald continued. "Someone, or more than one of you, has stolen a flag from the flagpole in the courtyard." The children were quiet, knowing how serious this was to these people. "Stealing, in this country, is a crime. Anyone found guilty of stealing will be punished, and the RCMP are here to see that they are." She lifted the strap from the dining table beside her and put it down again. "Unless whoever has done this owns up right now, I'll strap every child in this room before you go to bed, and all visits will be cancelled until we discover who it is and the flag is returned."

Nina had stopped breathing. Through the glass panels of the door the words were muffled but unmistakable. She watched the silence hang on the children, their faces slack. Without expression they told the story of accepting punishment and disappointment as generations of Doukhobors before them had done. Some of the families had already begun the journey to New Denver. It would be too late to advise them to turn back, even if someone was inclined to do so. They too would accept what had happened and return home, no less committed to the next trek to visit their children. The children were helpless, without the chance of making their case with reasoned argument, asking for justice, leniency for the guilty or mercy for the innocent. Nothing would change what Matron MacDonald was going to do. It was what the English did.

Matron said, "Does anyone have anything to say? If you don't own up now, it will be because of you that visits are stopped and your friends get the strap." She waited. "This is your last chance."

Nina opened the door. "It was me." Her voice was softer than intended, but the effect was electric. The room hummed with excitement.

"You!" said Matron. "Why would you do such a thing?"

Nina said, "You stole the coat my auntie made me, so I took your flag." The children erupted.

"I did no such thing. Come here, young lady." Matron grabbed Nina's arm, dragging her forward.

"Where is it? Where have you put the flag?" asked Matron.

"At the bottom of the lake." There were stifled giggles and tittering among the children, who did not know if fear or excitement was right. "I put stones in it and dropped it in the lake." The room gasped.

"I'll deal with you right now." Matron lifted the strap, and the children cowered. "Give me your hand."

Everyone got the strap sometime, Nina had been told, and everyone cried, even those who said they did not. It had become the common dread that boys denied, while girls huddled around each other for support. It would be terrible to cry in front of all the now silent faces before her. It was as bad as them watching her vomit through her nostrils. Pavel was also watching. It made her feel stronger, but why was he smiling? She smiled back at him and thought he must be proud of her for taking the flag and standing up to them. Other children were smiling. They were all proud of her, wishing her well and hoping she would get through this. She was no longer the spy in the camp. She had become the girl who fought back.

"This is no laughing matter, Nina," said Matron. "You're a thief and I'll take that smile off your face." The anger reddened Matron's face.

Nina obliged Matron and offered her hand. She watched Matron hold her by the wrist, straighten her back and lift the strap over her head. The room waited for the cruel slap that would arrive in the next second. Nina thought, in that moment of hesitation, there was nothing she should be punished for. The strap fell toward her hand with the weight of Matron's anger. Nina pulled her hand away and let the strap continue, clapping hard on Matron's thigh. The sound was softer against cloth than against a child's hand, but Matron yelped and jumped back in shock as the children caught their breath and began shouting and laughing as if Christmas and birthdays had all arrived.

Matron rushed forward, gripped Nina's wrist with the strength of the enraged and whacked her hand three, four and five times in quick succession, before Constable Flanagan held her raised hand.

"That's enough," he said, stepping between them and covering her hand with his.

Matron's fury turned on him. "Let go of her hand!"

Flanagan said, "She nearly drowned today and should be in bed."

"You will leave this to me." Matron raised the strap again.

He said quietly in Matron's ear, "End this now and I won't investigate her stolen coat."

The tension of Matron's anger eased and she released Nina.

"Go to your beds, all of you." She turned to Nina. "You come with me."

With Nina in tow Matron stomped across the courtyard, past the flagpole, toward sick bay. Constable Flanagan followed them. Matron turned to him as she walked.

"You won't be needed anymore, Constable." Flanagan continued walking. "I'm in charge here, not you."

They reached the door of the small single-storey office building and sick bay. "You can't come in here," Matron said. She held Nina roughly by the wrist.

"That's fine," Flanagan said. "I'll wait outside the door awhile."

Matron yanked Nina into the office block and pushed the door firmly closed.

April 19, 1957

CONSTABLE FLANAGAN BEGAN THE AFTER-LUNCH WALK TO SCHOOL. HE followed the children past the security hut, out of the dormitory compound, through the eight-foot wire mesh fence and on to Galena Avenue. The compound, lifeless without the children, fell silent behind them. Once he had finished escorting the children to school he would not be needed again until the end of the school day, less than three hours away. At the corner of Union and Seventh Avenue, the children turned toward school. Nina was just ahead, walking with a group of girls as he had not seen her do before. As they went through the school gates, she dropped off the group and turned to Flanagan.

"I hope you didn't get into trouble for Saturday."

"No trouble. Are you feeling better?"

"I am, thank you. Thanks for what you did."

"Don't mention it. It was pretty wicked of you to move your hand away." He could not help the amusement in his words. "Caused quite a commotion. Matron was sure to lose her temper with you."

"No," said Nina, "I didn't mean that. You stayed at the door until Matron went home."

Flanagan turned his head. "I thought Matron was upset by you nearly drowning, and then when the flag was taken, it was never going to be an easy night, now, was it? And then you moved your hand." Flanagan adopted a serious face, shook his head and looked grimly at Nina. "She needed someone to make sure she was all right, just for a little while."

"So you were looking after Matron," said Nina.

"That's what my report says."

"No need to thank you then."

"Definitely not. No need of thanks. You better get off to school before the bell rings." He watched Nina set off for the schoolhouse. "And keep your hands off those flags."

She looked back along the path. He had seen her like that years before in Perry Siding, running away from him with two children dragging behind her, but now the blue eyes gleamed with amusement.

On the way back a figure waited for him on the Union Street bridge. The smirk on his sergeant's face was a bad omen.

"Good afternoon, Sarge. Didn't expect to see you today."

"I didn't expect to have to see you again, Constable," the sergeant said. The disdain in his voice was clear. "Disappointed in you, Irish. Matron tells me you can't even watch the children get back from school without letting them get into trouble."

Flanagan said, "What trouble would that be, Sarge?"

"Apparently there's a woman a few streets from the dormitory who keeps contraband for the children, and you've done nothing about it."

"I know nothing about it, sir. Is she breaking a law?"

The sergeant stood closer. "The same problem, Irish. Wherever you go, you don't know what bloody side you're on. You're here for less than two weeks and already I have complaints. Come with me. We'll see about the bloody laws being broken."

The two men walked in silence, west toward Third Avenue and the house of the Green Witch.

OUTSIDE THE SINGLE-STOREY HOUSE THEY STOPPED. "IS THIS THE HOUSE?" asked the sergeant.

"I don't know, Sarge. I've never been here."

The sergeant looked askance at Flanagan and knocked on the door.

A woman opened the door and said, "What's your business here?" Her face, pale and wrinkled with the wisdom of years, moved little in the greeting. She held a .22-calibre rifle in both hands.

"I'm Sergeant Benson of the RCMP, and this is Constable Flanagan."

"What do you want?"

"We have reports that you're hiding contraband for the children of the dormitory."

"Contraband?"

"Yes, contraband. Food and other things that the children are not intended to have."

"They're not intended to have food?"

"No, they're not. Not that sort of food."

"What sort of food are you talking about?"

The sergeant paused and said, "Madam, we haven't been introduced."

"That's right, we haven't."

"Perhaps you would tell us your name."

"Perhaps you can get off my step."

"I won't be leaving until we clear this matter up." Benson stood undaunted in front of the Green Witch.

She said, "Suit yourself," stepped backwards and closed the door.

"Sarge, I think we should step away from the door." The two men moved off the step.

"You talk with the old girl." Benson gestured at Flanagan to go to the door again. Standing to the side and knocking gently, he waited.

The door opened. The rifle was still in hand. "So, I had the organ grinder, now what?"

"May I speak with you, please?"

"If you have a tongue in your head and can be civil with it."

"I don't know what's going on here. The sergeant tells me you let the children keep food here. The matron's complained about it. That's all I know."

"Let that one complain all she likes. She takes her share of what the children get."

Flanagan said, "It's true, then, what she says. The children do keep food here."

"It's true they steal things from the children. What will you do about that? Nothing, I expect." Flanagan remained silent and still until the woman relented. "I give them cookies when they come. What business is it of yours?"

"It's none of my business, but if I stand here long enough, the sergeant will think you're co-operating with us and then we can leave you alone, and we can tell the matron there's nothing to worry about."

Something changed in the woman's face. "So, you're not just a monkey."

"No, I'm not. Would you mind setting the rifle down? It makes me nervous."

Her body relaxed and she set the butt of the rifle beside her foot, as soldiers stand at ease.

Over her shoulder Flanagan saw pictures of family. Black and white, formal poses, military. "I see you have family in the army. They're proud-looking men."

"You're too young to have served," she said.

"Too young to make my mother proud," said Flanagan, smiling.

"I'd rather still be a mother than proud of dead sons."

"I'm sorry."

"Lost them both in the North Atlantic, on the way to fight. Didn't fire a shot. Pointless."

"I can't imagine what that must be like."

"I expect you can't."

"I'm sorry to have bothered you. I think we've been here long enough. Good day to you." Flanagan turned to go.

"Young man!" she said, causing him to turn toward her again. "You're about the age of my boys when they left me. The last time I saw them they were in uniform too." She paused. "I'll tell you what's going on and then you can tell me what you're going to do. We'll see if what they died for counts for anything." She fixed her eyes on him. "In my cellar, I have boxes of food for the children. Each one has a child's initials on it. It's their secret and I keep it for them. They get food from parents and they buy candy from the store. If they didn't keep it here, the staff would take it or the mean boys would have it off them. On the way home from school and on the weekends they come round and treat themselves. Sometimes, if a box is empty, I put a cookie or two in it. Now, what are you going to do? Arrest me?"

"No. That won't be necessary."

"He wants to arrest me," she said, pointing at the sergeant, now thirty feet away. "I could tell by the knock he reckons he can do whatever he likes."

"He thinks he's doing his job, that's all."

"Tell him these children should have the freedom my boys died for, and neither of you should be helping to keep them locked up for no good reason."

"I will."

"If he knocks on my door again, there'll be more trouble than he wants."

"I'm sorry to have bothered you, and I'm sorry about your two boys."

"Perhaps you are. We'll see," she said.

"Sorry, I still don't know your name."

"Don't you?" Her face broke into a grin. "I'm the Green Witch. Tell him that too."

Flanagan returned to his sergeant, who asked, "What was that about?"

"She told me she makes cookies and gives them to the children."

"That's all?"

"Yes, Sarge. That's it."

"Waste of bloody time."

"Yes, Sarge."

"You better tell the matron."

"Will do, Sarge."

April 21, 1957

ARINA SAT ACROSS THE DINNER TABLE FROM HER FRIENDS, AND ON EACH side they clustered. Spoons stirred idly in bowls, pushing lumps aside for fear it was not edible or, worse, meat. It smelled old and unwelcome. All the children had been raised vegetarian, but it meant nothing here if pennies could be saved by the addition of cheap meat not suited for market. At the head table matrons and staff openly ate the food prepared by the parents for their children. It was often like this and children learned to allow the injustice to pass, but there was something different about today. It could not be dismissed so readily in the light shone by resistance. This had found its way into focus and allowed resentment to simmer again.

Nina arrived at the table to be with Arina. The younger girls buzzed and shuffled to make room for the newest celebrity of New Denver Dormitory.

"The food smells worse than normal," said one girl.

"We could refuse to eat it," said another.

"We tried that years ago. There's always someone who eats it. They can't help it."

"And they stop our visits until we start eating again."

"What do you think we should do?" Arina asked Nina.

The girls would hang on Nina's words, if only she could think of some to offer.

"I don't think we should ask people not to eat. It's hard enough here for all of us," Nina said, stirring her bowl. "Anyway, there's no point doing it if we can't get everyone to do it." She brought her spoon to her mouth, allowed a little in and returned the rest.

Another voice leapt in excitement. "What was it like when Matron strapped her own leg?" They all giggled. "It was so brave."

"I wish I'd seen it."

"Why did you do it?"

"I'm not sure, really. It happened so quickly. I thought it was unfair," said Nina. "They shouldn't just beat us when they like."

"But you stole the flag and put it in the lake."

"They stole all of us from our families, take our food and clothes from home." Nina surprised herself with the sudden burn of emotion. "Maybe we should all have straps and whack their hands." The children laughed anxiously, peeking at the head table, hoping not to attract attention.

"At least you've done something," said Arina. The others listened. "What can we do?"

Nina had not meant to be in the middle of this excitement, but there was nothing to be done but accept it. She searched for something harmless they could do and something came to her. The young faces waited as she struggled to string the idea together. The matrons would threaten to make it worse for everyone. Matron would strap the whole group, blocking visits, preventing the children from doing things they wanted to do. Every protest, including her own, added more hardship but, she thought, it did not have to be a show of defiance.

"They take our clothes and give different stuff, don't they? Where do they get the clothes they give us?"

"I don't know. Never thought of it. They just give us shoes and things when we grow out of them."

"Well, if you lost a shoe, what would they do?" Nina grinned at them, pleased with her idea.

"They wouldn't send us to school without shoes; the school wouldn't let them."

"We'd have to have coats in winter."

Nina watched the understanding of her scheme grow on the faces of her younger friends.

"It would cost a lot to keep us all in shoes."

Nina said in English, with wide eyes, "We had better not lose our shoes."

Other children were leaving the dining room. The bustle of making ready for the day had begun. Nina put a finger to her mouth and whispered in Russian, "Share the secret, but only with the friends you trust." They stood together and headed for the door.

Nina stopped. Pavel was there among the boys leaving the dining room in a clatter. He stepped away from them and came to her.

"What are you smiling about?" he asked.

"The little ones wanted to do something to fight back, and we came up with a plan to lose bits of clothing they would have to replace."

"Like what?"

"Shoes and socks. The things they have to replace."

"Be careful," said Pavel. "I didn't like seeing Matron strap you."

"I don't care. It'll be all right. If lots of people do it a little, we can say the town children are taking things. We won't be blamed."

Pavel knew this to be true. They would never punish their own children, but the risk to everyone in the dormitory was real.

"Would you tell the boys? Just the ones you trust."

"Okay." They had found each other long enough to renew the connection, but Pavel was uncomfortable.

"What's wrong?" she asked.

"Well, we don't waste things. We shouldn't, should we?"

"But they're not our things," said Nina. "They take our things."

"I know, but still, it's not the Doukhobor way. I don't want ... I don't want us to be ... like them."

"You'll never be like them. I won't be like them. Promise." She could see he was still not right with it. "We must fight not to be like them."

A voice came from outside. "Pavel! Come on. We've got time for soccer."

"All right," he said. "I'll tell them." Then he was gone.

April 23, 1957

THE LIGHT STAYED LONGER AND THE WARMTH OF THE DAY NOW LIN-gered until the evening chill. Constable Flanagan waited at the gate as the children came scrambling out of the school at the end of the day. He began walking along with them, near the back of the group.

Up ahead groups of children chatted and cavorted. Boys pushed each other and then began kicking something along the street. They cheered the final thump of the object to the side of the road as if a win-ning goal had been scored. Only ten years before, Flanagan had been one of the boys playing to exhaustion with his school friends, arriving home gasping of thirst. Now he was amused to watch himself in these boys competing down Union Street on the way to the dormitory.

At the point on the road where the goal had been scored, Flanagan stopped to look at the object being treated as a soccer ball. It was a black shoe. *Strange*, he thought. *Who would leave one shoe at the side of the road?* He began walking toward the dormitory. Across the Union Street bridge another shoe lay, and he went to inspect it. It was brown, not the other of the pair. He began walking again and caught up with the children as they clustered together to get into the dormitory compound. A girl at the back waited for others to enter. Flanagan noticed she wore only one black shoe.

"Hello," he said, tapping her on the arm. "I think I found your shoe." She turned, scowling at him, and spoke in Russian. "Sorry, I don't understand. I found your shoe. It's on the road," he said, pointing at her foot and directing her attention toward the bridge. She turned her back to him. He touched her again. "Your shoe, it's on the road." She spoke again in Russian, this time a torrent of impossible syllables, and then turned away.

He spoke to an older girl. "Would you tell her that I found her shoe on the road by the bridge?" But the girl turned away and pushed to get into the compound.

Flanagan stepped back, not understanding what was happening. There was another child without a shoe, and another one.

7

Vancouver, December 30, 2017

"DENNIS?" SAID WILLIAM INTO HIS IPHONE. "IT'S WILLIAM ... I KNOW IT'S Saturday morning. We have to talk ... there's been a development ... we did come to an understanding, but there's something else ... I wouldn't be talking to you if it wasn't important ... not on the phone. We have to meet ... today ... I'll come to you ... this afternoon ... I know it's the weekend but it can't wait ... we all have other things to do but this is in your interest as much as mine. Okay ... I'll come to your house at three. See you then."

The swagger in Dennis's voice made William angry. He turned off the phone and remembered he had not been to Dennis's house and did not have the address. His anger had not yet subsided and the prospect of letting Dennis know he had forgotten to ask for it was too much to contemplate. The address would be in his employment records at the office but Cathy would have it, he was sure. She never minded being phoned on the weekend. Any distraction seemed welcome to her.

The heat of anger eased and William exhaled. It might be that Cathy was with Dennis at this moment. Images streamed suddenly through his head. Clothes being tugged and pushed, thick hands pulling and kneading soft flesh, bodies moving, yielding, offering ... William shook off the intrusion. It was unfamiliar. It seemed more difficult to concentrate these days and perhaps, he thought, it would take time to get back to normal. Lifting the phone again, he started to call Cathy and then changed his mind. He would leave it a few minutes until his body and mind settled.

3:00 p.m.

THE TESLA ROLLED OFF THE HIGHWAY INTO NORTH BURNABY, JUST A FEW minutes before three o'clock. Snow fell lightly on the windshield. The satellite navigation spoke gently. William tried to imagine how this would go. He had the advantage at the last meeting with Dennis just by imposing himself, but on this occasion he was on unfamiliar turf, and as Uri had so clearly suggested, the stakes were higher. The voice told him that he had arrived at the house. From inside the sanctuary of the Tesla, William took stock of the neighbourhood. It was unremarkable. The grey wooden townhouse at the end of a row was distinguishable from the others only for the need of paint. It peeled from the window-sills. Mildew grew at the foot of the step railing.

One light, upstairs and deep in the house, could be seen through the window. There was another at the back. William stepped out of the Tesla, walked to the door and rang the bell. No one came. He tried again and still nothing. He reached for his phone and called Dennis. It rang until the voice-mail script began. Standing back from the front door, William tried to see through the windows. He stepped farther back to get a better view of upstairs. There was no sound or movement. A passageway to the right separated the house and the next row of townhouses. William walked between tall wooden fences protecting the little backyard. The downstairs light was in the kitchen. He craned his neck to see over the fence, adjusting his position to survey all he could. The back door was slightly open, as was the gate into the yard. He entered and opened the door to the house.

The house was cold. The countertop and floor were soaked with water, chairs upended and a table knocked askew. William stepped carefully through the water. He made his way to the darkened hallway and saw a staircase on the left, a doorway on the right. He felt his way along the wall for a light switch. A fist emerged from the darkness of the doorway. William saw it momentarily before it connected with the corner of his jaw and crumpled him to the floor.

WILLIAM WOKE BEFORE HIS EYES COULD OPEN. HIS EARS RANG AND HIS head throbbed more than before. Through this he could feel his legs were cold and wet. Ideas connected loosely. Perhaps the liquid in his brain had drained out and soaked him. It might be blood, but if the blood was cold, it could not be his. There had been water on the floor and his clothes may have absorbed it. He recalled the punch. There was some stiffness in his limbs from being folded for a time, but he could not detect other damage. The punch, he thought, may have disturbed the site of the operation near his brain. William opened his eyes and tried to move his hand to check if there was clear liquid oozing from his nose. His hands would not move. They were tied behind his back. Dennis sat at the kitchen table, holding a glass and a short, fat bottle of whisky.

"What's going on?"

"I dunno," said Dennis. "Thought you would know. You said there was some kind of 'development.' A few hours later these guys turn up, spend half an hour slapping me around and pouring water up my nose before they say anything."

"What did they want?"

"Same thing you want."

"Did you give it to them?"

"Sure I did! They were going to find it whether I was alive or dead. I gave it up quick when they asked, when they finished having their fun, and here I am."

"Why tie me up?"

"You sent them."

"Why would I arrange to meet with you and send them?"

"To make sure I was here. Get the heavies to do your work. Turn up later and fuck with me. Have fun, right? Maybe it's what you like, eh? You like to be in charge, don't you?"

"It wasn't me."

"Maybe. We'll see."

"What do you mean?"

Dennis turned. "I mean, a few minutes of having water poured up your nose will help me work out if you're lying."

"No need for that," said William. "You already know money's being made somehow. Now you know that I am not alone in this. I have a partner."

"Who is it?"

The irritation cleared William's head. "Do you want them to come back and introduce themselves? The less you know and the less contact you have with them, the better. They're not like us. They don't have families and jobs and make a little extra on the side. This is all they do. It's what they are. You've seen how they work. For Christ's sake, untie me!"

William waited and watched Dennis, scanning his face for a flicker of falsehood. He pushed his chair from the table, stood and approached William, turning him roughly to get at his hands. The smell of whisky hung on his breath.

William felt the wet trousers flap against his skin as Dennis helped him up. "You're a fucking idiot," said Dennis, "to get mixed up with guys like that. I thought it was just you and a little scam."

"And I thought it was a quick way of sticking it to the taxman. It seems we both got it wrong."

Dennis sat again at the table and lifted the whisky to his lips. "I guess so. What do we do now?" he said, and then drained the glass.

William pulled a chair upright and sat across the table from Dennis. His wet trousers stuck to his legs. "Do nothing. Behave like nothing has happened. You'll get a bonus next month to help pay for this."

"No need for that," said Dennis. "It's just water. I don't think any damage has been done." He poured from the bottle and shifted his weight back in the chair. "Anyway, I've been thinking. I better look for another job. I'll put my notice in on Monday. I don't live with my children anymore, but they rely on me. Anyway, I should try again with their mother. I can't get mixed up in this kind of thing. If it all comes down, I don't wanna be there."

William acknowledged the pragmatism with a nod. It would be good all round if he left. "What will you say to Cathy?"

Dennis shifted in his chair. "It's not serious with her. There's not much for her to get over."

"Well, you'd better tell her soon. Maybe you can tell her you've been offered a new job and have to go without notice, and I'll say the same."

"She knows it's coming."

"I'll give you three months' pay and a reference if you need it, but the deal is you talk to no one about this." Dennis nodded. "One more thing. I have to ask this: Are there any more copies of the manifest?"

Dennis shook his head. "No, there was only one."

"You wouldn't keep one for insurance?" Dennis was already shaking his head again. "That would put us all at risk."

"No. They took the only one."

"Okay. I'd better get going."

Both men stood. William felt himself trembling with cold.

"I'll come in next week and sort things out in the warehouse," said Dennis. The swagger had gone.

"Thanks, that would be helpful. See you Monday." William headed for the front door.

Outside, sitting in the Tesla, William concluded Uri was satisfied with what his associates found in the house. Otherwise, the outcome would have been very different. He moved uncomfortably to prevent the wet trousers from making fresh contact with his skin and remembered he still had to retrieve the sprocket on the way home.

4:30 p.m.

IT WAS WARM IN THE TESLA AND THE SOAKED TROUSERS HAD, FOR THE most part, reached body temperature. He was not looking forward to stepping out. Large, damp flakes of snow fell, blanketing all that did not move. The dumpster was still where it was when he dropped the sprocket into it a few days before. William hoped it had not been emptied. He stepped out into the falling snow; in a few seconds his trousers became cold, and each step found a new patch sticking to his leg.

Inside the dumpster the sheen of black plastic bags could be seen forming a mound, pushing the lid ajar. He would have to dig to the bottom to get the sprocket, and there was nothing to be done but get in and toss the bags aside. The hinge squealed as the lid rotated open. William reached for the lip with both hands, stepped on a metal edge and hoisted himself into the dumpster. His bad shoulder took the strain without much discomfort, and he was in. The smell was tolerable and it seemed dry inside. Bending over the bags, he began pulling them away from the corner where he had dropped the sprocket and shredded papers.

"What the fuck are you doin'?" An angry voice emerged from the black bags behind him just as a foot made contact with his rear end.

The dumpster erupted as William overbalanced, falling out head-first. He caught the edge and swung his legs enough to break his fall.

"Fuck off! It's my dumpster."

From the pavement William saw the head and shoulders of a wild-eyed man enraged and staring down at him. "Fuck off!" Snowflakes drifted past the wild man. He had seen faces like that: angry, pale, cheeks hollowed out by drugs.

"I didn't know you were there," William said.

"Just fuck off. I don't care."

"I'm sorry. I don't want your dumpster."

"It's mine. Want do you want?"

William struggled to his feet. "I threw something away. It's at the bottom of your dumpster."

"If you threw it away, it's mine now."

"I didn't mean to throw it away and I need to get it," said William. "It's worth nothing to you."

"If it's worth something to you, it's worth something to me."

"I'll buy it from you." William reached for his wallet. "I'll give you fifty dollars."

"A hundred." The wild-eyed man sat in the dumpster. Snowflakes adorned his head now. The street light made him glow like a Russian icon.

"Okay." William pulled all the bills he had from his wallet, held them under a street light and began counting. I've only got seventy dollars."

"Then fuck off. It's mine. Come back when you've got a hundred."

"Just take the seventy dollars. Please."

"A hundred," said the wild-eyed man.

William stepped forward, hand outstretched with the money. "Just take it."

"The deal's a hundred."

Anger surged. "Have it!" William threw the money at the wild-eyed man and lifted himself on the lip of the dumpster. The man scrambled to prevent William from getting in, grabbing his shoulders and pushing him back. The dumpster leaned with the weight of two men on the edge and began falling. William stepped off and rolled backwards as the dumpster crashed on the laneway road. The snow-dampened quiet of the dark winter afternoon stifled the sound.

William sat up. Plastic bags littered the laneway. There was no movement from the open dumpster. The wild-eyed man lay face down and still. Both the man's arms were tucked under his body as if he had held the edge of the dumpster until impact, bringing his face to the road with terrible force. William approached on hands and knees.

The face could not be seen. Snow absorbed blood leaking from the ears along the line of the cheekbone. William rolled the head aside to offer some chance of air getting into the man's lungs and recoiled from what he saw. The upper jaw was crushed and had released the teeth, some broken, some whole. His breath was hoarse and blood spluttered from him. The wild eyes no longer aligned. Using his finger, William brushed bits of flesh and teeth away from the mouth to prevent them from being inhaled. It was all he could do for now. He had to get the sprocket.

William stood, pulled bags from the overturned dumpster and quickly got to the bottom corner. The smell in the bottom was of something sweet, dog foul and rotting fish. He rummaged in the dark, grabbing wet, slimy, freezing objects, some soft, others angular. There was no time for retching. After a few moments he had the sprocket in his hand and lunged out of the dumpster, gasping for clean air.

The wild-eyed man had not moved. There was more dark-cherry blood on the snow and rasping breaths came from his broken mouth. William knew he had to get away even though life was leaving this man. Even calling an ambulance would draw attention to him and the dumpster, and put others at risk. But could he let a man die for ten ounces of gold or the thirty dollars he did not have in his wallet? The cold seemed not to matter now. A thought arrived with the vivid clarity of blood on snow: Would Kelly ever know what had happened? Understanding would be unlikely. Would there be forgiveness for what he had already done? It had never before entered his mind. There had always been justification, a reason to rail against convention, ignore the expectations authorities imposed. He had always had faith in the righteousness of his entitlement to disregard them, to do as he wanted, to pay them back for betraying his people and crushing his father's spirit, but now, he felt his daughter watching and could not leave this man to die.

"Hey!" A voice from down the laneway caught his attention. "What are you doing?"

William turned, checking himself enough to avoid being seen in the cold light, and shouted, "There's a man hurt! Get an ambulance."

The voice left the laneway. An ambulance would be coming, bringing the fire brigade and police as was standard in Vancouver. At least Kelly would not be disappointed in him for leaving the wild-eyed man to die if she ever found out about it. It was hard to imagine how she would find out, but somehow, for the first time he feared she might.

William tucked the sprocket in his coat. Someone was getting help for the wild-eyed man, so, he reasoned, he was not really leaving him to die. William began walking toward the car, having not yet convinced himself this was true.

5:15 p.m.

THE GARAGE DOOR CLOSED BEHIND HIM AND BROUGHT A RELIEF THAT HE could not remember feeling before. The house had not been a sanctuary. It was a place to start, to store things, to plan, a base from which he could go and do what he wanted, but not a place to simply be, until today. He could fall asleep in the driver's seat if not for being wet and reeking of garbage. The truth of the day would have to be hidden somehow, if only he had the energy to create a story of how he came to be in this state. It occurred to him that he often seemed to be disguising his reasons for leaving the house or returning ruffled. The house door from the garage opened and Julie entered as William lifted himself from the Tesla. He had dreaded seeing her, but this too was a relief.

"We've been worried about you! Where have you been?" Her face narrowed with something between irritation and concern, and then she saw him. Dirty knees, bloodied shirt, trousers wet, and then the smell of the dumpster found her. "My God, what's that smell?"

"It's my hands." William raced to find a story to tell. "I've been in a dumpster."

"Whatever for? Are you all right?"

"Yes, I'm fine."

"There's blood on your shirt. Are you hurt?"

"Don't worry, it's not mine," said William. "There was an accident." A story was emerging as he spoke. "I saw a dumpster tip over as I drove by. There was someone in it, and he was hurt when it went over."

"You stopped to help?"

"There was nobody else there."

"Was he badly hurt?"

"I think so. He came down hard on his face. Completely unconscious and didn't move."

"Oh my God, was he all right?"

"I don't know. The ambulance was on its way when I left. It didn't look good."

"Let's get these clothes off you."

Julie reached for his lapels and pushed his coat over his shoulders. It brought her close enough for him to feel her warmth. He let the coat fall down his arms. She moved quickly to get his wet things off his body, yanking his shirt over his head. He tucked his chin in and allowed his body to bend to the pressure of her pushing and tugging.

"You're freezing," she said. "Get your pants off and get in the shower."

He moved slowly to help her, stepping on his heels and kicking off his shoes, undoing his belt. She dragged the trousers down and he lifted one knee and then the other to be free of them.

"You smell terrible!" The moment was gone. "Just leave everything and get in the shower."

"Where's Kelly?" he asked.

"In her room. She had a good day on the mountain."

"I wish I'd gone with her."

"She'd have liked that."

"Thanks for dealing with my clothes." He reached to put his hand on her shoulder. She pulled away.

"Sorry," she said. "Your hands." They both turned their noses up at the smear of blood, the filth and the stench.

"Not very appealing, are they?"

"Dirty hands never are." Julie smiled at him.

"I'll get in the shower." William left Julie in the garage to sort out his clothes. There was something going on between them that had been lost for such a long time.

The shower ran hot. William scrubbed at his hands to remove the smell, as persistent as the spray of skunk. Whatever he did, a hint of it lingered. He anticipated sleep being interrupted by his hand falling on his cheek, filling his nostrils with recollections of the wild-eyed man face down in the snow. He speculated that he had probably survived. It seemed unlikely there would be a Julie to drag off his clothing and bundle him into a hot shower. Julie opened the door of the bathroom and came in.

"William, what's this cog doing in your coat pocket?" she asked, holding the sprocket up to the shower screen. "It weighs a ton."

He cleared mist from the inside of the shower to delay responding while his mind raced. "Just leave it in the car. I keep meaning to leave it at work."

"All right. It stinks. I'll give it a rinse first. Are you hungry?"

"Oh yes. Starving."

"I'll get your clothes in the washer and make something for you. Your coat and trousers will have to stay in the garage."

Through the shower glass William watched her contemplate the sprocket. She was holding it under running water and scratching at the surface. It was more curiosity than the object merited. He suspected she was thinking what he was thinking. It was odd for the sprocket to be in his coat pocket. It was filthy with clinging grit and stank of dumpster. How could it have got like that when it had been protected in his coat pocket? She would know it did not make sense. He resisted offering an explanation and relied on the riddle falling in between the layers of their relationship where not making sense was tolerated without ever being spoken of. He thought, as he scrubbed his nails again, that so much of what he did happened in that space, where what he did and why he did it was deniable, ignorable or excusable.

WILLIAM REACHED FORWARD TO PLACE THE EMPTY BOWL OF SOUP ON THE coffee table, lifted the glass of wine and sat back on the sofa to watch the news on the television. It had been a difficult few days but he had done what Uri had asked within the time that had been allowed. There was still the issue of the visitation on Dennis, but both manifest and sprocket had been retrieved and the risk had been managed.

Kelly came down the stairs.

"Hi," he said.

"Hi. Mum said that you stopped and helped someone who was hurt on the road." She sat beside him on the sofa. Her closeness surprised him.

He pointed the remote at the television and placed his glass on the coffee table. "Well ... he must have pulled a dumpster over on himself, so I just stopped to help."

"Was he badly hurt?"

"I don't know. He had a nosebleed and had knocked himself out." The image of the wild-eyed man's face swept through him like a current.

"Did the ambulance come?"

"Someone did call the ambulance, so I came home. Nothing more I could do."

"Mum said you smelled like dog poo and rotten fish." Kelly smiled broadly.

"I think I did. Maybe I still do." William brought his hand to his face and sniffed. A trace remained, he was sure. "It'll take a couple of showers to get me clean again."

"Let me smell." She reached with both hands and he offered his. Kelly held the hand gently and very deliberately searched it with her nose. "Yep, dog poo, fish and ..." She gripped his hand to prevent him from whipping it away and contemplated earnestly before declaring, "Red wine."

"What vintage, do you think?" said William, allowing the game to play out.

She sniffed again. "Poodle and trout." He snatched his hand away and they laughed.

It seemed that each time he looked at her there was something else to see. "When did you get so funny?" He gazed at her.

"We can call it Hero's Red," she said, not wanting the game to finish.

"What do you mean?"

"You're a hero, Dad. We'll call the vintage Hero's Red."

"I don't think I'm a hero."

"Yes, you are. You stopped and saved a man."

"Well, I'm not sure about that."

"You didn't have to do it. Most people would have driven by, but you stopped to help him."

"No, Kelly, it's something anyone would do." The mood changed and Kelly seemed disappointed. Suddenly her closeness unsettled him. The responsibility of affection pushed him into turmoil, and he stood. "I better get on with a few things for work," he said, lifting his wine from the coffee table.

In his office he sat in his leather chair. His head pounded and his thoughts tumbled. He remembered as a young child seeing his father as an oak. There was such strength and conviction in everything his father had said and done. He had been all that every boy wanted his father to be until the collapse began, and then it was shame and disappointment. William had resolved to never allow that collapse to happen to him. To have his father's passion and commitment to anything that could be eroded was a weakness that might render him broken and pathetic. No, he thought, that wasn't quite right, but the next thought was hard to hold. He feared anyone being so loyal to him. There could never be someone as disappointed in him as he was in his father. Tears came close to the surface, and he felt hesitation in his breath and the trembling of his chin. Now Kelly had elevated him to hero status, and William realized she might have always done so without him ever noticing. It was too late to escape her affection, and maybe, he thought, it was too late to avoid failing her. *What would she think?* William allowed tears to run down his face. The strength of feeling was again a surprise. He hated the weakness and feared what was happening to him.

"What's happening with you?" Julie came through the door and William swivelled away from her. "I've never seen you like this. It must have really been awful." He nodded and tried to wipe the shine from his cheeks. There was no explanation required. She had offered him sympathy for what he had seen and he allowed it to run. "Don't turn away," she said.

He swivelled halfway back. "I'm all right now," he said. "I guess I'm still not right after the operation. I get tired, can't concentrate, and this howling in my ears is enough to drive me mad."

"Some people take months to get over a concussion. You've had a head injury, two general anaesthetics and two operations. You're just doing too much. I wish you'd listen to me."

"There's so much to do. I can't just let it drift."

"Sorry. We shouldn't be talking about your work. It was miserable finding that man. Was it bad?"

"His face was smashed in. Teeth and blood everywhere. I thought he was dead." The graphic image steeled him against shuddering tears. He could be the strong one in the face of someone else's horror.

Julie quivered. "Oh God! No wonder it upset you. Did you tell Kelly?"

"No, nothing like that. I just said that he knocked himself out. She thinks I'm a hero."

"Well, that's nice. Maybe you are."

"No, I don't think so." William closed his eyes, wishing the conversation would stop.

Julie said, "She wants to think of you like that. She's proud of you."

"I know," he said, without opening his eyes.

Julie stood. "You need to go to bed."

He allowed her to pull him to his feet and lead him upstairs to the bedroom. *No need to undress*, he thought, crawling onto the bed. *I just need a few minutes.* The last thought before sleep took him was a wish that the wild-eyed man survived. He had not wanted that to happen. He was responsible for too much already.

New Year's Eve 2017

THE SMELL OF COFFEE AND TOAST FOUND HIM. "WHAT TIME IS IT?" William lifted his head from the pillow.

Julie put the cup and plate on the night table and arranged pillows behind him as he sat up. Her breasts were close to his face, and through the sleepy fog, he noticed.

"Nearly ten o'clock," she said. "You haven't moved all night." She sat on the bed close enough for his hand to fall on her thigh. She held his forearm and inspected the marks on the heel of his hand. Her hands were warm and gentle.

"I slept like the dead. How did I get my clothes off? I don't remember."

"Guilty," said Julie, smiling. "Don't worry, I didn't take advantage of you. Actually, I don't think you even noticed."

"Maybe that's a good thing. I wouldn't want to disappoint." William smiled and then felt awkward on the ground he was treading and was surprised he had ventured there.

"It wouldn't have been a disappointment. How did you get these scratches on your hand and wrist?"

"I'm not sure," said William. He recalled leaping on the dumpster and falling back. "I suspect I got them the other night."

"You have more on the other hand." She reached across him, lifting the other arm for inspection. "There are bruises on your back too. What's this?" she asked, turning his face to see his chin. "You've got a bruise just there." Julie put her forefinger under his chin at the corner of his jaw.

"There was quite a lot of scrabbling around." William thought she didn't believe him but he had enough cover to slip this story through. "Thanks for looking after me last night. I was washed out."

"You need quite a lot of looking after at the moment. I've never seen you like you were last night." There was nothing to say to her. "Let's see your back. I've got some gel for the bruises."

He shuffled and leaned forward and she switched positions with him, perching at the head of the bed.

They had not touched in years, and yet this was not unwelcome. A sudden burst of cold gel under his shoulder blade startled him, but it was her hands—they were familiar, knowing hands, touching him as he used to be touched. Her hands worked into his back and pulled memories to the surface. The deep push of her palms shifting muscle in his back distracted him from the strangeness. William allowed the sensations through the long-established resistance, without knowing why.

"Where is Kelly?" he asked. Once asked, it seemed an awkward question, implying so much. It had come without thinking, as an unconscious wish for a long impasse to be broken. Now that it had found its way into the open, William wanted it to be broken.

"Downstairs," said Julie. "She'll be fine for a while."

WILLIAM CHECKED THE MESSAGE ON HIS IPHONE. THE EMOJI WAS THE same but the number was different. He called it and waited for Uri to answer.

"Hello, William. I thought we should speak. What progress have you made?"

"I've got it. When shall we meet?"

"Good. We can meet soon, perhaps Tuesday morning. Do you remember the meeting place we arranged off Welch Street near your office?"

"Yes."

"Good. I'll be there at nine. See you then." The phone went dead.

William noted that he had only mentioned having one item. Uri was unconcerned about the second item he was to have retrieved. It was confirmation that the manifest was already with Uri.

8

New Denver, June 16, 1958

FLANAGAN ARRIVED AT THE DORMITORY FOR ANOTHER MONDAY AND wondered when his purgatory would end. It was dulling to spend day after day on a detail better suited to a babysitter than a police officer. He had hoped he would be part of some rotation relieving him from this, but it had become clear, as weeks passed, that was not what his sergeant intended.

As he passed the security hut he noticed it was empty and locked. Mr. Nori was always there before Flanagan and had become his first stop of the day. There was always a smile and cheerful comment from Mr. Nori, who was endlessly kind and polite to everyone. Ahead, he could see the matron standing at the door of her office.

"Constable." Matron MacDonald demanded Flanagan's attention from a distance. "I need to speak with you."

Flanagan altered his course toward the starch-white figure. When he was close she said to him, "Good morning, Constable." It was the first time she had greeted him with pleasantry. "We have a problem and I'll need your help. One of the boys has become unpopular. It's not safe for him to walk to school by himself."

"What happened?" he asked.

Matron said, "We found out about that woman on Third Avenue. The one they call the Green Witch."

"I've met her, with my sergeant."

146

"Well, it was this boy who told us about her."

"She seemed a harmless old lady to me." Flanagan recalled how the fierce demeanour of the Green Witch had altered with the mention of her now dead boys.

"Somehow, the children found out he told us what she was doing."

"Brathadóir." The Gaelic term for "informer" came to his lips as if he had never left Ireland. For a moment he was steeped in memories. "We don't know she was doing anything wrong, but I guess it doesn't matter."

Flanagan understood precisely the implication of this. The boy had done something and, without knowing, changed the course of his life. He would for always be known as an informer, a collaborator or traitor—words not understood by schoolchildren but would, by increments, be first stitched to the boy and then branded on the psyche of the man he would become. Flanagan raged inside at those who had exposed a boy to this, persuading him to give up the Green Witch to the smiling white witch standing in front of him, and then carelessly allowing his peers to know.

"They call him Juda. It's Russian for Judas," she said, without discomfort or concern. "He's in sick bay now, too frightened to come out, or too ashamed to show himself. Either way, he still has to get to school this morning and it's your responsibility to make sure he gets there." She caught his eye briefly to emphasize the point.

"Do you know anyone likely to give him trouble?" he asked.

"Hard to say. They're all in on it."

"All in on what?"

"Nobody's talking to him. He's been shunned."

"Maybe he shouldn't be going to school today, if it's as bad as that," said Flanagan.

"He'll go to school if I say he'll go to school. You reminded me of my responsibility, and I'll remind you of yours."

Matron's righteousness nearly burst the buttons on her tunic. She had rehearsed that comment designed to slap him. The satisfaction it gave her was clear.

He chose to allow her the victory without retort and said, "Is he ready to go? I'll get him to the school gate before the others."

"I'll bring him."

"What's his name?" asked Flanagan.

"Marko," said Matron. "His name is Marko." She went into the building and returned with the boy.

Marko's face was red, his eyes puffed and wet.

Flanagan said, "Let's get you to school, so you can settle in early." He put his hand on the boy's shoulder and eased him into motion. Marko's body was stiff and trembling.

Flanagan turned to the matron and asked, "You're sure this is the right thing?"

"He'll go to school like everyone else."

In the short time Flanagan had been at the dormitory he had learned there was no charity for the sick. Children with broken bones had waited a day before being taken to hospital in order to confirm their injury was real and staff time would not be wasted on the journey. In whatever condition, children made their way to school. No one would say why this was so important, but Flanagan suspected the school attendance figures played a part. Marko's plight would never cross the threshold exempting him from school and in so doing challenge the precious attendance rates of dormitory children at the local school.

Flanagan and Marko moved off toward Union Street, passing the security hut on the way. A new face peered out of the window.

Flanagan stopped and asked, "Where's Mr. Nori?"

"He doesn't work here anymore," said the new face.

"Whyever not?"

"Not my business really. I was told he got too close to the children and they took advantage of him."

"That's ridiculous," said Flanagan.

"That's all I heard."

The new face seemed familiar. "Sorry, I should have introduced myself. Constable Flanagan." He offered his hand.

The new face shook it and said, "Benson, John," and smiled broadly.

June 27, 1958

IT WAS THE LAST FRIDAY OF THE SCHOOL TERM, WHICH MEANT CHILDREN
left school thirty minutes early. At 2:30 p.m. Pavel gathered up his
things and headed for the exit with the other children. There would be
time to get to the den they had made in the forest next to the dormitory, deep enough to be hidden. Those who shared the secret of the
den had moved their treats from the Green Witch's cellar to the den
to avoid the interest around her doorstep. Rumour suggested the girls
had done something similar, not far away.

Pavel turned right out of the school gate and began running toward
the church on the corner of Union Street, hoping to catch sight of
Nina before she disappeared into the town or across the bridge with
the other girls. He looked back up Seventh Avenue to see if she was following. Something caught his eye. A group of boys were running east,
away from the school, toward the hill beyond. The large figure of Sam
lumbered steadily behind his three jackals in pursuit of someone too
far away to make out.

From the corner of Union and Seventh, Pavel scanned the crowd
of children for the taller, dark figure of Constable Flanagan but could
not see him. Normally he would be at the back of the group, and lately
he would have had Marko at his side, but there was no sign of him
today. Up Seventh Avenue, the boys were in the distance. It could only
be Marko they were chasing. Pavel began running, his heart already
pounding, as he had never run before.

He was gaining on them until the trees took them in. If they
changed direction in the shadows he would not find them in time.
He shouted, "Marko!" With luck his friend would hear him coming. It was unimportant to Pavel that Marko had been shunned,
nor did it matter that there would be little he could do to stop
the boys even if he caught up with them. He and Marko had been
together in the same dormitory since the beginning, stood cold in
the shower as a punishment they did not understand and comforted
each other when their parents and people were cursed and belittled.

Now Marko was in trouble and he would go to him, whatever had gone before.

In the woods, he followed the noise of the boys, now laughing and shouting off to his right. The sound of groaning to his left stopped him and he pushed through brush to a hollow between tall trees.

"Marko," he said. "You all right?"

Marko could say nothing. His nose was bleeding and his teeth showed blood in his grimace of discomfort. The smaller boy held his chest and struggled for the breath punched from him. Pavel pulled him to a sitting position and held his shoulders. A minute passed before he could breathe.

"The policeman didn't come. They were waiting for me."

"Sorry," said Pavel. "I didn't see what has happening until you were near the trees."

"It's not your fault," said Marko. "No one else would have come." The tears had stopped. Marko took large stuttering breaths. Pavel stood and pulled him to standing. Marko spit blood and said, "And it wasn't me."

"What do you mean?"

"I didn't tell anyone about the Green Witch. It wasn't me."

"Who was it, then?"

"I dunno." Marko cleared tears with the palms of his hands and wiped the blood from his nose on his sleeve. His face was marked with mud and red streaks. "Everyone just stopped talking to me and I didn't know why. Only found out when Sam came for me after school."

"It was Sam that told you. What did he say?"

"He said Matron MacDonald told him I had been talking to her about the Green Witch. But I never. It wasn't me. You need to help me. The others have to know it wasn't me."

Pavel listened to his friend and allowed the words to fall into place. Why would Matron tell Sam anything, and why would Sam say something like that if it wasn't true? Pavel understood his friend to be just what he appeared to be. Not the smartest of his friends, nor was he committed to the Doukhobor way. Of all his friends, the time in New Denver away from his parents had done to Marko what the English had

planned for all of them, but he was not a liar or an informer, or someone who would break ranks. The only way he had survived all this time
was by being cautious and loyal to his friends. There was no reason for
that to have changed overnight. It had to be Sam.

Pavel said to his friend, "C'mon, I'll get you back," and put his arm
around him. Some of this did not make sense, but his friend was true.
He was sure of that.

2:55 p.m.

CONSTABLE FLANAGAN ARRIVED, CONFUSED AND TROUBLED, AT THE
Union Street bridge. Some children were already at the dormitory and
others mooched about on the street. Toward Slocan Lake, he caught
glimpses of children at play and recognized them as children of the
dormitory, but it was too early for any of them to be out of school. He
walked quickly toward the school, hoping Marko was waiting there.
On the way he asked some of the children if they had seen Marko, but
none replied.

At the school, a teacher was locking the door. He asked, "Have you
seen the boy Marko?"

"No, I haven't, but someone said he was waiting for you."

"Do you know where he went?"

"Sorry. Can't help."

"What happened? Why are the children out early?" asked Flanagan.

"Last Friday," the teacher said.

"What's that?"

"The bell goes half an hour early on the last Friday of the term.
Didn't they tell you?"

"No. They didn't."

Flanagan turned toward the gate and began planning his search for
Marko. Town to the right, hills to the left. Four boys walked past the
school heading toward town. They were laughing. One boy grabbed
another in play and, with exaggerated swing, punched him in the

stomach. The boy curled and groaned in mock agony and they laughed again. A third boy threw an uppercut into the air and made the comic-book sound of fist on chin: "Pfiff!"

They were excited, more so than boys jostling and fooling with each other in play. There was triumph in their celebration, as if they had scored a victory or conquest. The confusion Flanagan had felt a few minutes before was now sickness and horror. He had been late to escort young Marko and they had attacked him. Flanagan began running up Seventh Avenue, not wanting to find what he knew to be there, hoping the boy was not too badly injured.

For the second time in a few minutes, Marko's name echoed up Seventh Avenue into the hills.

3:55 p.m.

MATRON STOOD AT THE DOOR OF THE OFFICE BUILDING AS FLANAGAN, Marko and Pavel arrived at the dormitory. They were in no hurry. There was anger in their eyes. Dirt and blood still streaked Marko's face. Flanagan said, "Thank you, Pavel, for taking care of him." Pavel clapped his hand on Marko's shoulder and left.

Matron reached out to Marko. "Let's get you inside and get you cleaned up."

There was compassion in her voice. It was something he had not heard before. She glanced at Flanagan, avoiding his eyes. He followed her inside.

Sergeant Benson sat to one side of Matron's desk. He waited until she had ushered the boy through the building to the sick bay. "Well, well, Irish. I would get you a job licking stamps, but I'm not sure you'd be up to posting the letters."

"No one told me the children come out of school thirty minutes early on the last Friday of term, Sarge."

"It was your job to escort this boy to and from school. That was my understanding."

"Yes, Sarge."

"Then it was your job to find out about it."

"May I speak plainly, Sarge?"

"Please do, son. I want to hear what you have to say. It might be the last thing you say in the RCMP, so go on. Let's hear it."

"This was a set-up. There is another boy here, called Sam. Sam was told that Marko had been telling Matron about the Green Witch, that woman we went to see on Third Avenue. The others turned on Marko for giving secrets away."

"That's what happens to informers. The boy forgot what side he was on and got what was coming. You would know about that sort of thing."

"But Marko was not the source. He didn't speak with Matron about it."

"How do you know that, and what does it matter? Did he tell you and you believe it? Is this the best police work you can do?"

"The boy Sam and his friends were the ones who assaulted Marko. They were waiting for him outside the school. I saw them coming away from it."

"Had you been there, it wouldn't have happened."

"I've been with the boy every day this week and not a sniff of trouble. On the one day I'm not there, there's a posse waiting. It's suspicious."

"Of what?"

"Someone told Sam I wouldn't be there because I'd been kept in the dark. There were twenty minutes or so when Marko would be alone. They knew I wasn't going to be there. They were put up to it."

"Now, who would have done such a thing?"

Flanagan resisted speaking in case it was overheard but looked to the door that Matron had shut behind her on leaving.

"You better have some bloody good evidence for that accusation, son. You're saying Matron is suspected of conspiracy to assault a child. What's your evidence? Can any of this be proved?"

"We should speak with her and with Sam and Marko, for a start."

The sergeant stood. "We'll do nothing of the kind. Listen to me, Irish." The sarcasm had changed to a sneer of contempt. "There is only one thing to understand here. You're not up to it. You'll always be trouble for someone else. In my report to headquarters I'm going to recommend they bring your time with the RCMP to an end, for incompetence. You're a danger to others. If I were you, I'd get my resignation in first."

It had not occurred to Flanagan until this moment. His anger, having worked out what had happened to Marko, had obstructed the processing of a key piece of information on his arrival at the office. It was shame he had heard in Matron's voice and seen in her furtive eyes. The contrivance of a plan must have brought a sense of satisfaction, even vindication, to her, but now, as the cruel reality of it unfolded exactly as intended, the righteousness, faced with a bleeding child, was lost.

"Why are you here, Sarge? How did you know to be here today, at this time? Normally you'd be in Castlegar and it takes a couple of hours to get here. Matron would only just have found out that I wasn't at the school on time, but you knew to be here. You both knew, and you knew what would happen."

"Careful, Irish."

"You let a thirteen-year-old boy have the shit knocked out of him so you could get at me."

"That's enough. You're in enough trouble already." Benson's angry face faded to a smile. "You'll always be an outsider in the force. You don't know how to be loyal. But I'll say this for you, Irish, you're not stupid. Untrustworthy, but not stupid. More than I can say for most of the Paddies I know."

The punch landed in soft tissue below the sternum with a force that buckled the sergeant. His knees bent and he gripped his stomach, mouth open, searching for breath that was not there. The second landed at the side between rib cage and hip. He fell to his knees. There was whisky on the air pushed from his lungs. Seconds passed until Flanagan grasped the sergeant under his armpits and hoisted him into the chair.

Sergeant Benson wheezed, "You're done now, son. Assaulting an officer is serious business."

"You better have some bloody good evidence for that accusation. I hope you can prove it. I don't see any marks, and I don't see any witnesses either."

"Arrogant bastard."

"Don't bother with your report. I don't want your stench on me for another day. I'm out."

Flanagan left the office. Within three strides he regretted having struck the sergeant, however much he had deserved it. The injustice he felt for these children, for Marko especially, and for himself made it nearly defensible, but not really. It was wrong, no question, and not like him. Yet he had surprised himself with his inability to contain his anger in response to that final insult to his heritage. One injustice after another had gradually scrubbed away all that contained his anger. The effort needed to live to his own standards had not seemed so hard, but the crust of civility was worn through more easily than he believed possible. Even now he wanted to justify it and rehearse the righteous argument vindicating what he had done, but it was wrong to do so and he shook it off. Everyone, he thought, must be capable of violence when pushed to it, but that also was too easy, even if it had a little truth. This moment of weakness with Sergeant Benson would haunt him, but it had sealed his fate in the force. The choice to leave had been made and there was no going back on it.

As he approached the security hut it dawned on Flanagan what was familiar about Mr. Nori's replacement. The door opened and John Benson emerged smiling.

"Hello, Constable. Everything all right?" asked Benson.

"Just fine, thanks, John. Your brother's in there," said Flanagan, jabbing his thumb at the office building he had just left.

"He's my cousin," said John, still smiling. "He said he would be coming by today. I have him to thank for getting me this job."

For Christ's sake!

At the edge of the dormitory boundary the eight-foot chain-link fence loomed higher than usual. He thought there could be no justification for this place. Good people could not survive working within it. It was a place for the righteous to acquire unquestioned authority and for the ambitious to hide the truth on behalf of those above. For some, thought Flanagan, the role of caring for the vulnerable offered an opportunity to twist the purpose to suit their comforts. It was the best that could be said of any of them.

He stopped and surveyed the dormitory. Flanagan was not sure of his future but he was certain that he would not allow that fury to kindle again, and the front line of the RCMP was no place to struggle against being outraged. There was too much to be outraged about. He could never be one of those who allowed it to wash over them or would turn away from seeing what was there to be seen, because those above found it suited them. He would have to find another way.

Flanagan wanted to believe the children would manage. Of course they would not, but there was nothing more he could do here.

9

Vancouver, January 2, 2018, 8:15 a.m.

WILLIAM CHECKED HIS WATCH. IN FORTY-FIVE MINUTES HE WOULD SEE Uri in the car park of a dead factory a short drive from the office. There would be no cameras in that car park, and there would be no recording of the cars being there or images of the transfer of a sprocket from one car window to another. The security arrangements tired him, and yet he needed the reassurance it provided. The ratio of opportunity to risk had changed, or perhaps that ratio was no longer important.

William walked into the office hallway and up the stairs.

"Morning, Cathy. Good weekend?"

"Yes, thank you. William," she said, catching his attention before he disappeared into the office, "Dennis hasn't come in today. I don't know if he's sick."

William stopped in front of her desk and nodded. "Well, perhaps he's just late. Leave it awhile and give him a call. There's probably a reason." William thought better of letting Cathy know of Dennis's resignation.

"Did you see him on the weekend?" she asked.

"I did, yes. Why do you ask?"

"You called me to ask for the address. Was he all right when you saw him?"

William said, "He was fine. I'm sure he'll turn up."

"Shall I call him?"

"Give him a chance to get in, before we start chasing him." The disappointment on Cathy's face darkened the room. "Don't worry, one of the others will step up. The work will get done." William smiled as if that was her concern. "What's on the schedule today?"

Cathy flipped open the desk diary. "Two deliveries are coming in this afternoon. It's the climbing equipment and the kayaks. There's a problem with space in the warehouse. If we don't get something out this morning—"

"I'll deal with it. What's in the mail?"

"I haven't opened it yet."

"You get on with that, and I'll make sure they get on with the work in the warehouse." He was grateful to be away from the questions. "I've got a meeting this morning. I won't be long."

"There's nothing in your diary."

"That's because I arranged it on the way to work. I'll go through the mail with you when I get back." He smiled again and headed for the warehouse, thinking she would be on the phone to Dennis within the minute, but there would be no need to deal with her reaction until he returned from his meeting with Uri.

URI PULLED INTO THE CAR PARK AND ALONGSIDE WILLIAM'S TESLA. Windows lowered and Uri began.

"Thank you for coming, William." Uri passed the counterfeit cog to William. "We did it more quickly than expected. The others will be more confident in us. You have it?"

William passed the sprocket across. "I think you have the manifest." Uri nodded. "I thought you were leaving me to deal with that. What changed your mind?"

"I was protecting our interests," said Uri. "You are new to our business. Until now we have kept you on the outside, so you cannot be blamed. But it is different now that you know things. If you had gone to Dennis and he resisted you, what would you have done? He is younger than you, a soldier. You could not take things from such a man just by asking. Then what, William? He would know how valuable the paper was and ask for more, or make many copies, or do something. You see how I have protected you. Now you have not failed. I have not failed. We are all safe again. The others will be happy. We can go on as before." His face lit up.

It was true, thought William. He could not compel Dennis to do anything. "Did you have to waterboard him?"

"William, you are not experienced in these things. It is very persuasive and leaves no marks. When it is over, people are the same. No damage."

There was nothing to say. Nothing would be heard, and in any case, William acknowledged the bizarre truth in what Uri was saying. He tried to shake off the idea. "Well, I'm glad the problem is sorted out. Dennis is leaving the company. He said he was going to resign when I saw him, after your friends had visited. He was pretty shaken up and wants to get away."

Uri looked wistful. "So, you will have to find someone else in the warehouse. I have someone in mind for you. It would be good to have someone we know, wouldn't it?" He grinned.

"Well, he hasn't resigned yet. We'll talk when he does."

"Okay, William. Thank you for this." He raised the sprocket and smiled. "You did well to get it so quickly. The others will be pleased with you." The two cars pulled out of the car park.

It was a short drive back to the office. Enough time for William to piece together what he had done. Accepting Uri's justification of waterboarding Dennis on the basis of it being harm-free seemed reasonable at the time. Of course, it was not reasonable, but a problem that he might not have resolved had been resolved. Perhaps Uri's assistance was needed, and William was grateful for the help, but now he was complicit in torture as well as smuggling gold bullion. He had come a long way since setting out to launder money, evade taxes and allow counterfeit bicycles through his warehouse. Now he was relieved to hear that Uri was pleased with the outcome.

For the second time that morning he parked and walked toward the office. This time the titanium sprocket was in his pocket. Going through the doors and up the two short flights of stairs, he braced himself to deal with Cathy, who by now would have discovered her lover would no longer be working in the warehouse. It seemed such a trivial concern, but it would have to be dealt with.

She stood nervously at the door of the outer office as he turned the corner of the staircase. As he reached the top step the view of the room widened behind her. Two police officers stood waiting for his return.

Cathy said, "The police are here to see you."

9:30 a.m.

"WILLIAM KOREN?" ASKED THE OFFICER.

William nodded. "Yes."

"Perhaps we could speak with you privately."

"Yes, of course. Come into my office."

William walked into his office and the two female officers followed. Speculation filled his head, shifting his focus and fear from one terrible outcome to another. Deliberately, he peeled off his coat and hung it at the back of the door—anything to delay proceedings until his head and body settled.

"Please sit down," he said. "Can we get you a coffee or something?"

"No, thank you."

He smiled at them, edged around his desk to his chair and took a breath. "What's the problem?"

The lead officer began without preliminaries. "A red Tesla vehicle was identified at the scene of an incident over the weekend, and when we followed up on it, it was registered to this company."

"I have a Tesla, registered to the company."

"Are you the only driver?"

"My wife sometimes drives it, but she has her own car."

"Did she drive it over the weekend?"

"I don't think so. Look, I think you might be talking about the incident not far from here, on Saturday afternoon." The two officers remained passive. "I was heading home and saw a dumpster fall over. There was a man either hit by it or standing on the dumpster when it tipped. I just happened to see it so I stopped and helped."

"How badly was he injured?" asked the officer.

"He'd landed on his face and was unconscious, so I turned his head to one side, cleared his airway with my finger. He was in a bad way. Someone else arrived from one of the buildings in the laneway and said he was calling an ambulance. I left when there was nothing more for me to do."

"What time was that?"

"Sometime between four and five. I can't be sure. Do you know how he's doing?"

The two officers caught each other's eye. "No, we don't. Mr. Koren, we're not here about that incident, although it sounds like you did that man a favour." The silence was full. "Do you have an employee by the name of Dennis Mansion?"

"Yes. He's our senior warehouseman. He takes care of the inventory in and out of here. Why?"

"Did you visit his house last Saturday?"

"Yes, I did. About three, maybe later. I was there for less than an hour, I guess."

"Is it normal for you to visit an employee's home on the weekend?"

"Not at all, but there was something I had to speak with him about and I thought it better be done outside work."

"Why was that?"

William asked, "Can I ask what this is about, before we go any further? I'm not sure what you're getting at. Has Dennis said something?" He was being just a little too defensive, too early in this exchange. He checked himself and looked squarely at the lead officer, pulled his hands off the table and held them on his lap.

"No, no, we're not accusing you of anything, but there's been a serious incident and your car was at the scene. You'd expect us to follow up on these things. Do you mind telling us why you went to Mr. Mansion's home?"

"It's delicate." William lowered his voice. "Dennis and Cathy, my admin person you met, were having an affair. I'd gone to Dennis to ask him to stop."

"Would you mind explaining why?"

"It isn't helpful to have that going on at work. But I also thought Cathy's vulnerable right now and can be taken advantage of. She has enough going on in her life and doesn't need that."

"So you were trying to keep the workplace healthy."

"Yeah, that sums it up."

The officer's stern face broke into a smile. "And you came to her rescue."

"I don't know about that."

The stiffness of the officer had gone. "Not many employers would bother to do that on a Saturday. I wish more would be that concerned."

"I've heard the police have had their problems with that kind of thing." William knew it was a mistake as he said it.

The formality returned. "How did your conversation with Dennis go?"

"It was complicated."

"How so?'

"Dennis had been drinking and there was water everywhere. He had a flood of some kind and the kitchen floor was soaking."

"Any idea why there was a flood?"

"He didn't say."

"Did you argue?"

"He didn't like what I said."

"What did you say?"

"I told him that he should bring his relationship with Cathy to an end or I would bring his employment to an end."

"And how did he react?"

"He said he was going to resign, today, but I don't think he's been in yet. We agreed terms. I would give him three months' salary and a reference."

"When you left, how was he?"

"Drunk and a little morose, but we shook hands as I left and I wished him luck."

"It seems very generous to give him so much when you are about to fire him."

"I wasn't going to fire him if he stopped that business with Cathy. I think he thought he had made a mistake and was doing the right thing. It saved me a lot of trouble. Anyway, he's got obligations, a family he doesn't live with. Oh yes, he said that he was thinking of getting back with his wife. I just thought we could make it as easy as possible for everyone. What's going on? Has he said something different?"

There was another look between the officers. "Sometime late Saturday afternoon or evening, there was a fire at Mr. Mansion's home. I'm sorry to tell you that Mr. Mansion was found dead at the scene." William brought his hand to his face as if to prevent the sudden throb of terror escaping. "I'm sorry if this comes as a shock to you."

He was unable to speak or bring his thoughts to order. The policewoman continued. "Do you mind if we just ask a few more questions?"

"No. Of course. I'm just ... shocked." William remembered a conversation that had troubled him and thought, *What did Uri mean by "Then we decide what to do with Dennis"?*

"That's understandable," she said. "You may have been the last person who visited the house before the fire. Is there anything you can tell us that will help our inquiries? Anything about Mr. Mansion, or anything you saw that would help us piece together what happened?"

"No, just that he was drunk and there was water everywhere. Maybe the water got into the wiring. I don't know. I just don't know."

"Okay, Mr. Koren. Thanks for your assistance. I can see this has come as a shock for you. Our job was just to confirm that the Tesla was yours. Someone might have to talk with you again, and with Cathy, but we can leave it for now."

"Yes, of course."

"We'll see ourselves out." They stood and moved to the door. "Is the Tesla here?"

"Yes, it is, just outside, on the right as you walk out the front door."

"Good. We'll need to see it and confirm the licence number. Okay, Mr. Koren. Thanks again for your help." Both officers left, nodding at Cathy on the way out.

The door of his office was open and Cathy waited. He could feel himself trembling and wanted to put off telling her. He recalled Uri being quick to suggest a replacement for Dennis and staying quiet when told that Dennis was about to resign. At the same time the wild-eyed man came crashing down, Dennis's house was burning with Dennis in it. It could not be a coincidence. Now he'd had a hand in the death of a man—maybe two. The understanding of his daughter seemed a long way off.

THE POLICE CAR BACKED OUT OF THE PARKING SPOT AND MOVED INTO the traffic. The lead officer asked her partner, "What did you make of him?"

"He seems decent enough. Generous, eh?"

"'Generous,' you'd say?"

"With his secretary and giving a handout to the guy he's about to fire, just because he has a family. Most employers wouldn't bother."

"And stopping to help that injured man," the lead recalled. "He does come to the rescue a lot. Useful info about the flood and the alcohol. That'll help the fire investigation."

"Are we following up on the ambulance call?"

"We better make sure it happened and pass the information on."

It was unusual, the officer thought, for someone to be connected to two unrelated incidents within a couple of hours, each resulting in serious injury, which they just happened to be passing or visiting. Something was not right about this.

The patrol car stopped at a red light while she thought of the chances of such a coincidence. The light turned green and they set off again.

It came to her, and she asked her partner, "How does a young and reasonably fit man die in a house fire in the middle of the day?" She recalled that Mr. Koren had been having a conversation with the victim. "Surely he wasn't so drunk as to be incapable of opening a window and jumping out."

"Maybe he took something else," said the partner.

"Maybe."

11:30 a.m.

ONLY THE HISSING IN HIS EARS COULD BE HEARD ABOVE THE NEAR silence of the Tesla. Cathy had cried when told of the fire but it was not the flood of tears William had anticipated, and then she was quiet. It was more shock than loss. Consoling words were not needed, and William was grateful for not having to find them. She gazed out the window without focus until they glided to a stop outside her building. William stepped out to help her. She was already out but she accepted the arm he offered.

"Is there anyone at home?" he asked at the door.

"No," she said, opening her bag in search of keys.

"Let me."

She lifted the keys into his open hand, and he pressed the fob against the pad beside the door. It clicked open. She allowed him to usher her into the entrance hall and press the button for the third floor. The elevator arrived; doors separated and drew them in.

"I'd rather not be alone," she said, before there was a question of him leaving. "I don't want to be alone."

He would have to go back to the office sometime but he was connected to this in a way that he could not evade. It was like standing beside the wild-eyed man and being unable to get away until someone arrived to deal with the mess. He needed someone else to be responsible but there was only him. William thought she appeared to be on autopilot as she shed her coat and hung it, unzipped her winter boots and shuffled to the kitchen. He removed his coat and followed.

"Thanks for staying," she said. "Do you want coffee?"

"Let me do it."

"No, I'll make coffee," she said. "You phone work and let them know you'll be back later."

He collected his phone and stepped into the living room, thinking it was an odd and particular instruction. He heard the fridge open and close, water running, the kettle turned on. It was strange to be back in her apartment. As he returned he said, "When is your husband home?"

"He doesn't come home these days. Just when he wants something." She nearly smiled and continued making the coffee.

"I didn't know it was like that between you. I'm sorry," said William.

She turned two cups off the drainer, heaped four scoops of ground coffee into a glass pot and added steaming water and the silver plunger. He had thought she hoped for something more with Dennis, perhaps a life raft to drift away from a situation that was drowning her. It had appeared that it didn't much matter in which direction she drifted—just away from the life she had would suffice—but now it seemed the affair with Dennis had been something else.

"He hasn't left me. Not really. Since that thing with you, he comes and goes as he pleases. Leaves me money sometimes. This is just a hotel to him. A hotel with benefits."

The reminder of their affair came without protection or shadow of disguise. To be exposed to it reddened him.

He said, "That was fifteen years ago. I didn't think he knew about it."

"Twelve years. Of course he knew," she returned.

"Is that why he moved out?"

"That's what he said. Maybe he was going anyway. I'm not sure."

William grasped at an explanation. "We were younger then. The business was getting off the ground. It was exciting. It was never a long-term thing for either of us, was it?"

"You could have told me what it was."

"Surely you never believed it was." His appeal was hollow and he regretted being defensive.

"Did you ever wonder why I stayed with you all these years? Being paid a pittance, putting up with you ignoring me at work, and him turning up whenever he needed me to scratch an itch?"

"Why didn't you just divorce him?"

"Why doesn't Julie divorce you? Anyway, what would I do? Move in with you? I don't think so." The bite in her voice relented. "How do you think I pay for this? Where do you think I would be living on the salary you pay me? This is Vancouver!"

"I would have helped you," he said.

"Really! Well, that's good to know." The words lashed at him. "All this time I could have bent over the kitchen table waiting for you to pass by, on the way home to your wife and daughter."

He started at the recollection of the times he had done just that. Now pornographic memories arrived without asking, and he struggled to stow them away.

He said, "That's not what I meant." The fucking had been electrifying until the heat dissipated, and then it stopped. William realized it had ended as it had with Julie, suddenly and without ceremony.

"I didn't need your money. I could earn extra when my husband brought a friend with him." She turned away from William. "You men. All you bloody men."

"I wish ..." William hesitated, not knowing how to finish what he had started. The truth was that he had not wanted to know about her life, how she felt or what was bothering her. He had used every tactic to escape engaging her in conversation about personal things.

"I didn't want to cause trouble for you." His voice softened to share a memory with her. "I thought you enjoyed it as much as I did."

The turmoil of the morning seemed to leave her. "I always know what you want. No need to tell me. I always know." There was confidence in her frankness. "You want what you can take from someone. It's what you always do."

"Do you think I'm as bad as that?" he said, unsure where Cathy was taking this.

"If you can have it, why shouldn't you? It's what makes you success-ful. It's what makes you attractive."

"Maybe I shouldn't always have what I want."

Cathy came to his side and leaned on him. "I want you to have it. You said you'd help me."

William held his breath. He had evaded closeness with her since that time years ago. Disdain for her chaotic life meant just touching was getting too close, accepting responsibility. It risked being involved with her intense, meaningless emotions. But this time, he stood like a post for her to scratch and scent, remembering those other times: the hotel afternoons, the furtive shuffles in the office, her willingness to do anything. There was heat and discomfort in the recollection.

"Look, Cathy, we better not do anything." Something brazen and uncompromising was coming at any moment. Reason would leave him if he did not move. His head flooded with images of the things he should escape. "Maybe I'd better go."

"Not yet."

"I should go."

The words came without intent. It was too late. Her hand moved quickly under his belt and strangled his cock and scrotum like the neck of a chicken. The shock backed him up against the fridge and he gripped her arm with both hands as if to resist her and hold the sen-sation alive for as long as he could. She had said the magic words of wanting this: the promise of ecstasy, the hands on skin, abandoning vanity. It absolved him of everything. All resistance left him.

12:45 p.m.

WILLIAM SAT ON THE EDGE OF CATHY'S BED AND LISTENED TO HER MAKE coffee for a second time. A collage of random thoughts streamed in and out of his mind. He grasped at anything that would prevent him from thinking of what he had just done.

It was good that Cathy was not distraught at the loss of Dennis. The business would struggle with both leaving. He chided himself for the thought. It was pragmatic but too soon to say out loud. If Uri's colleagues had wanted to kill Dennis, they would have done it after waterboarding him. Once they had all they wanted, the opportunity was there to be taken. The best explanation of the fire was the water getting into the fuse box, or perhaps he had tried to fix the mess and ended up starting a fire. He had drunk enough whisky for that to happen. Nothing else made sense.

William reached for his trousers, wanting to be dressed before Cathy returned. Sex with two women in two days seemed improbable. Six months ago it would have been impossible. He grasped for something in his memory, something connected to the operation. The surgeon had said the tumour had messed with his hormones over years, and he would see changes when it was removed. Maybe, he thought, this was what he meant.

"No time for coffee?" she said, returning to the bedroom.

"I have to get back to the office. There are things to do. Will you be all right?"

She smirked with a hint of derision and then asked, "What will you do?" She placed the coffee on the side table beside him.

"There's nothing I can do, except find a replacement and carry on. He was leaving us anyway." It was the wrong thing to say. Cathy sat on the bed. "He told me he was going to resign. Family reasons," said William, standing and doing up his trousers, regretting that he had raised the issue.

"Is that why you went to see him over the weekend?"

William heard something coy or distant in her voice. He had said something that may have been hurtful and yet there was no emotion.

"Yes," he said, and reached for his shirt.

"Do you think I'm responsible?"

"He wanted to get back to his wife and kids." He pulled his shirt on and began buttoning it up. "Not sure what else was going on." William hoped that would be an end to it.

"It was my fault," said Cathy.

"I don't think so. People come and go all the time. How many people have we had in the warehouse in the last ten years? I've lost count. Everyone has reasons to stay or leave."

"No, I meant …"

William had no wish to fall into the emotional vortex Cathy was capable of, sucking up time and energy, leading nowhere. He could not get away quickly enough. The search for his socks and shoes began as he spoke.

"It was an accident, just a terrible accident. He wasn't keeping the house well. It was rundown, it needed paint, he'd just had a flood. There must have been lots wrong with it. Nothing to do with you. Really."

The cuffs of his shirt sleeve finally came together and he slipped on his jacket, relieved he was ready to leave. He said, "I really do have to go now."

"Just like that," she said.

"Cathy, c'mon. It's the morning of a working day and Dennis is gone. I can't just stay here. There are things to do." Cathy nodded in reply to him. "It'll be all right. We'll get through this." William leaned toward her, trying to be sympathetic without having to be intimate. "Take a day or two and when you feel settled, come in and we'll talk." Her silence offered a chance to escape and he headed to the hallway to collect his coat.

At the door something nagged him. It was odd of Cathy to think it was somehow her fault that Dennis had died. Even for someone like her it didn't make sense.

She was surprised to see him return to the bedroom. He asked, "Why would you think this was your fault? The fire, I mean." The question froze her. "I think you should tell me." A child could see that she was hiding something. "What do you know?" He closed on her and pulled her to face him, but she turned away. "What do you know? Cathy!" He twisted her shoulders square to his and spoke loudly into the side of her face. "Tell me!"

"What are you going to do?" she shouted back at him, pulling away. "Do you want to hurt me? Is that it? Slap me around. Make me beg."

William pulled away from her. It was the second time his anger had flared; the last time, the wild-eyed man seemed like he would be dead.

He said, "No. I'm sorry. I don't want to be angry with you."

"Always something you want."

"What?"

"It's always about something you want, isn't it?" Her words were familiar.

"Please, Cathy. Just tell me what's going on."

She said, "I told them you were going to see Dennis on Saturday."

"Who did you tell?"

"Your business partners."

His heart crashed in his chest; thumping began in his temples. "Who did you tell?"

"I don't know his name. He came to the office after Christmas and threatened me."

"Small man, accent, dark wavy hair?" Cathy nodded. "Two men with him?" She nodded again. "Did they hurt you?"

Cathy opened her dressing gown and lifted a breast from her bra. The nipple was livid, the underside of the breast green, blue and purple.

"Oh God," said William under his breath. "I'm sorry. I didn't think you would ever be affected."

"They frightened me. I have to tell them things when they ask."

"What things?"

"The phone rings and he asks me what you're doing, where you are, where you're going, what shipments are in the warehouse. That sort of thing."

"And you tell him."

"Yes, I tell him." There was bite in her. "They said they would hurt me again and tell my husband about Dennis."

"Of course you tell them. It's not your fault." William struggled to bring his thoughts under control. "Just do as they ask. Tell them what they want to know. I'll figure something out." He hoped it was reassuring enough to stop her from panicking. "It would be better if they didn't know that you told me. Just carry on as normal."

"Why would they hurt me?"

"It's how they work." It was, again, the wrong thing to say. William thought he was losing control of himself. He was normally in control of what he said, but everything seemed to be getting away from him. "It's not very likely. The important thing is to do what they say and you'll be all right."

"Like being married," said Cathy.

"Maybe so." He began walking to the door.

"Aren't you forgetting something?" she said.

"What?"

"You can leave it on the hall table. Whatever 'help' you want to give."

William took a moment to understand what she was saying.

"Think of it as a performance bonus. Tell the accountant. It might be deductible."

He reached for his wallet, emptied it on the hall table and left.

He had not before understood Cathy's vulnerability, or how close she was to being desperate, maybe homeless, or how she had lived with being constantly exploitable. Neither had he understood how it had disgusted and excited him in equal parts. It was not strictly her vulnerability to hardship that excited him. She had learned to embrace those on whom she depended, and in the moment of her embrace the vulnerability could go unseen, remaining outside of consciousness for the duration. Just the willingness could be attended to. It provided a special kind of thrill. Nothing you did with her made you accountable. Gratitude or apology was never needed.

With Cathy he had created the perfect arrangement of service without cost. She was the only asset and he had no obligation for the upkeep, until today, when she asked for money. It made him think of the chain of events he had set in motion. Her life on the edge of prostitution was connected to what he had done. There was no obligation, but the sense of being responsible would not shake off. She had shamed him by asking him to pay for services, and the act of giving her money clarified the nature of the transaction. It would not happen again. So he hoped.

7:15 p.m.

"WHO WAS KILLED IN A FIRE?" KELLY ARRIVED AT THE EDGE OF THE kitchen, having heard what was not intended for her.

"One of my employees. There was some kind of accident at his house."

"Did he really burn in a fire?" Kelly's enthusiasm for the lurid details caused William to start. The image was too close to what might be true.

Julie tucked Kelly under her arm. "People don't burn to death in fires. The smoke means they can't breathe. That's how they die." It was a better image but still beyond thinking.

William said, "I don't think we should be talking about it."

"Mum said you wished you'd gone skiing with me. Wanna go?"

"Yes, I'll go."

"Oh good! I'll get my stuff."

"You mean now?"

"We can go night skiing at Cypress Mountain. Well, you can ski and I'll be on my board."

"I'm not ..." William caught the expression on Julie's face. It said everything about what he always did—what he had become in this house. A promise never quite kept. The guilt of the day swept over him. If he spoke, tears would come. He turned and walked away.

"Where are you going?" asked Julie, the disappointment shaping the question.

The dangerous moment had passed. Disappearing into the living room, he said, "To get my gear. Are you coming?"

There was commotion in the kitchen as the family sprang into action. *How would Kelly manage?* She seemed confident enough but he did not know how to manage a blind person down a mountain on a snowboard. He should know by now. His ignorance, and his absence from her life, would be exposed soon enough on the slopes. He tried to think about the problem. Julie had once said how it works. Should he lead or follow her down the mountain?

"Don't worry," Julie said, arriving in the garage. "She's done this before."

It was not his decision to make. Kelly would make her own decisions, and he would have to do what he was told. It was the only way they could make it work between them.

January 4, 2018

WILLIAM OPENED THE FRONT DOOR TO SEE THE TWO FEMALE OFFICERS.

"Mr. Koren, I hope you don't mind us coming by your home."

"Not at all. How can I help?"

"Can we come in?"

"Of course," he said, swinging the door wide for them. "Come into the kitchen." The officers entered and stood in the hall.

The lead officer said, "We don't want to trail snow and mud into your house. This will be fine."

"How can I help?" William felt a small twist of discomfort in repeating himself.

"Thanks for telling us about the man falling from the dumpster. We followed up and found a Mr. David Kerrigan in Lions Gate Hospital."

Alarm flowed through William. "How is he?"

"He's going to live," said the policewoman. "But he'll be in hospital for some time."

"Has he said anything?" *Mistake*, he thought. *They'll wonder why I care.*

"I don't know. Someone else will be talking to him when he's able. Do you mind if we ask you a little more about that night?

"Sure. Glad to help."

"Just to clarify a detail, you said you stayed with Mr. Kerrigan until the ambulance arrived. We know the ambulance picked him up twenty-seven minutes after they received the call, and you weren't there when they arrived." William listened to her, forcing his eyes to stay fixed on hers. "The man who made the call said he saw you, or the person we think must have been you, just before calling and when he went back into the laneway, you'd already gone. So there was half an hour before the ambulance arrived when you weren't there."

"That may be true. I left before the ambulance arrived, but I never said I waited. There was nothing for me to do once the ambulance was called, so I left." William thought it was not convincing.

"Do you mind me asking, was it a good idea to leave the injured man alone?"

"It would only have been a minute or so."

The officer nodded without expression, but William felt the disapproval. Nothing said, no expression, but clear.

"You didn't know that," she said.

"No, I guess not. Perhaps I should have stayed."

"How long were you at the scene in total?" she asked.

"Five, ten minutes, or something like that, I guess."

"Would you mind me asking why you didn't call the ambulance?" It was the second time the officers had asked if he "minded" being asked. The two officers' faces were entirely passive.

"What do you mean?" he said, offering a little resistance.

"Sorry, Mr. Koren, we don't mean to suggest you did anything wrong, but we just have to tie up the loose ends. It's just that, if you arrive at a scene like that and find someone is badly injured, the first thing to do would be to call an ambulance. So we need to ask why you didn't."

William scrambled for an explanation. "Well, I'm not sure I have an answer for you. It was such a shock to see it happen, I must have forgotten."

"You forgot," she said.

"I can't explain it. I did spend some time checking to see if he was alive and moved the garbage bags away from him. He wasn't breathing well so I cleared his airway. Not sure how long that took. Didn't look at my watch." It was a cheap remark.

"Well, that would have taken a few minutes, anyway." The officer smiled at him as if that was just enough.

William sighed relief. "I've just remembered something. When I was at Dennis's house, I got wet when I slipped on the floor. Remember? There was a flood at his house. I had taken my phone out of my pocket so it didn't get wet and left it in the car when I went to help the guy. Sorry, it just slipped my mind."

"Okay, between the shock, the first aid and leaving your phone in the car, ten minutes could easily go by and it explains why you didn't call the ambulance." She smiled, and William thought three excuses were too many. "That's all we need to know. Thanks very much for your time." The officers reached for the door handle.

He said, "Sorry for making that complicated. I should have remembered the phone. I think that may have been why I left quickly."

"What do you mean?" the officer asked.

"I was soaking wet and freezing." William smiled at the two officers and wondered why he had raised it.

"Thanks for mentioning it. Just one more thing," said the officer. "You were heading home from your meeting with Mr. Mansion, is that right?"

"Yes."

"The ambulance reported picking up Mr. Kerrigan in the laneway south of Third Street. It seems like a way off the route from Mr. Mansion's house to yours."

"I was dropping in on work before going home. I couldn't remember turning the alarm on, so I thought I would check it." She was not convinced. "I wasn't far away."

"That's helpful," the officer said. "There's always something to do running a business."

"It's never-ending."

"Thanks again for your co-operation. Good night, Mr. Koren."

The door closed on the officers. William was sickened, rattled to the ends of his fingers, and his body swayed. Only his grip on the handle stopped him from sinking.

"Why would you go to the office soaking wet?" Julie drifted in from the kitchen. William turned to face her. "Well? It's an interesting question. The police must be thinking about it right now."

He could not answer and her gaze shamed him.

She said, "I thought you'd got wet in the snow helping that man. And why would you stop and help someone when you're in that state? You haven't stopped to help anyone as long as I've known you. So, why did you?" A long pause separated them until Julie relented. "I don't care about that really. Save it for the police. I want to know why you didn't tell me you'd gone to see Dennis, when you told me you were going to the office? And how did you get wet talking to Dennis?"

"I was going to the office after seeing Dennis." He thought it was thin but might be enough.

"Why didn't you just say that?"

"Because I was going to fire him, and I didn't want a conversation about it." William felt his confidence returning.

"What did—"

"That's the conversation I didn't want," he interrupted.

Julie took her time to respond. "I don't care what you want or don't want. You were there before the fire. You didn't tell me you'd gone there even when you knew he was dead." The word thudded against his chest. She stepped forward as if to fasten blame to him. "You're hiding something. Lying to me, lying to the police, pretending to be a hero."

"I never said I was a hero."

"Oh, my mistake. That changes everything! What are you then?"

He could, if he chose, overpower her with words or volume, squashing her contempt and sweeping the challenge aside, but the breath of momentum he had felt a moment before had gone. He need only turn away and walk, dismissing her relevance to all he would do, jettisoning accountability for all that he had done. It was in keeping with his past, but something had changed, preventing him from moving. It was not the lies that held him. It was that question, never before asked or heard with such clarity. The hissing in his ears started buzzing and his scalp shifted.

"I don't know," he said gently. There was nausea building with the noise.

"What don't you know?"

The light from the kitchen became unbearably bright. "I don't know …"

Julie's body lifted and turned sideways as if floating away, until she rushed toward him and cradled his head, shouting muffled words he could not make out. There was a sudden stop, pain in his shoulder, and then he was looking up at the ceiling. Julie looked down at him, silhouetted by the kitchen light. The glow closed around her until she was gone.

WILLIAM TWISTED HIS NECK TO SEE THE MOUNTAINS IN THE DISTANCE, across the water over which they flew. He said, "The fire didn't get us."

"No thanks to you," replied Owl.

"But I'd fall if I let go." William hesitated and asked, "Why didn't you drop me and save yourself?"

"It is not what I do."

"What do you mean?" asked William.

"We are what we are. We do what we do."

"What should I have done? Should I have let go and saved you?"

"If that is what you are."

"I don't know what I am," said William.

Owl said, "My mother was an owl, my father was an owl, I am an owl. It is all I can be."

"My mother and father were Doukhobors."

"Then you are a Doukhobor," said Owl.

"No, I'm not. I don't want to be a Doukhobor," said William. "Even if my parents were."

"You are ashamed?"

"I'm not ashamed!" said William. "The Doukhobors are good people. I just don't want to do what they do."

"Very odd," said Owl. "Not 'shame,' 'good' people, but you want to be only what you do, and not what you are."

"I don't understand. Am I only what I do? So what's that?"

"You are a cyclist, holding on to your hat."

"That's not fair. I'm more than that," said William.

"Really? What more are you?"

10

New Denver, August 2, 1959

BREAKFAST WAS OVER AND ALREADY THE AIR WAS HOT. NOISE AND CHAT-
ter tumbled out of the dining room with the children and into the yard.
Some looked to the lake to occupy them, despite the chill of the Slocan
water. Others would spend their time marauding in packs, open for fun
or mischief, whatever could be found.

Pavel had thought it would be a day to laze away, soccer with
friends, talking with Nina, but it was a visiting Sunday, which meant it
would be otherwise. She would be anticipating her auntie's arrival. As
with all the children, visits from home meant she would not be right
until hours after family had gone. Her mind would be at home and her
body in New Denver. It was never easy to have them apart. For Pavel,
it had been easier since the arrest of his father. Mind and body were
mostly together in New Denver, and home was hardly thought of. It
had become a dream left behind on the pillow.

Pavel had expected an excitable morning, but something was not
as it should be. The children knew more staff than usual were present,
but at this moment, none could be seen. The invitation to get on with
the day and the urgency to make beds and behave had not been heard.
Nina arrived at his side.

He said, "Not sure what's going on today. Have you heard anything?"

"Nothing," said Nina.

It was usual on Sundays to be more relaxed, but today the children felt a difference and limbo descended on them. Gradually the realization of being uncontained by staff caused inhibitions to fall away and a buzz began. Boys teased girls, jostling grew to careering into each other, competing for the ball became a life and death struggle, and laughing became near hysteria. Anger started when a little girl, felled by a random kick of the ball, began crying. The boys laughed and the girls stood square to them, threatening retaliation, bursting with defiance against their brothers and circling the fallen child.

Matron MacDonald and her staff emerged from the office and headed for the dining room. Some smiled; others did not. They gathered children as they approached the dining room, attracting the attention of everyone. Pavel anticipated all visits being cancelled. It would send children's minds into a spin and inflame every disagreement between them, but it had never been done like this.

"I have news for you all," said Matron MacDonald. "I've been told by the principal that many of your mothers have finally seen sense." She paused to emphasize the shaming of the mothers. "On Friday, they agreed with the judge in Nelson that you will go to Canadian schools, when terms start in September. So, you will be going home."

The children were quiet at first, not believing what they heard. Not just that they would be going home, but that their mothers would agree with a judge.

A voice emerged. "You mean we're going home with our parents, today?"

"I guess so, if your parents come this afternoon."

"What if our parents aren't coming?"

"As soon as it can be arranged, you'll be going home," said Matron. "If your parents are coming today, you better get your things together before lunch."

The noise erupted and laughing began. The yard quickly filled with children and whooping. A boy known as Popcorn stood on his hands, celebrating like a circus acrobat. Friends cheered.

Pavel watched the celebrations. It dawned on him that he had nowhere to go. The end of New Denver meant being shunted off to another place, somewhere else, with new people. It might be better, or worse.

"What's wrong?" asked Nina.

"Nothing."

A long second passed as he waited for her to respond. Nina was screening out the excitement in the yard and eyeing him carefully. "You don't have anywhere to go, do you?"

"I'll be fine," he said, smiling at her.

"You can stay with us."

"Will they let me?"

"Yes, I'm sure," she said. "They know your parents are still away. There's room for you, if you don't mind living in Grand Forks, with me."

The hesitation in her voice gave something away, but it was difficult to understand. Perhaps, he thought, she did not know of his affection.

He said, "Didn't know they'd moved to Grand Forks."

She seemed disappointed with his reply. "It was Auntie who went to the court on Friday. A month ago she told me she was doing it, but I couldn't tell anyone."

"Why?"

Nina spoke as if appealing to him. "Lots of people won't speak to her. Auntie said they had to move to Grand Forks to get away from them, and she thought if I told anyone, the same would happen to Arina and me. No one would talk to us." Pavel nodded his understanding. She continued, "I thought we would hear about it yesterday, but nothing happened so I thought she decided not to. But she did, and now we can go home." Nina smiled at him.

It was more complicated than that, they both knew. What her auntie had done could drive them apart, depending on whose family sided with what principle, or with this community or that. Whatever he decided now might or might not taint him always.

It was her eyes, and the hope he saw in them that all would work out, that allowed him to choose. He thought it was enough to be leaving New Denver and be together, and with that settled he sighed relief. Maybe it would work out. There was always hope.

He said, "We better get packed and tell Matron I'm going with you."

"Good!" she said, beaming at him before turning to a group of girls now squealing with excitement.

As soon as she left, panic swept through Pavel. New Denver might be over, but nothing was settled—not for him or his parents, and not for the children here who had struggled with and against each other for all these years. How would it be on the outside?

He caught sight of Matron MacDonald and two others in matron uniforms moving away, nearing her office. They looked down as they walked. It was unlike the usual bustling march that gathered and swept all before it. There was nothing righteous or insistent in their walk, and no threat of swift punishment in their manner. No authority was now vested in their uniforms, nor was there pride in what they had done. Everything about their progress moving away from the children suggested they knew.

They were knowers of what had happened in New Denver. As years passed there might be some comfort in nostalgia, but only among those capable of suspending what they really knew. It could never be shared with outsiders; at least the truth could not be shared with people outside of their huddle.

Behind them big Sam lumbered alone. Since it became known that it was Sam and not Marko who had given up the secret of the Green Witch, even his jackals had abandoned him. He stayed close to Matron. Now he would have to live outside with having been a bully and a Judas to all the people he knew. He was never to be trusted and would be lost to the other children for always. All of them would have to live in the world with what they had been in this place, where reputation had been formed and frozen. Each impression now hung like crystals in the eye of each child, deflecting the light and distorting what they would see.

THE HOT MORNING WENT QUICKLY. THERE WAS HARDLY TIME TO TALK TO everyone, and now families were gathering outside of the fence. Pavel searched for Nina from behind the phalanx of departing children heading toward the mournful singing that filled the air from Galena Avenue.

"Goodbye, Pavel." Matron Cody was smiling at him from just a few feet away. The blood drained from his face.

She approached and put her hand on him. "Soon you'll be too tall for me to touch your shoulder. Aren't you going to say goodbye?"

Nina arrived suddenly. "I've seen them. They're over there," she said, pointing to the fence. There was too much excitement for her to take notice of the disgust on his face, and she began running toward the gate.

"Well?" Cody asked.

Pavel turned to Matron Cody, still unable to speak, but a message passed between them. She removed her hand and stood stiffly to regain the dignity he had stripped from her with his silence.

"Good luck, Pavel." Her eyes lifted after Nina.

Pavel began following Nina. He felt Cody behind him and thought she would be there always.

Outside of the gate the singing stopped, and parents reached for children, some of whom had not been hugged for five years. There was awkwardness in some, but most grasped and kissed without shyness. Two women, both large and pendulous, stood as pillars outside the gate, naked save for their shoes. Each child ran the gauntlet of the women embracing all who filed by. The children could not believe what they saw, and some recoiled in horror at being enveloped by so much flesh, such intimacy, so suddenly.

Pavel shuddered and hoped Nina would not see that a different horror gripped him, or ever know why it was there.

Grand Forks, March 26, 1960

PAVEL LIFTED HIS SMALL BAG AND FOLLOWED NINA OUT OF AUNTIE'S house. It was the last of winter and wet snow squished under their feet. They walked along the sidewalk with coats open, allowing the heat from their bodies to escape the layers of clothing.

He said, "You don't need to come with me to the bus stop."

"I want to," she said.

Pavel knew she wanted to say something and the house was no place to say it. They walked in silence for long minutes and his mind wandered, waiting for her to begin.

These were his people and yet it was different among them. Pavel had a fragile place with this family but he, like the others, felt disconnected from the life they had previously lived. It was unlike the big bustling communal houses of his people, offering a full life, filled with rhythm and purpose. Nearly half his lifetime had passed since he had lived like that, but the memory endured, except in those moments of slipping between sleep and consciousness when he feared it may have been a dream.

Sunday prayers were constant but brought another change. The Union of Spiritual Communities of Christ had allowed them in to worship, but among these Orthodox Doukhobors there would always be suspicion of those who had been radical, and rejection of those who had been to prison.

Pavel was drawn to his friends in Brilliant, nearly three hours northeast of Grand Forks, and wedged between the Kootenay and Columbia Rivers. They were all boys from New Denver, locked in common step, motivated without direction, save for the guidance of the elders of the Sons of Freedom and their distant leader, Stefan Sorokin.

They stopped at the bus stop.

"How long are you going for?" asked Nina.

"Just a few days."

"You know it makes it harder for Auntie and Uncle when you go away. The congregation doesn't like it."

"It's me the congregation doesn't want," said Pavel. "Anyway, they're my friends and they need me."

"What do your 'friends' need you for?" She waited for a reply. When none came, she said, "Why won't you tell me?"

"Because you know what I'll say. You know what we're doing. The Fraternal Council gives us jobs to do, and we do them." Pavel lowered his eyes. "At least I'm doing something."

"I understand what you're doing," said Nina, closing the distance between them, "but I worry about you, and I don't want anyone getting hurt."

"I'll be all right. I make sure they don't get into trouble."

It was a lie, or nearly so. While it did fall to him to be the cautious one, he ran the same risks of being harmed or caught. Down the road he saw the bus coming to take him away.

"Auntie and Uncle don't want you to do these things. If someone is hurt, they won't let you stay."

"Then I'll live in Brilliant with my friends." His defiance was not intended as uncaring and immediately he regretted it.

"Without me?" she said flatly.

"Sorry. I didn't mean ..."

"Promise me you won't do anything that hurts someone."

The bus arrived beside them and the doors opened.

"I promise," he said and smiled awkwardly at her. He turned to step onto the bus, but she grabbed the front of his coat and lifted her face to his, kissing his cheek, so close to his lips. He wanted to kiss her back but stopped. It was not a sister's kiss and was an evolution of their friendship. It was what he had always wanted from her, but it surprised him.

Pavel stepped from her and onto the bus. The seat next to a window was free and he swung into it. Then he watched her as the bus hissed and rumbled from the curb. The whiff of diesel exhaust reminded him of seeing his mother from the window of the New Denver bus pulling away from Perry Siding. He was not yet ten years old when that happened, and it remained as clear as the crystal Slocan River. His mind filled with memories of New Denver and then, as Nina disappeared from view, returned to that kiss.

It would not be the same between them when he returned from his duty in Brilliant. Her affection excited him, but the prospect of the intimacy that might follow frightened him in equal measure. Matron Cody was still too close to thoughts of his affection for Nina. They were only seventeen and still living with her auntie and uncle. Maybe it was too soon to be thinking of it. There was time, he thought, before their lives became complicated with that.

February 16, 1962

IT DID NOT MATTER THAT THE CAR HAD BEEN THROUGH HARD TIMES. IT had been bumped, rolled and repaired, but everyone loved George's car. The guttural noise of the Chevy big-block v8 was unmistakable. It was, for all the friends, a thing of beauty. Although objects and possessions were not to be revered among their people, it could not be helped with George's car. From every angle it had something to please. Double front headlights and wraparound windshields front and back had the style of the time. The long lines drew the interest of passersby, whose gazes lingered as they walked. Huge doors opened like the mouth of a whale, swallowing friends clambering in. The wide bench seats welcomed them all, with enough room in the trunk for everything they might need. It was their transport everywhere, their clubhouse and their freedom to go.

Harry shouted, "Are you coming, Pavel?"

The friends exchanged glances. Something was going on. Pavel knew them all from New Denver. Each of them, George, John, Peter and Harry, carried their history in equal loads.

"Where are you going?" asked Pavel.

"Into Castlegar. I need to do something for my mother." Harry smiled broadly. "We're all going." His curly brown hair protruded from under his toque. "You should come." Harry emphasized the "you," adding an expectation in his voice.

"Why should I come? I've got things to do."

"So do we," came the reply. "Something important." Harry patted his coat gently and kept smiling.

Pavel understood. There was a job to be done, initiated from the elders, the Fraternal Council responding to a message from Stefan Sorokin, or it might just be mischief. The boys piled into the Chevy, George in the front with John, Peter in the back. He wished he were going with them, if only to stop them from getting into real trouble.

"Be careful, Harry. They are after you already," said Pavel.

Harry grinned at him and slipped into the back seat on the passenger side.

A voice emerged from inside the Chevy. "Go back to Grand Forks. There are always things to do in love." Laughter rose from the car and ape-like grins appeared at the windows, already steaming up on the inside. There was mocking in the laughter.

It was true, Pavel thought. His loyalty to Nina and the promise to her had put distance between him and the others.

"Last chance!" More shouts came from the Chevy. "Come on, Pavel, it'll be better with five of us. Sit in the front. She won't miss you for a few more hours. Come with us."

Pavel allowed the teasing to pull him toward his friends and he ran to the front passenger door and climbed in, as John shuffled along the bench seat. The five were off.

Pavel's thoughts yanked him away from their task. *Why did I get in?* The leaders had not briefed him, except that he knew the mission was in the service of the cause of his people and would let loose the anger of New Denver boys. Only Nina and obligation to her family had tempered his fury and prevented him from doing more with the militants.

Many of the valley's communal homes had been torched since the children were released from New Denver. Each night sparks drifted into the blue-black Kootenay sky. From time to time the sound of explosions trundled between the mountains like thunder. Many of his friends had been taken and were serving sentences for bombing or similar acts, exchanging places with their parents. Pavel shared the anger of his friends, none of whom could understand how the injustice could be ignored in a country claiming to be free. He had been between the militant Sons of Freedom and the Orthodox Doukhobors, until times like this when a side was clearly chosen.

The Chevy crossed the river and headed north toward Genelle, just south of Kinnaird. The sky and hill were lost in the blanket of grey. A solid figure of an RCMP officer held his hand up and waved the Chevy to a stop. He came to the driver's window and waited for it to open. All the boys listened.

"Checkpoint," he said without explanation. "Stop over there, please."

The Chevy rolled toward four more officers waiting.

"Do you think they know?" asked Harry.

"Be quiet," said Pavel. "They stop everyone from Brilliant."

George said, "Let them do what they usually do, and then we'll go." The temperature rose in the short distance the Chevy rolled to the waiting uniforms. Windows opened to let the tension out.

A second officer came to the window as the car stopped. "Turn the engine off and step out of the car, please, all of you. Bring your licence with you." The five of them climbed out of the car and began closing their coats against the cold. The standard-issue boots of the RCMP crunched the snow into the ground as they walked. An officer took the driver aside and waited for his licence to be produced. The others were waved toward two more officers. The senior man and one other leaned into each side of the Chevy and began searching—opening the glove compartment, pulling up the mats, yanking out the bench seats. The hood opened with a mechanical clunk as the spring released a hundredweight of steel, and then the trunk was open with the spare tire out and tools scattered behind. Ten minutes passed. The boys stood in the cold and watched the officers look in and under the car, removing all that could be removed.

The uniformed men came together briefly before the lead began walking toward the boys. Several others lifted the spare wheel and tools to the trunk. It slammed shut and the big doors crashed closed. The danger had not yet gone. The senior man arrived in front of the boys.

"Where are you coming from?" He already knew.

"Brilliant, but we stopped in Trail."

"What were you doing there?"

"I have a present to buy for my aunt," said Harry.

The officers fixed on him.

"Does it take five of you to buy a present for an aunt?"

"It does if you're Harry!" The boys stifled giggles.

The RCMP officer did not budge. "And where are you going?"

"Castlegar."

"What for?"

"We've got girls to meet."

The officer studied the face of each boy, as if scrubbing off the facade of innocence with his glower. "Okay. Just be careful. There's more snow coming tonight. On your way."

The boys loaded themselves into the Chevy and rolled up the windows. The v8 came alive with a rumble and off they moved, north toward Castlegar. Clear of the checkpoint, they began laughing hysterically. The excitement released by their RCMP encounter filled the car and lifted their spirits. Pavel was first to settle.

"Did you see his face? They're on to us. I think we should call it off."

"Too late," said Harry. "We gotta do it. It's been decided."

"We should talk about it, at least."

"Nothing to talk about. We'll do this and go into Castlegar, like we told 'em. Stay for a while and come back to see the mess. There it is." Harry pointed at the sleepy post office in Kinnaird, now closed. It was quiet in the neighbourhood, and dark. "It will be easy—too dark for anyone to see us. When it goes off we'll be in Castlegar." He began fumbling with his jacket.

The target seemed without problems and the sight of the empty street eased the tensions in the car. So often in New Denver Pavel had felt like this. A tide was moving, all could see, but nothing would stop it. He was helpless again and wanted this to be done.

A white flash, sudden noise beyond imagining and skin-blackening heat arrived without notice. The Chevy seemed to bend in the middle, doors whipped open and the roof lifted into the air. Soft billows of smoke followed the now dead car to a standstill and then climbed up and up.

In the front passenger seat Pavel searched for his ear, unaware of his scalp having been peeled back to the crown of his head. He was unable to hear or think clearly and waited for the world to make sense. The front bench seat had folded, squashing him into the footwell and forcing his breath away. To his left John was up against the dashboard. His face seeped blood through blackened flesh. George struggled to untangle himself from the steering wheel. Pavel pushed the seat back and fell out of the car, his blood dripping from his chin onto the snow. Finally his breath returned. He stood and looked into the back of the Chevy. Harry and Peter were unconscious. Their heads had fallen back and to the side.

Pavel approached the rear door. Harry had been behind him. Flesh and bone from chest to pelvis had gone. Pieces of Harry were everywhere. To Harry's left Peter sat lifeless, one arm mangled beyond recognition, his body smoking. Pavel could not hear his own cry and recoiled from the image. Stumbling from the car, he headed toward the river. There was somewhere he had to go, to wash his ear, to get help, to get away, to do something. He had to speak to Nina. She needed to know what had happened.

Nelson Courthouse, April 1962

"YOUR EAR IS LOOKING BETTER." NINA PUT HER HAND TO PAVEL'S FACE AND was careful not to touch the livid scar tracing red in front of his ear and into the hairline. He took her hand and pressed it against him. "How is your hearing?"

"My head is still ringing, but I'm all right." He could not hide his sadness.

She said, "I'll come and see you at the Mountain Prison."

"If that's where they send me."

"It will be. They built it for Doukhobors. That's where you will be."

Pavel marvelled at the certainty. Of course she was right. The Mountain Prison was built to be indestructible by fire and to house Doukhobors who refused to work at the command of government authority. That is where he would go.

She was trying to keep the conversation flowing. "I'll see you every week or so. We'll talk about everything, just as if you were home. Lots of women will come. You'll hear us singing, just like our parents sang when they came to New Denver."

Pavel heard the enthusiasm in Nina's voice but struggled to lift himself to it.

"What did the lawyer say?" she asked.

"He said I might get five years. They want to make an example of us." Pavel felt his emotions wobble but Nina's gaze held him. She would not let herself waver in this moment. He felt he had let her down by going with his friends, and now they would be separated. Five years seemed like forever.

"We'll still be young when it's over. I'll be waiting for you. We'll still be young."

"No, Nina, you mustn't. You must find someone and get on with your life. Mine's gone; please don't waste yours on me."

"Yours is not gone and you don't choose for me, Pavel Korenov. I'll make my own choices." Her mock indignation caused him to ache for the loss of her. "You told me not to give them everything. 'Always keep something for yourself,' you said. Well, keep me and I'll keep you."

Of course she would wait for him. "You don't have to. Really. I'll understand, and I'll be happy for you."

"Stop this! We know how to live with it. All our people do. Have you forgotten?" She pulled his two hands into the space between them and placed hers flat on his, palm to palm in mirror image. "Remember?" She brought their thumbs together and rotated her hands until their forefingers touched. They brought their lips together through the diamond space and remembered the kissing fence where their affection sparked.

Pavel felt his courage returning. Her hands held his face. The thick Russian unbridled kiss connected him to all that was good and wholesome about Nina and their people, transcending his sorrow.

The loss of his friend Harry and the disappointment of being without Nina for five long years could be endured with this kiss. He felt a rush of optimism. He could survive prison, especially as so many of his people would be there, and many of those he knew from New Denver, including his friend Paul. There was a prospect of a life, maybe even children, when this was over if he could be strong and keep true. He would draw on Nina's strength and be strong for her. It was a reason to continue.

He asked, "How are the others?"

"Like you." She smiled. "Everyone is confused. Some have been told to confess to everything and others tell them to stay quiet. It's impossible."

"No, I meant from the car."

"They were cruel to Harry's mother. She had to identify Harry's body. They uncovered his whole body. He was in pieces. She saw everything." Pavel winced with the recollection of his last glimpse of Harry. "They put a picture in the paper of his body with his mother identifying it."

"Why would they do that?" he asked.

"To teach her a lesson—to teach all of us a lesson. Someone even said she taught him to be a terrorist from the time he was a baby. All of us have been educated to be terrorists by our mothers, according to the English."

"It's the English who have taught us everything." Pavel shook his head, unable to tolerate the cruel depiction of his people.

"It's not what our people are. Always remember."

"I'll remember, all right. And I won't let them forget."

"Neither will I."

A door opened and a large man in a blue uniform said, "It's time."

They stood without breaking eye contact. He felt strong enough to stand in front of the judge and keep his sadness and anger in check long enough to be sentenced.

11

Vancouver, January 5, 2018

WILLIAM LOOKED UP AT THE CURTAINS FALLING FROM THE CEILING, defining the allocation of hospital space he had occupied since the previous evening when he passed out. It was quiet, for all the movement outside his space, and peaceful, for all the suffering in the cubicles nearby. The medication washed away most of what troubled him and allowed him to observe without feeling.

Soon he would be returning to the outside world, where the turmoil he had created would not end. He could not escape what he had done and wished it could just be over. The thought of ending it did not seem so bad. There was something decisive in bringing his time on earth to an end. Was it possible that his father had the same thought?

William had claimed nothing in common with his father until this moment. The mellowness of his mood allowed the contemplation of a commonality. It opened him to long-hidden thoughts, returning unfiltered or unobstructed by pride or anger. All of his father's past was not his, so he had contended. The commitment to others, the obligation, the grinding faith and, most of all, the trust or hope that justice, even fairness, might prevail would not be allowed by William as his father had allowed it. The world was not a place for such naïveté and weakness, he was sure. Yet he and his father had arrived at a point, each before his time, where ending was an option. William tried to push away thoughts of his father and the frailty they might share, but they would not leave him.

It must be the drugs, William thought, checking his watch. It was 7:00 a.m. He would be discharged as soon as the ER consultant came by. He forced himself to get off the bed and began dressing. He had to get grounded again and attend to the opportunity this hospital visit had afforded him. Julie would be coming soon, but there was time.

It had not been very long since the wild-eyed man had surgery. William calculated he would still be somewhere in Lions Gate Hospital. He walked to the hospital reception, asked after David Kerrigan, claiming to be a brother-in-law, and got the direction he needed.

At the ward entrance, he chose his moment to enter, moving quickly past the desk and along the corridor. The hospital reception staff were unlikely to remember him, but the ward staff might. Better if he went unseen. William walked steadily, as if he knew his destination. In one of the rooms was a man with the right hair and bruised face, criss-crossed at the nose with white strips. He opened the door and entered.

The man in the bed was motionless, save for the hoarse breathing expanding his chest. *At least he's alive.* The hospital gown exposed wiry white forearms and the nut-brown hands of someone who lived on the streets. On the plastic band around his wrist was the name "Kerrigan, David," a number and a date of birth. William thought it might not have been a good idea to come to this room. The task, he recalled, was to stop Kerrigan from talking to the police of their meeting. It was not a chance Uri would leave unguarded. William shuddered at the thought of what Uri might do in this situation.

He examined the bruises on Kerrigan. The colour of plum shaded his eyelids like thick mascara. His cheekbones bulged and dried blood caked the tip of his nose. There was nothing he could do with David Kerrigan, the man who slept in dumpsters and defended his space to near death. William noticed the purple eyes watched him.

"I owe you a hundred dollars," William said. Through the purple swelling the whites of Kerrigan's eyes grew as large as they could. "Yes, it was me in the laneway when you fell out of the dumpster."

William pulled his wallet from his jacket and removed five green twenty-dollar bills, folded them in half and lifted the bundle so both could see. "This concludes our deal"—Kerrigan reached for the money and William pulled it away—"which no one ever needs to know about." He returned the money to the line where their eyes met. "Do we have a deal?"

Kerrigan eyed the money and then the wallet. William had anticipated this. He removed another five green notes and Kerrigan nodded his approval before snatching the money and hiding it under the hospital blanket. He reached for a pen and pad by his leg and wrote, *What was it?*

"It had sentimental value," said William. He hesitated. "Can I ask you a question?" Kerrigan shrugged. "Why do you live outside like that?"

The writing started again. Kerrigan lifted the pad and shoved it toward William's face.

Fuck off.

"I'M MAKING A HABIT OF PICKING YOU UP FROM HOSPITAL," SAID JULIE, smiling at William from the driver's seat. He smiled back and watched the street through the smoked glass.

The Tesla passed through the streets unheard and unnoticed. He was insulated from sights and sounds of people struggling to get through the days. William had constructed his life to achieve this. His disconnection from obligation and separation from those with less money was his life's work, if only he had understood what he was doing. It had become his crowning achievement, and it shamed him now that it came to mind.

Kerrigan returned to his thoughts, and William began scanning the sidewalks for people like him, wondering about the life Kerrigan led. What did he eat? He had descended into a life of subsistence—grabbing each small opportunity, treating all comers with equal hope of taking something, be it food, comfort or status, from the encounter. Each was in such short supply that the smallest morsel was prized beyond any common value. It led William to think of those working in the offices they passed. Like him, they would sweep by in cars to private homes with views toward Vancouver Island over the tankers that squatted in Burrard Inlet or English Bay. It was discomforting to think that people like Kerrigan would be invisible through those windows, but down here, as they drove west along Marine Drive, he looked closer and, unmistakably, they were there.

It was after 10:00 a.m. The morning rush had ended and the business people were indoors. William picked out a scruffy man leaving middle age, wearing blue jeans, a black jacket and soft shoes. He seemed aimless and moved slowly, before disappearing from sight. Another one appeared, this time smoking and incongruously wearing trainers. A third man appeared in ill-fitting black leather in blouson style, track pants and soft black shoes. His brown-grey hair curled stiffly on his collar. There were more of them everywhere he looked, middle-aged and older men, wandering the streets in the uniform of the dispossessed, with nothing to do. He had not seen them before. There was something terrifying about the number of men without purpose. He thought how awful it would be, to have nothing to do, and yet it seemed he was working toward having so much money he need do nothing. He had forgotten what he was grasping for, unless acquiring money, buying things, competing against everyone for more of something and being disconnected from everything was the point. Maybe he was not very different from David Kerrigan, except there was no pretense in Kerrigan's life as there was in his own. William closed his eyes, feeling upside down.

His phone dinged. It would be the emoji he had been dreading. Uri was beckoning him back into the world. Another shipment was due and arrangements would have to be made, but Uri would have to wait until he was home. They stopped at a red light and then pulled away when it turned green.

"I've never seen that before," said Julie.

"What's that?"

"You didn't look at your phone."

"Maybe I should make a habit of it," said William.

"That would be good," she said. "I told Kelly that you went to hospital for a checkup, about the operation."

"I didn't see the surgeon. Another doctor saw me."

"What did he say?"

"He said there was no problem with the operation." The question reminded him that so much had happened since the tumour had been removed.

"So, what was it?" she asked.

"They don't know for sure." William searched for a way to say it. "There was nothing physical." He waited for the implication to settle with her, hoping there would be no lecture.

There was relief in her voice. "I knew something was up. You've been different." She was quiet for a moment. "I wanted to help."

"There wasn't very much you could do."

"To be honest, it hasn't all been bad," she said. "I mean, I'd rather be like this with you than to be just cut off."

"Like what?"

"You've needed us more. I've worried about you more, being under so much pressure, but I haven't felt frustrated or angry with you, with us, with work. At least you've been human."

Would she be as concerned about me if she knew what I've done? thought William. It was true that the connection between them had become more intimate, and he had felt the relief of being at home with Julie in a way that he hadn't for a long time. But he had thought this was something to do with the tumour, or with her, and nothing to do with him.

Julie said, "I know there's lots going on at work you don't want to talk about, but can I ask one question?"

William nodded. "Okay."

"Is it very bad, the trouble we're in?"

"It could be. I'm not sure yet, but it could be."

"I'm worried that you're in a different kind of trouble. Not just the business. Am I right?"

"That's two questions, but the answer's the same."

"I'm glad you told me. It won't come as a total shock if something happens."

William knew that something might happen, but what absorbed him was the way she said it. There was no castigation. It was solid, matter-of-fact, totally accepting, without fear or judgment. It was not what he was expecting.

January 8, 2018

WILLIAM ARRIVED AT THE WAREHOUSE TO START THE WEEK. IT WAS QUIET. He retrieved his keys from his pocket and let himself in, closed the door behind him and then headed for the security panel before the alarm started. The quick steps from door to panel annoyed him. Every demand the system, his system, required of him, rankled. The pleasure of thrusting himself into work had gone. There had been a time when he could hardly wait to turn the key, bolt upstairs or into the warehouse and start sorting, asking, deciding on whatever was next. All of this with the phone stuck to his ear. The buzz of building the business had been heroin to his system. Nothing and no one else had mattered.

He wondered if Cathy would be coming in. They had not spoken since his visit to her apartment. The thought made him cringe. In his office, he phoned her—no answer. The voice message invited him to leave a message.

"Hi, Cathy. I was wondering how you are. Let me know if you're coming in today. Don't worry if you're not up to it yet, just let me know. Take care."

It was odd. She always answered. The phone rang in his hand. It was an unfamiliar number. William hesitated before answering it, but if it was Uri it could not be avoided.

He accepted the call. "Hello?"

A brusque male voice asked, "Who is this please?"

It was not Uri or anyone he recognized. His mind began racing with possibilities and then doubt about the wisdom of answering at all.

William said, "You called me. Who is this?"

There was silence on the other end, and then, "This is Constable McKinnon from the RCMP Integrated Homicide Investigation Team. You just called a number we have an interest in. I need to identify you."

"My name is William Koren. I was phoning one of my employees, who hasn't shown up for work. Is there anything wrong?"

McKinnon spoke again. "Mr. Koren, I wonder if you could come to our office in North Vancouver. You could help us with an investigation."

"Look, I have a business to run—"

"Mr. Koren, we're speaking to your employee right now. When you phoned her, we picked up your number and phoned you back using this line. You'll also know of another employee who died in a fire at his home."

"Yes, of course."

"So we would appreciate your co-operation."

"Sorry, I'm trying to keep the business running. We've had a lot of disruption. When shall I come?"

"This morning, if you can," said McKinnon. "We are on East Fourteenth Street?"

"I know it."

"Thank you, sir. Just ask for me, Constable McKinnon in the IHIT, and I'll come down for you."

"Okay. I'll see you in about an hour."

William put the phone down and tried to keep his mind from jangling long enough to plan all that he had to do before going to the police station. The sooner he could get Cathy back to the office, the sooner he could get on with things. He began thinking of the questions they might ask. The thought emerged suddenly: What might Cathy be saying? Dennis might have said something to her about his discovery. She also knew about his connection with Uri. He could only believe she would say nothing. They could say nothing about Uri. Nothing.

"THANKS FOR COMING," SAID MCKINNON. "I SHOULD HAVE SAID WE'D PICK you up, but you coming here saves us a lot of time."

William followed McKinnon into a barren room—three chairs, one table—and sat down. "That's all right. Glad to help," he said, relieved the RCMP had not shown up at the warehouse.

"Sorry about the surroundings." McKinnon smiled. "Our headquarters isn't here; we just borrow rooms when we get involved in a case. This is all they had."

"It's fine."

"So, we have Cathy with us now, and I need you to confirm some information that she has given us."

"Okay."

"She said she has worked with you for more than thirteen years."

"That's true," said William. "She has been very loyal. Been with me from the start."

"Can you describe the role she's been in?"

"Well, she's the information hub for me and the company. She's my admin assistant, but she also runs the diary for me, receives information about deliveries, in and out, takes messages, opens the mail, brings together files."

"How many employees do you have?"

"Under twenty, but it can vary with the season and how busy we are."

"What exactly do you do?"

"We import high-end sports equipment, mostly from Asia and Europe, and distribute all over Canada."

"Is that a competitive market?"

"Oh sure. It's very competitive."

"How has the company been doing?"

"Well, we're still in business. That says something. Do you mind me asking what this has to do with Cathy and Dennis?"

"Just background. We always have to start these investigations with family and business to understand what we can follow up and what we can ignore." McKinnon smiled again. "I'll bring it back to Cathy. How much contact does she have with the other employees?"

"Not that much, really. She communicates with Dennis"—William hesitated, having forgotten Dennis was gone—"the warehouse manager, quite a bit, because she gets the notification of comings and goings that he has to manage in the warehouse. Otherwise she sees me every day and sometimes the people we contract in for payroll, health and safety, bookkeeping and so on."

"Can you tell me about the relationship between Cathy and Dennis? How did they get on?"

William thought of avoiding this one by pretending to be ignorant, until he remembered the conversation with the two women police officers. It was bound to get back to McKinnon. "Well, that was a problem," he said.

"How so?"

"I'm sure she told you this, but they were involved."

"Romantically?"

"I'm not sure how much romance was involved, but yes, I think so."

"And why was that a problem for the company?"

"It's never a good thing to have that going on. It was becoming a distraction for them at work." William felt his face flush with hypocrisy. "In fact, that was why I went to see him at his home on the afternoon of the fire."

"You went to see him at his home, on the weekend?" asked McKinnon.

William thought that was a strange thing to ask. McKinnon would have known that he had called Cathy for Dennis's address. "I explained this to two officers, from West Vancouver, I think. I was concerned about her and I wanted to speak with Dennis about bringing that relationship to an end, or I'd have to let him go."

"How did that go?"

"He said he wanted to get back with his wife and children anyway, so he offered to resign. I agreed to pay him something and give him a reference. That was it."

"How long were you there?"

"About half an hour. I had a glass of whisky with him and we shook hands. It didn't take long."

"Anything else you want to tell me about that meeting?"

"The timing was a little awkward. You must know there was a flood at his house. Water everywhere, in the kitchen. He was busy dealing with it when I arrived and didn't hear me at the front door, so I went round the back. Lights were on and the door was open."

"Did he say what had happened?"

"No. I don't think he did."

"How did you get on with Dennis?"

"He was a good worker, ex-army, reliable and doing well, until this. He'd been with us for about eighteen months or so and fit in well. I liked him."

"Do you know if he gambled, had debts or was in any kind of trouble?"

"Money was a problem for him, I think. He was supporting his wife and children. He didn't live with them. It couldn't be easy. He liked a drink, but it wasn't a problem at work. He smoked but I don't know of anything else. Nothing that showed at work."

"One more thing. When you told Cathy about Dennis, how did she take it?"

William noted that McKinnon already knew it was he who had told Cathy about the death. Maybe Cathy had told him. He said, "She was pretty strong, not as upset as I thought she'd be." As he said it, he wished he had not. "She can be emotional, but she seemed to be shocked and numb rather than upset. She just went very quiet. I drove her home and she said nothing."

McKinnon stood and said, "Thanks very much for coming in."

"Is that it?"

"No. I'm going to ask you to stay here for a minute while I get one of my colleagues to take a formal statement from you. We need the detail for the investigation. I just wanted to meet you myself and get a little background. Can I get you a coffee?"

"No, thank you. Any idea when Cathy might be ready to go? I could give her a lift to work if it won't be too long."

McKinnon seemed to be frozen. "I'm afraid Cathy won't be coming back to work. I thought you understood."

"Understood what?"

"Cathy's been charged with the murder of Dennis Mansion."

William sagged under the weight of that word. "It can't be. It couldn't be Cathy." It was more than he wanted to give away.

McKinnon was quick to spot it. "Why do you say that?"

"I don't know. I've known her for so long. I can't imagine her doing something like that."

"It's a shock when people we know do bad things, but there's always a reason. Anyway, I'm sorry it's come as a shock to you. I should have made that clear at the start. Just wait here and my colleague will be along shortly. Thanks again."

There was nothing for William to say. McKinnon left him alone in the barren room.

How the police came to believe Cathy might have killed Dennis was a mystery. He understood enough of police work to anticipate their interest in intimate partners, but she would be free if they knew what he knew. If that emerged, everything would be lost. His daughter, Julie, the business, everything was at risk. Cathy might go to prison, perhaps for life, to prevent it from coming out. The realization emerged that she would have to go to prison if he was to be saved from being seen for what he had become. He felt sick. It was not simply that he could choose between giving up all he knew to save Cathy or live with being responsible for her conviction, but it was all that he had done to her without really being aware. That she had wasted her aspirations and affection on him had evaded consciousness.

A decade ago, he would not have cared even if he had been conscious of it. She had never let on that her marriage had failed as a result of their affair or that she was in such financial hardship as to be pimped out by her husband, as and when it suited him. Then, somehow, the worst of all things was the recent torrid encounter at her apartment. It was easy to respond to her need, her sense of being lost and wanting to anchor herself to something warm in the way that she had always needed, but it was not something she had control of. He allowed himself to take what was on offer because there was nothing precious or fragile in his keeping of Cathy.

He looked around, taking in the scuffed walls and scratched table of the room. It was a room for police, criminals and lawyers to do the business of hiding or uncovering schemes and grubby ambitions of the weak—peeling the pretense of truth and righteousness from the proud and selfish. He had left behind those people from his childhood who would recognize this room for what it was. They might say that those who pushed God from their hearts would find themselves here. They were right, and here he sat.

William stopped abruptly. He had not thought of God without swelling anger for two decades. The faith that had destroyed his parents' marriage and his father, whom he was only now beginning to understand, could still not be forgiven, and yet the light it shone on him now meant something. It was shame, he thought. Obligation to others and being part of a community had been lost to him since leaving Grand Forks and the Kootenays. He had succeeded in business by allowing his pride and anger to excuse all that he had done. Not since he was known as Dmitri Korenov had any of the values of the Doukhobors meant something. He had dispensed with it long ago with the resolution to serve himself as the English Canadians had helped themselves to everything his people had achieved.

His phone rang. The number was unfamiliar but it would be Uri. William took a breath and put the phone to his ear.

"We'll have to be quick. There's been a problem."

Uri was measured. "What problem, William?"

"Cathy has been arrested for the murder of Dennis. She is being interviewed now. I'm at the police station, waiting to be interviewed."

"I'm sorry to hear it, but why is this a problem for our relationship?"

It was always exasperating dealing with Uri. William said, "I have no idea what she will say or what Dennis may have told her, and she's being interviewed right now."

"Sometimes you make things right by doing nothing. Let nature take its course. It's unfortunate for Cathy, but she got involved with Dennis, and this is what happens."

"I can't just let her go to prison."

"Of course you can. You will protect yourself, your family and your partners. We can rely on you."

"I'm still concerned about everyone being dragged into this if we don't help her somehow."

"You mustn't worry, William. If we help her, we draw attention to ourselves. We have a partnership with Cathy too, and she understands what has to be done. We did this without you knowing, when she came to the warehouse while we were there and saw us."

"She never said anything."

"Of course not. That was part of our agreement. She has a family; her children are important to her, so no need to worry."

William reeled at this threat to Cathy's children and understood it applied equally to Kelly and Julie. "Right."

"And, there is no evidence. We rely on each other for this. It's true, isn't it?

"Yes."

"That's how we work. You understand now, the way we do things is important. Even if Cathy says something, you will say you don't understand what she is saying. There is no paper, no records. She doesn't know my name. There is nothing, so don't worry."

"Okay. I better go now. They'll be coming back soon."

"We will talk again when you have finished. I'm glad we can rely on you. Bye, William. Don't worry."

William erased the call history on his phone and slipped it into his pocket. The hope of redemption was gone with Uri's cordial menace. There was never an option of doing right by Cathy. It had been foolish to consider it.

The door swung open. Two RCMP officers arrived, a man in uniform and a woman in civvies. They introduced themselves, taking the seats at the table, and explained what was to happen. They were professional, businesslike. William struggled to concentrate on what they were saying. He looked and nodded, leaving autopilot in charge, his mind elsewhere.

"Mr. Koren?" The woman added volume to her voice. "Are you all right? Do you understand what we are saying?"

"Yes, yes, I understand. Sorry, I'm not concentrating very well. It's been a shock. Can I see Cathy?"

The woman hesitated. "Why would you want to see her? She's been charged with the murder of one of your employees. Anyway, she's being interviewed." Her brow was furrowed. Her scrutiny bored into him.

"Does she have a lawyer? If she doesn't have a lawyer, maybe—"

"She's been given every opportunity to see a lawyer and one is coming."

"Look, I just feel a little loyalty to an employee who has been with me a long time. That's all." William's explanation raised something about his relationship with Cathy, which he knew was dangerous ground.

"Perhaps we should get on with your statement, and then we'll see about Cathy."

12

September 1, 1966

IT WAS NEARLY OVER, BUT DESPITE THE RELIEF HE WOULD FEEL STEPPING out of captivity, it was a mournful moment. The hunger strike among Doukhobor prisoners at Agassiz Mountain Prison had taken a toll, including Pavel's friend and companion from New Denver. Paul had slipped away without a tussle after a hundred days of protest. Pavel had never understood why Paul had died and he had lived. In this time of departure, remembering Paul brought the guilt of surviving, and now he was leaving the essence of his friend inside the prison. He remembered saying goodbye to Paul at the chain-link fence when he had aged out of New Denver on a cold day nine years before, saying he would eat enough for everyone. The irony of his death was shuddering.

There was so much confusion inside the prison at the time of the strike. Even now Pavel struggled to remember what it was about. Elders offered conflicting messages. Their leader, Sorokin, was said to have sent messages discouraging—or was it encouraging?—co-operation with the police, but no one had seen physical evidence of the messages. Another faction, working with the RCMP, encouraged people to unburden themselves through confession. Some had confessed to crimes they had not committed as well as crimes they had. Others told tales on their brothers, believing assurances from the police that there would be resolution of their problems. Somehow they had been fooled into believing that laws, procedures and decisions of the courts in Canada would be put aside, as if all of it were at the discretion of someone who could be persuaded by what was right. Perhaps, Pavel thought, it is what people have to believe when so much of what has happened to them feels unjust.

They had gone on hunger strike with the expectation of provoking a government inquiry into these false promises in return for confessions, but it was never likely to succeed. The hunger strikers knew this at the beginning, but as the days went by, the confidence of the righteous gripped them all and squeezed any doubt from them, until Paul had died. At the time it seemed they might all die for the cause, but now, standing at the edge of liberty, the purpose was unclear. What was that sacrifice serving? A question clouded the joy of Pavel's liberty. *What was Paul's sacrifice for?*

Some of the women, Nina among them, begged the men to give up the hunger strike after Paul had died, and they did. Otherwise more would be dead and unable to stand at the gates, waiting for freedom.

Finally the gate opened. Pavel offered Paul a last, silent farewell and walked out of Agassiz Mountain Prison. Over the threshold a clear vista in front of him appeared to go on forever. He was like an infant, insignificant, standing at the edge of a field of corn. Away from the smell of cabbage and the sweat of men, the air was fresh.

At the end of the driveway Nina emerged from a car that had stopped nearly a hundred yards away. She began walking toward him. His focus narrowed. All he could think of was the time he had wasted away from her. He wanted to lift his legs and run but they had not recovered their strength since the strike. It was all he could do to carry a small case and walk the hundred yards to greet her.

They came together carefully, allowing an embrace and gentle kiss. "This is done now," she said. "And we're still young."

"I don't feel so young."

"You will." She smiled at him, took his bag and his arm and walked away from the gate.

Nina's uncle had driven her to collect him. He sat stiff at the wheel without acknowledging Pavel.

As they reached the car Nina said, "It's complicated. I'll explain later."

The rear door swung open, they both slid in and slowly the car pulled away.

On the right side of the road a village had been created with a long line of tents and haphazard structures four or five deep, all of which had appeared since the strike. Hundreds of women had come to either support loved ones or plead with them to give it up and survive at least. Some tents had chimneys that smoked idly. The women gathered in small groups, huddled over endless chores and conversation while standing in mud. All burdens were shared and no one was alone.

Pavel said, "We heard of the women's village, but it was hard to imagine. So big! So many people."

A loud slap on the driver's window startled everyone inside. Arina's face, pleading and shouting, looked into the car.

"Please stop! Please stop!" said Nina.

The car did not stop. Arina's father glowered directly ahead without speaking. Nina opened the window and extended her hand and Arina took it. They squeezed each other's hands as the car rolled on, Arina trotting beside.

"How's Mama?" she asked.

"She's fine."

"Give her my love."

"I will. Take care of yourself," said Nina, as the speed increased and separated their hold on each other.

Arina shouted, "You too. I love you, Papa." The words entered through the window and filled the car with discomfort.

Nina grasped Pavel's hand and spoke to him. "Arina joined the trek when it came through Grand Forks." Nina glanced at Uncle. "She was asked not to go, but she went with them to Vancouver. When the hunger strike started, the trek came to the prison. Arina helped them set the village up. She lives here now."

Uncle said, "She's made her choices."

It was the last word. Uncle and Auntie were leavers, not to be trusted by the Sons of Freedom of the tent village, many of them from

Krestova, and previously friends. The Orthodox community of Grand Forks were also suspicious of Uncle and Auntie because they had given a roof to Pavel before he was arrested. Pavel recalled this suspicion as the reason Nina had asked him not to go to Brilliant and suddenly felt embarrassed. Then Arina had joined the trek, against their wishes, and their daughter was lost to them. Uncle and Auntie lived on a thin edge of tolerance in Grand Forks only because of this sacrifice and Auntie's role in ending the time in New Denver.

Some of the women of the tent village looked into the car as they passed by, curious to see Pavel and gauge the well-being of their own men, still inside, by his pallor. Others turned away to make their point. He had not been out an hour and had not travelled a mile into his new life and already, Pavel realized, the causes and sides people chose enclosed them like the chain-link fence or the walls of the prison he had just left. The causes and choices were so many that no one was free to move. Somehow, it seemed that being inside was an easier option. From the back seat, Pavel could see Nina's uncle in the driver's seat, reflected in the rear-view mirror. He was crying, but nothing would be done or said. No movement outside the choices made would be possible.

Pavel let time go by until they had reached the main road. "I'm sorry," he said, loud enough to be heard in the front. Uncle tilted his head to glimpse Pavel in the mirror. "It's kind of you to pick me up. I hope it doesn't cause you trouble." Uncle nodded, appreciating Pavel's understanding. There would be trouble for this favour.

"I can't stay with Auntie and Uncle, can I?" he said to Nina.

"No, you can't. We've already thought about it. You can stay with me." Nina's words were plain and delivered with a tone of this having been decided. She paused long enough for it to sink in. "If I'm going to see you or be with you, neither of us can stay with them." She waited for him to reply and when he did not, she said, "I have a little place where we can stay." She watched him carefully. "You do want to stay with me?" It was the first time she had sounded in doubt of anything.

"Of course I do, but how will we live?"

"I have a job. You'll get one too. It's what other people do."

It was simple for Nina, who saw the world clearly, and he allowed her optimism and bright eyes to see for both of them.

The trip to Grand Forks flashed by. The speed of Uncle's car seemed extraordinary to someone who had been nearly stationary for so long. From time to time Pavel closed his eyes to escape the quickness of changing landscape. Nina insisted on opening the window in the back. It had caused his hair to flutter and the smells from fields to find their way into the car, blowing away any lingering scent of Mountain Prison.

His head filled with the machinations of being out. As they neared Grand Forks only the complexity of his situation was clear. Where was he placed among the fences and choices made by others? There was not much room for him to move. He was not Orthodox and not with the Sons of Freedom. Nina had fully joined him in this limbo, and now they would live together, which brought its own fears.

In the centre of Grand Forks, before the bridge, the car turned south off Central Avenue toward the Kettle River and stopped after a few streets. Nina said, "We're here. This is my place ... our place." She was smiling and proud, as if nothing else mattered. "It's around the side."

Uncle straightened his body as he got out of the car and received Nina's embrace. There was no one on the street to see the display of affection that might compromise any remaining trust in his commitment to a peaceful Orthodox life.

"Thank you," she said and stepped away from her uncle.

Uncle extended his hand to Pavel, who took it firmly.

"Thanks again," said Pavel. "I'm sorry to have caused you trouble. Not just today. You were kind to me and I should have been more grateful."

Uncle said, "You can't help being trouble. We're all trouble to someone these days."

Pavel thought for the first time that Uncle's place in Nina's life had been neglected. He said, "Do you mind this? Do we have your blessing?"

He gestured to the door and the new life Nina had planned for them. "She's your niece."

"It's not for me to mind. She wants to be with you, so it must be." Uncle shrugged with helplessness. "Our women are stubborn as the men. That one won't be stopped if she has something in her head."

"I know," said Pavel.

"Take care of each other. It's all you have now. Each other and God."

IT WAS A SIMPLE ARRANGEMENT, LIKE A LEAN-TO. THREE WALLS TACKED on the side of a single-storey house created a wooden space smelling of cedar and pencil shavings. The roof leaned under the eaves of the main house and extended past the outside wall, forming a small porch facing west. Inside, the house was divided into two rooms and a tiny bathroom. One room was a kitchen and the other a bedroom. A light bulb dangled in each space. Nina had acquired a melamine table with strip metal edges and chrome legs, and two yellow vinyl chairs. Not very Doukhobor, but it did not matter, just as it did not matter they were neither new nor matching.

In a drawer were two knives, two forks, two spoons and a pair of scissors. The top shelf of the cupboard had two plates, two cups and two bowls. The second shelf stored pots and pans. Below was a wooden box with an assortment of tools, a pair of pliers, hammer, short saw and assortment of screwdrivers, surely a parting gift from Uncle. A half-size fridge, humming and trembling, dominated one corner of the kitchen. Inside, it was stocked with enough to keep them going for a week or so. Without asking, Pavel knew the fridge, and the sewing box he had seen under the bed, would be a contribution from Nina's aunt, who never failed to provide what was required from whatever she had. It made Pavel slump with the recollection of how good these people had been to him and how he had not returned that generosity.

Nina pulled the two vinyl chairs onto the porch and arranged them just right. "Sit with me," she said. "The sun catches this spot."

The evening sun shone red gold on their faces, and the stress of years began draining from them.

Pavel exhaled a deep breath and kept his eyes shut against the light. "You've been thinking of doing this, haven't you? You and me sitting here."

"Yes, I have." She smiled without opening her eyes. "What did you think about?"

"I tried not to think about outside too much. Keeping your head inside the walls is easier. Just like New Denver."

"I'd forgotten," she said.

"Do you ever think of the dormitory?" Pavel asked.

"Sometimes it comes, when I don't expect it. I still don't like swimming very much."

"You nearly drowned sinking that flag." They were both smiling. "That was so great."

"Me drowning?"

"No, no, the flag. You were a hero. Everyone wanted to be like you." Pavel stopped short of saying he had also wanted to be like her, to be brave and fight back as she had done. It had been this inspiration that had drawn him to Brilliant and to follow the commands of the Fraternal Council, but she could never know it.

"And you were the father, and took care of them," said Nina. "You told stories at night, didn't you?"

"How did you know about that?"

"Everyone knew," Nina said.

For an instant Pavel was anxious of what else everyone knew.

"Let's walk to the river." She took his hand and tugged him off the porch.

"Why?"

"Because I want to," she said, tugging him again. "Something else I've been thinking about."

"Will we do everything you've thought about on my first day out?"

"Maybe," she said. "Maybe not."

They stepped from the porch and walked south, away from the town, between the trees and across the grassy flood plain to the stony edge of the Kettle River. Nina left shoes on the bank, rolled up her trouser legs and waded into the water. Then she turned to Pavel and waited in expectation. Like an old man he dragged his shoes off and stepped in. The sensation captured all of his attention and they began laughing. Suddenly he was young again.

The helplessness and inertia that come from confinement would not be an option for him. He understood this for certain. She would encourage and nurture him to discover that life could be good, and was starting by exposing him to sensations the earth could provide. Wind in his hair, sun on his face and the chill waters of the Kettle River on his feet were stirring his senses to feel joy again. *How could she know to do this?*

On the bank she picked up their shoes, then began walking toward town.

"Wait a minute!"

"Who needs shoes?" she said. "The grass will dry your feet."

He ran to catch up with her and realized he was actually running—not like he used to as a boy, but still, he could jog. Up ahead, Nina moved like she was born to run. To his eye each step had balance and grace. Each movement flowed into the next with a languid ease. From the moment they had met in New Denver he could not stop looking at her.

At the porch, the last light was failing. Nina went inside and Pavel sat on a vinyl chair, hoping life with her would always feel like this. Nina appeared at the door.

"Are you coming in?" she asked.

"It's been a good day. I don't want it to end." That was true, thought Pavel, but not completely true. As the sun set, apprehension of bedtime rattled him.

Nina said, "I'll get ready for bed. I have work tomorrow. Don't be long."

There was time to think, but it would do no good, Pavel knew. This moment had been contemplated without resolution. He did not want Nina to know of Matron Cody, the things they had done and the deal that was struck. The only good thing about prison was it had delayed what Nina might learn about him and Matron Cody. She would know only if he told her, but he feared something uncovering him. Someone could know, just as they knew of his storytelling. Nina might simply be able to tell. It had no logic, but felt more likely than not.

The door opened and Nina emerged onto the porch. She wore a long, thin nightgown and was backlit by a single candle from inside. Without asking, she grasped his hand and turned to go in. He hesitated as he had done before following her to the river.

"Do you think I'm not frightened, like you?" she asked, her question sounding vulnerable. "Come on. Please. The sooner you come to bed, the sooner I can stop shaking." Nina pulled him again and he followed.

She was shaking. Her trepidation distracted him momentarily. Hands touching lightly trembled together. Nina moved easily onto the bed and slipped under the sheet. He stopped at the edge and began undoing the buttons of his shirt. He recalled Matron Cody, her face painted and cast in blue light from a New Denver window. It had been the sureness of her every move and authority to justify it that had rendered him helpless and dogged his memory. Nina isn't her! Even so, he feared the thoughts intruding on him and that Nina would read him like pages in a book.

Her face glowed warm in the light of the candle. She waived no authority, and nothing needed justifying. Her desire to join them together, however it could be done, was all that drove her. Nina watched him undo the buttons, her eyes appealing to him to share the need. Pavel wanted to feel it. She was beautiful, pure, inviting him to step into the water, but he was stained, and struggled to join her. The foreboding closed in on him as the buttons were undone. He hesitated to allow the shirt to fall.

"I want to fix something with you," she said.

The horror of her knowing something stopped his breath. "What do you mean?"

"You must know what happened to some of the girls."

His relief was immediate. "In the gym, on weekends. I heard things about girls having to play rough games with the staff. Basketballs being thrown at them and the touching that went on. It was rumours. We didn't know if it was true."

"It was true," said Nina, acknowledging her place among the victims. "For every bad thing that happened to me in the gym, I want to make it better with you. Will you help me ... make it better?"

Nina had thought about this too. A simple calculation to purge the memory of abuse had been constructed. She would overlay each bad memory with a good one as if it were as simple as laying a new rug over the damaged weave of an old one. Pavel thought it was as good an idea as any he had heard, and realized it was the only idea he had heard on the matter.

Nina diverted her gaze from his face to the shirt and back again. Her urgency in reaching for him, as his shirt dropped, surprised him, and he felt her desperation. She pulled him over the edge of the bed, unwilling to wait another moment to be chest to chest. Her breasts squeezed against him as if it would save them both from something.

"Wait, wait," she said, and pushed him away before sitting up, lifting her nightgown over her head and discarding it. She drew him in again, dragging her breasts back and forth across his chest, as if to touch every part of him with every part of her. Her eyes closed and her body writhed against him, gripping one of his legs between hers and rolling back and forth.

He had never imagined her like this. The strength of her hold on him was fearsome, the intensity of her need infectious and compelling. The foreboding became lost in her passion and now his obligation to put it right. Whatever she needed, he would put it right.

PAVEL LAY IN THE DARK WITH NINA TUCKED IN THE CROOK OF HIS ARM. It had been awkward and clumsy but as tender as their experience would allow. At least it was over, without trauma, and he had managed to keep thoughts of Matron Cody away for most of the time. Now he felt the bed softer than he was used to and his mind raced. The previous four years had begun to recede like a nightmare decaying from the moment one wakes. It would stay alive only if he worked to recall it and keep the details crisp. The alternative was to allow the memory to crumble, resist the recollection, the angry rehearsal of all that was unjust, and simply let it go. As Nina had calculated, he would repair each painful recollection by overlaying it with one that was better.

This was the question Nina had asked, perhaps without knowing. It was an invitation, to start again, to leave the struggle and all that went with it. They might be happy living as independents, like the English Canadians. There was love and joy to find in things around them. God would be no less important. They could work and have a simple life. The sun would shine and the rivers would run just the same. It felt nearly right, if only he could let it go, and if only he deserved to be without obligation to the cause, whatever that had become.

It meant letting go of so much, but then here he was with Nina, away from the Sons of Freedom and shunned by the Orthodox people of his past. What was the purpose of holding memories if they no longer connected him to those people? For the first time he thought it might not be important to hang on to it all, except what, then, was the purpose of Harry being blown apart in the Chevy and Paul starving to death? It had to mean something.

Pavel shuffled gently out of bed and stepped onto the porch, hoping cool air might clear his head. The night was black as could be, and haunting sounds arrived from the woodland. His memory of New Denver, Krestova and Mountain Prison were each a crucifix of sorts. They were reminders of suffering, of Paul and Harry's sacrifice for a cause he could not quite define beyond the injustice. Even so, his crucifixes were every bit as real to him as Jesus's suffering was a reminder to Catholics of their faith. He tried to order his thoughts.

The Doukhobor tradition was clear. God should reside within people and not in icons of any kind. His people had rejected such objects centuries before, but it had not prevented other "icons," like his crucifixes, from being created in their minds and held sacred among them. Was there a difference between a physical object and a memory, if their effect was the same? Both endure over time, both obstructed and distracted from the true way. There was no difference he could see.

Maybe, he thought, it was no longer an obligation for him to carry these icons in memory. He could remove them from sight and place them in a drawer. It was someone else's task to hold that memory and keep that cause alive. He could be free to be with Nina, and not be responsible. Someone else would be.

There was something reassuring about the pieces settling in a way that justified his effort to let go of what had gone before, if Harry's and Paul's deaths would not be lost. Only one question remained. Without the obligation to the cause, what would be his purpose? Without a community or communal home to find a role within, was it enough to be with Nina? It might be, thought Pavel, if there were children.

Nina called for him to return to their bed. Somewhere from the riverbank, an owl also called to him.

13

Vancouver, October 5, 2004

PAVEL LIFTED HIS HEAD FROM THE NEWSPAPER AND STARED OUT THE window of his tiny apartment. The trees he could see were hanging on to their green, edges of leaves curled brown and yellow. Many had given in to the autumn wind, falling where they were taken.

There's no point, thought Pavel. It was a hopeless struggle and no energy should have been spent fighting against it. Dulcie McCallum, the ombudsperson for BC, had given them such hope in 1999 with Public Report No. 38, a resounding call for the injustice of New Denver to be put right, but the attorney general, Geoff Plant, would not say what had been recommended. Everyone knew what was right, but right did not matter to these people. Pavel returned to the newspaper article. Geoff Plant was quoted:

"I extend my sincere, complete and deep regret for the pain and suffering you experienced during the prolonged separation from your families."

Complete and deep regret, thought Pavel. *It's nothing.* The children of New Denver, now men and women, would see it as nothing. For all that he and they had endured since leaving New Denver, this was nothing but another betrayal.

He checked again the date of the paper and found the names of eleven children from New Denver attending the Parliament Buildings in Victoria to hear the statement read by the attorney general. There was no mistake. It was the occasion they had all waited for. How stupid they were to believe it would be the start of being whole again.

He yearned to leave the bitterness behind and do what was normal: to connect to family, be the father he could not be, go to work, stop the bloody medication, feel part of something not tainted with being a victim. *It would be so good*, he thought, *to talk with someone without having all of this shit in my head.* Not many spoke of it, but it was what they all felt. *Would it not just stop!* If not for themselves, then for their children. So many of their children had been driven away.

He was reminded of his son, Dmitri. The boy, now a man, had been let down and had taken his anger to Vancouver to dissipate in that anonymous place, without purpose as any of his people knew it. It was something else to be guilty about, and yet he could not solve the hurt that stopped him from being as he should without the apology—a real one, not this damned statement of regret. Anger flared and he crushed the paper in his hands. He had seen so many stories in newspapers casting his people in a way that absolved the English Canadians from what they had done.

From his pocket he drew a lighter, flicked it with his thumb and put it to the top corner of the offending paper. It began slowly and then became like a liberty torch. Without thinking he jammed it in the kitchen waste and watched it burn. There was smoke in the room, and fire started roaring as the alarm began. A hanging towel began to burn beneath a plywood cabinet. The gathering cloud swirled above him, leaving enough room to sit and watch the convection sweep the flame higher. There was no fear and no motivation to get away. Whatever happened next did not seem to matter.

August 6, 2006

THERE WAS NOTHING LIKE RIVERVIEW HOSPITAL IN THE LOWER Mainland. The sloping acres had flowing lawns and broadleaf trees grown large with a hundred years of sanctuary. It had become home to thousands of people struggling with their mental health. At its largest, five thousand people lived there with a dedicated community of staff. For all of them it was a complete life. The buildings were square, imposing, exaggerating the institution's strength and rendering as insignificant each of the people living there. Admission signalled the end of agency as an individual, and so it was with Pavel Korenov.

Someone, he thought, must have believed such symbols of strength would be reassuring to those living with mental illness, or perhaps it was the outsiders to be reassured by the sense of enduring power of the institution designed into the buildings. Symbols of their strength were everywhere, and none seemed connected to the truth of things. These people had no use for humility, doubt or shame, except in those who were called patients. *Perhaps not all of them*, Pavel thought. *There is kindness in some.*

His lawyer had said it was a kindness to be sent to hospital rather than prison. Choosing to be described as mentally unfit or deemed mentally incapable of forming intent, or whatever words they had used to demean him, they had said, was a good thing. Apparently it was his only defence against the charge of arson in which he had disregarded the risk to the lives of others. Pavel's history of imprisonment for possession of explosives would guarantee a life sentence to be served in prison. His lawyer had said, "Why put yourself through a trial when the outcome would be against you?" The doctors would say he had attempted suicide when the balance of his mind was disturbed, and Pavel had agreed to what he thought would be a shorter stay in hospital. However, the medication, the electric shocks and the boredom caused him to think he could no longer look after himself. This, he supposed, was what they had meant by it being a kindness. *If only the kindness would end.*

For all their treatments, the dreams could not be stopped, nor did he want them to stop. His nighttime torment was not to be shared or treated as a symptom. His disappointment and fear were not to be recalled as an illness. It was his life and had value of a kind, even if it meant he wrestled with the sheets of his bed as if they were spirits entangling him. No matter that he woke soaking from fear and the struggle to save himself. The intensity of his fight was all the intensity he had, and he would keep it. Pavel sat in the cavernous day room and recalled every detail of last night's struggle with such clarity that he might have been sleeping. The muscles of his arms and face tightened and twitched with the memory.

It always began with Pavel the boy surveying the earth from above. It was covered in snow, spread like a tablecloth to the east of New Denver. To the west, the long silver Slocan Lake ran north and south, butting up against a mountain range on the eastern edge. People moved slowly between the buildings of the old sanatorium, and then he was among them. Children played and snowballs flew. They stopped and gawped at Pavel. Their mouths smiled, bleeding on sad white faces.

A girl said, "We can't go home. Can you help us?"

"What can I do? There's nothing I can do," said Pavel.

"Then why are you here?" she asked.

A boy said, "My mother stripped naked and walked in the streets." There was defiance and pride in his eyes. "And burned the house down."

In his dream Pavel knew what was coming next and clenched his teeth.

A wave of voices rose from the yard, claiming that parents were walking naked in the street, and then snow began flying.

"Look! There they are." The children pointed through the eight-foot chain-link fence surrounding the compound, children on the inside and adults outside. Three rows of tall sinewy men stood to the right and three rows of robust women on the left, naked in the snow, frozen together like chicken legs from the freezer. Still eyes stared endlessly at the children. From open unmoving mouths the drone of sacred Russian song emerged. Under the deep tones there were chirping sounds. Pavel saw the children crying against the fence, dangling by their lips on the frozen steel, like fish hanging in a drift net. Miles in the distance buildings burned orange, yellow and black.

In the dream Pavel turned to run, but the ice and snow prevented traction and quickly he was down, scrabbling, clawing at the ground to get away.

A woman's voice shouted, "Take him inside!" Two Mounties were on the boy and began dragging him out of the yard. He struggled against being pulled away, but he was no match for the two men.

In the hospital day room Pavel gripped the arms of his chair and closed his eyes in fear of what he would now see. The Mounties pulled him backwards up steps and through a doorway. He kept his head down until the door slammed, enclosing him in a room. He raised his head, not wanting to look but having to see. Harry lay on a table, all the flesh of his torso lost. His eyes watched for what Pavel the boy might do. There was nothing to be done except allow the helplessness of terror wash over him, grind his teeth and grip the arms of his chair.

Footsteps approached: two people, tapping on the linoleum floor and echoing in the cavernous day room of Riverview Hospital.

A nurse said, "I'm not sure how long you'll want to stay. He doesn't seem to be having a good day today."

"I won't stay long," said a familiar voice.

A chair scraped up beside Pavel and he waited until his son, Dmitri, spoke.

"Hello, Father. How have you been?"

Pavel glanced at his son—a glimpse of the boy he had abandoned was all he could endure—and began crying.

April 29, 2013

NEARLY ALL THE PATIENTS HAD DEPARTED FROM THE HOSPITAL, NOW formally closed. The last patients waited for new residences to be made ready. The imposing structures on the Riverview site and uncompromising organization of the community had none of the enduring qualities of the past. Now the edges crumbled like autumn leaves. Large buildings stood empty save for their occasional use as filming venues for movies Their disinfected aroma lingered but the smell of mice, mildew and dust grew. Pavel contemplated that musty whiff and imagined thousands of beds made and unmade, the flakes of men and women combing hair, removing socks, scratching at dry skin now trodden into floorboards, falling between the cracks. The smell rose again as if reminding the world that they had lived here. Tomorrow he was scheduled to move to a new place, after eight years of meandering the grounds. The prospect revived defiance, not yet wholly extinguished.

Pavel had settled to being in Riverview, but at the worst of times the horrifying metaphor of the place preoccupied him. The hospital had been built a hundred years before, in the same years his people had marched across Alberta to the Kootenays, driven from Saskatchewan, in their efforts to live according to their customs. They had found themselves dominated and controlled by government and institutions insisting they abide by rules governing how they lived. Obedience had been demanded, assimilation was required and dissent led to certain disadvantage. A century later Pavel regarded the beautiful trees and lawns of Riverview Hospital, listened to staff and patients celebrate the end of these days and thought nothing had changed. It was, for a patient in Riverview, as it was for all the Doukhobors since their arrival. The choice was to go along with what others wanted, or extinction.

There had been an expectation of an apology for the treatment of the New Denver children arising from them taking their case to the BC Human Rights Tribunal, but yesterday the judgment, and the disappointment, had come with a visit from Nina. A seventy-six-page judgment had concluded that the confinement, beatings and abuse the children had experienced had not been a matter of discrimination. In his darkness, there was humour. It seemed that British Columbia treated so many people cruelly that, indeed, they had not been discriminated against.

He had been wrong to pin any hopes on this. He always knew the tribunal could not offer an apology, whatever it concluded, but the pressure on government to live up to its own Human Rights Tribunal might have led to something—hope, at least, but that was the problem. He smiled at the realization he had avoided for so long. He had learned to live with disappointment, as his people had done over three centuries, but he could no longer live with hope.

His mind wandered, remembering Nina, the mop of hair and piercing blue eyes that had arrested him in New Denver all those years ago. She had offered hope to him there, while he was in prison and afterwards. He could not live up to all that she was or break from the hope that their leader, Sorokin, had offered, and which he followed. When that was smashed, it was too late to go back. He had been driven from Nina, not by disappointment in her but by the hope Krestova and his people could be renewed. *Thank God she was strong enough to look after Dmitri.* He pushed his family from his thoughts as more than he could tolerate.

It was time. All the staff were in, many more than usual, celebrating the closure. They did their best to keep the anxiety of tomorrow's move manageable by being present, keeping things light, special food, a few speeches, and having medication at the ready. More staff meant that each one accepted less responsibility for keeping an eye on what was going on. It was an opportunity.

Pavel left the ward without speaking and made his way to the tree he had chosen. It was an enormous copper beech. The leaves rustled and whispered above him as he gathered the rope he had taken from the filmmakers weeks before, threw one end over the chosen branch and tied the other off. He worked quickly, fearing only that he would be found and stopped. He estimated the height of the noose from the ground, adjusted the knot, pulled it close to the trunk and began climbing the few feet to a place he could cling onto, before placing the noose around his neck.

Something shuffled above him in the branches and he looked up. Without thinking, he said, "Don't worry, I won't hurt you." Then he thought, *How ridiculous to be talking to an owl,* and let go of the trunk.

14

Grand Forks, January 8, 2018

IT WAS NOT SOMETHING THAT WILLIAM COULD EXPLAIN, ALTHOUGH HE felt it keenly. Neither were there coherent thoughts of why he should be making the journey to Grand Forks to see his mother on this day and at this moment, except that it was the only thing he wanted to do.

Somehow his mental construction had been fixed for the last two decades, believing that she would be there always. It was, as so much of the world he had made, a convenient assumption absolving him of responsibility and obligation. He had left the police station and gone directly home to leave the Tesla, which did not have the range for his journey, and pick up Julie's Mercedes.

The travel time was nearly six hours, a little more with a single stop for gas and something to eat. Now, the last light of the day completely gone, he drove south down the Crowsnest Highway to meet the Kettle River at the first of seven sweeping bends beginning on the western outskirts of Grand Forks near the edge of the forty-ninth parallel. He slowed to find the unmarked turning on the right, off the highway. Unless you knew it was there, you would fly by the unadorned turning without a thought. It was a cemetery for the Doukhobor people.

Through the hedgerow separating it from the highway, the slice of land between road and river was wide enough for a dozen cars to park side by side on the gravel. The lights of the Mercedes illuminated nothing in front but a blanket of snow that stretched as far as could be seen. William stopped the car, left the lights on and stepped out into the crisp night, pulling on his coat and tucking a scarf around his neck. The sound of the Kettle River rushing along could just be heard. In the same ravine, the sound of an owl haunted the night.

Nothing marked the way and he strained his memory to orient himself. The last time he had visited, it was autumn and daylight. He had waited until the group of friends, celebrants and his mother had left before showing himself, making his way to his father's newly dug grave. At the time he had not wanted to be inveigled into justifying his departure to those who might question him, but now it seemed more likely he had been hiding shame. Among normal people it could be masked by his affluence, the cut of his suit, his designer sunglasses and the Omega on his wrist, but it could not be hidden from these people, who cared nothing for all he had or had become. Somehow, William thought, it was fitting that he had arrived in the dark.

A shed to the right at the edge of the ravine offered a waypoint from which he might recall the place of his father's grave. He crunched the snow toward the memory. Each marked grave lay flat on the ground, some with the smallest of arrangements to allow flowers to stand. Even in death it was important for these people to accept an equal and humble place among others, but it meant only the indentation of the quilted snow blanket revealed the place of each grave.

William squatted down at the spot he thought he remembered and brushed the snow away. The lights from the car were too far away to help him. From his coat he pulled his iPhone and turned on the light. His memory was wrong. At the next grave he swept the snow off and was again mistaken. The date was too new. He should have known that more people would have been placed in the neat rows since his father had been laid here, but for a minute he felt the panic of a child lost from his father in a crowd. It was ridiculous, but still he could not help but rush three rows to the next grave and then two rows to the next, sweeping the snow away, as if it covered all that would save him.

He was much deeper into the cemetery than he remembered when his finger scratched snow from the letters of another small flat stone.

Holding his iPhone at an angle to cast shadow in the marks, he read the name: Pavel Korenov. He placed his hands on the stone and allowed the urgency of the search to drain from him. The freezing cold of the stone went unnoticed and he spoke as if his father were listening.

January 9, 2018

OUTSIDE HER APARTMENT WILLIAM HESITATED AND CHECKED HIS WATCH; ten thirty in the morning was not too early, but he thought he should have given her notice. He had no idea what to say or how to begin, except he knew a connection with her must be made before the chance was lost. For all he knew she would turn him away. It would not be the first time one Doukhobor had turned their back on another. He was beginning to think he could return tomorrow and was stepping away from the door when it opened. A handsome grey-haired woman with piercing blue eyes looked at him.

"Dmitri," she said, "do you need help knocking at your mother's door?"

"No. It's been so long, I didn't know what I was going to say to you."

"Well, if you need help with that too, you'd better come in." Nina reached out with both hands, pulling him over the threshold and lower until she held his face in two hands. She planted a solid kiss on each cheek before embracing him.

Squeezed tightly by his mother, William felt overwhelmed, wondering how he could have forgotten this and at the same time squirming with the discomfort of doubt that he was worthy of it.

Just as quickly Nina released him and beckoned him in. "Now come in. Sit down."

The small apartment was perfectly ordered, practical as much as comfortable. Solid furniture was draped in knitted blankets and crochet throws. Pictures stood on a sideboard. His father, Nina's parents, aunties and uncles and the image of a Japanese man smiled from the top row. He knew from his mother's stories that it was Mr. Nori, one of several Japanese security workers at New Denver, who had been cherished by his mother and all the children in the dormitory for his kindness. There were pictures of William—then, Dmitri—as a boy, reminding him of times he had abandoned. A radio played CBC in the kitchen. In front of the compact sofa was a coffee table with cups, saucers and biscuits.

"I'm sorry. You're expecting company."

"Only you."

"How did you know I was coming? I didn't tell anyone."

"We still look out for each other," she said. "A car was seen in the cemetery last night and someone checked early this morning. They called to say a few stones had been cleared, but the clearing stopped at your father's grave. Only one person in the world would sweep the snow from your father's gravestone, other than me. It had to be you."

"I'd forgotten which one it was. With the new graves, it confused me."

She said, "You were seen at the funeral too, after we had all gone." He shrugged sheepishly. "You could have come by last night. I wouldn't have minded."

"I thought you might not want to see me."

"Why ever not?"

William shrugged a second time, to reveal his helplessness. "It's been so long. I felt I might not be welcome."

"We've had lots of practice waiting for our people, haven't we?" Nina smiled as if the twenty-plus years that had passed had done so in a blink and meant nothing. It was true that the hallmark of a Doukhobor was patience. They had waited for leaders to arrive from exile, for parents to come home, for children to be returned, for promises to be kept, for boats to come and for justice, with the same patience with which they waited for crops to grow. They had waited two centuries to be allowed to toil in the earth and live a peaceful life, and some were still waiting. She continued, "I hoped you would come and see me. Not all of the young ones come back, but we hope. We hope for all of you."

"I didn't think of there being others. I should have known."

"Oh, sure. We hear of the young people who have left. Some are doing fine; others not so much. Will you have tea or coffee?"

"Coffee, please." William felt strange in his mother's home. The greeting was warm enough but somehow, as Nina made coffee in the kitchen, there was something familiar and something missing. His mother was practical as always but nothing more, save for the first greeting.

As if listening to his thoughts Nina said, raising her voice from the kitchen, "Don't think I'm not full of joy for you being here. I am. I did my crying early this morning when I got the call and I'll do the rest when you've gone. But now we can talk, for a while, until you feel you must go again."

William felt the push and pull of his mother's words. At first it confused him but gradually he began to understand the reserve in the air. A ratio had been carefully calculated between welcoming him without creating an obligation to stay and a commitment to something more than he might tolerate. Only the effusive kisses at the door crossed the line, from which she quickly drew back. She had retreated into her plan of benevolent neutrality. He had walked into a scenario with trepidation, not knowing she had contemplated his arrival a thousand times with only him in mind. He had done no preparation and, to his discomfort, had not thought of how his mother would feel, just that her disdain of him might drive him away.

The cutting of ties with his family and the Doukhobor people had unmoored him. He knew this now. He had floated alone, determined his own direction, and because of this, there would be no pursuit of him or pleading with him to stay. Nina would be as neutral as she could manage. He felt a sweep of the insignificance that had angered him as a young man unable to influence his father's affection for him, and then fear of being alone, which lurked in the background ever since he left. Finally it came to him that she was holding her emotions in check; otherwise they would burst from her chest. He must be careful with her, he thought.

Nina carried the mugs from kitchen counter to coffee table and instructed her son to sit. She took a chair and left the sofa for William. "How have you been?"

"Lots has happened," he began. "You have a granddaughter."

"Oh, how lovely. What's her name?"

"Kelly. She's fourteen. A snowboarder. She's funny, and sweet." William could not remember having described Kelly in this way before. His thoughts had been uncharitable until recently, always finding her limitations, and now the pride in his voice surprised him. "She's losing her sight, unfortunately. There's not much that can be done to stop it."

"Oh dear. Well, fortunately you don't have to see who loves you to know that they do." Nina tilted her head as if to suggest it was unimportant to the love she could offer.

"It doesn't hold her back. She goes to parties and even plays soccer." William did not want to tell his mother he had not watched her play.

"And does snowboarding, you say. She sounds lovely. Do you have a picture of her?"

"Maybe." William pulled out his iPhone and began searching. Before starting he knew there were no pictures, except those taken of Kelly as an infant. "I guess not. Sorry, I should have thought to bring some."

"Never mind," Nina continued, unable to hide the smallest purse of her lips. "Are you still with the mother?"

There was something knowing in the question. "Yes. Her name's Julie. It's amazing, but we are still together."

"But she doesn't know you're here."

"What makes you say that?"

"You said you didn't tell anyone about coming." She paused. "Has something happened for you to travel all this way so suddenly?"

"So much has happened."

Nina allowed the pause to linger only a few seconds before changing tack. "There's a recent scar under your eyebrow."

William put his hand to his forehead and stroked the livid line there. "I fell off my bike, and when I went to the hospital they discovered I had a little tumour near the brain. It wasn't very serious, but it needed an operation."

"Your father had a scar a bit longer than that one. Are you okay now?"

"Yes, I think I'm fine now, but I haven't felt the same since." William was about to say something about the operation being the start of the turmoil—how he had changed and how the things he had done all came back to that. "There's no end of problems. It's difficult running a business on your own."

"It must be."

"Maybe the operation explains why I'm not concentrating, and why I seemed to be losing it." He paused. "I was fine, then I had the operation and now I'm not so fine. It makes sense to me, but sometimes I'm not sure."

"It sounds like it would help you make sense of things, if it was that simple. Or maybe you weren't as fine as you thought you were. It's hard to see ourselves, I know." She smiled. "You didn't come all this way to talk about your operation. Or maybe you did; that's fine too."

"I'm not sure why I came." He paused, then admitted, "That's not true. I've come to say I'm sorry."

"For what, exactly?" asked Nina, locking him squarely in her gaze. "It's enough that you have come." She watched him. "Ah, you haven't come to say sorry to me. That's what you were doing last night in the cemetery."

Everything he did, William thought, revealed his inability to consider how it affected someone else. It had become a habit that only now had become embarrassing. His fumbling explanation to his father at the grave was nothing but self-justifying, and he had missed what was in front of him. "I owe you an apology. It's been too long. I shouldn't have just left and I should have come to see you."

"I've missed you, all right. Every day, especially since he died, but I know you have a journey to finish and I have to wait. But you've come about your father this time."

There was no point in hiding it. "I've spent most of my life angry with him and trying not to be like him. I never understood why he wouldn't stay with us. Then I hated him because he was gone. I guess I was ashamed of him."

Nina asked, "All of this anger and still you visited him in Riverview Hospital?"

"How did you know I visited him in Riverview?"

"Because I did too. The nurses told me you had been."

"You visited him in Riverview?"

"Sure I did, every month or so."

"They didn't tell me."

"I asked them not to. I didn't want you to stop coming. They said you once brought a little girl with you. I thought it might be your daughter." Nina smiled. "How did you know he was there?"

"There was something in the paper about a man arrested for arson and his name was mentioned," William explained. "It was easy to find him with that. I just felt someone should visit. You're right. If I'd known you were visiting, I might not have. I don't know why."

"It was kind of you."

"How did he get so ... lost?"

"It's a long story. Are you sure you want to hear it?"

"I've come a long way."

Nina began, "I knew Pavel as a boy and a young man, when he was strong, full of courage. You didn't know him then. The things he did for others in New Denver would have made you proud. Even after that he was so strong for everyone. But our people, well, they were always divided. My parents were in prison, and I lived with Auntie and Uncle. They had broken away from the Sons of Freedom and moved here from Krestova, but not everyone accepted them in Grand Forks. Even though they took me out of New Denver and put me into English school they were still part of the trouble.

"My parents, when they were released, went back to Krestova and left me with my auntie and uncle, who took your father in too. They had looked after me for the years I was hiding from the police. We all felt cut off from someone in those days.

"When Pavel was released from Agassiz Mountain Prison I brought him to Grand Forks, but it was difficult. He was shunned, and because of that the Orthodox Doukhobors would have nothing to do with me. Auntie and Uncle couldn't have me in their house, so your father and I lived together. We weren't married but it didn't bother us. We were happy for a while.

"Pavel would go back to Krestova sometimes, which Uncle hated, but I couldn't go there with him. I was a leaver. It didn't matter that I was in New Denver. My aunt and uncle were leavers, and when I went to them, I was a leaver. That was it."

William asked, "Father went with you, but he was not a leaver?"

"He had sacrificed himself to their cause and had a place among them. He had spent all that time in New Denver, got himself blown up on a mission and went to prison. For some it drove them away from the Sons of Freedom, but not your father. It bound him to those people. I tried to pull him away from all of that, but once it's done you can't undo it. They're stuck together. It took me years to understand that."

"But you were in New Denver too," said William.

"Not for very long. I wanted to be with my friends in New Denver. I can't tell you how lonely it was hiding for those years. But when I was finally taken, they were already together, like a gang. I could speak good English and the other children thought I was a spy at first. They wouldn't tell me things or let me in, in case I told the matrons. Pavel never believed that. He'd speak to me."

Nina continued, "All my friends had changed. They were tough—streetwise, you'd call it. New Denver made them cruel. I was just a little girl when I got there and had to toughen up pretty quick. It didn't help that Auntie was the leader of the group who took us out of New Denver. So, Pavel couldn't stay away from his friends."

William said, "He couldn't be with us, but he could be with his friends in Krestova or Brilliant. It doesn't say much about us."

"Don't be too harsh with him. He was only a child when all this happened. I thought I could fix it, but it was too late. He was lost when he came out of prison, maybe before that. I just thought I could love him better, but I couldn't. All of those children and all those families have scars."

"Krestova wasn't a happy place, was it?" asked William. "He was always upset when he came from there to stay with us."

"Krestova had been through so much. They just needed someone to lead them out of their anger, but there were divisions. It got so complicated. There were Sons of Freedom, mostly the elders or older people, and Reformed Doukhobors, who were mostly young people who followed Stefan Sorokin. Your father believed in Sorokin. He wanted to lead them away from violence. Pavel was part of the group of Reformed Doukhobors. Do you remember any of this?"

"I remember," said William. "I was about ten or eleven when Sorokin died. Father was upset. There were stories he told me about miracles Sorokin had performed. People about to die in hospital and getting better, that sort of thing."

"Yes, there were stories like that. People, like your father, loved him, believed in him. When he died, your father was one of those who tried to keep things going, and he was there all the time. You were about thirteen when he said he couldn't come back, but he was already gone—had been for a few years."

"He wasn't always in Krestova, was he?"

"No. Something was happening in Krestova and he ended up leaving. I didn't understand it all then and I'm not sure I do now, but something terrible happened that upset everyone."

"What was it?"

"Well, I've had to piece it together because Pavel wouldn't talk to me about it. Even when I visited him in Riverview he couldn't talk about it."

"Did something happen to him?"

"Not directly. The story is that some young men went to your father, I don't know how many, and said that Sorokin had been touching them—their privates—and doing other things. Pavel couldn't believe it at first, but then when so many others spoke about it, he came to think it must be true. Then he tried to get others to believe it and help these young men, but they wouldn't accept it. They just couldn't."

"Why not?"

"You have to understand the people in Krestova had suffered for their beliefs and felt righteous in their cause. They were proud of keeping true to what they believed but were struggling to be a community again. Undermining the reputation of Sorokin, especially like that, was the same as undermining their community. So, they were angry with your father for trying to destroy the progress they'd made. I guess that's why so many people couldn't bring themselves to believe it. All that suffering and commitment to their cause would mean nothing if it were true. Even the young men were accused of lying. It was terrible. Many of them left. The community was in pieces. Hardly anyone came to worship, congregations dropped off." Nina lifted her eyebrows and shrugged in exasperation. "How can you worship together or even say God's in your heart when the leader of your community has done that and the victims are called liars and cast out? Well, you can't. In the end, Krestova was broken and no one was strong enough to help them heal from it all."

"What did Father do?"

"He felt betrayed by what had happened and couldn't stay. Pavel wanted the community to face what had happened. When they turned on him, it was a betrayal and against all he believed. He had heard that a few of the young people had moved to Vancouver and were in trouble. He went to help them. He shouldn't have gone. He wasn't up to it."

"What do you mean?"

"He was broken too. He went to Krestova to hold himself together with a dream of the community being whole again. When that went bad, it was the end. It wasn't long before he was nearly destitute, sometimes living on the streets."

William streamed the image of the wild-eyed man in the dumpster, the musty young man in Tim Hortons who had woken him up, the aimless army of dispossessed middle-aged men who walked the streets of Vancouver.

"I went to find him several times, but he wouldn't speak to me, or come back to Grand Forks. He became preoccupied with the idea that everything would be settled if the government would apologize for what happened in New Denver, as if it would make everything right again. It didn't happen. BC wanted to avoid paying compensation, so a statement of regret was made. It was another betrayal and it drove him mad. Eventually he was diagnosed."

"What with?"

"At first it was schizophrenia, then it was depression and then it was something else. It was always changing so they could give him electric shocks or more drugs. It didn't matter. Anyone who knew what had happened to him understood why he was lost. For Pavel, who had given so much to the cause of the Doukhobors, 'they' had taken every-thing, even his childhood."

"Who's 'they'?"

"Canada, British Columbia, the RCMP, English Canadians. It went further than that. He was scarred by everything, even the stories from Russia. Every hardship done to our people he carried as if he were, I don't know, responsible for making it good."

"Is that why he ..." William hesitated.

"Hanged himself?" Nina said matter-of-factly. "You don't have to be gentle with such things. I've seen too much to be coy about it. The hospital told me it was his mental illness, the depression, they said, but it was nothing of the sort, to my mind."

"What was it?"

"Maybe you heard something about this on the news, but there was a time when there was again talk of an apology happening and some compensation had been worked out. Our people couldn't agree on the details and it didn't happen. It was the last straw.

"Your father used to say, 'They can't take everything from you,' and 'Don't give them everything.' I just thought he meant outsiders would take everything if they could and you had to hold something back— keep something for yourself. It's not like Doukhobors to think that, but that's how it became. I never understood, really, but he wasn't talking about things or even secrets. He was talking about what made him Pavel Korenov, a man, a human, a Doukhobor. I think, after all that went on, and then the apology didn't happen, the only thing he had left was himself. Everything else had been worn away, and then he was in hospital. The doctors with their shocks and drugs were taking away what he had kept for himself. He took his life, the core that made him, before they did."

They sat there quietly. William recalled his anger and disappointment at this man, Pavel Korenov. How unjust it seemed now. He had resented and then disregarded his mother as being the only other person able to remedy his anger but failing him, and this too was unfair. The blue eyes that scrutinized him without judgment, and with compassion, could have helped him understand all this, if only he had stayed and been open to it.

"Would you like more coffee?" she said. "I'll make some fresh. There's more to talk about."

LESS THAN TWO HOURS' DRIVE WEST OF GRAND FORKS, WILLIAM PULLED the Mercedes to the edge of the Crowsnest Highway at Anarchist Mountain Lookout, just east of Osoyoos. He stopped the engine and stepped into the near-frozen air. The light had just started to fade, darkening the blue of a clear sky. Wisps of long white clouds drew the eye north along Osoyoos Lake to the rich farmland snuggled between barren white hills. He sucked the cold air in through his nostrils and made his eyes water. Cold tears trembled at the corners of his eyes. The rattle of new information settling in his mind had eased. Pushing aside the old bricks on which he allowed his presumptions to rest had been exhausting. Room had been made for all he had learned, and for now the turmoil of that effort was gone. The unfolding labyrinth of memory and emotion would be calm until he encountered another jarring inconsistency within him that could not be ignored.

He had thought that since his operation he had been losing his mind, but now it seemed he had only just found it after all this time. His life had been madness from the time he left for Vancouver years ago, and only by returning to Grand Forks had he found the prospect of sanity within his grasp.

There was also succour in knowing his father's final act was one of his own volition. For William, it had always been understood that his father had a weakness. He had abandoned his family, wasted his life in futile obligation and finally ended it, because he didn't have the strength of character to do otherwise. It was this he had railed against. For the hospital staff it was an act borne of a diseased brain, for which they had little responsibility save for spells of being watchful, or negligent; it had seemed not to matter which. So easy had it been to point a finger at hospital staff.

For his father, William now understood, it was an act of defiance in which he deprived his tormentors of the satisfaction of finally snuffing him out. His chest expanded with pride on behalf of his defeated father. He had never before felt pride in the recollection of his father or allowed the memory to force tears out, but his mind lay unprotected by the anger needed to shut out all he did not normally allow. Tears crumpled him. Squeaking sounds of a child escaped him and were whipped away by the wind. There was no strength to interrupt the flow or prevent hot tears welding his father's life and death to all he had become. He was his father's legacy, and all he had to show was his misunderstanding of everything.

The chill finally overcame the emotion. His wind-raw cheeks registered the cold and his body shivered. William returned to the car and started the engine. It was still four hours' drive to Vancouver, and it reminded him that there would be people there worried about his absence. He reached for his phone and saw it was dead. Scrabbling in the armrest, he found the charging cable and plugged it in. William lifted his chest and pushed out all his air. He pulled onto the highway to begin the final swooping turns into Osoyoos. As he passed over the lake bridge from east to west, the iPhone sprang to life, dinging over and over. He turned into AG Foods car park and inspected the screen. There were twenty-one messages, an emoji from Uri and thirty-four missed calls. He would have some explaining to do.

William decided to make one call to his home and let Julie know where he was. He pressed the screen several times with his thumb and the call connected. The voice-mail message replied.

When it was done, he said, "Hi Julie. Sorry for causing you some worry and borrowing your car. I've been in Grand Forks visiting my mother and I'm heading home now. There's lots to talk about. Again, sorry, I'll explain when I get home." He looked at the Omega on his wrist. "I should be there before eight. Please let Kelly know everything is fine."

The list of missed calls was long—some from work, some from Julie and others he did not know—and he decided not to bother replying. Tomorrow would be just as good.

WILLIAM NOTICED THE HOUSE WAS IN DARKNESS EXCEPT FOR THE ONE light they left on to deter burglars. The outside security lights detected his arrival and flooded the surrounds with flat light. The garage door opened. The Tesla was not there. It was eerily quiet as he stepped out of the Mercedes next to the rack of bicycles all in a row.

"Mr. Koren." A voice spoke from the garage door.

William turned to see Constable McKinnon and two uniformed men.

"What do you want? Sorry, you made me jump."

"You weren't answering your phone, so we had to come over. We tried many times to reach you."

"Sorry, I went to visit my mother in Grand Forks, my phone ran out of juice and I didn't notice. What do you want?"

"We'd like you to come down to the station with us."

"Look, I only just got home and I've given you a statement already."

"I know, but you know how these things go. There are always details to sort out."

"I'm very tired. Can't it wait till morning?"

"No. I'm sorry, Mr. Koren. It can't."

"Can I just tell my wife what's going on?"

"She's not at home, Mr. Koren. We were here earlier and she told us what time you would be arriving, but she didn't want your daughter to be alarmed."

"Why would she be alarmed?"

"RCMP at the door, I guess."

William looked at the faces of the three men opposite him and understood. "I don't have a choice here, do I?"

"Well, we are asking you to accompany us to the station voluntarily. Let's just say that, without getting more complicated."

15

Vancouver, January 10, 2018

THIS TIME MCKINNON SAT OPPOSITE WILLIAM IN THE BARREN ROOM.

"May I call you William?" he asked.

"That's fine."

"Remember that this interview is being recorded. Now, I want to go over some of the things you said last time you were here. You described your relationship with your long-standing employee Cathy. Is there anything you omitted to tell us or would like to add to your statement now?"

It was obvious in the question that they knew something, but what exactly Cathy had said was not clear. In the hanging pause inviting him to reply, William thought it was not likely Cathy would say anything about Uri or the shipments. She was likely to say something about her relationship with him. It was pointless denying it.

William said, "Years ago we had an affair. It was when the business was starting and for most of the time it was just me and her. It was an exciting time, full of energy." He felt his face redden, conscious of how lame this must be sounding. "It was a mistake and I shouldn't have let it happen."

"How long did it go on?"

"Hard to say exactly, but more than a year. Something like that. Less than two."

McKinnon said, "Would you like to say why you didn't tell us about this the last time we spoke?"

"You didn't ask me about it, and I'm not very proud of it. An affair with your secretary is a bit of a cliché, isn't it? But mostly I didn't want my wife to find out. I thought if I mentioned it, she would find out."

"You don't think she would be very forgiving?"

"She's put up with a lot, but I don't really know. It's just, we've been distant for a very long time, and only recently we turned a corner."

"You stopped seeing Cathy romantically but kept working together. Is that not unusual?"

"I can't understand why she stayed. Maybe she needed the money. I would have understood had she left, but that's for her to say. I was grateful that she did stay. The business benefited. I benefited."

"So you have some affection for her."

"Yes, of course. The business is tough, and she stuck in there when it was very difficult. I value that."

"Is that why you arranged for a lawyer to represent her?"

"What? I don't know anything about that."

"You didn't instruct a lawyer to represent Cathy?"

"No."

"You did ask about her having a lawyer last time you were here."

"Because I wanted to make sure she had good advice, but I didn't do anything about it. If a lawyer showed up, it wasn't me."

"Okay, let's leave that. So we have established you had an affair, lasting more than a year, but continued working together."

"Yes."

"How did you feel about the affair Cathy was having with Dennis?"

Suddenly the danger was clear to William. "I thought it was a bad idea, and I asked Dennis to end it."

"Why would you do that?"

"It was a distraction to them both and to the business. I didn't know what was going on, but one morning I suspected them of getting together at the warehouse, just before I came in. They were flushed and,

I don't know how to put it, ruffled. Anyway, it was enough to convince me of what was happening. Not good for business, but also I thought Cathy was going through a difficult time in her marriage. She seemed unhappy much of the time and I thought she was vulnerable."

"You told two of our officers that you were looking after the workplace, being a responsible employer, making it safe, so you went to Dennis's house on a Saturday, the afternoon of the fire, to get his agreement to end the relationship, or you were going to let him go. Is that right?"

"Yes, pretty much."

"Wasn't Cathy married when you had an affair with her?"

"Yes." William squirmed.

"Was that different? If having sex with Dennis makes it an unsafe workplace, it was pretty unsafe when you were doing it."

William squared up to the challenge. "That's fair. It's not really different, but I did see the mistake and stopped it, eventually."

McKinnon nodded. A long silence held them fast in the moment. "The problem is," he said, "the affection and the sexual relationship between you and Cathy had not really come to an end, had it?"

William tried to hold his stand on shifting ground. McKinnon had prepared as thoughtfully for this conversation as William's mother had prepared for his return. He had felt the same trepidation in front of her. McKinnon said, "On Monday, after you had been told by our officers that Dennis had died, you took her from work to her apartment and had sex with her. Is that right?"

The reply stuck in William's throat, and McKinnon continued. "Be careful how you answer, William. You will have guessed that we have Cathy's statement. We're waiting for DNA evidence confirming that statement and we'll have to wait a few days to know for sure. But you already know what happened. You could tell us now. Did you have sex with her on that Monday?"

"Yes. I should never have let it happen."

"Asserting your rightful place as a dominant male lion over his pride." McKinnon's mockery grated on William, as it was intended to do. "Is that a reasonable comparison? Kill off the rival and mate at the first opportunity."

"It wasn't like that."

McKinnon opened a file on the table and pushed three photographs toward William. The bruising on Cathy's breast was every colour of purple, green and yellow. "From where I'm sitting, you could be just another beast in the jungle. Or would you prefer me to say, a jealous lover wanting to get rid of a younger rival, and angry at his 'unfaithful' partner?"

William inspected the pictures slowly and carefully, making time to order his thoughts. There was relief for him in the photographs. They would not have shown him these pictures if Cathy had told the police the truth of how she got the bruises. There would be no questions to discover what William knew about the incident or the men who did it. He thought it could only mean that McKinnon was trying to rattle him—an old-fashioned shakedown to test a theory that Cathy was protecting him by taking the blame for the murder they both committed. It hung on the presumption of their continuing relationship.

He said, "Cathy showed me the bruises when we were together. They were old bruises then, and even older now. Anyone can see that. I thought her husband had mistreated her, or Dennis, but it doesn't change what happened between us. We had sex. It was an emotional time and hard to explain. It shouldn't have happened, but I let it happen."

"You let it happen? That suggests you were passive, perhaps a victim of some kind of ambush."

"Of course not, but I asked her to stop a dozen times. She was just very demanding, persuasive. I was weak."

"You asked her to stop?"

"A number of times."

"I guess 'No' doesn't mean 'No,' even for women."

"That's what happened."

"She persisted and took advantage of your ... vulnerability. Is that it?"

"I wasn't vulnerable. I was weak. It was pathetic of me not to walk away, but that's how it happened."

"So, let's just sum this up, to be clear. You want us to believe that Cathy is told, for the first time, that her lover has died in a fire, and within an hour or so she is insisting that you have sex with her in her apartment. Is that what you are saying?"

The incredulity in McKinnon's voice made preposterous all that William might say, but William felt confident that if McKinnon had anything of substance, mockery would not be needed.

"It sounds strange, even to me, but it is true." It was impossible to make ground with this man, he thought. "Look, there's an explanation, but I don't want it to sound like another excuse." McKinnon waited. "I haven't had sex in years, maybe ten or more, just haven't been interested, but recently, with my wife and with Cathy, it's started again."

"Explain. Why do you want me to know this?"

"You want to know why I had sex with Cathy. Well, there's a reason."

"Go on," McKinnon said, his expression flat with skepticism.

"Before Christmas I had an operation. You can see the scar here." William traced the line of the scar under his eyebrow. "There'll be hospital records. It was a tumour, and it was causing trouble with my … hormones and whatever. It took away my interest in sex completely. When they took it out, the hormones recovered. I'm not used to it. It was a surprise to me when things started happening again. It's the only reason it happened with Cathy. In my mind it's been over for a long time, but on that Monday, I realized it hasn't really been over for Cathy. All these years I had no idea. I wanted to keep it that way. I know I should have walked away, but I didn't."

McKinnon leaned back from the table. "It's hard to believe, William, because you haven't been candid with us. You didn't tell us about the affair or that it ended, but now you want us to believe it ended. Then you say that Cathy drags you into her bed after hearing her lover died in a fire, and you let it happen, on this one occasion, because she still loves you and because of your hormones. It sounds like you're making things up as you go along."

"It must sound that way to you, but it's true."

"If you weren't jealous of Dennis and Cathy getting together, what did he have on you?"

"What do you mean?"

"You've gone out of your way to get rid of him, quickly and generously, as I understand it. Another way of looking at this is you were trying pretty hard to shuffle him off. If it wasn't about Cathy, what was it about? What did Dennis know, William? Was he blackmailing you?"

The word paralyzed William. If McKinnon knew of the shipments, he thought, all would be lost. "What are you talking about?" he asked.

McKinnon said, "If Dennis knew about your affair with Cathy, he might tell your wife and her husband." William struggled to control a long exhale of relief. "Maybe you two achieved what you wanted to achieve and were pleased with yourselves. Maybe you were celebrating together, in bed, having dealt with the danger."

William's confidence grew with McKinnon casting his line. "Why would I celebrate his death? I'd just made a deal with him to leave. I was paying him off. It was done. Over. He didn't need to be dead to achieve that."

There was another pause before McKinnon said, "That's what you say. No one has any evidence of you making a deal with him. It was something you said after he was dead, and we know what you say can't be relied on. A jury might think you haven't been straightforward with your wife, your employees or the police. You're just ... not very honest."

Another stretch, thought William. "I don't know what they'll believe, but they'll know I wasn't there when the fire started. Cathy would never say that I was."

"Because she's protecting you?"

"Because I wasn't there!"

"You didn't have to be there when the fire started."

"What do you mean?"

"Dennis was dead before the fire started. Skull was broken. He was found at the bottom of the stairs, as if he had fallen, but the injury that killed him doesn't match the fall. So ..." McKinnon hesitated to let William absorb the implications. "You could have been there when he died. That's what we call a slam dunk: motive and opportunity, but in your case it's even better. The motive is connected to an opportunity that you conjured. You phoned Cathy to get his home address. You phoned Dennis to make sure he would be there. You went to his house, on a Saturday, to get him to stop seeing Cathy. You even said it yourself, to a number of people, including me. There was nothing accidental about the opportunity. Chance wasn't involved. It was all quite deliberate."

"That's ridiculous. It's what you do when you are about to let somebody go before the following Monday. Anyway, why would I make it so obvious where I was going if I was going to murder someone?"

The door of the barren room opened suddenly and a note was passed to McKinnon. Everything stopped while he read.

"Well," he said. "The mysterious lawyer is back—this time for you. We'll have to suspend this interview while you speak with her." He stood. "Interesting, isn't it?"

"What?"

"Our two suspects. One confesses to everything, and the other denies everything, but both with the same lawyer."

AS HE STEPPED OUT OF THE TAXI THAT BROUGHT HIM HOME, FATIGUE overwhelmed William. It was not the close call it might have been, but the disguise of deceit weighed heavily. William distracted himself and began scrolling through his messages to find something from Julie. The short messages all asked that he make contact as soon as possible. A message from the hospital caught his eye. It invited him to check his voice mail to find a follow-up appointment with his surgeon later in the week. There was nothing substantial from Julie in his messages. She may have left him a note on the kitchen table, but more likely a terse email awaited him. He began spinning through the clutter of his inbox. There it was.

William—I don't know if you will get this. If you do, it will be because you
have not been arrested. The police were here looking for you and I told them
you were on your way home from Grand Forks. They told me not to contact
you until they had spoken to you, which they will have by now. They said you
and Cathy were suspected of being together and both involved in the murder.
I knew you were in trouble but I didn't appreciate how serious it was or that
you were involved with her. I can't tell you how hurt and saddened I am.

I have taken Kelly to my parents' so she would not know of you being
taken away from the house. If you are out, please stay away from us. Collect
your things and leave in the next couple of days. We'll be all right until you
are out. I need time away from you.

Julie

William cursed the deliberately clumsy McKinnon for disclosing
his theory to Julie. Just a little discretion might have saved him, and
Julie, from this. It was part of McKinnon's style to unsettle people. His
iPhone dinged and William checked the screen. An emoji and number
beckoned him to call. He rang and Uri answered.

"William! I'm glad you called." Uri sounded jovial. "We haven't
talked for a long time. Too long."

"I thought, with the police sniffing around, it would be best if we
weren't in contact."

"Good, William. Thank you for being careful. How was your talk
with the police?"

William wondered how he could know it was over, but then it was
obvious. "I'm out of the police station now, on the way home. Thanks
for the lawyer."

"My pleasure, William. We look after each other; it's what partners
do, Cathy also. But what did you say to them?"

"They were trying to link me and Cathy, saying we were in it
together and Cathy is protecting me. They've got nothing."

"The lawyer says the same. She says you did well, but Cathy confessed
before the lawyer saw her. She told them about your ... relationship. A

pity. We would have asked her not to involve you. Did you learn any-thing about what they know?"

"Cathy hasn't said anything about you. They don't know about you or the shipments. I feel sure about that."

"Good, William. That's very good. What makes you think that?"

"They asked if Dennis was blackmailing us, but they thought he was threatening to tell Julie and Cathy's husband about the affair. Nothing about the business."

"Excellent. Thank you for telling me this. It is the end of it, I think, but if they try again, say nothing without the lawyer."

"What about Cathy?"

"There is nothing to do about Cathy." Uri left it hanging, waiting for William to understand.

"What did the lawyer say about her?"

"You must let her go. There is nothing you can do," said Uri.

It was true, thought William. She was lost, but he had to know. "Do you know what happened?"

There was an audible sigh from Uri. "Okay, William, but after I tell you, we let it go."

"Agreed."

"It is only what the lawyer has said. Cathy was in the house with Dennis when you arrived—she was upstairs. She listened to the con-versation with Dennis. He said to you he would leave her and go back to his wife. Cathy was upset when she heard this. When you left there was an argument between them, and she hit him with something. He fell down the stairs. She set fire to the house, hoping to cover it up. It was foolish and not enough."

"She's confessed to all this?"

"She has. She is gone, William. There is nothing to do."

Uri spoke again. "I must tell you something, William. Cathy believed you did this thing with Dennis, letting him go, because you wanted her for yourself. She thought you wanted to stop her having a life with him because you were jealous. Later she was angry with you because she was mistaken."

William heard the words "Oh God" escape his lips without intention. Her ferocious seduction of him made some sense.

"You are feeling badly now, but you must leave Cathy alone. She will think you are just trying to make yourself feel better and it will make her more angry with you. You know what women think. You have had your pleasure with her and now you want her to help you feel better about what you have done. She will say more to the police if you make her more angry."

Lessons in human emotions from Uri were a paradox, and yet he was right. "Okay. Thanks for telling me, and for the advice. I'll say no more about it."

"The next shipment is coming in two weeks. You need to be ready. I'll send you replacements for Dennis and Cathy—people we can trust. Don't worry. Business as usual, eh, William?"

"Yes, of course. Bye, Uri."

The coldness of Uri's understanding and the consequences for Cathy were typical of him. He spoke as though all of life were merely a journal of events, each without real meaning but needing to be known and understood before one moved on in pursuit of the next opportunity. The chaos left behind mattered not at all. William could not prevent himself from thinking they had that in common.

Cathy's urgency, her nonsense talk of knowing what he wanted, the coyness she displayed when he told her of Dennis's intention to return to his wife and the contempt as William departed all made sense to him. It was her big play for him and the comfort she might salvage without Dennis. It was clumsy, visceral and persuasive in the moment but nothing more. He recalled his single interest in getting away from her when the rutting stopped. Ashamed, he had exited quickly. She might have expected to be with him after killing Dennis, or perhaps her seduction of him was simply desperation, bubbling up from the chaos driving her. In either case he was responsible. He had driven a wedge between Cathy and her husband years before, reducing her to chattel in that relationship, but now what life she may have had was lost to her, and he was entwined with that course.

William sat alone in bed with his laptop on his knees. An apple, a block of cheese and a shower had revived him sufficiently to consider one final task before sleep. He wrote:

Julie—I want you to know that I had nothing to do with Dennis's death. Cathy has confessed to his murder and setting the fire. The police thought I was involved with this because I had been in his house that afternoon, and recently, as you now know, Cathy and I had sex. I feel ashamed about this. She told the police about it, and now they have some evidence. There is no point in denying it to you or them. The bottom line is, there is no relationship between Cathy and me, and I am no longer a suspect, according to my lawyer.

I am truly sorry for the Cathy thing and accept responsibility for the hurt you feel. I have been a fool, not just over this but in just about every way possible. I learned just how foolish on my trip to Grand Forks. I spoke with my mother for the first time in twenty years. I wish I had gone sooner.

On Thursday at 2:00 p.m. I have an appointment with the surgeon who operated on me before Christmas. He said there would be changes from removing the tumour, and I am sure you have noticed things being different. I have struggled with these changes in addition to being weak and foolish. If you have the smallest hope that we can/may, in time, recover from this, please come to the meeting with the surgeon and listen to what he has to say.

Love, William

It was a Hail Mary, but with damage already done there was little to lose. He wanted his email to read in a straightforward way, without the blemish of excuse or justification, but on reading it again, he found this was impossible. In any case, he wanted her to hang on to the possibility that not everything he had done was within his control, so this would have to do. He took a breath and pressed Send.

He closed his eyes and fell into a restless sleep.

WILLIAM DANGLED BELOW THE OWL AND SURVEYED THE EARTH BELOW. As far as could be seen, grey-black mountains folded the earth. Their rivulets and lumps were etched in snow. There was nothing inviting about falling among them, but it was not fear that he felt.

"If I let go, it will be the end, won't it?" asked William.

Owl blinked at William as if surprised by the stupidity of the question.

"Or a beginning," it said.

"I want it to end."

"No, you don't," said Owl.

"What do you mean?"

"I mean it's not what you want."

January 11, 2018

WILLIAM AND JULIE SAT STONE-FACED IN A HOSPITAL OFFICE. THE DOOR opened. A smiling man in pyjamas and surgical hat, with a mask tucked under his chin, arrived suddenly.

"Mr. Koren. How are you? And Mrs. Koren, nice to see you too. I'm Dr. Franklin, the surgeon who saw you before Christmas, remember?"

"Yes, I remember." William recalled the smiling eyes and round nose above the mask of the man now sitting in the chair opposite.

"Tell me, how you have been? Have you noticed anything, a runny nose, bad headaches, stiffness in the neck or shoulders?"

William tried to focus in the blizzard of leading questions. "Just headaches from time to time, and whistling in my ears."

"How do you manage the headaches?"

William said, "Tylenol works okay." He watched Dr. Franklin's head nod approvingly. "Can you do something about the noise in my ears?"

"Tinnitus! Almost everyone gets it sometime. Not something we've found a cure for. I can refer you to someone, but in the end, they'll try to sell you hearing aids you don't need. The best thing is to learn to live with it, I'm afraid."

"It drives me mad." William smiled awkwardly.

"It drives all of us mad. Is there anything else you'd like to tell me?"

"There is something," William began, conscious of Julie's silent presence beside him. "You told me that I might notice changes after the operation. Well, I've noticed that I seem to say things without thinking. I'm not concentrating as well as I did. Not all the time, but I blurt things out that I'd normally keep to myself. It isn't like me." William paused. "Sex is different too."

Dr. Franklin's face became serious for the first time. "How so?"

"Julie and I had not been ... active for a number of years, but it started again. There's been nothing for about ten years and suddenly ... it started." William could not help feeling like a schoolboy.

"That sounds like a good thing," said Dr. Franklin. Julie's expression caused him to reconsider. "But I'm guessing it's more complicated than that."

"It is more complicated. I've made it more complicated." William saw the concentration on his face and understood there was something that did not add up in Dr. Franklin's calculation.

Dr. Franklin said, "The problem I have is that the kind of disinhibition you have described won't, I'm sure, be connected to the tumour or removing it."

"I thought you said I would notice some changes like this."

"Well, I did say something like that, but that was before we had the tumour out and could examine it. The reason we removed it was because it was quite large, about the size of a small fingertip, but that is considered large when it's near the brain. The problem is, these things continue to grow. Eventually it would have pinched the optic nerve and caused all sorts of trouble, so it had to come out. I had thought it was possibly of a type that secretes and interferes with the endocrine system, which regulates lots of functions in the body. That might have explained your disinterest in sex and then recovery of that interest when it was out, but it wasn't of that kind, and neither was it malignant."

William felt a wave of disappointment and then anxiety that Julie would hear this. "Something has to explain it. I thought it would explain why I've been dreaming more and feeling more emotional. I've even thought I might cry sometimes. Just not like me."

Dr. Franklin moved his head from side to side. "I've heard people say they were irritable before the operation and less so after it, but this is most likely because they're tired much of the time, which can happen with secreting adenomas, but not yours. I don't think being emotionally labile following the removal of your kind of tumour has been reported, certainly not to me." Dr. Franklin moved closer. "Remember, there's trauma involved in the operations you've had. It takes time to recover and sometimes it opens people to discovering new things about themselves." He shrugged. "An operation can focus the mind on what's important and what's not. Best not to search too hard for an explanation."

"So why have I been so different?" William asked.

"That," said Dr. Franklin, "is not a question for me. I can only tell you that there is no physical reason to do with your brain or the tumour we removed. There'll be other reasons and I'm not qualified in any of them to comment. Talk it through with your family doctor or perhaps you might think of going to counselling; maybe it'll help. Is there anything else I can help you with?" He smiled broadly.

William wondered what the doctor would think if he knew of the havoc his words would cause. Julie continued to sit motionless next to him, allowing the doctor's message to percolate within her, confirming every dread, justifying each angry thought, extinguishing the last of hope.

Dr. Franklin continued. "Well, if there is nothing more, let me take a quick look at the scar." Lifting his nose in the air to examine William through his half-glasses, the doctor stood against his patient, tilting William's face upward, as if to kiss him on the forehead or cut his throat. William thought either intimacy would be comforting. Dr. Franklin stroked William's eyebrow with a thumb. "It's fine. Very good. I'm pleased with the outcome," he said and released him. "I don't think I'll need to see you again, unless something changes." He smiled, moved toward the door and leaned back awkwardly, extending his hand toward William.

William reached for the hand. "Thank you."

"Good luck, the both of you." He waved incongruously to Julie, who smiled thinly, and was gone.

Julie and William sat side by side for about ten seconds. Then Julie lifted her bag from the floor and her coat from the back of the chair and left without speaking.

3:00 p.m.

STEPPING OUT OF THE HOSPITAL INTO THE COLD WAS FRESH. WILLIAM walked from the hospital, drew in the air and found himself at Tim Hortons on Lonsdale Avenue. He bought a double-double and moved to the counter to arrange his cup sleeve and plastic lid. People around him moved mechanically through the lineup with solemn faces, masking most of what they were. They were all strangers to each other, and that was just fine by William. His family was now lost to him, which should have been a terrible thing, and yet there was something about not having to struggle to save it that released him from the tension of trying. What remained was the need to salvage a relationship with Kelly. Julie would probably allow it, but before he turned to that there was something else to resolve.

If only I could wash my hands of Uri, thought William. The relentless cycle of deliveries, each one a doorway to jail for most of his remaining life, was not what he had anticipated or agreed to. Neither was the death of Dennis, or Cathy's plight. Without disengaging from Uri, there was little chance of keeping with Kelly. It seemed unlikely that Uri would grant him a free exit, especially now that he had moved closer to the centre of the operation.

Outside Tim Hortons a man stood with his hand out. He was tall, gaunt, with tangled hair and clothes gone grey with life on the streets.

"Any change?" said the man.

As the man smiled, William winced at the first glimpse of yellow teeth. An image of the wild-eyed man was drawn from memory, his teeth smashed and face bleeding.

"Sorry," said William. "You startled me." He reached into his pocket and delivered a small handful of coins into the man's palm.

The man offered meagre appreciation with a nod and a glance. William usually avoided the panhandlers that proliferated on the streets of Vancouver, his resentment too easily overcoming the truth of their disadvantage. They were aggressive or lazy or unsuccessful people, all designations worthy of contempt. Most of them, he had thought, arrived in Vancouver because the weather was better than elsewhere in Canada. There was a choice made to come here and beg on Vancouver's streets—and why should he have to pay for it? The truth and their circumstances were seldom this convenient. He had known and denied this most of his life. Then he recalled his father, who might have been standing outside on the pavement, collecting the change offered from people's pockets.

William said, "What do you need for today?" It felt awkward and unnatural to say it.

The man looked him up and down, expecting patronizing concern or a tirade of righteous indignation of the kind he often heard before being asked to move on.

"Something to eat, and a place at the shelter tonight."

"How much will that cost you?"

"Twenty bucks, maybe thirty."

William pulled his wallet from his coat pocket, opened it and began counting. It caused him to recall having more money hidden away than he could possibly spend without drawing attention to himself. He lifted all the bills from the wallet and held them out. "Take it."

The man shuffled and reached out with trepidation. "Are you sure?"

"Yeah. Just take it, get something to eat, some clothes and a couple of nights' rest."

"How much is it?"

"I don't know. Two or three hundred. Enough to get you going."

The man let go of the money, sank to his haunches and began crying. William looked around, conscious of the people on the street walking by, and bent down in front of the man, who tried to speak but could not.

"You okay?" William asked.

The man struggled and then spoke. "You don't have to."

"You can use it more than me."

"Can I buy something for my children with it?" asked the man.

William had never thought of people on the streets having anything other than a hard and lonely life, brought on by their own failure. This man had people more important to him than his own welfare. The idea of being able to buy them something had caused more gratitude than he could tolerate.

"How many kids do you have?"

"Two. Two boys."

"Do what you like with the money." William forced the money into the man's hand. "Buying them something is a good idea. I've got to go. Good luck." He stood up.

"Thank you," said the man. "Thank you."

Walking away, William recalled that he had money at home, and lots of it. Each month an envelope with cash was handed to him. He had used it wisely, first to pay down the company debt in small amounts and then to nibble away at the mortgage until it was meaningless. It seemed important not to pay off anything completely or do it too quickly. There was no need to draw attention to his new cash flow. When those tasks were done the money accumulated without a plan to spend it. Had he thought about it, the calculation of how many counterfeit bicycles passed through the warehouse would not have added up to all he had been given. It was within his power to have known more was going on, but he had pretended otherwise. Now having the money was a burden. He had thought about what might happen if the police found it. It was not illegal to keep cash on the premises, but Revenue Canada would want its share, and an explanation. The solution grew slowly at first and then became so clear that no other made sense. It would have to go.

The prospect of dispensing with the money brought another relief. The money was what he worked so hard for but it was not what he needed, and the effort of struggling to get and keep it was no longer required. But what had it been for? William had always felt it had been a struggle against something: not to be like his father, not to be constrained by a community for whom tradition and ritual were tormented by disagreement, not to allow himself to be trampled into oblivion as, it would seem, was the fate of the Doukhobors at the feet of government. His struggle had never been for something, except wealth, and that was only a symbol of his defiance. All that he had become was not what his family or his history had invited him to be. In the eyes of all those who had brought him into the world and tried to anchor him to values, it was worth nothing. He had not needed the help of brutal governments, squabbling factions or troubled parents to sink the hopes of all he might have been. He had untethered himself and run unaided into the push and shove of uncaring tides, where he had been a "success." At least, he thought, nearly everything was exposed to him as it had not previously been and the fresh air was cool on his face. He continued toward the car, head buzzing.

Julie, he thought, could never have understood the part she had played in this. She would have been disappointed to know the truth. He swayed with the realization that he had allowed her to spend most of her adult life with him, have his child, and all that time he had been dedicated to something else of no real value. He owed her in ways he could not repay. Suddenly sorrow caught up with him. An ache began squeezing, too low for a heart attack but too strong to dismiss. He stopped against a pole, grimacing, and waited.

Finally the discomfort passed. Minutes before, he had felt the liberation of her leaving, but now he caved to the physical pain of grieving her loss. Maybe he would feel the same about burning the cash he held. Knowing he must be cleansed of it would not prevent him from thinking of reasons to keep the money. It seemed he was capable of believing anything that was suitable, and he resolved to guard against that temptation. He would start at home, as soon as he could.

7:30 p.m.

IN WILLIAM'S GARDEN FLAMES DANCED WITHIN THE RUSTED OIL DRUM, warming his front while the cold air chilled everything not exposed to the fire. He stood solemnly, dropping cash into the fire in small enough bundles to ensure it burned to ash. Occasionally he added sticks from the garden and pieces of timber from the garage, and stirred the cinders to keep it hot. Glowing sparks rose into the sky and drifted away. The last of the dollars fluttered from his hand into the flame. It was gone, all of it. There was no evidence left of any connection with Uri and their activity together.

He recalled the trouble and energy expended in covering his tracks. He had not anticipated how modern bills might resist the fire and thought it was fitting that it took some effort to remove the stain of dollars he had hidden. The smell and slime he had encountered at the bottom of the dumpster when scrabbling inside to find the sprocket had stuck to his hands for two days. No amount of washing could clear it. Kelly had thought it was funny. What was it she had called the smell, as if it were a bottle of wine? It came to him: Poodle and Trout. It made him smile. Blood in the snow and the sound of the wild-eyed man landing in the laneway were difficult memories to scrub away. He thought of sitting with Dennis on the afternoon before he died. The bright light of his flooded kitchen, cold wet trousers sticking to his legs and head throbbing, not realizing that Cathy was upstairs. *What a stupid thing to do,* thought William of Dennis making a copy of the manifest. *What was he thinking?* It had caused trouble for everyone. And then he recalled that Dennis might still be alive but for the connection with Uri. He recalled the shredding he had done, mixing it with other papers before putting it in the dumpster. *Should have burned it*, he thought, staring into the embers of thousands of dollars. It didn't matter now. It was well buried in landfill or incinerated somewhere.

The thought stopped him and his stomach fluttered. He had discovered what Dennis had done when he noticed the photocopier was on in the office. He searched his memory for the sequence of events after printing the copy of the manifest. He had done the shredding and the disposal, but he had no recollection of deleting the electronic copy from the hard disk in the copier. *It must still be there.* The best possible evidence of fraud, or money laundering, or tax evasion, or whatever it might become in police hands, sat waiting to be discovered. He had to deal with it tonight, right now.

10:30 p.m.

PEMBERTON AVENUE IN NORTH VANCOUVER WAS QUIET. THE SMALL BUSIness district off the busy drag of Marine Drive had closed for the night and the usual swarm of white vans and pickup trucks had found their way home. William began his turn toward the darker street of the warehouse and office, cutting the corner of the intersection. It was a mistake. The oncoming cyclist arrived, all in black, without warning. He yanked the wheel of the Mercedes, braked hard and stopped as the figure came down on the hood and rolled off to the side. The black figure rose quickly, picked up the bike and began running with it up the road.

Still rattled, he continued the turn into the street, parked across from his warehouse and took stock of what had happened. It had been a close call. Had he rolled two more feet, the figure would have been under his wheels and another life gone because of all of this, but that was not what troubled him. In the split second of seeing the cyclist flash across the headlights and fall over the hood, he knew who it was and had suspected there would be more work to do.

William locked the car and began jogging to the office and ware-house. The glint from the glass-panelled door told him a door was open, but the alarm was silent. From his upstairs office window a light flickered. Now he ran. Through the doors the smell of gasoline filled his nostrils. A red plastic jerry can lay on the floor. He bounded up the stairs, the cackle of burning and the smell of smoke growing. The fire was in his office, now burning intensely. A deafening alarm began.

He tried to process all of the information and order what had to be done. It was likely the security system had recorded the dark figure entering the building with the jerry can and also rushing out. There was evidence to be dealt with. He must make it appear as though it were a break-in and get to those tapes. There was so much to do before the fire department arrived along with the police.

William ran downstairs, closed the door and turned on the sec-urity alarm. He swung his foot at the bottom glass panel of the door. Nothing. He kicked again and rebounded off the double glazing. A metal doorstop caught his eye and William thumped the window with it. Still nothing. Then he remembered to strike at the corner of the pane. The glass shattered and the alarm burst into life. Security and fire alarms screamed in tandem; lights began flashing. The next task was to collect the jerry can and get up the stairs.

Flames were inside the inner office where Cathy had spent her time. He pushed the red plastic container toward the fire and began searching her desk for the keys to the video cabinet. *Where has she put them!* Right-hand drawers, nothing. Inside the left-hand drawers the temperature was hot, but no keys. On the desktop there were pots, a notebook and small plastic containers, which he dumped and picked through until he found the little plastic tab that told him he had the one he needed. A remnant of gasoline in the jerry can ignited suddenly and the left side of the desk erupted. It was now fully in the room with him. William bent down at the cabinet and felt the heat through his jacket and shirt. The cabinet opened easily. He began pressing the eject buttons and stacking the tapes in the crook of his arm. Turning toward the fire, William flinched at the temperature of the air on his face. His eyes closed involuntarily until he gathered himself enough to toss the tapes toward his office into the fire.

William turned to the photocopier. It was off. It seemed madness to turn it on but there was no choice. He threw the switch and was grateful the electricity had not cut off. There was nothing to do but wait for it to be ready. The flames were advancing. *Why isn't the sprinkler system coming on?* Someone had turned it off, and he tried to remember where the stopcock was. In the pause it gave him, William realized the solution to his problem. Without the warehouse, there could be no deliveries. His value to Uri would be gone, but he had to keep the fire at bay until the evidence was destroyed. He remembered a fire extinguisher at the top of the stairs and went for it.

William returned and opened the compressed cylinder at the desk. Cathy's desk was overcome, fed constantly with heat from the inferno of his office. His effort was despairing. With his foot he pushed the desk a few feet away toward the hottest spot in the room. Only the partition wall prevented the whole second storey from being alight. He moved around the machine to put distance between himself and the fire. The alarms still wailed. He pulled his jacket over his head and peered out, protecting his hands from the heat and burrowing his nose into the cloth of his jacket. Finally the light from the photocopier travelled back and forth, signalling it was ready.

Turning his shoulder against the heat, he moved between the copier and the desk. The plastic of the machine was smoking on one side. The acrid smell and taste of burning plastic had reached him, but now he stood at the display with the fire close. Paint from the ceiling began falling in crispy flaming curls like autumn leaves. One landed on his hand, burning into the skin. He flicked it away. The fierce heat pushed through his trousers and to the backs of his legs.

The copier menu was plain enough. He pressed Menu, then Options, selected History, then pushed the falling debris away before scrolling through to Delete All. He clicked OK and stepped away from the machine toward the door. It was done.

Looking up, William realized the blaze had travelled above and behind him, lapping at the door by the stairs and blocking his escape. There was no time to hesitate. He had to plunge through the flames, or perish. Something fell and he spun around to look behind. The copier was still on. The display read Confirm Delete History, but it was too hot and too far away to reach.

Fucking machines! It was too late. His last thought as he ran toward the stairs was to wonder if it was right to have broken the glass and gotten rid of the jerry can and tapes before deleting the manifest from the copier. It might have been his undoing, but he did not regret it. He was hopeful the dark figure on the bicycle had not been hurt as he bumped her with the car. She would be clear of this if she got home without incident and claimed to know nothing when questioned. It was something to hope for.

He leapt through the doorway. The fire licked his face as he flew headlong down the stairs to the first landing, where he lay crumpled and still.

January 12, 2018

ARMS AND LEGS REACHED UPWARD AS IF SUSPENDING HIM FROM ABOVE. It took a moment to understand the arms and legs were his. He was hurtling from the sky, looking up at the blue, when Owl came into view and began circling. To William's right and over his shoulder the North Shore mountains seemed small and lay quiet, far below. To his left Vancouver appeared moulded like Lego on a kitchen floor.

"Am I falling?" he asked. "Of course I am. I've let go of the hat." He craned his neck to see where he might land and then realized the futility of the effort. All control of his landing was given up on letting go.

Owl came closer and William asked, "Will it hurt when I land?"

He strained to hear Owl and thought he heard, "The fall is more painful."

"Why?"

"Remorse," said Owl. "Pain of a kind. Stops when you land."

"Then I am in pain. I regret everything," said William.

"Too late," said Owl. "Too late."

"Maybe I can make up for it ... be different."

"How?" asked Owl.

"I don't want to be William Koren anymore."

"Ah," said Owl. "That's what you don't want, and it will not do."

William's descent quickened, leaving Owl circling high above him. The hissing noise in his ears became a roar. Tearing wind caused his clothes to ripple and flap along his limbs, the Omega flew from his wrist, his pockets emptied and a shoe yanked from his foot, disappearing in the distant blue.

Faster and faster William fell, now buffeted by hot winds. He began shouting, before it ended.

"I'm sorry. I'm sorry, it was wrong of me. I made mistakes." Wind whipped hair against his face, lifted his eyelids, entered his mouth, inflating his cheeks. He turned his head back and forth against the turbulence and roaring in his ears.

Owl lunged into the trail of debris. "No, that will not do. We are all sorry. It will not do."

The air burned William's skin as he neared the ground. Smoke and then flame from his back surrounded his body, engulfing arms and legs.

William shouted, "Help me, please!"

"You don't have much time," said Owl.

The volume of noise was now so great he could not hear the words that came screaming from him. "I am a Doukhobor! I will let God into my heart, I promise."

"Too easy!" said Owl.

William's clothes began shredding from his body. "I am a Doukhobor. My name is Dmitri Korenov." Fire and smoke trailed behind in a long plume in the sky. His flesh burned; his hands blackened and peeled.

"Still too easy," said Owl.

The fear was gone, the pain lost in the noise and turmoil. With his remaining breath he said, "My name is Dmitri Korenov. My father is

Pavel Korenov. My mother is Nina Korenov. I am their son. I am their son." Over his shoulder William saw he was now level with the mountain peaks, his time nearly over.

Owl's face appeared close to his. "What do you want?"

William said quietly, "I want nothing."

"Good!" said Owl. "You may have nothing, and the peace it brings. Now, you can have anything you want, providing it is nothing, and everything. What must you have, Dmitri?"

"It's too much to ask."

"What must you have?" said Owl. "Say it!"

William said slowly, "I ask …"

"FORGIVENESS." WILLIAM WOKE, LIFTING HIS HEAD OFF THE BED, AND, without knowing why, began crying a fearful cry with all the terror of an abandoned child. A nurse with large round glasses and a face mask peered down at him.

"Mr. Koren, don't be frightened. Just lie back and try to stay calm." She waited for him to relax into the bed. "You're safe now. You've been in a fire, but you're safe now. This is Vancouver General Hospital and you're in the burn unit. We're looking after you. I'm Ellen and I'll be your primary nurse." She reached for a plastic cup of water and held it to his lips.

She had the gentlest of voices. It helped him control the emotion. He cleared his throat and asked, "How bad is it?"

"You've been burned in a few places, but you'll make a good recovery. You'll have to help us by staying calm and keeping everything clean. That's the important thing."

William saw his arms and legs suspended in the air.

Nurse Ellen said, "You have some bandages to protect you. Your hands and one side of your face and ear have been bandaged. There are a few more bandages on the backs of your legs. That's why your arms and legs are elevated, so there's no pressure on them."

"That sounds bad to me," said William.

"You'll make a good recovery. We're very good at looking after injuries like yours." He could hear her confidence through the face mask.

"I thought it was over."

"You survived a close call. Fortunately you fell downstairs and out of the smoke, so your lungs are fine, and that's why you lived through it. You must have had some good karma stocked up." Her voice embraced him without knowing the irony of what she said.

The pain of his wounds intruded and she was quick to see it. "Your injuries can be quite painful if we don't stay on top of it. You'll learn to help us with that too." She fiddled with the bag and tubes hanging beside his bed. "I'll tell the doctor you're awake and be right back." Her face smiled through the mask. "Oh yes, the police. Are you up to seeing them?"

William thought there were things he needed to work out beforehand; most of all, he wanted to speak to Julie, before the police did. "I don't feel up to it. Can we put it off?"

"Sure we can. I'll tell them you're being seen by the doctor just now. We'll keep them off for a day or two. What about your family?"

"Would you call my wife and ask her to come in, maybe tomorrow?"

"I can do that too. She has already called to see how you are." Nurse Ellen smiled and left with quick steps.

William felt overcome but it was not the pain. All that had happened and all he had done, and yet this Nurse Ellen was kindly to him. It was nothing he deserved and hard to understand. She would, he thought, recognize the tears that came to him as trauma and pain, but she would be wrong. It was the second chance that made him cry. He did not want the relief of death. He had things to do with the life he had been wasting and nearly lost.

January 13, 2018

THIS WAS ALWAYS GOING TO HAPPEN. WILLIAM WAS HELPLESS TO PRE-vent it, but the moment could not have been more difficult. Nurse Ellen had protected him for a few days, which had given him time to prepare himself, but he had not figured on dealing with this scenario.

Julie stood by his bed, and he desperately wanted to speak with her and guide her in not incriminating herself in interviews, except Constable McKinnon stood behind her, waiting his turn and listening.

"Can we have a few minutes alone?" asked Julie.

"No," McKinnon said. "A crime has been committed; you're both witnesses, possibly suspects. We can't have you speaking privately."

She said, "What does it matter? I thought man and wife can't be witnesses against each other anyway."

"You're mistaken. In Canada married people don't have to tell us about what's been said between them, but they're compelled to tell us what they saw and what they know."

William saw Julie sag under the weight. Neither was sure if McKinnon was right, but neither had the knowledge to challenge him. Julie looked at William as if there was something she wanted to say stuck in her throat. His mind raced with all that she might know about the house being paid off, what she might have seen on her occasional visits to the office, what she might have known about Cathy, something he had taken home. *That's it. The sprocket.* It was long gone, but still a danger. She had seen it, inspected it and wondered about it. Perhaps she had understood what it was. A single mention of it would have the police crawling over his business records, searching everything and maybe even discovering the electronic copy on the manifest, still on the now blackened photocopier.

William said, "Never mind him. Thanks for coming. How's Kelly?"

"Very worried about her father. They told me not to bring her because all the bandages can be really upsetting for children."

"They don't know Kelly." Both parents smiled.

"You better tell me how you are. She'll want a full report."

"I feel lucky. It could have been much worse. They say I'll have a little scarring, but in a year I should be fine."

Julie was nodding and then the thin smile faded. "I want to say—"

"Don't say anything. You don't have to. It's me who should be sorry."

It was true that he was sorry, but the interruption had achieved a purpose.

"Sorry that you'll have to spend time getting Kelly through this, dealing with the insurance and talking to the police." William watched Julie's face crunch in surprise at his mention of the police. "There's nothing to worry about. Just answer their questions and tell them everything you know." She did not understand why he was saying this and looked at him as if it could not be true. "You're not connected to the business, so don't worry. You should take my keys, in case you have to go to the warehouse for any reason." William braced himself for the mistake Julie might make by revealing she had her own keys. "The only other keys are in the building somewhere." There was a change in her face, as if she understood.

"Where are your keys?" she asked.

"Ellen will know—the nurse you spoke to." Julie nodded.

"So, get the keys from Ellen and tell Kelly she can come any time she likes."

"Okay."

"And don't let these people," he said, thrusting his chin toward McKinnon, "tie you in knots. Just answer their questions and tell them everything." The smile he was forcing cracked the scab by his ear, but realization appeared on her face.

"I will," she said. "I promise to tell them everything."

"Would you get Ellen to come in, please? The drugs are wearing off."

MCKINNON STOOD BESIDE THE BED. HIS COLLEAGUE WAS AT THE DOOR. The greetings were over and inquiries as to how he was feeling followed their usual path. Further politeness had no purpose, and so the questioning began.

"Why did you go to the warehouse so late in the evening?" Constable McKinnon made no effort to hide his skepticism.

William said, "My wife had left me and I didn't want to be in the house. I was trying to keep busy and there are always things to do at the office."

"So you arrived at the office and immediately saw evidence of a break-in."

"The front door was open, glass was broken and there was flickering light upstairs."

"What about the alarm?"

"The security alarm was on," said William.

"Then what happened?"

"I went upstairs and saw the fire in the front office, my office, and went to investigate."

"And?"

"I went for the fire extinguisher on the staircase and tried to put it out. I couldn't stop it. The fire alarm started."

"It sounds like you had plenty of time to get out, but you didn't. Why not?"

"Well, I thought I would be able to rescue the CCTV tapes, which might tell us who it was."

"Did you get them?"

"Yes, but I left them behind." McKinnon's expression invited more. "I didn't see the fire get to the staircase behind me. I got the tapes out of the recording machines but then I was trapped. So I dropped the tapes and jumped through the doorway into the stairwell."

Constable McKinnon studied William. "You've had quite the few weeks, haven't you? An arson at one of your employees' homes, and he dies. You were there just an hour or so before the fire, but your secretary, or maybe I should say your lover, confesses to it. Then your wife leaves you and your business burns down, also arson, just as you turn up. Remarkable timing. Just leaving or just arriving, but never there at the moment it happens."

William remained quiet.

McKinnon continued. "Is your business in debt? We can find that out, but it's easier just to ask."

"No, the business is going well ... was going well."

"Are you or your family in debt?"

"No. I'm square at the bank, mortgage is almost paid off, and there won't be much on the credit cards."

"Was the business insured for fire?"

"Of course."

"How much will you get?"

"I couldn't tell you. Really, I don't know. I don't even know if they pay out for arson."

"Perhaps you should have found that out before you set fire to it."

"Why would I try to put out the fire and risk my life if I'd wanted to burn the business and collect the insurance?"

"You wouldn't be the first person to fake an injury to make it look like you're innocent."

"There's nothing fake about the injuries I have."

"No. Maybe you overdid it. Who else has a key and the code to the alarm?"

"The code would be known by the people who work there. Me, Cathy, Dennis, a few others, some who've left. Not sure about the keys."

"What do you mean?"

"Well, Cathy and I have one each and she kept the spares. They're given to people from time to time for weekend deliveries or when maintenance people come in the evening. Lots of people would know they are kept in Cathy's desk." William felt his burns sting as he recalled the set Julie kept at home. He hoped she would see the danger and send them flying from Lions Gate Bridge as soon as she got home.

"Do you have records of who had them?"

"I think we kept a little book of who had the keys out."

"You kept records?"

"I left it to Cathy. She had the book on her desk."

"And now that's gone in the fire. It doesn't sound like a very secure system."

"No, I guess it wasn't."

Nurse Ellen arrived. "Officer, not too much longer." She moved to the edge of the bed and adjusted the drip hanging beside William.

McKinnon ignored her. "Does your wife have keys?"

"No." William kept his tone even, as if it were nothing. "She hasn't been to the place for years, except to drive me there sometimes. She worked there at the beginning but then she stopped."

"Why's that?"

"She looked after the home and I looked after the business. That's all." It was not enough. "Our daughter was born, and we could afford for her not to work in the company. She's a full-time mum."

McKinnon was unconvinced. "Okay. There'll be a full investigation and I'm sure we'll want to speak with your wife and you again."

"Of course. I won't be going anywhere."

"One more thing. One of the glass panels on the outside door was broken."

"I saw that. I thought that's how they got in."

"Maybe," said McKinnon. "But the broken glass was on the sidewalk outside. You would think that glass broken from the outside would be found on the inside of the door, in the hallway."

William felt his skin respond with sweat, and a new pain began at the edges of his wounds. "I have no idea. Maybe the firemen dragged some of it outside when they pulled me out."

"Very good, Mr. Koren. Maybe that's what happened. We'll have to wait for the report to be sure. You've certainly got an explanation for everything."

That was true, thought William. He was very good at saying what was untrue as if he believed it were true.

16

West Vancouver, August 2, 2018

THE CELLPHONE RANG WITH THE OLD-FASHIONED JINGLE OF A DESKTOP cradle phone. Julie recognized it and answered it without looking.

"Hi, William. Okay, she'll be right out." She hung up, irritated that her manner was too familiar. It was difficult to maintain the balance of the emotional distance between them while remaining close enough for Kelly to know that her relationship with her father had her approval. She shouted, "Kelly, your dad's here."

Kelly bounded into the kitchen, asking, "Did he say what the surprise was?"

"Nope. I'm completely out of that loop. All I know is that you were going for a picnic. Here's your backpack. Let's see, hat, water, lunch, sunscreen, jacket."

"I won't need the jacket. It's too hot."

"It's lightweight and in the backpack. Just take it."

"Oh, Mum!"

"Use it to sit on and don't argue. Just go."

They went to the front door together and kissed briefly as it opened.

"Have a good time."

"I will. Bye, Mum. Thanks."

Julie watched her daughter skip down the steps and along the short path to the sidewalk as if she could see. It had been a hard few months for Kelly, who disliked the absence of her father.

William's car was not outside as expected. A curious man was looking at her. He was clothed head to foot in light jungle gear, a sun flap draped from his hat, and then she realized it was William leaning on his surprise.

Julie had not anticipated what he had brought, and it caused her heart to lift into her throat with a joy that could not be explained. For now, it was enough to anticipate her daughter's reaction and to know what it would mean to her.

William said, "Over here."

Kelly altered her direction and followed the sound to him. "Hi, Dad," she said as they found each other. "Can I hug you yet?"

"Sure you can. Just be gentle with me."

"So?" Kelly waited briefly for a response. "Where are we going? What's the surprise?"

"I'm sitting on it."

"What?" Kelly's arm reached behind him and found a seat and then the crossbar of a bicycle. Her eyebrows came together and confusion emerged in her voice. "A bike! Dad, I can't ride a bike anymore."

"You can ride this one."

"How?"

"You work it out." William stepped away, leaving her holding the seat and handlebars.

"It's heavy."

"True."

She felt the front wheel and breaks. "But it's high-tech, titanium bits maybe. Road race wheels?"

"How do you know that?"

"Different metal, different temperatures."

"Very clever. Keep going."

Kelly giggled. "I'm joking!" and then rocked it back and forth. "Really long frame." She moved behind the seat and felt the second set of handlebars. "A tandem. It's a tandem!" Without knowing exactly where he was she reached out to her father with one hand, pulling him close.

"Careful, careful," said William, holding his damaged face and ear away from the embrace.

"Is it really ours?"

"If you like it, it's really ours." He would have to sell one or two of the sophisticated machines that now collected dust in Julie's garage, but that did not matter. This was more important than all of those.

"I don't know if I'll be able to do it."

"It's just like riding a bike. You'll be fine."

"Thanks, Dad." She kissed his cheek.

William handed Kelly a helmet and held the tandem firm while she got on.

Julie shouted, "You be careful now."

"We will."

"Bye, Mum."

Julie felt her daughter's pleasure and wanted to join the squawking celebration in the street and pedal off with them for a picnic on the grass next to the ocean, but it was too soon. It would be a long time before that was possible, if ever. William had changed for the better. He was lighter, easier with himself and connected to others. Perhaps it was the close call in the fire, the business being lost or his move back to Grand Forks, near his mother, that had changed him. Still, the barrier separating them would remain.

There were things unknown and unsaid that lingered in the space between them. Julie still worried that something more and very bad would come from the sprocket William had brought home that night. Whatever that single piece of gold implied, it remained unknown and unsaid to the police. Nor had her part in the warehouse fire been discussed. William's contrary instructions to get rid of the office keys she kept at home and say nothing to the police suggested he knew she had been there. It also looked as though he had been injured covering her trail. There could be no other explanation for the details that had emerged, but it had not been discussed.

Of all the discussions they might have, the one she wanted most was about the loss of his business. It had not been the response she would have anticipated, and it could be understood only by speculating that the fire had unburdened him in some way—enough to see and appreciate other things. It made her think there was something to learn about William, and it was enough to hope that the changes she could see in him would endure.

She watched from the door as Kelly waved goodbye. There was unsteadiness as they started out, but then, as if wind filled their sail, there was momentum, and they were off.

AUTHOR'S NOTE

THIS NOVEL IS DEDICATED TO THE DOUKHOBOR PEOPLE IN CANADA AND especially the survivors of New Denver, British Columbia. They fled persecution in Russia and arrived in Canada in 1899 with the help of the Quakers and also Leo Tolstoy, who provided the proceeds of his novel *Resurrection* (1899) to help their journey. (See "The Hand of Tolstoy in Canada," https://bit.ly/2D2E6GJ.)

The immigrants had accepted the certainty of an agreement with the Canadian minister of the interior, Clifford Sifton, that they were exempt from military service and would receive large blocks of land, in what would become Saskatchewan, where they could live according to their customs. They would not have come without this understanding. However, in 1905 the federal government changed. Frank Oliver replaced Sifton and disavowed the agreement, insisting that Doukhobors accept conventional citizenship, or the land would be taken from them. About two-thirds (five thousand) could not accept this and migrated to southeast BC, abandoning farms, brick factories, mills and homes. It was the first major schism among these people in Canada. The second was the emergence of the Sons of Freedom, who were determined to be true to their beliefs and the original agreement with Canada, and fought to persuade other Doukhobors to do the same.

From 1953 to 1959 about two hundred children of the Sons of Freedom were taken from their families and confined in a repurposed sanatorium in New Denver, BC. Life was never the same for them, and the impact on their children and community continues to this day.

(See "The Doukhobors in Canada from 1953: The New Denver History and Background," https://bit.ly/2D24EYO.)

However, this book is not simply about the Doukhobors or Sons of Freedom. It is a story of how we become what we are, from generations ago—how our sense of self and place in the world is corrupted with the destruction of lineage and continuity. We see this plainly enough among displaced peoples and Indigenous cultures around the world, but it is true of all of us. If we look carefully we can find that thread, drawn through years, decades and generations before us, which influences the choices we make every day.

I hope this book may raise again the issue of reconciliation between the people of Canada and British Columbia on one side and Doukhobors on the other, especially the New Denver survivors. The original wrong, in Canada and BC, has been the treatment of the Doukhobor people as a whole. The tension between the Sons of Freedom and the Orthodox Doukhobors is a painful distraction from the first truth of this injustice. Saying this does not diminish the hurt experienced by the New Denver children, but it would never have happened without the original betrayal of all the Doukhobor people in Canada and BC.

While the Doukhobor people now live easily and productively in Canada, the legacy of the past stays with them. They still wait for an appropriate response from the BC and Canadian governments. Every child knows how this must begin: you must say sorry for the wrong that has been done.

PHOTO BY JACQUELINE MASSEY

ABOUT THE AUTHOR

B.A. THOMAS-PETER IS CANADIAN BUT LIVED IN THE UK AS A TEENAGER
and eventually trained there as a Clinical Psychologist. His work
focused on providing help to children, adults with mental health dif-
ficulties and the families of the elderly in need of care, before moving
into the field of forensic psychiatry. He spent eleven years as Honorary
Professor of Psychology at Birmingham University before moving to
Oxford as Director of the Regional Forensic Psychiatry service. In 2010
he returned to Canada as Provincial Executive Director of Forensic
Psychiatry for BC.

Thomas-Peter has published in many anthologies and peer-
reviewed journals. He has been a regular contributor to international
academic conferences and has contributed to the development of the
Forensic Psychology profession in Australia and the UK. He currently
lives on an island on the west coast of Canada, runs a small consultancy
and spends most of his time writing.